DEVIL DON'T GO

GO

A TANNER YORK THRILLER

ANDREW KENNING

DEVIL DON'T GO

A TANNER YORK THRILLER

ANDREW KENNING

Published by
DYK Publishing, LLC
Raleigh, NC

Devil Don't Go
Copyright © 2024 by Andrew Kenning.

Library of Congress Control Number: 2024922026

ISBN: 979-8-9914197-0-3

For information contact: DYKpub.com

Edited by: Scribendi.com
Cover and interior design by: Miblart.com
First Edition: 2025
10 9 8 7 6 5 4 3 2 1

For my wife Debi,
une femme inoubliable.

NEWS FLASH – WXNG-TV, CHICAGO

"... For more on a developing story coming out of the Fuller Park neighborhood, let's go live with Meghan Orr."

"Thanks, David. On the city's South Side, where eleven-year-old Elijah Washington was walking home from school, eyewitnesses saw two adult males lure the boy into an alley near his home and execute him with two shots to the back of the head.

"Police say the two men were from a rival gang and were retaliating for the actions of Elijah's father, Derek Washington.

"Sources tell us the dispute was over contested turf. We have learned that the father is not cooperating with police, and no charges or arrests have been made.

"Police Superintendent William Cooper has been taking heat from citizens and from the city council on whether he should continue as the superintendent or retire. Under his tenure, the crime rate has gone up, especially in low-income areas, as has gang-related violence. At the age of sixty-two, Cooper is perceived as having outdated methods, according to one councilperson. In response, Superintendent Cooper had this to say:"

"I'm horrified by the actions of some people, but what happened here is beyond belief. We have leads; we have camera footage we are going through as I speak. We will exhaust all efforts in tracking down the killers of this innocent boy and will bring them to justice. Thank you."

"The superintendent did not take questions. We caught up with Elijah's grieving mother, and she had this heartfelt message to share:"

"My little boy... why would they take my little boy? This needs to end... the violence in this city sickens me. An innocent child pays for a grown man's sins... why... for what? Hope... the people need something... some hope it will end. Someone needs to shine... shine a light... someone needs to shine a light on this city and watch the cockroaches run."

"It will certainly take the city a long time to recover from this tragedy. Reporting live from the South Side, I'm Meghan Orr for WXNG-TV News."

ONE

I was nine when I first wondered what it would be like to die. That was my first thought when I turned onto snow-packed Illinois Route 71 and didn't see any cars. Were they all dead, or had everyone already hunkered down in the small town of Kickapoo, Illinois? I was eager to get indoors myself. WXNG-TV News had forecast a significant snowfall event for Friday night into Saturday morning. Most areas were looking at twelve inches, but places outside the city of Chicago, like Kickapoo, could see twenty.

Two miles down the road, I stopped at an intersection. I sat there a bit, watching a mix of fog, rain, and snow cover farmers' fields. Maybe I shouldn't have stopped for dinner with Frank, after all. If I turned right, it meant a longer drive, but it would also be more tranquil with flatter roads. If I went straight, I'd have to navigate what the locals call the Roller Coaster. That stretch of road twisted up and down. It was a narrower, steeper, and shorter way home and a lot more fun to drive. But in weather like this, taking that route would be risky at best, if not deadly. The Roller Coaster reminded me of life—the good and bad times that one goes through. But what joy life could bring if one were daring enough.

Kickapoo's topography was a bit different than other places in Illinois because of its canyons—twenty in total. It was surrounded by flat farmland, but tens of thousands of years ago, as the glaciers melted, rushing water stripped away everything except the sandstone that made up its many canyons. Hiking trails, wildlife, and that quaint small-town feel were just what I needed after spending a week in the city. I liked the quiet isolation it offered, the rustic vibes.

I stepped on the gas and headed straight on into the fog. The gray mist surrounding my vintage '72 Ford pickup made visibility five, ten yards—tops. The truck's headlights did little to help illuminate the road, even in the absence of streetlights. Tricky sharp and curvy turns were coming up. My hands gripped the wheel tighter than usual.

As I traveled down the road, cutting through the weather, icy snow pellets made a tapping sound on the truck's exterior. Moving at top speed, the wipers only cleared the view for a moment at a time. I squinted at two red specks on the right side of the windshield that slowly came into view. They were faint at first but grew larger and more significant as I drew closer. It took a second for me to realize that those specks were red taillights, and I was heading straight for them.

I hit the brakes, and all four wheels locked, causing the back-end to fishtail. I cranked the wheel hard, see-sawing left and right to avoid impact. The truck started spinning out of control.

The road ahead bent sharply to the left and had a steep banking. I spun across the oncoming lane, sliding down the opposite shoulder. The back of the truck bed hit a tree and stopped me on a dime. My body continued in motion until the seat belt locked and dug into my shoulder; I winced from the jerk. I was facing east—the opposite way I had been going. The pickup must have done one and a half full revolutions before coming to a stop.

As the fog lifted a bit, the outline of a car up on the top of the banked turn in the road materialized. The red glow from the rear taillights hung suspended over the roadway while the other half of the car draped over the guardrail. We must have hit the same patch of ice. They went up and over the turn. I went down.

I moved the truck to a safe spot. The fog moved eastward, clearing my field of vision a bit more, and I could see someone in the other car's driver's seat. I checked my cell phone but had no signal.

Approaching the car, I found the doors were locked, and the motor was still running. I had no way of getting into the vehicle. Knocking on the window, I shouted, "Hello, are you hurt? My name is Tanner York."

No response.

"I'm going to smash the window so that I can open the door."

I found a rock and proceeded to bang it against the passenger side window. It chipped the glass a little, but that was all. Gripping the rock with both hands, I reared back and thrust my arms down with all my strength, and the rock cracked the window like an egg. Repeating the action, the window eventually exploded inward, and hexagonal bits of glass sprayed over the passenger seat and floor.

Sticking my hand through the broken window, I pressed the unlock button and heard the click of the door's lock release.

I headed for the driver's door.

"Hey! Hello! Can you hear me?" The woman's head moved. Her seat belt was still intact, and there were no signs of blood on either the windshield or her. Feeling her neck, her pulse was faint.

I should wait for the first responders and not move her. I checked my cell—still no signal. If a car hit her now, she'd be pushed into the canyon.

"Hello?" I put my hand under her chin and raised her head. She moaned, and her eyes opened.

"Can you hear me? Are you hurt? You need to get out of the car. It's not safe here."

"Whhhhaaat," she slurred, "my fffffffffir."

"Was someone with you in the car?" The fog was thick again, and searching now would be dangerous. The conditions would be this bad or worse throughout the night.

"Can you walk?"

"What's... going... on?"

"You've been in an accident. You're in danger just sitting here. Are you hurt?" My fingers began to stiffen and numb from the cold.

"My wrist... I can't... think," she muttered.

Realizing that she was a sitting duck, I took a chance on saving her myself. I got the seat belt undone, helped her out of the car, and carried her over to my truck. After I buckled her in, I set up some flares around her vehicle to warn oncoming drivers.

With that done, I climbed into the truck and fastened my seat belt. I quickly glanced over and saw her staring at me. I cracked a smile just as her eyes rolled back and she passed out, head slumped against the door. "Shit! Hey! Don't pass out on me." I didn't have any medical training but figured this wasn't good. Fumbling with the keys, I finally got the truck started, slammed my foot on the gas, and raced to the ER.

CHAPTER

TWO

It had all started four hours earlier on a cold, windy day in Chicago when my old '72 Ford pickup roared to life. Not even the bitter Chicago air that was typical in late February could stop it from firing up. That old truck and I had made some great memories together. Frank Brannon, my best friend, had helped me restore it over a lot of late nights at his service station, drinking beer and sharing some laughs from our boyhood days. Frank had broken a few fingers putting in the transmission. We had invested our blood, sweat, and smashed knuckles into returning it to a pristine condition. I drove the pickup on weekends when I headed out to Kickapoo, Illinois, which was a sleepy country town eighty miles southwest of Chicago. It was a perfect getaway spot for me when I needed a break from the city. I had a three-bedroom cabin that sat on five acres of woodland. With the severe weather that was due to come in late that night, hitting traffic getting out of town would be tedious, so I left work around two and put the busy city behind me.

I called Frank on the way.

"Hey, Ty, what's up?"

Tanner York was my real name, but everyone called me Ty. When I was a kid, my mother would put my initials on all my stuff, so people assumed my name was TY.

I lived on the sixty-ninth floor of Lake Point Tower, which was right on Lake Michigan, by Navy Pier. During the week, I worked for the law firm of Westcott, Ackerman, and Rockwell, or WAR, as the firm's investigator. It wasn't as glamorous a job as people thought. I spent tons of hours in my office fact checking backgrounds on cases. Occasionally, I tailed people and took photographs of them doing various things they'd rather keep private.

I hired Frank on occasion to help with surveillance. He had a military background—the details of which he kept to himself— but I knew he'd spent time at the FBI Academy in Quantico. He wouldn't tell me what he'd done or what he'd seen, and I was his best friend. All I knew for certain was that whatever it was, it had left its mark. He owned and operated Frank's Auto Repair out in Kickapoo.

"Not much. I left work early. Is Robert coming?" The three of us had made dinner plans for that night. It being a Friday, we'd usually go to the Bison Head Tavern in Ottawa, which was the next town over from Kickapoo.

"He said he was. You know him, though."

"Yeah, I hear that. I'll meet you there."

"Sure enough, and I have some news."

"Great, save it for when I see ya."

Frank and I had been friends for more than forty years. We grew up on the same block; both of us were orphans. A car accident claimed the lives of my parents, whereas someone gunned down his parents. Frank was born on the South Side. His dad was in a gang, and his mother was always strung out on drugs. I'd never had an African American friend before I met

Frank at school. The other kids would pick on him because of his skin color.

One day, Frank and a bigger kid got into it. I felt this was unfair, so I stepped in. The bigger kid knocked me down hard and fast. When I looked up, Frank was on him like nobody's business. Ali would have been proud of how quickly his fists flew. When it was over, my leg hurt so bad that I fought back tears. It had gotten twisted when I fell, and Frank helped me limp back to my house. He'd made fun of me the whole way home, but I didn't mind. From that day forward, we would look out for each other—or rather, Frank would look out for me.

Another thing we shared was a friendship with Robert Fields. He was another orphaned kid who'd lived a few blocks down from us. Robert was now the executive assistant to the governor of Illinois.

I'd hit the interchange of I-55 and I-80 in an hour. Not too bad. My spirits lifted. Only forty-five minutes to my exit. I started thinking about the last session I'd had with my psychologist, Dr. Sabrina Renfro. We'd talked about my lack of a relationship; she wanted me to register for an online dating site. My fiancée had died twenty years before, and it had been challenging to overcome. Things hadn't been fruitful in the romance department ever since. I'd mentioned to Dr. Renfro that I'd been thinking about asking Bridget out for dinner. She owned a bookstore I frequented, Bridget's Book Nook, in the Loop downtown. I stopped there before heading out to pick up my weekend book haul. We'd talked some, but she'd had a lot of customers to attend to. Everyone was picking up books for the stormy weekend ahead. I ultimately lost my courage to ask her out, but I promised myself that I would, eventually.

I'd made excellent time on I-80, reaching my exit in only thirty minutes. In Ottawa, the Bison Head Tavern had a prairie chic ambiance. The restaurant wrapped around two huge copper kettles that they used to craft their own beer. The bartender, Vinny, recognized me, so I grabbed a seat at the bar and ordered a Blanton's bourbon. My drink of choice was bourbon, neat, and I preferred Kentucky bourbon. Five minutes later, Frank showed up.

"You made great time. Let me guess," Frank said, pointing to my glass, "Blanton's."

"Where the hell is Robert?" I asked.

"I'll have a Winter Porter," he told Vinny. "You know Robert, Ty, always late and then later. How's your asthma? This cold air can't be good for it."

"I'm fine. I've learned to live with it. Got my Combivent right here." I patted my shirt pocket. I'd had asthma all my life; my inhaler had saved me more than a few times.

"I have another car project, if you're interested. A '69 Dodge Charger. Needs a lot of work, though. Body's not bad. Up for it? Feel like turning some wrenches and bangin' some knuckles again?" Frank asked.

"Count me in. That Chevelle we did is damn sweet."

"You take it out every now and then?"

"Sure, but not in this shit I don't." I gestured at the dirty, gray snow that was heaped along the curbs outside.

"So, any chicks on the horizon? And not the blind dates Margaret sets you up with."

"Chicks? Christ, Frank, I'm fifty-one. Guys our age don't go for 'chicks.' Women would be the term you're looking for. And some of Margaret's set-ups have been fairly attractive."

Frank chuckled. "Whatever. You've got to get out more. You have a great job, not that you need it with all the money you have already. Live at Lake Point Tower, and you have an awesome huge cabin in the woods. And lastly, you have me as one hell of a great friend. That alone should attract a woman."

"I'll put your name down on my résumé the next time I'm interviewing potential dating prospects."

"Buddy, you know I love ya, so I'm telling you straight up. Karin's been gone now for what, twenty years? I get it, you got dealt a bad hand. But don't you think it's time for someone? What does your therapist say? About the bookstore woman? You keep mentioning her, and Lord knows you spend a fortune in that place."

I sighed. "My doctor's been telling me to sign up for online dating, too. Bridget's nice, and I've been thinking about asking her out, but I'm happy with the way things are in my life. I'd rather not screw up the friendship I have with her. If I ask her out and it doesn't work, it might get awkward. What about you, Mister Casanova?"

"I'm seeing someone, but it's complicated." His face softened. He looked through the mirror behind the bar.

A burst of laughter escaped me. "What? When did this happen? And what's complicated mean? Is this the news that you had for me?"

"Yeah. She's young. She's trying to get out of her current situation. I'm trying to help her out with it. This would be a great time for you to ask Bridget out. We could double date."

I was happy that Frank had met someone. He'd had relationships before but none with younger women. Good for him.

"Did you see the news about that kid getting gunned down? Still think it's an educational issue and not a gun control issue?" I asked to change the subject. Frank continued to stare into the large mirror behind the bar.

After collecting his thoughts, he said, "Yes, I do. If we educate our young people and give them a path forward through education, it will reduce the amount of violence. Right now, they have nothing. There should be gun safety classes in schools. I would've ended up the same way, but being in a foster home in a better school district was my ticket out. Maybe it was a good thing my parents died."

Frank looked down at his phone and showed me a text from Robert: "Need to cancel guys." I looked up at Frank, he was shaking his head with a look of disgust.

"I knew it." Frank muttered.

"Well, next time," I said, doing my best to hide my disappointment.

Frank left, and I stayed for one more bourbon. I was finishing up my drink at the bar when two guys walked in. Both wore black suits under their overcoats. One was tall and the other short—they looked like the gangster version of Laurel and Hardy. I looked at Vinny, who shook his head, letting me know that they weren't regulars. They sat down beside me and ordered the eighteen-year-old Glenfiddich single malt scotch on the rocks.

The taller of the two craned his neck toward me and asked, "Hey, pal. How far is it to this fucking place called Kickapoo?"

"Oh, about thirty miles east of here," I lied. Whatever they wanted in Kickapoo, I wasn't going to help them find it. My guts told me these guys were trouble.

Squinting, he said, "Thought we were closer. GPS must be off. Fucking foreign cars for ya."

"Judging by the name, it must be one shitty town," the short one said. The taller guy burst out laughing. Several of the bar patrons looked our way.

"Hey, what are you gonna tell, you know, him?" the short man asked.

"I'll call him and tell him the truth."

"Oh shit, he's not gonna like that, Hal."

"Let's drink up and get the fuck outta here. My kid's got basketball practice in the morning, and I don't want to get stuck here if they close the fucking roads."

"Sure, Hal. Hey, did you hear about the plumber who overdosed on Viagra? His wife is takin' it pretty hard." The shorter man began to laugh at his own joke. Once again, the patrons turned and looked.

The taller man threw some money on the bar and got up to leave. He turned and looked at me, and I saw a tribal tattoo on his neck. "Hey buddy, here." He handed me a red business card with Big Al's Wrecking Service, a phone number, and a website address written on it. On the bottom right corner was the word 'Cairo.' "Looks like you could use it." They walked out.

I wrote Hal on the card and stuffed it into my pocket. On my way out, I paid and thanked the bartender.

Outside, the air temperature had dropped, and it was getting foggy. I had about five miles to go. I could feel the warmth of my cabin from here. Whatever those guys wanted in Kickapoo sounded like trouble. They followed my directions and headed east. I headed west.

THREE

The ER waiting room was chilly. I wondered if it was a trick of the mind as I watched the snow fall. Concerned, I stayed, wanting to see if she was all right. I could call someone for her. She must have taken the curve too fast and lost control. I hadn't smelled any alcohol in the car or on her breath. She must have hit some ice on the road like I had. When I arrived at the hospital, I called Frank to see if he could get her car off the guardrail so no one else would run into it. A nurse headed my way.

"You can go in now," the nurse said. "Are you a relative? Only relatives are allowed in the back." She whispered, "You look like a nice man, but the doctor on duty is a stickler for the rules. You look like you could be her..."

"Uh, brother?" I suggested, keen to find out the woman's condition. The nurse nodded and walked me to the back.

"Doctor, this is her, uh—" she looked at me.

"Brother. Tanner." She left me with the doctor.

"After a thorough examination, we found no broken bones, no concussion, no internal bleeding, and no lacerations. There was some mild bruising from the seat belt. She'll be sore for a few days. She complained about her wrist; I diagnosed a mild sprain. We wrapped it up. Gave her some pain meds through the IV. She's groggy now but resting. We'll be releasing her soon. Take her home, and use ice packs on and off for the wrist—it will help with the swelling and pain. I'll send her home with some painkillers and anti-inflammatory meds in case she needs them. Follow up with her regular doctor in about a week. Any questions?"

"No, thank you, Doctor. I'm glad she'll be all right. Did she say anything about what happened?"

"Not about the accident, but she mentioned a friend a few times. She got lucky." We shook hands, and he left. The nurse returned.

"Unfortunately, we had to cut off her clothes, although we try to damage them as little as possible if we can. The hospital keeps some spare donated clothes, which is what we used to dress her—nothing fancy."

"Thanks, I appreciate that. I'll make sure I bring them back and a few more to help out."

"Oh, that would be wonderful. I'll let you visit for a bit and get her discharge papers ready." She turned and left the room.

The fluorescent fixture in the center of the room hummed. Its harsh bright light would send a photographer into a fit. I flipped the switch off. The soft overhead light above her bed cascaded down in a non-threatening glow. The IV machine and heart monitor beeped a steady rhythm. They bandaged her right arm for the sprain and taped up her left forearm to hold the IV catheter in place.

I grabbed her purse by the nightstand and opened it, but there was nothing out of the ordinary. Her wallet had sixty-two dollars in cash, two credit cards, and some business cards. I flipped through some pictures, presumably of family or friends. I found a vape pen and a keycard for WXNG-TV News in Chicago. She had an Illinois driver's license as well.

"Well, let's see who's taking up my Friday night." I scratched the day-old growth on my chin. "Five feet, six inches, a hundred and seven pounds, and born on July 7th... calculate the years... which would make you twenty-eight. North Side Chicago address; nice neighborhood. And your name is Samantha S. Rhodes."

I looked around the room for a chair, pulled it up beside the bed, and studied her. I watched her chest move up and down as she breathed. She would sometimes make a sound, like a moan, or take a deep breath. Reaching over, I squeezed her hand, and to my surprise, she squeezed back.

I thought about leaving; I was sure they could find someone to call. But for some reason, I stayed.

Leaning over the bed, I brushed a strand of hair from her forehead. Her wavy hair was golden butterscotch in color with a balayage of sandy blonde tones. The scent of strawberry and something else I couldn't immediately identify wafted around me. My nostrils flared as I inhaled deeply and recognized the smell as mint. Strawberry and mint—an odd combination. But it added a nice touch of freshness to her girl-next-door features.

My eyes investigated her as they scanned her body, adding her up like a math equation. It totaled to a high number. She looked self-confident and intelligent, but with an innocence that had not yet been tested by the modern world. The dusting of freckles that traveled across the bridge of her nose gave her a hint of cuteness. Her eyebrows were full and plucked to perfection—not a single one was out of place. Her lips were dry and pale pink, and the top one was slightly thinner than the plumper bottom one.

Beginning to stir, she moaned and tried to speak, so I moved in closer to hear what she had to say. A faint voice got one word out: "Ad-ee." The nurses came in and removed her IV. Still groggy from the pain medication, they put her in a wheelchair. I told her I was her ride home. After being discharged without a hassle, they gave me a bag of her belongings, and we headed to the truck. I buckled her in and called two hotels, but they were both booked solid all weekend. The snow had started to fall fast and heavy. An inch had accumulated already.

Her eyes fluttered open as she said, "Hi." Her voice was shallow. "Hello."

"Just drop me off at my place." She undid her seat belt, slid over to me, and put her head on my shoulder. The scent of strawberry and mint filled my senses. I made the call that I'd take her to the cabin instead, and we'd figure it out from there.

Our journey was uneventful. She needed help getting around, so when we arrived, I carried her to the spare bedroom. She was light, and it felt good to help her. The hospital had dressed her in a man's red-and-black flannel shirt, which on her was more like a robe. The navy-blue sweatpants she wore were long and baggy. White tube socks she had on tied the whole mismatched ensemble together. I put her to bed, covered her with blankets, and let her sleep. I went to the kitchen, got some Blanton's bourbon out, and poured myself a drink.

The hand on the wall clock slid past midnight when I poured my second drink. I'd sleep on the couch just in case Samantha got up and needed me.

FOUR

The dog never took his eyes off the pale man with the athletic build as he circled the plywood table with an aluminum strip wrapped around the edge. Overhead, the fluorescent light fixture flickered, its ballast buzzing to the point of annoyance. A gang member belonging to Lucifer's Disciples, sat nervously in a chair. The pale man surveyed the yellow grease-stained walls that were typical of housing in Chicago's Austin neighborhood on the West Side.

"I love dogs, don't you? Well, I guess that's a stupid question because if you didn't, you wouldn't have one. What's his name?"

"Butchy, man."

"Butchy. What kinda name is that for this magnificent creature? He should have a name like Zeus, Poseidon, or Thor."

"My son named him. You know, about that—"

"We will get to business in a bit." He kept circling the table. "First, I'd like to get to know you." He stopped and looked at a picture on the wall. "Is this your family?"

"Yeah man, leave 'em alone, mothafucker."

The pale man tilted his head. "Your son. He looks... funny, or something."

"He has Down's, man. He's a good kid."

"Oh, I see. He's retarded." The pale man turned with a thin smile.

"Man, why you got to use that mothafuckin' word, man?"

"Because that's what he is. No?"

"No, he's got this... condition, man."

"Condition. Never heard it described like that before. Say, when you found out he was retarded, did you ever think of taking him down to the lake and drowning the little fella? You know, make it look like an accident?"

The gang member bolted up.

The pale man pointed at him. "Sit down, DeeDee. You don't wanna make me sit you down. You fucked up, and you're in some serious shit. Don't make it worse for yourself."

DeeDee sat down, wiping his face with his hands.

"You know, Rottweilers aren't aggressive by nature, but old Butchy here does not seem to like me much." Butchy's eyes never wavered, not even when he licked the drool from his dark lips.

"He's a trained killer."

"Is that so? How'd you train him?"

"I only feed 'em every third day. Keeps 'em hungry."

The pale man stood behind DeeDee. His right hand slipped behind his back and produced his Black Widow knife. Its handle, black and gold with spider web etching, made for a solid grip. Its single bloodthirsty edge was clean and curled up to a sharp point. The pale man took DeeDee's right wrist and placed his hand on the kitchen table. "Hold still," he said. Before DeeDee could register what was happening, the knife penetrated his skin, slicing through the plywood table and out the bottom.

DeeDee screamed, "Mothafuck. Aghhhhhhhhhh. Mothafuck."

"Let this be a lesson to you and your tribe, asshole. It's this simple. We sell guns, and you buy them. If another gang wants guns, they buy them. You don't go sharing the guns. How many fucking times do I have to tell you pricks? No sharing! These guns aren't your fucking girlfriends."

"Fu... fu... ck you." DeeDee was shaking; his right hand was stuck to the table. Blood ran to the table's lip, dripping onto the linoleum floor.

DeeDee was breathing hard. He watched the pale man's eyes but they revealed nothing of the events that were transpiring. Out of nowhere, the pale man had another knife in his hand. This one was a Bowie survival knife with a nine-inch blade. One side was clean while the other had a row of saw teeth—perfect marching soldiers—that were razor sharp on a slotted blade.

"And it pisses me off that you don't feed that dog." He reached for DeeDee's left arm. DeeDee tried to resist but his mellow, drug-addled reflexes were no match. The pale man held DeeDee's hand flat on the table, put the clean edge of the knife on DeeDee's middle finger, and looked him in the eyes. "I'll make this quick."

"No, no... Ughhhh."

The knife sliced down. The blade cut easily through the flesh, tendons, and nerves, but it stopped at the bone. DeeDee jerked to free his right hand, but the Bowie blade held firm. The pale man applied more pressure to the knife, but it would not cut through the bone.

"Damn it," he said. "I thought for sure this would've done the trick."

"No... no... no." That was all DeeDee could muster.

"Oh well. Guess I'll have to saw through it." He flipped the knife over and began to use the jagged edge to saw through the bone. A few cuts later and the finger was off.

"There." He then twirled the knife and slammed it through DeeDee's mangled hand.

Butchy cowered in the corner as his master sat trapped and writhing in pain.

"So, no sharing, right? Can't talk, huh? Nod. Good. Excellent. I'll be on my way. Give my love to the family. Hey, Butchy. Here boy." Butchy's ears perked up, his head tilted, questioning. As he looked up, the pale man took DeeDee's finger, held it up so Butchy could see it, and then tossed it to him. The hungry beast eagerly caught it mid-air and chowed down. Butchy's lips smacked as his teeth crunched through the bone. After a few bites, the bloody digit was gone.

DeeDee watched in silent horror and passed out.

Outside, darkness was descending on the city. The pale man took a deep breath of cold air and immediately felt better. His message had been sent, loud and clear. The phone buzzed twice before he answered.

"Well. What?" the pale man said.

"It's Hal. We're coming back to the city. I got some bad news. We hit the wrong car. It wasn't the right girl."

"What? Moron. I gave you everything you needed to get this done." His fist gripped the phone.

"It was the wrong car and girl. She wasn't the one in the picture you gave me."

"Did you search the car for the codebook?"

"Yeah, we didn't find it either."

"Fuck. I need that codebook back."

"I know. But it wasn't the right car, and it wasn't that whore, Addison Martin."

FIVE

Samantha slept through the night. When morning came, I dialed up Frank. He'd been able to get her car to the garage before hunkering down for the storm. He'd call back later with a report.

I made a pot of coffee and hit the shuffle button on a Spotify playlist on my phone. Its Bluetooth connected to my stereo. The soft classical music created a rich background. I put some more wood on the fire and then went to the front window to watch the snow fall. While sipping my coffee, I heard the floorboards creak behind me. I turned just as a fist was flying at my face. My reaction was too slow, causing it to connect with the left side of my jaw. I dropped my mug, and it smashed on the floor. Another fist hit my midsection. Before I knew it, I was up against the glass with my hands around my head for protection. She tried to get in another jab in my ribs, but her fist connected with my elbow instead, and I heard a slight scream.

"Samantha, stop," I barked, peering over my clenched fists. She stood there defiantly, swaying slowly in a side-to-side motion. Her arms with their balled hands looked like two mini cobras ready to strike.

"Who the fuck are you, and where the hell am I? How do you know my name?" she said in a stern, raspy voice.

I relaxed my hands and showed her my empty palms; a sign of surrender. "My name is Tanner York—Ty. I found you on the side of the road on Route 71. You must have hit some ice and slid off the road. You're in my cabin in Kickapoo. I got your name from your driver's license because the hospital needed your info. Do you remember anything?"

She looked at me warily. I moved slowly and kept my distance. The music and crackling of the logs on the fire filled the room with sound.

"Yes... I think so. Someone helped me... you? I remember the doctors and nurses, and now I'm here." She looked down at her baggy clothes. "Whose clothes am I wearing?" She moved a step closer, looking like she was ready to attack again.

"Whoa, easy. I mean you no harm. Here." I motioned for her to come over to the kitchen bar and sit. "Your clothes had to be removed by the nurses so the doctor could examine you. The nurses dressed you in whatever they had lying around. Sorry, they did the best they could. All your things are here. Look—there's your purse. Check it out. You'll see it's all there."

She went through her purse with diligence. She often looked up at me to make sure I was staying put.

"And my car?"

"Your car is at Frank's Auto Repair, and it's going to need some work, I'm afraid."

"I'll call a cab or Uber."

"They won't come out here because, as you can see, it's snowing quite a lot. We're up to ten inches, at least according to the weather report. They've already closed most of the roads. I'm afraid we're snowed in for the day. Cell service is a bit sketchy, but your phone is on the counter charging up."

Her eyes widened, and her mouth opened as she looked out the big bay window. Just loud enough for me to hear, she muttered, "No way."

"I have plenty of room and plenty of food, and you're more than welcome to stay. It's no problem."

She looked at me apprehensively with her cognac-colored eyes. "You're not going to kill me, are you?"

"No, ma'am."

Her eyes scrutinized me. "Who are you again?"

"Tanner York. You can call me Ty."

"How do I know you're not the guy who caused the accident?"

"I'm not, but you're free to examine my truck. Other than one on the rear quarter panel, there's not a scratch on it. If I was going to do something to you, I've had more and better opportunities to do so since the accident, don't you think? You are completely free to go, I'm just not sure how you'd leave." Her demeanor softened a bit.

Samantha looked out the window again, evaluating her options. She turned and looked at me for a time. "I'll need to make some calls. And if need be, I'll fight dirty. My dad sent me and my sister to self-defense classes."

"I'll keep my distance, Samantha. I believe you could kick my ass if you wanted. Your kung fu is strong. Do you know that?" She stood there, eyeing me up and down, weighing her options. She looked around the cabin. Not a thing was out of place. It wasn't the type of dingy lair in which the bad guys on TV hold their victims hostage.

"Well." She bit her lower lip, and her eyes flared up at me. "We'll have to make it work. And everyone calls me Sam, or Sammy."

"Then... that is why I shall call you Samantha."

She thought about it for a bit. "Fine. I like that. Can I take a quick shower? And have something to eat? I'm kinda hungry, and you can catch me up on what happened last night in detail. I must look a mess." She brushed the curtains of hair out of her face.

"You look great," I said, rubbing my sore jaw.

As the night devoured the day, the glow from the fireplace offered a soft and warm respite from the cold. The sounds of Beethoven's "Fifth Symphony" filled the void. She told me what she remembered, driving along Route 71 in the fog, seeing a bright light, like a flash of lightning, losing control of the car, and hitting the guardrail. Then me pulling her out of the vehicle.

She made several calls when the reception was available. Everyone told her to sit tight—they weren't coming for her until the storm had passed. She called her sister in Florida to let her know where she was and what had happened. We concluded that she was lucky—it could have been worse—and that we would ride out the winter storm together for another night. Conditions would be better tomorrow, and they'd have the roads cleared by the afternoon.

I put the last of the logs on the fire. The flames seized the wood in a chokehold, and the wood popped in protest. I would need more firewood soon. It was cold outside and the winter nights were long.

"Beautiful place. Didn't know cabins could be so cool. You have a lot of books." Her fingers roamed over my book collection displayed on the floor-to-ceiling bookshelf.

"Do you read much?" I asked.

"Constantly." She looked around the cabin, restlessly moving about. I couldn't take my eyes off her. She made sweats and flannel look like lingerie.

I took a few blankets out of the closet, putting one on the floor next to the leather club chair that was my usual spot to sit. I put another blanket on the matching chaise. Bottled water was on the coffee table for us, and I took my place on the floor with the chair supporting my back.

"This is nice," she said, rubbing her hands together in front of the fire. The effects of the trauma were wearing off. She sat on the chaise opposite me.

"Yeah. It's a normal Saturday evening in the winter for me," I laughed.

"Is there a Mrs. York? Or a girlfriend I need to worry about busting in to catch us as we lounge in front of this romantic fire?"

"No, I'm a single man. It's only the owl and me."

"Owl?"

I got up and motioned for her to follow me to the front window. The moon was full, and the snow was acting like a giant reflector, making the darkness glow ghost white.

"There." I pointed.

"Oh, he's beautiful," she cooed.

"He sits in that oak tree from time to time. I was thinking of naming him after Dashiell Hammett, the writer. But I guess that's silly. I don't even know if it's a him or her owl."

"No, I like it. Dashiell, or Dash. That's what we'll call him."

We headed back to the fireplace. Samantha was warming to our situation.

"What about you? Your boyfriend tracking you on some cell phone app?"

"Ha, boyfriend. I wish. My work schedule doesn't really allow for a social life. Even if it did, it would be the same old story. Men my age don't get it. I'm at work at all hours, and then I get accused of cheating."

"I saw your keycard for WXNG-TV. What do you do there?"

"I'm a PA—a production assistant—for the news department, now. Have to think fast on your feet. I work during newscasts, edit video, do floor directing, and run cameras—all that stuff and more."

"Wow, that's quite the workload. I watch WXNG-TV News all the time. I see Meghan Orr on there a lot reporting on the shootings. Do you know her?"

"Sure, I know Meg. I was her intern for a summer. She's a good reporter, but the hours suck. Meg wanted to be called at any time of day, regardless of what anyone else was doing. Her goal is to become a news anchor, ASAP."

"What did you do for her?"

She sighed. "Well, I set up interviews, did research, and went out on location. And I did the coffee runs, of course." She smiled, staring into the flames.

"Where did you go to school?"

"I went to FIU—Florida International University in Miami. Got my BS in Broadcast Journalism there. While doing that, I was a Miami Dolphins cheerleader for two years. That opened up some modeling work in print magazines, stuff like that. Then I did the intern thing at WXNG. After graduation, I had a short reporting gig in Milwaukee, but I found that I didn't like it. Then WXNG called me. They'd always liked me and offered me a reporting gig, but I said no. As it turned out, they happened to have a PA job open as well, so I took it."

I grabbed the poker and tended the fire. My mind was forming a mental picture of what she'd look like in an orange and aqua cheerleading uniform.

"So, what do you do for work?" she asked. "Let me guess. You're a writer and living out here helps you think and create remarkable worlds of wonder."

"Not quite. I work for WAR—it's a law firm in the city. I have a condo in a high-rise, which is where I stay during the week. Just come out here on weekends and holidays. I do research investigating for the firm."

"Wait. What?" Her face light up. She sat up on the edge of the chaise, eager to learn more.

"I investigate for a law firm. Downtown."

"Really? You might be just the guy I'm looking for."

"How do you mean? Are you in trouble?"

"No, not me. But my friend Addy might be," she said.

That name triggered my memory. "You mentioned a friend when I found you. Is that who you were talking about? The doctor also said you asked about a friend, and you said 'Ad-ee' to me in the hospital. Why are you out here?"

"Addison Martin is my best friend. I call her Addy for short. She's been missing for a little while."

"Did you call the police?"

"Not yet. Addy disappears occasionally. She's kinda flighty. One time, we didn't hear from her for more than six weeks. When she finally got in touch, it turned out that she'd been in Europe all that time. She works in sales or something, travels from Chicago to Vegas a lot, and sometimes she goes overseas. But the last time that I talked to her, she seemed different. Desperate. Addy and I have a mutual friend out here, and I was hoping she'd seen her. I couldn't get ahold of her on the phone, so here I am."

"By 'we,' do you mean her family?"

"I mean our circle of friends. Addy's not connected with her family. But I should call her dad, I guess. She's closer to him than she is to her mom." She blinked and smiled at me. It was the first real sign of being at ease that she had shown since she'd arrived.

"That might be wise."

She raised her eyes to meet mine, biting her lower lip. "You could help me find her."

"I usually don't do side jobs outside of work. Going to the police would be your best option." I forced a smile.

"Come on. You could probably find her quick. That would give me so much peace of mind. I'll pay you, of course." She took her eyes off me and stared into the fire. "I probably couldn't pay you your normal fee, but I can call my dad and work something out." Her eyes locked with mine. They challenged me to say no. "Please," she whispered.

Something about this girl sent a thrill up my spine in a way that I hadn't felt since Karin had died. She had a spark. And I liked it. I wanted to say 'Yes, I'll help,' but the voice in my head was sending out a warning blast not to get involved.

"We need more firewood. I'll be back." I got my coat, put my boots on, and fled outside to avoid the conversation. It was still snowing, and the wind had picked up, making it almost blizzard-like. I scooped up a bundle of wood, headed inside, and filled the wood bucket. Samantha wasn't in the room when

I returned. I hoped she wasn't mad. What could it hurt to check around a bit? I had a few contacts I could call.

When I finished putting the second load of firewood by the fireplace, I took off my outdoor gear and sat back down to warm up. Samantha returned and curled up on the chaise, absent were the sweatpants and socks. I noticed she had undone a few buttons on her shirt that were not undone when I had left. She wanted me to look and notice that she wasn't wearing a bra. There was a definite shift in her demeanor—she seemed to switch from playing defense to offense when she found out my occupation. Did she think using her sexuality would sway my decision to help her?

"Not sure if I mentioned this earlier, but I still have my cheer outfit hanging in my closet. And to answer that question you have swimming around in your head, yes. It still fits, Ty... ger." A proud smile framed her face. "Has anyone ever called you that? Tiger?"

My face flushed red. "Uh, no."

"I could really use your help, Tiger. Please." Again, we locked eyes. She bit her lower lip, waiting for my answer.

My better judgment screamed at me to say 'no.' But...

"What I meant by an 'investigator' is more like I sit in an office on the computer and look through law books." I couldn't stop myself. "We have lots of software at the firm, some of it the police don't have access to. It might be able to track her down. Give me her full name, and if you have a picture, that will help, too."

Her face lit up again. It made me feel good to make her happy.

"Thanks, Tiger." Her eyes sparkled. Before I knew it, she was off the chaise and hugging me. She kissed my cheek gently, and the thrill I felt in me amplified. She had me hooked, and we both knew it.

We watched the fire dance together in silence. I looked over at her and smiled, and she smiled back. I realized our silence wasn't uncomfortable but enjoyable. It was excellent spending time with someone—her—like that. Sometimes you can get to know a person by what they don't say.

"Uh, I need more water, do you want anything?" I broke the trance, got up from the floor, and headed to the kitchen with a limp.

"You okay? You're limping."

"Ah, it's just my knee. Old sports injury. When I sit like that it gets stiff."

"I hope that's the only thing that gets stiff tonight," she giggled, captivating me with her playfulness. She followed me into the kitchen.

"I'm sorry, but you totally set me up for that one. I like to tease, and I feel comfortable with you—is that okay?" She grabbed her purse and pulled a vape pen out. "I'm going to take a hit or two, it's odorless. Would you like some?"

"No, I have asthma."

"I don't smoke cigarettes, this just helps me relax—it's good shit. Taking a puff or two will set me up for the night. I'd rather take this than those pain meds they gave me. This is better for you, anyway. Are you sure?"

"I'm sure. Water?" I didn't want to get into the pros and cons of vaping or marijuana with her right now.

"Do you have anything stronger?"

"Beer? Wine?"

"Stronger?"

"You a bourbon girl? I have E. H. Taylor bourbon, it's barrel proof though."

"Very specific, Mr. York. Can you tell me the number and age of the barrel it came out of?"

Shaking my head no, I asked, "How do you take it?"

Laughing again, she said, "Neat, please." That surprised me even more. Most people can't take barrel-proof bourbon without water or ice. From my experience, most young people are more into craft beer than straight liquor, or those fancy mixed cocktails the bartenders put smoke into.

I poured two glasses of neat bourbon.

"These are cute glasses, they're tulip shaped," she said as she swirled the liquid around.

"They're Glencairn glasses. Made in Scotland, they're designed for tasting whiskey..." I could see I was losing her and stopped. "Sorry."

She raised her glass. "To my hero," she bellowed. "Thanks for saving my life out there, taking me in, and taking care of me. And for helping me find Addy."

"Cheers. To warn you, this bourbon is 129 proof, so it's got a bite to it." We clinked glasses.

"I'm a big girl, I can take it." She winked and took a large gulp, but as soon as she swallowed, it came right back up. She coughed, spraying the alcohol all over me while making a sour face. It ran down her chin, neck, and chest. The floor took most of it.

I reached for a towel and handed it to her, patting her on the back. "Told ya it had a bite."

"I guess I'm used to the cheap stuff that's watered down," she coughed.

She wiped her face and neck with the towel.

"That was embarrassing. Sorry about that, I'll drink it slower this time." Dropping the towel on the counter, she started back to the fireplace.

"Uh, you still have a little..." She turned, and I pointed to her general chest area.

She pulled the front of her shirt away, revealing her cleavage.

A few droplets of bourbon trickled down the valley between her breasts. I couldn't help but watch the liquid slide over her smooth skin.

"Here." I brought the towel up from the counter, my eyes never leaving the traveling droplets.

She took the towel and wiped it all away. "Don't mind me, I'm a bit goofy." Again, she giggled. She turned and headed over to the fireplace. She was now sucking me into her little game. I was her mouse to play with. My curiosity took control. I wanted to see this play out.

"Would you be a love and bring me my glass? Sit next to me, okay?" She batted her lashes in a way that would make the hardest of men bend to her will.

Crossing the room to walk toward her, I held out her glass. "Slow, this time."

"Yes, sir," she said, giving me a mock salute.

We sat on the floor facing one another, sipping our bourbon. I poked at the fire and added another log. Looking at her more closely, I realize that I hadn't noticed until now how big her eyes were. The radiance from the fireplace illuminated her right side; the darkness of the room shadowed her left. I drank in every drop of her beauty thirstily, feeling the pull of not just a want but a need. I was trying my damnedest to resist, but she had a deadly combination of good looks and wit. It was a double-barreled shotgun pointed straight at my heart. Would she let me down easy or let me have it with both barrels?

"You're a creative kinda guy."

"How do mean?"

"Well, you read, you listen to classical music, and I would imagine you have to be creative in your job."

"Yeah, I like the arts."

"Let's play a game. Here, face me. Let me tell you what I see." She didn't wait for an answer. "Hmm. On one side of your face, the light from the fire shows me a man who is pure, good, and kind. It's a worn look, but not from age—it's from experience. A man who has seen tough times but gotten through it. Serious gray eyes that know right from wrong but sometimes do wrong things to make it right. I see someone who provides for himself, his family, and others. His is a face you can count on and trust with your life. But it's also the face of someone who can be taken advantage of precisely because of those traits.

"On the other side, the dark side, I can't see anything. But I can feel an aura; there is a presence there. It's a part of who you are. It's dark and cold, haunting you—even tormenting you. Alive, moving about inside of you; it's its own being. Is it pain? Do you use it as a shield so no feelings can penetrate? The light can't take over that side because you don't want it to take over. You feel it's your protection, your armor. It wants control. A tormented tiger lurks within."

"Well, I guess we've made it past the small-talk stage," I said.

She laughed. "Did I make you feel uncomfortable? I didn't mean to. When I interned, part of the job was reading people. You needed to know who would make for a great interview and those that wouldn't."

"No, you've been entertaining. It's good to be uncomfortable sometimes. Gets the blood going."

"Now it's your turn. Tell me. What do you see when you look at me?"

"I see a young woman—"

"Ohhhh, you've got to do better than that."

The heat from the fire was drawing the moisture off the wood, causing it to hiss and pop. The classical music that was playing in the background seemed to reach a crescendo as I spoke.

"Well, I see a *beautiful* young woman—"

"Continue."

"—whose glowing face can light up a room. She has eyes you can get lost in. A warm smile that would melt any glacier. It's a face full of life, laughter, and love. A free spirit who's willing to take chances and make people happy in whatever way she can.

"Your other side is not so dark. It's ashen and has some secrets. You like mystery; you like games. You're a cat, and the world is your mouse. Which makes me wonder if I'm one of your mice. It's the side where that right hook introduced itself to my jaw." She giggled. "It's still sore, by the way." I rubbed my chin for dramatic effect.

We fell into an easy silence that was broken only by the crackling of the wood on the fire and the music.

"It's getting late," I said. "I've kept you up, and you need the rest."

She shook her head. Hair went everywhere. The chaotic tangle of her tresses combined with her carefree attitude made her irresistible. She moved closer, and I could feel her breathing. She took my left hand in hers, leading my hand to her chest, passing it through the gap between the red-and-black flannel shirt. With great care, she placed my hand on the bare skin over her heart. She wore no bra. I could feel her warm, silky skin, and my thumb slid under her small, firm breast. My touch caused her breath to quicken, her heart galloping in my palm.

I raised my head, looking deeply into her eyes.

In a soft whisper, she said, "See, I'm all right. Still breathing. You've taken great care of me, and I'm forever indebted to you."

Her eyes narrowed, one side of her mouth curled, forming a sly smile that went beyond sly—like a crafty serpent. A serpentine smile.

"Let's play another game. Would you like to tie me up... Ty?"

I held her by the shoulders and pulled her to her feet. My right hand grabbed a fistful of velvet hair and pulled her head back. Lust burned throughout my body, and I could think of nothing else. A soft gasp of surprise escaped her lips.

"Now you listen and you listen good." I looked into her eyes, and they grew hot with passion. "I don't mind this whimsical game we've been playing, but a man can only take so much. I can only take so much. Your actions and words have consequences. Do you understand?" I shook her gently. "Don't you understand that once it starts, it can't be stopped? Once you open yourself up, only pain follows. I won't do it again. Do you hear me?"

"Take me," she purred.

I kissed her hard. My free hand grabbed flannel, and in one fell motion I ripped her shirt open. Cupping one of her breasts, my index finger and thumb pinched the nipple awake. She responded by biting my lower lip. Samantha's hand reached down for my crotch, in a frantic search found the stiffness in my pants, and stroked it. Her fingers fought the restraint of the button and zipper. Once she had succeeded, my pants fell to the floor.

Still engaging in our tongue tango, she hopped up, wrapping her legs around my waist and her arms around my neck. My hand went underneath her bare rump to support her. She cradled the back of my head with her hands and pulled me into her chest. My mouth explored the valley of her bosom. She moaned as my tongue flicked and played.

She pulled my head back and went in for my neck like a vampire. Her mouth worked feverishly. I carried her over to the chaise lounge and laid her down. Standing over her, Prokofiev's "Romeo and Juliet No. 13, Dance of the Knights," played, setting the mood. I felt the flames licking out heat and the light illuminating Samantha's body. She looked so beautiful in the glow. She made herself available to be admired. Every part of her was exposed by the open shirt. Her eyes were hungry, and her serpentine smile was ready to devour me. I stumbled back, the bourbon affecting me. She looked so young, so wrong.

The tempo of the music reached a climax as all the instruments collided into a crescendo of madness.

"Not like this. What happens after? I've let this go too far." I pulled up my pants, tucked in my shirt, and zipped up. "You're too young—"

"I'm tired of boys," she shouted.

"I'm sorry. I shouldn't have done this."

She shook her head, tossing her hair into a tumble that spilled over her shoulders. The dancing light from the fireplace revealed a lascivious face with spirited eyes.

"Okay, Tiger, you win. Besides, I'm a bit tired." She gathered herself, kissed me softly on the cheek, and retreated. In one last moment of whimsy, she flipped up her shirt, flashing her bare bottom as she disappeared into her room.

I closed the glass fireplace door, took our empty glasses to the kitchen, and gave myself one more pour of bourbon. Walking to my bedroom, I couldn't decide whether I should lock myself in.

NEWS FLASH – WXNG-TV, CHICAGO

"In a brutally violent and snowy twenty-four-hour period, Chicago police reported thirty shootings. There were ten fatalities and twenty wounded this weekend. Meghan Orr has the latest."

"Thank you, David. Among the ten killed were children and teens. Of the thirty shootings, twenty-three were gang related. Four others were robberies, and three were attributed to domestic violence.

"I am currently in the Austin neighborhood, where you can see behind me the most recent crime scene. Police are still unspooling the barrier tape as this shooting happened mere moments ago. What began as an otherwise happy family gathering ended on a deadly note. The victims, an eight-year-old boy, his aunt, and his grandmother, were waiting at a bus stop after spending time with relatives in celebration of his aunt's birthday. As they waited, a shootout apparently erupted between rival gangs. What we do know is that a stray bullet hit Edgar Lamar in the head. His grandmother, Rosie Reynolds, was struck in the leg, and a bullet grazed the neck of his aunt, Dianne Wharton. Edgar was immediately taken to hospital where we have just learned that he passed away.

"Police are still looking for more casings and evidence. But for now, the snow is making the investigation difficult.

"And earlier, on the South Side, two separate triple shootings took place about two hours apart. The first happened in the Englewood neighborhood. Three men were sitting in a car when shots rang out. One man was hit in the left shoulder, the second in the leg, and the third in the mouth.

"The other triple shooting was a drive-by. A silver-colored car pulled up alongside a small group of teens who were playing in the snow. Someone in the backseat pulled a gun and opened fire into the group. Three teens were hit but were able to find cover. No word yet on any of the victims' conditions.

"I spoke to a man who lives close to where the drive-by occurred, and he said the following:"

"I just can't believe this, all this shootin' goin' on. There's violence everywhere. We can't let our kids walk to and from school anymore. Or play outside of their homes."

"I'm afraid the recent spate of violence isn't showing any signs of cooling off, despite the chilly weather. Reporting live from the Austin neighborhood, I'm Meghan Orr for WXNG-TV News.

"Thank you, Meghan. Now let's get an update on the weather..."

SIX

Frank's Auto Repair was a time capsule of rural Americana—a snapshot of the old Route 66 days. The roadside dust on the wooden structure had been replaced by wet, gray snow. The place had modern repair equipment like the big-city garages, but out in Kickapoo, service stations still sold gas. Fuel pumps chimed with every gallon dispensed. The customer service was unlike any elsewhere. Frank would come out rain or shine, hot or cold, and fill your tank. He'd check the oil and wash the windows for no extra charge. On occasion, Frank would take payment in kind for the repairs he did for the less fortunate.

The roads were cleared early, so we headed over to the garage Sunday morning. Samantha pilfered some personal items from her car and then made some calls in the garage office. Frank looked at the damaged car on the hoist.

"Look at the back end." Frank pointed at the car.

"Wow, that must have been some hit."

He lowered the car from the hoist to show me the damage to the left rear quarter panel.

"We had a hard time getting it off the guardrail, and it caused some undercarriage damage."

"You've seen a lot of wrecks," I said. "Doesn't this seem excessive? I mean, driving down such a twisty road in those conditions means that speed wasn't likely a factor."

"What are you getting at?"

"Samantha said she saw bright lights, like lightning, in the rearview mirror before the crash. Those were probably—"

"Headlights?" Frank said.

"Most people drive slow in severe conditions."

"Are you saying this was deliberate?"

I shrugged. "Hit from behind? Pushed over the rail?"

Samantha walked into the garage. She had on one of my coats and the same navy blue sweatpants, but she was wearing a clean shirt of mine because I'd ripped the red flannel one. She had a way of moving that made people take notice—she commanded attention, and she knew it.

"It kinda stinks in here." She crinkled her nose looking at us like we should do something about the odor.

"Sorry. It's an auto garage," Frank said.

"Hey," I said, pointing to the rear of the car. "You got lucky."

"Yeah, I've never been in a bad wreck like that before."

"Remember you telling me about the bright light you saw—like lightning?"

"Yeah. So?"

"When I hit the ice, my truck fishtailed, spun around, and slid down, following the bank of the curve. Correct?"

"Sure, if you say so." She sounded annoyed.

"Your car was on top of the bank over the guardrail. The brightness you saw was another car's headlights—the mirrors caught the lights. A car hit that back bumper and pushed you over the guardrail. What do you think, Frank?"

Frank's slow nod confirmed my theory.

"Great, a hit and run. I guess the question is, how do we find this individual? Call the cops?" Samantha breathed deep to help dissipate her nervous energy.

"Let's stay calm," I said. "We can go through the proper channels. Frank will take good care of your car. He'll order the parts and have it fixed in no time."

"What about the cost? My insurance will skyrocket."

"Let's not worry about that. The most important thing is you're okay. It could have been worse."

"Hey, let me tell ya. This guy here," Frank said as he slapped me on the back, "he's one of a kind. Ty's a great guy, and he'll work hard to figure this out. There aren't many guys like him around. I'm gonna get started and order those parts." He headed to the office.

Samantha looked at me and said, "Hard worker, huh?" Her serpentine smile formed as she turned and headed outside to call the insurance company. I watched her go with a devilish grin of my own.

I stood there looking at the car. Something wasn't quite adding up. Samantha's car had been struck hard. Why the hit and run? How damaged was the other vehicle? Was this an accident? Or was it deliberate?

I joined Frank in the office where he was on his laptop, looking up parts. Samantha came in behind me.

"The insurance company is closed, so I left a message. I don't think it would be a problem to have Frank make the repairs," she said. "But regardless, I'll make sure Frank gets paid. So, can we go now?"

"I wanted Frank to take a look at my truck," I said.

"But I need to go home and get into my own clothes. I'm tired of wearing baggy men's clothes. Not that I don't look exceptionally hot in them."

"Ty," Frank said. "I gave it a quick once-over earlier, and it's cosmetic. I know what parts I need, although they'll be hard to find, so you're good to go."

"Appreciate all the help, man." I shook his hand, and Samantha gave Frank a big bear hug. Heading for the door, something caught my eye—a red piece of paper on Frank's desk. A red business card. I flipped it over; it said Big Al's Wrecking Service, and the word Cairo was written in the corner—the same card the tall guy named Hal had given me at the bar.

"Hey, Frank, where'd you get this?"

"Uh, you know us repair guys, we all stick together. You never know when you may need a part for something vintage. We all call one another, ya know?" He seemed restless. He took the card out of my hand and put it in the drawer.

"Okay. Thanks again, Frank." Feeling uneasy, I left and headed to the truck to drive Samantha back home to Chicago.

SEVEN

I headed into the law offices of Westcott, Ackerman, and Rockwell first thing Monday morning. The law firm had its own building on LaSalle Street, close to the Chicago Board of Trade. Known as the WAR Building, I was told that Frank Lloyd Wright redesigned the public entryway in the early 1900s. It was stunning; a decorative scheme of arabesque patterns in white Carrara marble made it pleasing to the eye. It gleamed white and gold but had the musty smell of old money.

I arrived at the office at six, eager to find Addison Denise Martin, the friend Samantha had been searching for. Samantha had sent me a text with a photo of Addy. I checked all her social media platforms, and the results were fairly ordinary: pictures of family and friends, meals in some fancy restaurants, but no new posts in the past few weeks.

I also checked the facial recognition software we had and checked with my contacts at the Secretary of State's office for any outstanding warrants or citations. Some investigators search websites like Zabasearch, iTools, and Wink People Search—but I even checked the deep web using Pipl.com. I had access to all the programs you could want to use to find someone, but I kept hitting dead ends. I wanted to check out Addison's apartment, since maybe I could find something before the police could. Samantha was coming to the office at around eleven, and I wanted to be able to tell her that I had found some leads. But first, I had to attend the Monday morning update meeting.

WAR's conference room was exceptional. Entering through double glass doors, the centerpiece was a twenty-five-foot solid oak table. Surrounding it, or guarding it, you could say, were high-backed Italian leather chairs. The extravagant designer glassware held our imported bottled water from Iceland. As Julius Ackerman, the founder of the firm, was fond of saying: "The best law firm in Chicago needs the best people and the best office in town."

Another part of my job was running background checks on potential new hires. I had a few to report on at the meeting. The partners always followed my recommendations on whether the applicant was right for our firm. If you wanted to work for WAR, you needed to impress me the most.

Punctuality was important to me. I always tried to be the first to arrive at meetings. My father had taught me that reliability was key to being a person of integrity. William Westcott was second to arrive.

"Morning, Ty. Some storm. Glad you made it in." Westcott's gruff voice did not reflect who the man was inside. His brilliant legal mind and courtroom strategy were responsible for the firm's ironclad reputation. But get him started on his grandchildren and it was hard to shut him up.

We talked while he shuffled through papers. "Bottom line is," he said, "I think I'm too old for grandkids." He smiled and winked.

"Aren't we all?"

As the others filed in, my nervousness grew, even though I'd done this a hundred times before. As more of a backstage person, I'd never been one to speak in front of crowds. My morning coffee was essential to finding balance and propelling me through meetings like this.

In came Julius Ackerman, chubby and graying at the temples. Hot on his tail was his legal assistant/legal administrator, Jillian Sinclair. She was five-eight in heels with jet-black hair styled in a bedhead bob. I wondered if her messy hair reflected what life was like for her outside the office. Known collectively as the J-Birds around the office, they were never far away from one another, but their relationship was more father–daughter than anything else. If someone asked me who ran the place, I'd answer Jill. She kept things on schedule and made sure the partners were where they needed to be. Jill was one of the few people I talked to regularly in the office.

"Okay, are we all here?" Julius said. "Randolph will be joining us later."

The partners and associates reported the progress they'd made on their old and new cases. That was where I'd get hints of what was coming my way—cases I'd be working on, witnesses I'd be vetting, and phone calls I'd have to make.

The first question for me came from one of the younger attorneys about the cross-examination prep that I'd been doing on the Rodney case.

I cleared my throat. "Henderson has an offshore account that wasn't disclosed, with some large deposits being made right around the time of the incident."

"Excellent," William said.

The young attorney exhaled a sigh of relief. "Thanks, Ty. Dig further, locate all his assets. Real estate, accounts, vehicles, artwork... hell, even a plane if he has one. I want to know where this guy eats, sleeps, and... well, you know what else."

"Done," I said.

Ten minutes into the meeting, Randolph broke in. Arms outstretched flamboyantly, he bellowed in his irritating voice, "Morning everyone. Happy Alooooooha Monday."

Us Chicagoans have many quirks. We commute twenty feet in the air on an El, not a train. We know our highways and expressways by name and number. We love retro furniture—especially chairs with orange plastic seats and chrome metal legs from the sixties. They're not for sitting on but for standing guard ceremoniously, like Beefeaters at the Tower of London. Because when you've shoveled the snow from your parking space, you want that space back when you return.

We believe the Willis Tower is still the Sears Tower and that it's still the world's tallest skyscraper. The phrase 'lake effect' sends terror through our veins. Pizza is a meal that should be eaten with a knife and fork—not folded up like a snack. And ketchup should never be put on a hot dog.

Another Chicago institution was Randolph Rockwell, ace attorney for the firm.

"Morning," everyone replied in varying tones, except me.

"How's our top attorney this fine, fine morning?" Julius asked.

"Living the dream, Julius, living the dream," Randolph said.

"And taking names?"

"You betcha." Hearty laughs ensued. Randolph shaped his hands into pistols and gave everyone 'the guns,' as he called them.

Randolph and I went way back, but not in a good way. Her name was Karin Weaver, and she was my fiancée some twenty years ago. We'd had a great, fun-loving relationship. Karin was so beautiful, a real natural beauty. One fall Sunday, I was set to watch the Bears–Packers game, and she had been acting weird for the past few weeks. She'd asked me to take her shopping that day because she wanted to show me something. We argued about it. It was one of those stupid arguments that all couples have—quick, and easily forgotten. She went anyway, I stayed home. An hour later, I got the call from the County Sheriff. There had been an accident, and he told me to get to the hospital, fast. But I didn't make it in time. Karin died before I got there. Hit by a drunk driver. He'd blown through a red light, according to two eyewitnesses. His name was Joe Holiday, and he survived with nothing more than a few scratches. He was still living in Naperville with his wife and had two kids—last I checked, they were both in college. He never spent a second in jail, never got fined, and never got convicted. All thanks to an arrogant, self-centered, pompous-ass lawyer by the name of Randolph Rockwell. Julius had hired Randolph about ten years ago, and Randolph was always reminding me that he owed me a favor. I knew that the guilt ate away at him, which made me happy.

After the fanfare of Randolph's entrance, the meeting settled back down "So, Jill. Where do we stand with the celebration party? The congressman will be here at three p.m. sharp," Julius said.

"Yes, after lunch I'll put up the decorations. At two-thirty, I'll pick up the cake, the caterers are coming at two-forty-five. You can give your speech at three-fifteen or so, and we can eat and celebrate after that. Sound good?" A firm smile creased her face.

"Excellent. Always to the point, Jill," Julius said. "See if you can find someone to help you."

"It's okay, no prob—"

"I'll do it," I said. "I'll help."

"Ty? Really? That would be great. Is that okay, Jill?" Julius asked.

Her firm smile softened "Sure, I guess."

"Way to go, Tyster," Randolph said, giving me the thumbs up. I rolled my eyes.

"Excellent, excellent. Now, let's move on to the new hires. Uh, Ty, whatcha got?"

"You want to talk about this now? We don't usually discuss this in front of the whole team."

"It's okay. We have the party later, just give us a brief rundown," Julius said.

"Aren't you going to tell him," Randolph said, pointing at me, "about my new—"

"Later, later." Julius hushed him and motioned for me to continue.

"So, we had a lot of applications for an internship. They all seem fine, even the one from Harvard Law where Randolph went." Randolph turned around, his smirk approving the dig I gave him.

"Well, he's hired then. I'll take him," Randolph said.

"He is female, and she has a 5.0 grade point average," I said.

"Even better." Randolph's sly smile inflamed my nerves. "All the girls want to work with me." His eyebrows danced up and down. "I can teach her so much." His booming laugh took over.

"That's quite the sexist comment, even for you, Randolph." The heat in me spiked. "You should know better. Julius, William— don't we have a zero-tolerance company policy on this?"

"I was joking, Tyster. Come on, everyone knows that." There was a spatter of nervous laughter.

"Okay, let's settle down. We'll shelve the new hire discussion until later in the week. And Randolph, my office after the meeting," William said.

The meeting wrapped up soon after that. Everyone buzzed with excitement about the party we were having in the afternoon to celebrate Randolph's big win on the high-profile Ainsworth case. Everyone but me. I headed to my office to get some work done.

I needed coffee and headed to the kitchen for a fresh cup. Jill was there, staring at the wall, deep in thought in some faraway place.

I grabbed her shoulder and said, "Hey come back to earth..."

"Ouch," Jill shrieked.

"Sorry. You, okay?"

"Yeah, Preston used me like a jungle gym over the weekend. At thirty-six, I'm not as flexible as I used to be." She rubbed her shoulder. "You were in early. I saw your office light on when I came in."

"Oh, I had some work to do. How was your weekend? Did they cancel the soccer game? It was indoors, right?"

"Yes, indoors, but they didn't cancel. We braved the aftermath of the storm on Sunday and went to the game. He did great—scored a goal and held his own with the bigger kids. Then we had to book it over to Caprice's piano recital. She had some trouble with the song she's learning. I just need to get on her to practice more. We watched TV, made pop—"

Jill's story was interrupted when Peter Pozniak from payroll came in and announced, "Hey, Ty, your appointment's here." Jill and I looked up and saw Samantha leaning against the door jamb.

She breezed in dressed in a pencil skirt with a slit, of course, and a blouse with a modest neckline and long trumpet sleeves.

She walked over and kissed me on the cheek. I fumbled for words, and she turned her attention to Jill.

"Hi. Samantha Rhodes. Nice to meet you." She shook Jill's hand.

Jill responded with surprised eyes. "Jillian Sinclair. Likewise."

"Can I get a cup?" Samantha pointed to the coffee maker.

"Sure, let me get it for you," I said. "How do you take it?"

"If you're referring to the coffee, I like it strong, creamy and sweet, please." She pitched her serpentine smile and a wink my way.

Jill looked at me over the rim of her mug. "So, how long have you two known each other?"

"We met this weekend. Tiger here saved my life." Samantha entwined her arm with mine. "My hero." I could feel the heat rise in my cheeks.

Jill spit out her coffee. "Tiger?" she muttered, while grabbing a towel and wiping the brown liquid off her chin. She pushed up her sleeves to wash her hands.

"How was work this morning?" I said to Samantha.

"Don't change the subject, Ty. Please, tell me about what heroics our marvelous Tanner York performed. Or is it now Tiger? Like the golfer? But you don't golf." Jill acted confused.

I blurted out, "It was Friday night, and—"

Randolph entered with his World's Best Lawyer mug in hand. Eyeing Samantha, he hovered around her like an eager hummingbird searching for sweet nectar from a beautiful flower. "Well, hello. I'm Randolph Rockwell. It's a pleasure to meet you. You've come to the right place if you seek representation. We're the best law firm in the city. And in case you're wondering, Rockwell is the R in the W-A-R that's on the building. That's me." His eyebrows glided up and down a few times.

"So, this is where they keep the good-looking lawyers," she said coyly.

"We strive to be the best in all aspects, my dear. Has anyone given you the tour yet?" Randolph took Samantha by the arm, walking her slowly out to the hallway.

"Randolph," I said, "it's an office building. What tour?"

"You know, my office has a spectacular view of the city. It would be a shame if she didn't get to see it."

"Ta." Samantha threw her head back while being led off by her captor.

I made a move to follow them when Jill grabbed my arm.

"Where do you think you're going, bucko? Get back here." She wagged her index finger back and forth.

I turned back, shoulders slumped.

"Never mind about my weekend," she said. "Let's hear about yours, Tiger."

Jill and I went into my office for more privacy, and I told her all about the past weekend's adventures. She listened, riveted. I decide to tell her everything. Even the hard come on by Samantha. I needed a friend to give me advice.

"Wow, that's quite the story, but shouldn't you call the police?"

"I have one more thing to check. What do you think of her?"

"Looks like you two are hitting it off. She's young, but nowadays a May-December romance isn't so frowned upon.

Take her out on a date, let time work it out. This is a good thing, Ty. Be happy."

"We'll see how it goes. She's young. It might be a problem."

"Take the advice my grandma gave me once, go for it. Some days, I wish I would have listened to her more often."

A familiar sound of knuckles on wood rapped twice. Julius stood at the door.

"Um, Ty, this young lady is here to see you. Randolph had a call. It was a pleasure meeting you, Sam."

"The pleasure was all mine, Julius."

Julius left, and Samantha leaned against the doorway. Her eyes locked onto mine. She was so pretty just standing there. My eyes took her in. "So, did the big shot lawyer sweep you off your feet? Are you captivated by his brilliance?"

"It was a big office, with a spectacular view of the city. I got asked to lunch with Randolph, Congressman Ainsworth, and Randolph's new assistant at the Signature Room on the 95th floor of the Hancock Building, no less." Her voice was slow and relaxed. She wouldn't take her eyes off mine.

"Randolph has a new—"

"Wow, that's something." Jill seemed nervous. I sensed a high degree of tension in the room.

"I told them I had plans with you for lunch to discuss our... missing person." She moved toward me, our eyes hadn't unlocked since she had returned from Randolph's office.

"Jill, will you come with us?" she said.

"Oh, no. You two should go," she said. "You know, three's a crowd." Jill moved to leave the room.

Samantha put a handout to gently catch her arm but never broke the lock she had on my gaze. "Please, I insist. I'd like to get to know you better. In fact, I think we have a lot in common."

"Like what?" I asked.

"You, of course, silly."

Jill nodded slowly. "I... I guess. Okay, let me get my coat."

"Excellent." Samantha released me from her stare.

We had a good time at lunch; there was lots of laughing and joking. Jill was different— more relaxed and open with her thoughts, feelings, and opinions. I was happy that Samantha and Jill got along. Jill told us stories about her kids and all their funny antics. Samantha and I laughed so hard we had tears in our eyes.

Jill and I headed back to the office to get ready for the party, and Samantha went back to the news station.

"She's lovely, Ty. I think you guys would be perfect together."

"I'm beginning to believe that."

Samantha and I were going to meet up later and go over to Addy's apartment. When I got back to my desk, I took out the red business card that the man with the neck tattoo had given me and thought about the similar one I had seen on Frank's desk. I called the number.

"Yes?" said the man's voice that answered.

"Can I speak to Cairo?"

"If you want to talk to Cairo, you need to book on the website."

"Well, I have this card with..."

"Use the website. No appointments over the phone."

Click.

Congressman Richard Ainsworth came from a wealthy family, and his political career was impressive. He had started out as a local politician, and then he enjoyed a short term as a state senator before landing a spot in Congress. He had held on to that office for some twenty years, never losing an election. The press loved the guy. About fifteen years ago, there had been talk that he might run for president, but he never did. He was approaching seventy-seven years of age but looked a hundred and seven. The other representatives called him 'Old Man Dickey,' which was a nickname that he hated, and no one dared to say it within earshot of him.

He was at the party to thank everyone for the hard work they'd put into securing him a verdict of innocent of the murder charge he'd recently faced. Right as the pressure was mounting for Ainsworth to resign his position, I had found some crucial evidence that proved he was innocent. But, as always, Randolph got all the credit.

As Ainsworth worked his way around the office shaking hands, he approached me, looked me square in the eye, and extended his hand. I took it with gusto, and by the grimace on his face and tightened jaw, I could tell my grip had been a bit too hard. His hand was corpse cold, dry, and bony. He asked my name, and I said, "Tanner York, a registered voter who believes in term limits."

"Smartass," he whispered so only I could hear. Julius looked at me with 'we'll-talk-later' eyes.

After the hip-hip-hooray speech, I got lost in the kitchen and started the coffee. Wealth was abundant in the office, but we still had a coffee maker that only brewed one pot at a time.

Jill walked in. "How's that coffee coming? Done yet?"

"We should really upgrade our coffee system," I said.

"At first, I thought you were being such a nice guy for offering to help, but then I realized that you just wanted an excuse to get away from Randolph and the party, right?"

"Is it that obvious?"

"How about that speech Randolph gave? I would have thought he'd at least share some of the credit with you." She poured the fresh pot of coffee into a carafe.

"He's always been a dick," I said.

She laughed. "Don't say that too loud. You'll get called into the boss's office next."

"Right. I practically live there." We both laughed.

"Thanks, by the way, for putting Randolph in his place at the morning meeting. That type of talk could cause real problems for us if the wrong person overheard it."

"You're welcome."

Peter showed his face once more. "Hey, Jill, Mr. Ackerman's looking for you."

Jill clutched her chest. "Jesus Christ, Pete, you scared the hell outta me." His eyes darted around like a fugitive on the run. Pete had always been the anxious sort. Randolph called him *Pee Pee*, which didn't seem to bother Pete. He'd laugh with Randolph like a kid trying to gain acceptance from the cool kids at school. His head was too small for his bulky frame. What had always puzzled me about Pete was the women he was often with. At plus-one company events, he'd show up with some of the most attractive women I'd ever seen. He wasn't all that good-looking—he was nervous and sweaty most of the time. But then again, what did I know about attracting females?

"Okay. Thanks, Pete," Jill said. "Ty, let me see what Julius needs, and I'll be right back." Jill turned and walked away without waiting for a reply.

Jill and I met back in the kitchen to start the cleanup when his highness barged in.

"There you two are," Randolph said. "Come on and join the party out front, there'll be plenty of time to fuss around in here later." He gave Jill a big inappropriate hug as he said it. "So, how's the family doing? Hubby good? The kids doing okay?"

"Yes, we're all fine and dandy." Jill pasted on a fake smile and escaped his embrace with grace. "Remember, we've talked about the no hugging rule, Randolph. And lay off the booze, you reek of it. This is an office party, not a boy's night out."

"Sorry. I must fly. Ta." He left the kitchen.

"We should go mingle for a while." Jill went to leave but quickly turned back and smiled. "You're right—he is a dick." She gave me a little wave and left. I didn't see her for the rest of the day.

I went out to the party and mingled by talking to a few people about sports and politics. But it was nothing significant or energizing. The party broke up and people started to head home.

I felt a faint tap on my shoulder. I turned and saw it was Peter. "Hey, Mr. Ackerman wants to talk to you before you go." He left as quickly as he had appeared.

I put on my coat, made sure I had my keys, and headed over to Ackerman's office. I thought about our relationship. Julius Ackerman was like a father to me, and his wife Margaret was like my mother. They were the ones who had looked out for me after my parents died. My dad had worked for Julius as an investigator, but they were more like brothers than anything. The Ackermans were always over at my house, or I went to theirs. I was raised by my aunt on my mom's side, but Julius and Margaret were a big part of my growing up. My aunt never cared for Julius, and I never found out why.

The only time I had ever disappointed Julius was when I dropped out of college. I had given it a try, but it wasn't for me. I did learn one thing in college, though—girls and bourbon were my two weaknesses. So, Julius had hired me to do various jobs around the office, but what I really liked doing was the investigating.

"Ty, my boy, come in, come in." Julius got up from behind his desk and gave me a big hug.

"I'll be brief. I know you want to get going."

"No rush. How's Margaret?" I asked.

"Fine. Thank you for asking, and thanks for being such a sport and going on a few of the blind dates she's fixed you up with." He sat on the edge of his desk. "Listen, I know Randolph can be a bit of an—"

"—ass?" I finished the sentence for him.

"Well, yes. But he's a damn good lawyer. He gave us a big win, and we're lucky to have him. But I know the part you played, my boy, how you helped crack this case wide open, and that's the important thing. So..." He reached across the desk and handed me an envelope.

I opened it. It was a check for ten thousand dollars. I puckered my lips and sucked in air. "This is way too much."

"You've earned it." He smiled big and rubbed my shoulder like a proud papa.

"But the others—"

"Everyone involved will be getting a bonus, even our custodian. Not everyone will be getting as much, but they will be getting what I feel is appropriate for their role."

"Now, as for these new hires. I know you have strong recommendations, and you've hired a lot of great people for us, but Randolph wants this certain assistant, so I said it was okay."

"What? I really have to object. Why didn't I know about this?"

Julius held up a hand to stop me. "Let's see how it plays out. If it doesn't work out, all the blame lands on Randolph. I told him this already."

"This is highly irregular. We never hire without proper vetting." My inside temperature soared when hearing this news.

"It's okay; you've nothing to worry about. We decided this on our own and we'll own it if it goes wrong," he said in a paternal tone. "When you have time, run the proper background checks. And if he doesn't pan out, we can deal with it then."

"By then it'll be too late."

Julius gave me a hard stare.

"Fine," I said with a twinge of irritation. "On another matter, you really need to talk to Randolph about what comes out of his mouth. It offends people. And one day, it could hurt the firm."

"Point taken. I know William has already talked to him about it, but I will too. And thanks for looking out for us. You are just like your father. You know, we were like brothers. He always looked out for us. I really do miss him," he sighed. "It's getting late, and Margaret is making lasagna for dinner. Come on, I'll take you to meet our new man."

We walked down the hall until we reached our destination.

"Ian Smith, this is Tanner York. We all call him Ty."

Ian got up from his desk and straightened his suit. He briskly walked over and shook my hand. "Pleasure to make your acquaintance," he said.

"Nice to meet you; this is a great place to work. You'll enjoy it. Julius takes excellent care of us."

My inquisition of Ian Smith started with a bit of light conversation, and I pegged him as ex-military based on his fitness level and politeness. He called me 'sir' a few times. But I was still going to check out his background, right after I found Addison.

As we walked out of the office, Julius asked, "Ty, Sam told me that you're inclined to help find her friend, Addison?" He rubbed his chin with his hand, contemplating his next thought.

"She's been missing for some time. I thought I'd poke around a bit," I said.

"Are the police involved? We should hand this over, no?"

"We're going to check Addy's—Samantha's friend's— apartment tonight. If I don't find anything, I'll call the police."

"Good, good. Glad you're helping such a nice young woman. Yes, yes. Margaret will be so thrilled that you have a nice friend." A big smile revealed his white capped teeth. It was hard to be mad at him.

"Say hello to Margaret for me."

"Will do, will do. But please, keep me posted."

I headed for the elevator, but a tug of my arm spun me around.

"Ty, hey man, if there's anything I can do to help, don't hesitate to ask. I'm new, but I want to help in any way I can."

Ian spoke more casually than he had only a few minutes before. There was something in his sneer that made me uneasy.

"Well, thanks. For now, I'm okay."

"Wow, a missing persons case. That sounds interesting. I'd love to be involved. What did you say her name was? Addy? Maybe Addison?"

"Yeah. Uh, sorry, I gotta get going."

He looked me dead in the eyes. "That Sam is sure something to look at, huh? Lucky guy." He punched my shoulder a little too hard. "Randolph introduced me earlier this afternoon. Was she a cheerleader or something?"

I sized him up, again. "Funny, she never mentioned meeting you." The elevator pinged, and I stepped in as the doors opened. "Nice seeing you again," I said, turning around as the shiny doors closed. Ian's face had a disturbing yet contented appearance. His strange, crooked smile revealed a hint of malice.

Ian Smith's skin tone was odd as well. He was unusually pale—even for a Chicagoan in the dead of winter. The pallor of his milky white skin sent a shiver down my spine.

CHAPTER

EIGHT

"You're the luckiest bastard in the world," said the old man on Ian's screen. "York's gonna lead you right to that bitch, Addison. He'll probably open the front door and invite you in, if you ask."

"I know." Ian's pale face cracked a smile. He sat on the brown leather couch in his apartment sipping a 2010 Spottswoode Estate Cabernet Sauvignon.

The man peered sharply at him. "You didn't want that lawyer job, and now look. It's going to be the best thing ever, and it was my idea." The face on the screen stared hard through the monitor. "So, you want to tell me why my evening has been interrupted?"

"You need to tell your guys to back off Hyde Park tonight so Hal and Artie won't have any trouble when they take Addison down, old man."

"You were supposed to do that last time, you know, out in Kickapoo. And stop calling me that. I've given years of service to this city and I deserve respect."

"My guys had a massive snowstorm to deal with out in Timbuk-fucking-tu. They did their best. It was a silver car, just like you said."

"*A* silver car, not *the* silver car. Did you just pick any silver car driven by a woman to run off the road? Asshole. Talk about drawing unwanted attention—"

A woman's voice interjected. "Gentlemen, please. Watch the language. Do what Ian asks, and clear the streets. And let me remind you two, Tanner York stays alive."

"Yes, Madame Zoe," the two men said in unison.

"What about Addison's friend, the one he's with?" The old man on the screen asked.

"If she gets in the way, take her out," Madam Zoe replied.

"Shame. A waste, really. What I could do to her..." Ian sipped his wine, deep in thought.

"You're disgusting. I don't even want to know what goes on in that wicked, perverted, racist mind of yours," the old man said.

"Ian, where are your men now? Are you sure Addison will be there?" Madame Zoe asked.

"We have eyes on York. One car is following them. Once we know where he ends up, they'll call Hal and Artie in so they can do their thing. York only mentioned that they were headed out there. I'm hoping she's there. If my guys encounter York how much trouble is he going to be?"

"Not much. He's not one to get involved," Madame Zoe sighed. "Too bad, I liked Addison. She was a great earner for me. Well, let me know when she's dead. And again, Ty doesn't get hurt. When are the Syrians coming to check out the demo?"

"Couple of days." Ian said.

"Good. When the Syrians land, take them straight to the farm." Madam Zoe left the call.

"Hey, dickhead. Get it done this time," the old man said. The screen went dark.

Ian picked up the computer and threw it across the room. Plastic exploded, spraying the room with bits of debris. He didn't like the *old* talking head on the screen. He swore that the guy's days were numbered.

He was bigger than this small-time shit. Madame Zoe wanted more, too. They could run this business together, just the two of them, and eliminate the other guy.

Free from interference, his men would take full advantage tonight. Hal and Artie would handle the apartment, and the others would watch the street. Ian poured himself another drink and decided to call Madame Zoe back to have her send over a girl. He ordered a blonde-haired slut wearing a cheerleader outfit.

NEWS FLASH – WXNG-TV, CHICAGO

"... and we go live now to Meghan Orr, who is on the South Side with more on that tragic shooting."

"David, police have confirmed that one thirty-year-old man is dead tonight as the result of a shooting that took place in the Washington Park neighborhood. It appears to have been a gang initiation, but police haven't yet confirmed a motive.

"An eyewitness who wanted to remain anonymous said that the man was walking down the street with his wife and two young children when two teens approached them and one pulled out a gun. The witness said there were some heated words exchanged and they could hear the man pleading with the teens.

"According to the witness, the teen with the gun shot the man in the head twice, and then he and the other suspect ran off. I asked this person approximately how old the victim's children were, and they replied that they were 'under five.'

"Neighborhood residents are outraged. They want more to be done to stop the violence in their communities, but police say it is an uphill battle when witnesses refuse to come forward for fear of facing retribution. One neighbor told me that everyone is considered fair game out here.

"Reporting live from the South Side, I'm Meghan Orr for WXNG-TV News."

"Thank you, Meghan. Now, in Washington today..."

NINE

I made a quick stop at my apartment before meeting Samantha. I sensed trouble on the horizon, and this time I wanted to be prepared. Besides, we were going to the South Side of Chicago, and some parts aren't too friendly. I picked up my Beretta and inserted a fifteen-round magazine, secured them in my shoulder rig, and headed for the door.

I waited out front of Addy's Hyde Park apartment for Samantha. The neighborhood was part of the 1893 World's Fair where electricity and the Ferris wheel made their debuts in the United States. The buildings in this area were of a neo-classical and Beaux Arts architecture.

As predicted by the weather report, a light snow had started to fall. They had said on the news that we were in for a light dusting but no significant accumulation.

Samantha arrived via taxi, and she had changed her clothes since I'd seen her that afternoon. Dressed for style, not warmth, she wore painted-on torn blue jeans, a tight and low-cut black shirt, and a black leather jacket. An oversized bag hung low over her shoulder, and to bring the whole outfit together, she wore black boots with four-inch heels.

"It's freezing out tonight," she said as she kissed me and unlocked the building's front door.

"Why didn't you put on warmer clothes? Although, I must say, you've certainly warmed up my night by wearing that outfit."

She smiled and gave me a wink. "That's why."

The elevator was out of order, so we hit the stairs to the third floor. The apartment was number 307. Samantha didn't hesitate to unlock the door.

I did a quick search, checking first for any occupants. The place was empty. It was clean, things were all put away, and the hardwood floors were shiny and free of dust. In the kitchen, there wasn't a single dirty dish. The contents of the refrigerator were few, with just yogurt, almond milk, and kale. What else would you expect to find in a fit young woman's fridge? The bathroom was just as tidy as the rest of the place. I found the color palette of the apartment pleasing. Light blues, whites, and pale yellows brought a freshness to it.

Samantha started in Addy's bedroom. I took the second bedroom, which was more of an office. The rosewood desk was particularly eye-catching. The fine materials gave the first indication that this was no ordinary desk. They make guitars out of rosewood, which is very expensive. The drawer faces featured traditional Chinese carvings. It had eight drawers with a pull-out flat board for extra workspace. Unless this was a family heirloom, it had to be worth a few grand, easy.

"Oh my God." Samantha screamed.

My hand reached for my Beretta in its shoulder rig, and I raced to the bedroom. "What? What is it?" I burst in energetically.

"She has Christian Louboutin shoes. And Louis Vuitton. And not just one pair of each—several."

"Damn it." I released the grip on the gun. "I thought you were in trouble."

"I'm serious," she protested. In her mind, this was a sign of trouble. "A whole wardrobe of top designers. She has Valentino, Gucci, Ralph Lauren, and Versace. Her bags are Coach and Prada."

"Okay, so we've established that she has some nice clothes, but we're here to find evidence that we can use to locate her."

"This is a clue that something's going on. How can Addy possibly afford all this stuff? She's never mentioned it, and I've never seen her wear any of these pieces."

"Maybe she wears it for work? Or…"

"Or what?"

"She might have a sugar daddy or something?" This seemed the most logical conclusion to draw in a city of this size with so many wealthy men.

"And not tell her best friend? I think not. We tell each other everything." There was no light in Samantha's eyes anymore. I didn't like it.

A car door slammed outside, so I headed to the front window. Two men got out. One was tall, the other was short. Alarm bells rang in my head. My brain raced, making the quick connection that these were the same guys from the Bison Head Tavern. Was Addy what they'd been looking for? I also had a hunch that they were the ones who'd forced Samantha's car off the road. My guess was they'd mistaken Samantha for Addy, and they'd somehow figured out that they had crashed the wrong car. And now they were headed our way. Did they want Addy or Samantha? Maybe they thought she was a witness.

"We gotta go, now! We got trouble." I took one quick scan of the desk, looking for something, anything with a clue. I found a date/address book, snatched it up, and put it in my big coat pocket.

"What's going on?" Samantha asked, holding a bag.

"We've got company coming." I took her by the arm and headed for the door. "What are you taking?"

"Shoes and a bag—she owes me for what I'm going through."

We headed down the stairs to the second floor, and I heard the click of the door to the stairwell.

"Wait." Looking around, I spotted a small janitor's closet in the second-floor hallway. I opened the door, and the aroma of disinfectant hit us hard. The closet was small—one person could barely fit, but two was pushing it. Inside were brooms, buckets, mops, and a circuit breaker box on an unfinished wall. It was dusty, damp, and littered with mouse droppings. I put the brooms and the buckets out in the hall to give us more space.

"Get in."

She looked back, wide-eyed. "Seriously? These clothes aren't cheap."

I pushed her inside. After a few quick adjustments, I managed to close the door. It was tight, but neither of us was complaining.

"Well, I did want to spend a cozy night with you," I said, trying my best to ease the tension.

"All you had to do was ask. You didn't have to go through all this trouble for me."

Muffled voices from the men downstairs filtered through the metal vents at the top and bottom of the door. They must be looking through the mailboxes for the apartment number.

"How did they get in without a key?"

"Guys like that don't need a key." Our bodies were touching in places that start fires you can't put out.

My crotch tingled as she pressed her leg into it and that serpentine smile etched across her face, ready to strike. Her hands began to roam my body.

"So, is that a gun in your pants or are you just happy to see me?"

"Both. The gun's a little further north."

"Yikes. You brought a gun?" She let go, and her body stiffened with fear.

"This is serious." Her eyes narrowed in agreement. We heard footfalls on the stairs. The hardwood was giving in to the weight of the men as they ascended the staircase, the old wood complaining in a loud, creaking voice. The muffled conversation grew louder with each step.

"Come on, it's right up here," one of them griped.

"Hey, did you see *Talented America* last night?"

"Naw, I don't watch that reality show crap."

"Oh man, you should. Those female judges wear them low-cut dresses. Man, lots of boobs showin'. I swear I saw one of them bitches had a nip slip last night."

"Glad you got your rocks off. When we finally find this bitch, I'm gonna make sure that knife cuts a little deeper. I'm tired of this goose chase."

"Hey Hal, would you look at this? Someone left the brooms out. Doesn't anybody give a shit about doing their job right?"

"I don't give a fuck, Artie. We got other stuff to worry about."

"It's a trippin' hazard. What if the power went out and there was a fire and everyone had to evacuate? Someone could trip, fall, and hurt themselves."

"What?"

"Well, then the fire department would have to send someone in and risk their lives to get that person out. All because someone didn't finish their job by putting the brooms back."

"That's fucked up thinking. Where you going?"

"I'm gonna put these brooms back."

The floor moved under our feet as the man approached. I hadn't imagined that Samantha's eyes could get any bigger than they were, but they had. My right arm was pinned against the closet wall. I tried to reach for my gun. I looked at the doorknob and saw that it had a turn lock on the knob. Wrestling my left hand over to the lock, I flipped it one second before I saw the knob turn and hit resistance. The man tried again, wiggling the knob in the hopes of unsticking a swollen door.

The lock held.

"Come on. Forget it."

"Well, at least I tried. My conscience is clear."

The conversation grew faint as they moved along up the stairs. I waited a few more seconds and unlocked the door.

"Let's go," I said.

"Were those guys talking about Addy?" Her fingers were entangled with mine as we moved down the hall to the stairs.

"Afraid so. At least my gut tells me that."

She stopped and jerked her hand to free herself.

"What are you doing?" I didn't let go.

"I want to ask those guys what they want with Addy and find out what's going on." Her voice was brisk and anxious at the same time.

"Addy's not home, and you must trust me that I will find out what happened. But for now, we have to get out of here and to a safe place. I know these types of men—if you go up there now, they'll kill you before you can close the door behind you."

Putting my hand on the side of her face, her shoulders relaxed, and the tension left her body. Her eyes filled with tears as she looked at me, accepting what I had said was true.

"I'm scared," she said in a soft voice.

"Me too."

We got out of the building and walked quickly toward the truck. Halfway down the block, a car pulled out of a parking spot and headed straight for us. The cold, crisp, clean air was about to heat up with gunpowder, bullets, and mayhem.

We were in trouble. One hand reached for the Beretta, the other one shoved Samantha into an alley.

"Whatever happens, stay down," I shouted.

As the car passed, I saw two men—one in the passenger seat and the other in the back—leveling their weapons, cocking them, and letting them talk.

My Beretta cleared my holster and I knew I had fifteen shots and no more. My first shot missed, and the second hit the car's front quarter panel. I could feel and hear their bullets ripping by. One caught my overcoat, kicking it up like a flag on a breezy day.

Standing my ground, I did not attempt to move, hide, or get out of the way. Everything around me blurred. I envisioned a major league pitcher washing out the crowd, being totally in the zone. Something took over. Moving forward on feet I no longer controlled, I fired my third shot, hitting the windshield but catching nothing important. The fourth and fifth shots connected to the front door, but again didn't slow down the hail of bullets coming from my new playmates.

Hot spent shells flew out of my Beretta, clinking as they hit the ground and coming to rest, making perfect melted circles in the powdery snow.

As my vision narrowed, I saw that their instruments of death were compact, spraying out a message I wasn't interested in receiving.

The Beretta flashed, kicked, and sent my answer back to them with every squeeze of the trigger.

My sixth shot missed. The seventh shot resulted in an explosion of reddish-pink mist in the front seat. The man dropped the gun as his arm went limp, his body bobbing and weaving around inside the car. The backseat assassin continued to fire aimlessly as the car jerked and jolted.

My eighth, ninth, and tenth shots caught the tail end of the car as it passed. The backseat assassin stopped shooting as the car went down the block and out of sight.

I had fired a gun plenty of times before, but never at anyone. It came easily to me, which I found disturbing.

My breathing was heavy and my heart pounded so fast it hurt. The chilly air hit my lungs as I inhaled deeply, causing me to cough. I took a puff from my inhaler.

Walking to the middle of the street, looked down, and saw the weapon that the thug had dropped when I shot him. I picked it up—a Mini Uzi, still hot.

Now I had one.

"Holy fuck, that was awesome," Samantha screeched as she came running. She threw her arms around me and held on tight.

"Are you okay? Are you hurt?" she asked.

"I'm all right. You?"

"I'm fucking shaking. Look at me, I pissed myself." She had. "Man, you showed those guys. Fuckers better not mess with us. Let's take down those two guys in the apartment."

When she said it, panic bolted through me. I'd forgotten. We still had to deal with them.

"Here, put this in your bag." I dropped the Uzi into her bag and zipped it closed.

"A souvenir?"

"One fewer gun on the streets." I took her hand and headed toward the alley. "Your friend is in some deep shit."

The alley was dark, but the moonlight reflecting off the snow gave us just enough light to see. Halfway down the alley, we slowed our pace so as not to draw attention to ourselves as we headed for the truck. We were holding hands and inching our way closer to the alley's end as my truck came into view. I picked up the pace just as we approached the last building before the alley opened onto the street. We stopped dead in our tracks when two men—one tall and the other short—emerged from the doorway.

TEN

"Hey. Did you two hear gunshots?" the tall man asked as we proceeded through the alley. The darkness gave us some cover.

"I think so. It was back there," I replied. I put Samantha behind me to shield her. We continued to walk, my hand itching for the Beretta.

"Uh, where are you two going? This is not the best neighborhood to be walking down an alley at night," the short one said.

"We're from Ohio, we just met up with some friends, and now we're going to get a bite to eat." With Samantha close, I decided the smart play was to be cool. "Any good places to eat around here?" I asked.

"We ain't from this neighborhood. Might be better for you to leave," said the short one.

"You look familiar. Do I know you?" The tall one pointed at me. "You look familiar too, sweetie."

"No, we're from out of town," Samantha said. "It's our first time here."

"Hey, would ya look at that." The shorter man moved in closer. We stayed in the shadows. "That's some piece of ass you got there, mister. Hey honey, do all the girls look like you in Ohio? It might be worth taking a trip out there."

"Sure, we eat all that corn, you know."

"Oh, that's funny. She's a riot. Isn't that funny, Hal?"

"Shut the fuck up," the tall one said.

"Have a good evening." Nodding at the men, I pushed Samantha ahead. I could feel their eyes following us.

"Hey, stop!" the shorter one commanded.

I turned, my mind racing, calculating the best possible outcome in this situation.

"I gotta know something," he said while the taller one wrinkled his nose at him. "How'd a guy like you—no offense, but you ain't all that special looking—get a hot broad like that? I mean come on, she's a ten in any state, 'cept maybe California."

Before I could come up with an answer, Samantha shot back. "He's got a big cock." She took command, grabbed my hand, and led me off to the truck.

Laughter erupted from the alley, cutting the tension in the crisp, frigid air. Even I had a bit of a smile on my face. As we got into the truck, we heard the short man say, "I like that bitch."

Her body was shaking; I wasn't sure if it was from the cold or from the evening's recent events. The truck's bench seat offered little comfort.

"I might have ruined these shoes." She held them up, showing how the straps were twisted from her tight grip.

"I've never shot anyone before," I replied, numb.

"It was them or us. I think you made a wise choice. And thank you." She sat close, almost on top of me, squeezing me tight.

"For what?"

"Saving my life, again. I owe you so much."

"We need to go to the police. I think you need to let Addy's family know that they need to file a missing person's report. She's in some shit that I can't fix. I'm just a researcher from a law firm, and I have no training in detecting crime. Those men are hard. They're using Uzis—fucking Uzis. It's a war we're not going to win. If they find out who we are, they'll make us disappear rather easily."

"You haven't even started looking properly. Sometimes you need to shine a light on where the bad guys are, watch for a mistake, and now that we have a clue—"

"What clue?" I gave her a puzzled look.

"Someone knew we were coming here." She put her head on my shoulder. "Addy's in trouble. How many more girls are in trouble? If we keep digging, we may not like what we find. But we need to try. Will you do that? For me?"

We sat in silence for a few minutes. What she had said echoed in my brain. Like it or not, I was in this fight. Having her by my side was all the reason I needed to continue. Suddenly, chimes went off, making our hearts pound and bodies tingle with fear. It was my cell phone.

"Ty, it's Frank. The car's ready."

"That was fast."

"I'm going to leave the keys in the usual spot. I'm headed out of town, so I wanted to get it fixed before I left."

"Out of town? Where—" Frank hung up before Ty could finish the question. "That's odd," he said.

"Who was it?"

"Frank. Your car's ready."

"Great. Thanks. I can get a ride out there. You've done enough for me already."

"I'll take you. Frank sounded weird, he said he was going out of town. Besides, you don't know where he keeps the keys."

"No, I brought you into this, and you could have gotten hurt or worse. It's my problem." Samantha pulled back a bit.

"Are you fucking kidding?" I pulled the truck over. "I'm not going to let anything happen to you. We'll figure it out, but we need to play this smarter—whether it's us or the police, someone needs to find Addy before those guys do. We need a plan." I held up Addy's address book. "And this might help."

ELEVEN

I chuckled at the sign outside Bridget's Book Nook that announced: 'Our post-apocalyptic books have been moved to current affairs.'

The bell above the door announced our arrival.

The building was old with creaky, worn-out hardwood floors. Aromas of strong coffee, ink, and wood fueled my mind with inspiration. Opening a book could transport you to a faraway place. I felt at home there. Safe. Chopin played in the background. The store had a mood that a big chain bookstore couldn't match.

We found a round oak table in the back corner and soon it overflowed with papers, a computer, and unfinished coffees. We'd ended up at Bridget's Book Nook after we'd made a quick stop at the news station where Samantha kept a change of clothes so she could get out of her urine-soaked jeans. She'd asked someone in the office if anyone had reported a shooting in Hyde Park, but no police activity had been reported in that area. We needed to decompress and figure things out. I didn't want to take her to her apartment in case we were being followed. Bridget's was close and public, which seemed safer.

"I'm going to get something. Need anything?" Samantha rose from her chair.

"No, I'm good." I watched her walk off in her newly acquired heels, banging out a rhythm on the worn hardwood floor. The short guy was right—she was out of my league. I rethought calling the police now. What would I tell them? That I'd shot someone who'd been shooting at us from a car? Would I tell them about the two men, Hal and Artie? Tell them about Addison and her suspiciously expensive wardrobe? They'd take us in, and I wouldn't see Samantha again. I needed more time to think.

I opened Addy's address book. Big Al's Wrecking Service, I gasped, as I held up a familiar red business card.

"What's that?" Samantha said, sitting back down with a hot vanilla latte.

I told her about the three red cards with 'Cairo' written on them that I'd seen since last Friday. There was a definite connection.

"Did you web search it?"

"No. I called the number, but the guy on the phone was no help. Then I got sidetracked."

"You investigate for a living, and you didn't look it up online? I think Mr. Ackerman is paying you too much." She smiled.

"Whose side are you on, anyway?"

Just then, bells rang out. We both jumped—my hand reached for my gun while Samantha crouched for cover, digging in her bag for the Uzi. A customer walked through the door and headed to the cafe. We were a little keyed up, to say the least. We looked at one another and laughed. I wondered what Samantha would have done with the Uzi had she pulled it out.

"Here, pass me the laptop. I'll do it." She hammered on the keys, and I flipped through the address book. It really wasn't an address book at all—it was more like a schedule book for appointments with dates, times, and names penciled in.

"This is interesting. There's a bunch of names with X's next to them. Some have more than others. And you know what? The names are all male." I seemed to be speaking to myself. Looking up, I saw Samantha's eyes go from pinpoints to colossal. Her hard stare indicated she'd made a discovery.

"What is it?" I said.

She turned the laptop to face in my direction. Scrawled across the screen was: BIG AL'S WRECKING SERVICE.

The homepage text offered 'beautiful, dazzling companionship' for corporate events, reunions, and other functions. Basically, it was an escort service.

She clicked on MEET THE GIRLS. The screen displayed names like Sapphire, Payton, Vicky, and Cairo.

"There. *Cairo*," I said.

We waited for the page to load like dogs waiting for a bone.

"Oh my God!" Samantha cried, attracting the attention of the other patrons, who turned and looked at us. "That's Addy. What the fuck?" She pointed in disbelief.

"How can you tell? The face is pixelated." I clicked through the pictures. All were sexy, and a few were naked as they advertised their wares. But not a single one showed a clear facial image.

"Trust me, it is. I know her body as well as I know mine, and that's Addy. She has a beautiful face—you saw the picture I sent you. Why would they blur it out?"

"Makes it hard to ID anyone's illegal activity," I answered.

"Illegal activity?" she questioned.

"Because this is probably prostitution, and that's illegal."

We read Cairo's bio.

"Hello, I'm Cairo, a 24-year-old, 102-pound brunette bombshell with a graduate degree, successful career, and a zest for life. My personality is vibrant and my laugh infectious. I'm fun, with all-natural, toned, and athletic curves. I'm the girl next door with a naughty secret... the perfect mix of sugar and spice. I'm equally comfortable in my tennis shoes as I am in my Louboutins..."

The entry went on at some length, making flirty promises interspersed with blurbs about her height, weight, measurements, and other attributes.

"Are you kidding me? She's not twenty-four."

"That's what bothers you about this?"

"Oh, you mean about weighing one hundred and two pounds? Yeah, no way on that one either."

At the bottom were hourly 'donation' rates, including some for couples and 'special rendezvous arrangements.' Hourly rates ranged from the low- to mid-four figures.

"Well, now we know how she can afford her wardrobe," I said.

"I'm keeping these shoes," Samantha snapped.

"Did you know she was doing this?" I asked.

"No, of course not." She raised a hand to her forehead. "Oh, Addy, what have you gotten yourself into?"

"My guess? It's about money. She could've ripped off the wrong guy. Her pimp, maybe."

"She's so beautiful in these pictures, how could she not be earning enough? What do we do now?"

"We take the direct approach. Make an appointment with her and see what's going on."

"I'll come with."

"I don't want to scare her off if she sees you come barging in. Those guys are going to find her eventually, and I don't want you near them when they do. I want to figure out the situation," I continued. "I'll let her know you're concerned and have her call you when I'm there. Then you can talk to her, and maybe we'll be able to convince her to come with me and resolve this thing."

I looked up to see Bridget making her way over to us. Her auburn hair blazed with intensity as it was illuminated by the different sources of light in the room. She looked stunning.

"Hi, Ty," she said. "I didn't know you were coming in tonight."

I shut the laptop and stood to distract her from what I'd been doing. "Just working on a case with my, um, *client*." It sounded unbelievable.

"Uh, nice." She looked at Samantha. "Was the latte okay?"

"Oh yes, we've had several. I'm Sam, by the way."

"Oh, sorry," I said. "Bridget this is Samantha Rhodes, my... friend."

"Hi, nice to meet you. Well, I can see you're busy." She hesitated and turned to me. "If you want to finish our conversation from Friday, I'm more than ready to. And I promise no distractions. Anytime. Well... see you around." She waved, turned, and left.

"You like her, huh? You got all flustered when she came over. Is she your ex and you still have feelings for her?"

I sat down and focused on the computer.

"She's cute, you should ask her out. On second thought, maybe I will."

"Uh... can we get back to this?" I opened the laptop.

"Sure." Samantha's eyes were locked onto Bridget, and she watched her work awhile. I looked at Samantha. It bothered me that she wanted me to ask Bridget out. But her last comment puzzled me. Was she into women, or was she trying to shock me? I couldn't care either way. You are who you are. Make no apologies for it.

We filled out the form together and sent our request for Cairo's services. At closing time, we packed up and hesitantly stepped outside.

Samantha's place was secure, with a guard and a concierge stationed twenty-four seven. I pulled into the underground garage next to the entrance to the lobby. The security guard came up to the window.

"You can't park here." He was firm and direct. I lowered my window.

"Hi, Wendell," Sam said.

"Oh, hello, Ms. Rhodes. Didn't see you. Is everything all right?"

"Yes. How's the family?"

"Great. Everyone's fine. Thanks for asking." Wendell smiled widely. He was a large man—like an offensive lineman for the Chicago Bears. It appeared that he and Samantha had a good rapport. I felt confident that Wendell could handle trouble well.

"Hey, Wendell, my name's Ty." I offered my hand. "Has anyone asked if Ms. Rhodes was home tonight? Any strange vehicles been hanging around?"

"No, it's been quiet. You know, being a weeknight and all. Are you in trouble Ms. Rhodes? Did something happen to you?" Wendell's wide smile slide to a straight firm line.

"No, Wendell, Ty's just messing around." She threw a look with wide eyes and arched eyebrows, waving a hand in dismissal.

I parked in a visitor's spot and followed Samantha up to her apartment. After she unlocked the door, I told her to wait in the hall. She didn't, of course, but then again, she had an Uzi in her bag. She had a great place; it was well-kept with a modern decor. And even better, there were no unexpected guests waiting for her.

"Well, you got me home," she said.

I grabbed her and kissed her. No more messing around. I couldn't take any more. My body was on fire. Her full, wet lips locked onto mine. Her tongue was eager to explore. Our feelings for one another were beginning to unravel from the evening's excitement and the newfound discoveries that were bringing us closer together.

Our goodnight kiss led to our hands roaming wherever they wanted. I was ready and willing. And then she pulled a one-eighty on me.

"Easy, Tiger," she said. "Maybe we should go on a date first. You haven't even asked me out. You had all weekend. What's a girl to think?"

"A date? More games? Well, I've been kinda busy, shooting up Chicago and all. You didn't seem to need a date at the cabin, if I remember correctly." I was beginning to think she was crazy.

"Don't you want to take me out on a date? I'll get dressed up all sexy so you can show me off. You can put me on display for the world to see. I'll wear my new shoes." She made starry eyes at me.

She drove a hard bargain. "All right. We'll go on a date. And if we're taking this slow now, let's find Addy first."

"Deal." She kissed me. "Bye, Tiger."

"Uh, can I have the Uzi before I go, please?"

"Oh, sure." She put the gun in a reusable shopping bag, kissed me one more time, and pushed me out the door. I waited until I heard the door lock before I left.

The caramel-colored liquid curled like a wave inside the glass, tumbling over onto itself. This was my third pour of bourbon. I was drinking it neat and fast, waiting for the cops to break down my door and haul me off to the Cook County Jail. Unwinding from the night, I replayed every bullet that I'd fired.

The hot shower did me good, and the bourbon did me better. I went to Big Al's website once more. Addy had a secret, and trouble followed her.

I pulled Addy's date book out while I sipped my drink. I went through the names again, but the names never changed, no matter how many times I looked at them. Two names stood out that I wished weren't there: Richard Ainsworth and Frank Brannon. Samantha's friend had a secret; my friend had a secret. Someone I'd known my whole life. What was Frank into? Did he send those two guys after Addy?

All the other names had from one to three stars next to them. Frank's name had ten. I reflected on the conversation we'd had at the bar only a few days earlier. He'd said he was seeing someone who was young and that it was complicated. He'd also said that she was getting out of a situation. Was it the escort business? Was she running from the cops? Or something worse.

NEWS FLASH – WXNG-TV, CHICAGO

"... we now head over to the West Side of the city for a report from Meghan Orr."

"Thanks David. Nine people, including five teens, were wounded early this morning in separate attacks on the South Side and here on the West Side. Two people were critically injured just before 5:40 a.m. near an Englewood memorial for a sixteen-year-old boy who was fatally shot earlier this month. Police said a forty-year-old man and a forty-one-year-old woman were standing near the memorial when a dark van drove by and opened fire. The woman was shot in the leg and stomach and the man in the chest, arm, and hand. They were taken to Stroger Hospital where the man died and the woman remains in critical condition.

"The police have cordoned off the north end of the block, which includes the memorial with candles and balloons for the teen.

"Police say no one is in custody but they do have leads.

"In another incident, a nineteen-year-old man was wounded by gang-related gunfire in the Fifth City neighborhood; he was taken to Mount Sinai Hospital and is listed in good condition.

"Reporting live from the West Side, I'm Meghan Orr for WXNG-TV News. Back to you, David."

"Meghan, is there any word on arrests being made in connection to the nineteen-year-old's shooting?"

"No, David."

TWELVE

My head protested as it left the pillow. It was slow moving—drinking is a young man's game—but I wasn't yet old enough to admit it. I made coffee and took the cup over to the big windows of my apartment. The city sprawled before me, on fire from the morning sun. Coffee by the window. This was my morning ritual.

I flipped on the television for the news. There was a report of gunshots heard in Hyde Park but no mention of any police activity.

I'd call Samantha later to check on how she was doing. We promised to answer each other's calls as a safety measure. I decided to pay the congressman a visit at his office. There was no word from Frank.

It was a beautiful day for late February in Chicago, with mild temperatures in the high forties and plenty of sunshine. The streets were beginning to fill with people on their way to work, earning their keep in this madding city we call home. The city reminded me of a hub, with people moving in and people moving out. Visitors came from all walks of life—Chicago's a significant interchange with an ebb and flow, keeping time with the rhythm of the street din.

The Fast Track Diner stood on a corner a few blocks away from my place. I picked up a paper and headed to one of the booths I frequent.

"Hi, Mr. York. Coffee?" Emily was a waitress in her last year at the University of Illinois at Chicago, or more known as, UIC.

"Hi, Em. Yes, coffee would be great."

"So, what will it be today? The Denver omelet with cheese or the two eggs with corned beef hash?" She poured my coffee.

"Let's do the corned beef hash today."

"You got it." She headed toward the kitchen.

I read my email, finished my breakfast, and drank about a pot of coffee.

"Here's the check. No rush." Emily always had a smile on her face. From what she had told me, she had a 4.0 GPA, so it wasn't going to be long before she'd be out of here and ready to start a career.

"Thanks. Have a great day, Em," I said. The bill was just short of fourteen dollars. I threw down a couple of twenties and left to get the truck.

I pulled the truck into the parking garage off of Wacker Drive, which was close to the congressman's office. A kid from the valet took the keys.

"Hello. How are you today, sir?" the young man said.

"Hi, are you sure you're old enough to drive..." I spotted a name tag, "Jordan?"

"Sure am! I'm nineteen. Been driving for a while." He got in the truck, and I turned back around.

"Hey, Jordan. Here ya go. Put it in a good spot." I handed him some bills.

"Thanks, mister. That's the biggest tip I've ever got." His smile revealed the braces that mom and dad had bought him.

I turned the corner and headed north onto Michigan Avenue. Halfway down the block, I arrived at United States Congressman Richard Ainsworth's office.

"Hello, may I help you?" an elderly woman asked in a soft voice.

"Hi. Ty York to see Congressman Ainsworth."

She looked at her computer, then at a piece of paper on her desk. "Well, I don't see your name. Do you have an appointment?"

"No, but I've some urgent business to discuss that I'm sure the congressman will want to hear about." I flashed a smile.

"Well, I'm afraid that without an appointment the congressman won't be able to see you."

"It will only take a few minutes, ma'am. I assure you, it's urgent."

"Is there a problem?" asked a large security guard.

"No," I told the guard. "Please tell the congressman that I represent his lawyer, Randolph Rockwell, who sent me to talk to him about... Cairo."

Randolph's name seemed to spark some interest, if not raise an eyebrow or two. The woman held up her index finger to the guard, giving him the sign to 'wait a minute.' She picked up the phone, relayed my message, and hung up.

"The congressman will see you now." She waved her hand toward the metal detector. I went through, and then the guard hand-searched me. Finding nothing, he led me down the hall. The guard rapped his knuckles on the enormous wooden door.

"Yes, come in," said the voice on the other side of the door.

"I'll be right outside," the guard said, letting me know I wasn't wanted.

"Great."

"Hi, Congressman Ainsworth. Do you remember me? Ty York, with WAR Law"

He looked irritated. "I only have a minute. Whatever it is, please be quick, son."

"Okay. I want you to stop looking for Cairo. Call off the dogs."

"Who? I don't know what you're talking about. One shout to the guard outside and I'll have you thrown out."

"Cairo, the prostitute you've been seeing? Now does that ring a bell? I have her schedule book with your name, dates, and times written in it. You saw her a lot. Shame on you, Congressman Ainsworth. I'm willing to go to the press and shed a bright light on the whole thing." My insides churned as I waited for an answer. I went from shooting someone to now threatening a US congressman. *Not too bright, Einstein.*

He let out a hearty laugh. "The Ackermans speak so highly of you, and now I see why." His face looked tired. "Let's cut the crap and get to it. I'll buy the book. How much?" he said, blank-faced.

"Two million, cash. And you're done with Cairo." Add blackmail to that list.

"That's a bit steep. I wonder what your boss, Ackerman, would say about your little side job..." The congressman's last words trailed off.

"I wonder what your wife and all those registered voters would say about *your* side piece?"

"You got a lot of balls, kid. I can have the money ready in a few days. But be warned. If anything happens to that book between now and then, I'll have the CIA, FBI, and the whole fucking US government up your ass and up the asses of everyone you care about for the rest of your life. I'll be in touch. Now get out."

That threw me. He didn't put up a fight or deny it. "I don't want you seeing Cairo again," I said.

"Oh, you have my word. I'm done with her. There's plenty of young pussy out there that will sleep with an old man like me... if the price is right. The payment's for the book—there may be names in there I could use as leverage to advance some political issues I'm having trouble with in this wretched city. I want that book."

"I'll see that the money gets put in the hands of good people." I left, and the large guard all but threw me out of the office. That was too easy. I knew I needed to find Addy, fast.

Jordan was still in the parking garage.

"Hello," he said.

"I'm ready to head out." He took my ticket stub.

"I parked it in a good spot, just like you asked. If you want to wait over there, I'll swing it around for ya. You might as well wait in the warm sun." Jordan was off before I could say a word.

I walked over to stand in the sunshine, thinking about my date with Samantha and what we could do. I'd take her to an excellent restaurant, and maybe we'd go to a show or a concert. Inside and out, I was content in that moment. I knew I wanted to start a relationship with her, which was a big step for me.

Jordan pulled my truck around, and I started to walk toward it.

Suddenly, a bright flash blinded me, and an unseen force picked me up and twisted me completely around, its power propelling me through the air. My overcoat resembled a cape, but it didn't help me fly. My arms flailed erratically and my legs bicycled, trying to find the earth below. I landed on Wacker Drive like a Navy fighter jet on an aircraft carrier deck. Hard. The energy of the blast pushed me along the rough concrete. The scrapes and cuts caused by the slide painted a crimson mask on my face.

Rolling onto my back, the loud ringing in my ears gradually replaced the din of the city I was used to hearing at this time of day. The immense heat from the blast warmed the cold breeze coming off Lake Michigan that washed over my body.

THIRTEEN

"Ty, can you hear me?" said a sweet voice from the clouds.

My eyes fluttered, fighting hard against the swollen flesh that prohibited them from opening.

"Ty, nod if you can hear me. You're in the ER at Rush University Hospital. Can you hear me?" The angel's voice was getting louder.

"Yeeessss," I was able to say through my cottony mouth with its burnt and cracked lips.

My eyes could barely make out a form—a figure emerging from the fog. The sweet voice had a shape.

"Hi. There you are." I looked into bright grass-green eyes surrounded by a pretty face and a short mop of messy hair. It was Jill.

"Water," I said.

"Sure, here you go. Just a little sip." Jill helped me get the straw in my mouth. "Julius is distraught, so he sent me over. You scared us. The cops called the office. What happened?"

"The truck exploded. I..."

"You're awake, that's a good sign." A doctor came into the room. "Your wife here was very insistent that she see you. Just take it easy. You have a bruised chest, a slight concussion, and some other scrapes and bruises. You have two lacerations on your face that required stitches—one on your forehead and another on your cheek. But nothing that should keep you here overnight. You're a fortunate man."

"Wife...?" I looked at Jill. "Must have hit my head harder than I thought."

Jill mouthed the words 'watch it' to me, it hurt to laugh, but it was worth it.

"We only let family see patients down here," said the doctor.

"Doctor," I said. "Jordan..."

"I'm sorry. He didn't make it. Was he a friend?"

"Yeah." An innocent life lost. He'd seemed like a nice kid. My body was numb from either the drugs or the news. Maybe both.

"I'm sorry, Ty. What can I do?" Jill squeezed my hand.

"Does Samantha know?"

"Not yet. I just got here. I'll call her now, give me the number and I'll go pick her up." She smiled down at me.

"Thank you. You're a good... wife."

"Doctor, he won't be discharged for a few hours yet, right? I'm leaving to get his...sister." Jill put on her coat.

"He'll still be here when you get back," the doctor said.

"Okay. See you soon then. Get some rest." Jill waved.

"Oh, honey, no kiss?" I said in my sweetest voice, trying to pucker my crusty lips.

She walked over to the bed slowly and deliberately. Her eyes narrowed, and she looked at me like a kid who had just been double-dog dared. The doctor stood there waiting. There was no getting out of it.

"You asked for it." She leaned down and planted a full, deep kiss on my lips. Pain flared in my mouth. She darted her tongue like a snake and gave me a look of smug victory.

"Happy?"

She left me with my eyes watering from the pain and my mouth agape from the shock. I had often wondered what it would be like to kiss Jill. I liked it.

My cell buzzed on the veneer of the side table next to my hospital bed—a 312 area code number I didn't recognize.

"Yes?"

A male voice asked, "May I speak to Tanner York?"

"Speaking."

"This is Mike from Big Al's. Got your form here, but Cairo is no longer with the service. Do you have another girl in mind?"

"What happened to Cairo? I need to see her."

"I don't know, these girls are flighty, man. Probably met a guy and thinks he's the answer to her prayers. But when he starts beating her, she'll come running back. They always do." He sounded confident. "Look, her friend that she started with is available. She's exactly the same—they could be twins, man."

"So, they know each other?"

"Best buds, you know. But Erika has blonde hair, bigger tits, and she's shorter. Other than that, she's the same. Interested?"

Maybe if I saw this Erika, she'd give me a lead or two if I explained that Cairo was in trouble.

"Sure," I replied.

"I figured you would be. She won't disappoint." He laughed. "Be in the Water Tower area one hour before your appointment this Friday at 8 p.m. I'll call back then with the details. Got it?"

"Yeah, got it." He hung up.

I called Frank's cell. Still no answer.

I heard a familiar *clack, clack, clack* coming down the hall. My guess? Louboutins. The spirited thwacks continued to build until they'd reached my room. And the title of this intoxicating symphony was Samantha Rhodes.

"Well, don't you look a mess, brother dear." Samantha cringed as she looked me over.

"Some people say it's an improvement. You look great, by the way. I'm officially the beast in this duo." We embraced, the strawberry mint smell was back, and it made me feel better. She pulled up a chair beside the bed.

"Jill's parking the car. On the way here, I told her everything. I know better than to ask you to stop looking for Addy. But I'm worried now that we're in just as deep as Addy is." I didn't like the look of concern on her face.

"We can't be sure this is linked to Addy."

"Bullshit. What was your life like before you met me? I doubt you were being hunted by some crazed ex-wife of one of your firm's clients." She got up with her arms folded across her chest and turned away. I could tell she was holding back tears. "Look, Jill's husband's going out of town on business tonight, and she offered to let me stay with her and the kids. But I think I should stay with you to help you recover. What do you think?"

"You stay with Jill. I think that's a good idea."

"But..."

"No buts. Until I'm strong enough, it might be better if you were out of town."

"Need I remind you who kicked whose ass the first time we met?"

"I know honey, please." I knew she was disappointed, but she agreed.

Jill entered the room and stood on the other side of the bed. We talked a little more and made a plan for Samantha to take up temporary residence in the suburbs. Jill lived in Oak Brook in a gated community about twenty miles due west of the city.

The doctor came into the room. "Mrs. York?"

"Yes?" Jill replied.

"I signed the discharge papers. The nurse will be in soon to take your husband out in a wheelchair. Be well, Mr. York. Follow up with your family doctor."

"Thanks, Doc."

Samantha looked befuddled. "Mrs. York? You two have some explaining to do. Although this," she made a circle with her index finger around the three of us, "could be fun." Samantha flashed her serpentine smile.

The glacial air outside took my lungs by surprise and made me cough, triggering pain that shot through my chest. Weak legs barely carried me to Jill's car. Samantha helped buckle me in the back seat. She rested her head on my shoulder, holding tight to my arm.

"I'm sorry you had to go through this," she whispered. "I'll take care of you."

"So, where to?" Jill said.

"My place," I said. "It's 505 Lake Shore Drive."

She punched it into her phone's GPS and off we went. Zigging and zagging through the cars and people proved tricky in downtown Chicago, but Jill handled it with ease. I called ahead, and two employees were at the entrance of the building to meet us. I didn't want to take any chances.

"Lake Point Tower? This is where you live?" Jill asked.

"I'm impressed," Samantha said.

One doorperson helped me out of the car. "Mr. York, I'm so sorry to hear about the accident," he said. "If there's anything we can do, don't hesitate to ask."

We walked to the reception desk as both women took in the sizeable and ornate entryway, with its tall glass windows, big leafy magnolias, and other exotic plants.

"Hey, Marcus. These are some close friends of mine. Can you grant them full access to my apartment with parking and get a couple of keys made up?"

"Sure, Mr. York," Marcus said. "I'll just need some info."

"And, uh, make sure they're well taken care of." I handed Marcus a hundred-dollar bill.

After the girls were all set up, we hit the elevator.

"Hi, Mr. York. Hey, what happened to you?" the elevator attendant said.

"Just a little accident. I'll be good in a few days."

"Great. Going up. Floor sixty-nine." He pushed the button. As the doors closed, I could see Samantha's serpentine smile curl at the corners of her lips in the elevator doors' reflection.

"Mmm, sixty-nine. How yummy," Samantha purred.

Jill tilted her head my way. "My, that even excited me." We all laughed.

Lake Point Tower sits east of Lake Shore Drive. Three arms form a Y-shaped structure with exterior walls made of tinted glass. The concept behind the building was 'Park in the City,' and it features a two-acre park housing a playground, pool, duck pond, and waterfalls.

The elevator doors opened. My place was down the east hallway, all the way at the end. The entry faced east with a broad, double-curved view of Lake Michigan. My place was two apartments merged into one, so I had a whole end cap. The master bedroom and living room were on the north side with views of Lake Shore Drive and the John Hancock Building. The office, kitchen, dining room, and two spare bedrooms were on the south side with views of Buckingham Fountain. The dining area had a view of Navy Pier.

"Awesome. A girl could get used to this," Samantha said.

Jill seemed a little uneasy getting too close to the floor-to-ceiling, ten-foot windows that surrounded the apartment. "Talk about keeping secrets," she said. "I'm not sure if I should be mad at you or thrilled for you. What a view. My kids would freak out."

"You can bring them anytime. You should come for the air and water show. The perspective you have when looking down at the airplanes is very different. Sometimes the pilots wave as they zoom by."

"Yeah? How cool." Jill's eyes had a spark in them that I hadn't seen in a while.

"Help yourself to anything, ladies. I mean it. Feel free to use the place all you want. You're welcome anytime. Get to know the guys downstairs—they'll help in any way they can, and a bribe of cookies never hurts. The point in bringing you here is to give you guys access to my place in case something happens. I pushed the congressman hard today, and blowing up the truck might have been a message from him to me."

"Why didn't you tell the police that?" Jill asked.

"I just bribed a United States congressman. Don't think that would go over too good."

Jill's phone rang. "Excuse me." She went off to answer it.

"Boy, I pegged you for a Peter Parker-type guy, not Bruce Wayne," Samantha said.

"I'm neither. I can assure you."

"Well, when do I get to see the master bedroom, Tiger?"

The master bedroom was ensconced in earth tones. A California king bed in dark cherry with English detail dominated the room. The headboard was solid wood, upholstered in tufted button leather in a shade the designer called *espresso*. Matching dressers and nightstands rounded out the bedroom set. A black leather club chair and reading lamp stood in one corner.

We walked into the room with her arm around me tightly. "I was so upset when Jill told me what happened," she said. "You scared the shit out of me. I cried all the way to the hospital. Don't ever do that again." Her eyes welled up with tears. "I tried to put on a brave face. You saved my life twice, then you almost got killed. For me. And I'm crazy about you."

"I feel the same. I kept thinking about you when I was in the hospital. Today, I was sent a message, but I have to find Addy and get justice for that kid from the parking garage," I said.

"Promise me you'll be careful." She threw both arms around me and hugged.

"I will. I have an appointment tomorrow with the escort service. They said Addy wasn't available, but her friend Erika was. Maybe we'll get more answers from her. Saturday, we'll go get your car. I hope we'll run into Frank. He's not answering his phone, and I have a funny feeling that Frank's disappearance is related to Addy's. Frank's name is mentioned in Addy's book. He told me he was seeing someone young and that it was complicated. Have you heard from any of Addy's friends? Family?"

"No. I called, but no one knows anything. It's like she completely disappeared."

"Yeah, I think Frank has something to do with that."

Samantha moved over to a dresser, running her finger over its carved rope accents. "I like the bed, and the headboard has a lot of padding for when you start throwing me around in it. I won't bang my head."

We heard Jill come into the bedroom.

She cast her eyes around, taking it all in. "Nice room. Looks comfortable."

"Oh, this will work just fine," Samantha said, pulling one of my ties out of a drawer. She turned to face us, wrapping each end of the tie around her hands, then snapping the middle tight.

"What do you think, Tiger?"

"Work for what?" Jill asked.

"Tying me up." Her smile coiled once again.

"Oh, if you want me to go…" Jill gestured toward the door.

"No, that's all right," I said. "Can you take her to your house? I'm in no condition to tie anyone up tonight. I want a shower, dinner, and sleep. Tomorrow, I have an appointment to go to. I turned to Samantha. "You'll be safe at Jill's. Lay low for a few days. But keep in touch."

Samantha took Jill's arm and led her out of the room. "Let's swing by my place first, and I'll pack a few things. Then we can be on our way. And I'll treat us to dinner tonight. Whatever the kids want."

"Great, no cooking. They'll want pizza, no doubt."

"Then pizza it is. Let's leave Tiger alone. Tomorrow he has a date—with a prostitute."

Jill's head swiveled back to cast a glance toward me. "You two are just weird."

NEWS FLASH – WXNG-TV, CHICAGO

"... just after 4 a.m., four men in a black SUV were driving outbound on the Dan Ryan in the local lanes when a red SUV occupied by two men pulled up beside them and opened fire. The black SUV returned fire and the moving shootout began. The two vehicles traveled several blocks while exchanging gunfire before the black SUV exited at 37th Street, heading eastbound and coming to a halt at Stateway Park. Now, as the camera pans out, you can see that the black SUV is riddled with bullet holes. All four men in the SUV were shot and rushed to area hospitals. We are waiting for word on their condition.

"Police are asking anyone who witnessed or has information about the shootout to call police headquarters at the number listed on the bottom of your screen. Looks like March is starting out the way February ended, with gun violence on the streets.

"Reporting live from the South Side, I'm Meghan Orr for WXNG-TV..."

FOURTEEN

The pale man stood six feet, two inches tall with six percent body fat. In his early thirties, Ian Smith believed in working out daily, eating right, and taking care of himself. He detested those who did not. Fat people were loathsome creatures—lazy and disgusting. There was no place for them in this world. Especially obese women. How could a woman expect to be respected if she had no respect for her own body? Men should have standards for women since they were inferior to men.

Hal and Artie, whom he'd met while in the Marines, were still out looking for the girl that was causing him to have sleepless nights. They had made it through some tough times together when they were over in Afghanistan. He knew they were reliable men and would find Addison. She was a fine specimen of a woman and met his criteria for what a woman should be. Slim, attractive, and obedient to men. Michael, from the escort service, knew his taste in women and did an excellent job by sending her to him. If he could've had more time with her, he'd have been able to break her in right.

But Hal and Artie would find the noscy bitch and kill her instead. It would serve her right for snooping around in his things. The codebook she'd stolen contained sensitive information that could get him in trouble. Once she was gone it would be smooth sailing. The thought of her death aroused him.

Ian took his shirt off and put it on a hanger. He buttoned the top button and brushed away some lint before putting it in the closet for the next time.

He had told Madame Zoe about this new idea he had for the Syrians. She loved it. He liked her, she took great care of herself for her age. The other partner, the old man, not so much. He was getting too bossy.

He undid his belt. This small-time shit of selling guns to street gangs was getting on his nerves. He wanted more—a bigger score. More of the pie.

The partners wanted him to blend in more with regular folk. They lined up a job for him so they could paint him as an upstanding member of society. No one would be the wiser. Well, fuck that. He was above all that. Ian Smith was a gun lord.

He removed his pants, folded them by the creases, put them on a hanger and into the closet. He caught a glimpse of himself in the mirror and liked what he saw. His pale, naked body was clean-shaven. The shadows formed by his six-pack gave his stomach the definition he exercised hard to maintain.

Two tattoos decorated his body. On his right bicep was the eagle, globe, and anchor of the United States Marine Corps. The eagle held a ribbon in its mouth. In red ink, it read: 'Semper Fi.' Below the tattoo were the words: 'Operation Iraqi Freedom.' On his left deltoid was a crying angel. She was kneeling with one wing broken. A permanent reminder of Broken Wing, his favorite mission in Afghanistan.

Ian couldn't help but admire his form, fondling it. He was perfect.

His deal with the street gangs was simple. He'd supply the guns, they'd supply the money. But they had to go and fuck that up, so he had to sell them a lesser product: AK-47s and AR-15s made in China. But those were still pricey, so some type of compensation was needed to make the payment they owed. Last time, the Gangster Rappers could only come up with two-thirds of the money. For the rest, they would supply him with a gang member who wanted in but hadn't yet been initiated. He asked for a fifteen-to-eighteen-year-old black male. He liked the dark ones. Fuck those Mexican bastards. They're worse than fat people. He hoped this one was a wiggler. He liked it when they resisted.

He walked down the hall to the spare bedroom. He liked the way his penis flopped against his thighs as he moved.

In the bedroom, he gazed upon the naked black teen lying face down, spread-eagle on the bed, with his wrists and ankles tied to the bedposts. Versed, the twilight drug, was wearing off, but the teen's screams through the tape were still muffled. He struggled to get free, much to the delight of the pale man.

He picked up the tube of Astroglide lubricant from the dresser. An evil crease cut a line across his clean-shaven face. He closed the door with authority and said, "Hi, I'm Ian. I hope you like to wiggle."

FIFTEEN

With shops and restaurants standing shoulder to shoulder on both sides of the street, Michigan Avenue is the city's consumer hot spot. The sky above was black, but the sparkle of the lights made the street bright as day. I walked through the canyons of tall buildings, engulfed by the sensation of being in a mineshaft, looking for the mother lode—which in my case was information that would lead to the whereabouts of one Addison Martin. The noise of the city buzzed in my ears. As instructed, I was in the area one hour before my appointment. I'd woken up sore from the beating I'd taken yesterday, but the pain was getting better. At a bar I stumbled upon, they had an impressive variety of bourbons, unfortunately, Blanton's was unavailable, so I settled for a pour of Four Roses Single Barrel.

I'd opted for casual attire that evening—jeans with a classic herringbone plaid shirt in blue. As a force of habit, I'd brought my overcoat with me, although it was now sporting a few bullet holes, giving it a true Chicago flair.

The surrounding sounds faded away as my thoughts wandered to Jordan and his family. Knowing that he'd died hurt more than my physical injuries. It brought back some bad memories for me.

I realized that I was falling into that dark pit of depression, and I tried to use as many of the tools I'd learned in therapy to pull myself back out. I needed to focus on the job at hand.

I had two options for approaching Erika: one subtle; one threatening. Margaret always told me that you catch more flies with honey, so I'd try that first. Besides, I didn't think I could pull off the hardass approach in my current condition.

I'd checked in with Samantha and Jill earlier. They seemed to be getting along fine. They did some shopping and played with the kids—that sort of thing. Jill reported no strangers or people following them. All was clear. My phone rang.

"Be at the Remington Hotel on Superior Street five minutes before the hour. I'll call with the room number. Got it?"

"Yeah." He hung up. I headed out.

The deal seemed to be that they kept the conversations short, probably from fear of phone tracking. I imagined the next call would come from a different number. I found the hotel and sat in the lobby, reading a paper someone had left behind. There was an article about what great things Congressman Ainsworth was going to do to make our city bigger and better, but nothing about making the city safer. He was another issue I'd have to deal with and soon. I got the message loud and clear that he wouldn't be paying up. Since the explosion, I'd been constantly looking over my shoulder to see if I was being followed. This place looked clear. Then the phone rang.

"Are you at the hotel?" the man asked.

"Yeah, I'm here."

"She's in room 1620. Repeat it."

"Sixteenth floor, room 1620," I said.

"Wait five minutes, and then head on up."

In the elevator, I punched sixteen.

I walked down the sixteenth-floor hallway. The carpet was maroon with cream-colored swirls. The air was heavy with VOCs, or volatile organic compounds—new carpet smell. Room 1620 was on the left side. I knocked and waited.

"Come in, please." I stepped inside the two-room suite and saw that the door to the bedroom was closed. The curtains were drawn, and the only light came from candles and a lamp with the dimmer switch set to low. The candle flames flickered as I arrived.

A pungent odor occupied the room—it smelled of fruity florals and creamy vanilla with a dash of bitter regret from a lot of bad decisions made. The door closed behind me, and I turned to see a pretty woman in an emerald bra with black lace and matching panties. She ambled over to me, her long straight blonde hair swaying. Sapphire eyes highlighted the smoky eyeshadow that was swept over her lids. Spicy red lipstick moistened her full lips. Her choice of makeup complemented her warm golden-beige skin tone.

"Please, let's get comfortable. Take off your coat. My name is Erika," she said. I detected the hint of a Southern accent.

I draped my coat on the chair.

"Here, I'll hang it up for you. Do you need to use the washroom? It's right through that door." She put the coat in the closet. I was to have the money in an unsealed white business envelope with no names and place it on the counter next to the sink. I washed my hands, checking out my mug in the mirror. Things were healing but not fast enough. When I came out, she came up to me and gave me a big hug and kiss on the cheek.

"Let me just freshen up, and I'll be out in a jiffy." She disappeared into the bathroom to check the payment. I wondered what she'd do if the sum was light. I imagined a bodyguard busting down the door, cracking my neck. She came out and stopped in the doorway, leaning against it. "I think it's time we got relaxed, don't you?" she delicately said.

I couldn't help comparing Erika to Samantha. Erika's breasts were more abundant and enhanced, which was not my thing. Her hair was lighter, and she was shorter—even in heels. Her hips were a bit wider.

"I like your outfit. That color works on you." A compliment never hurt.

"Aren't you sweet. There's a big misconception that blue works best with blondes, but it's green that works the best. At least for me." She tossed her head back with a little laugh, and dimples appeared every time she smiled.

She sat on the couch, giving me a playful look and motioning with her finger for me to come over. I sat, and she swung her leg over mine, straddling me. My sore ribs were starting to hurt.

"Uh, I'd like to do..." I gently pushed her away.

"A man with a plan, I like it." She smiled, her teeth were perfect and white.

"Let's talk a bit."

She moved off me but stayed close.

"You're not one of those religious freaks who thinks they can save me, are you? Cause if you are, you'll have to leave." Her mood changed, and her body stiffened.

"I'm not. I'm currently searching for Cairo, your friend. She's missing, and I'd like to know if she's all right."

"I don't know any Cairo. Besides, I'm right here." She thrust her chest out, inches from my nose.

"Mike said you were friends with Cairo. I know her real name is Addison, or Addy, Martin, and she's from Winter Park, Florida. She has brown hair, blue eyes, and dropped out of FIU to do this."

Erika pulled her chest back, looking at me without expression. She was tough to read.

"She may be in danger, and two men were looking for her a few days ago at her apartment in Hyde Park. They also blew up my truck yesterday—that's what happened to my face. My friend—my client, rather, is just worried. Any info you can give me to find her could save a life. Maybe mine." My voice lowered as I ran out of breath, but my last comment seemed to resonate.

"You can keep the money, no matter what," I added.

She was quiet for a while, then she said, "So, tell me who's looking for Cairo. What's her name? I might know her."

"I never said it was a she, and I can't do that. I could give you a couple hundred more if that will help with your memory issues."

"A girl could always use a few more bucks. What did you say Cairo's name was?

"Addy."

"I admire you for not giving up your friend or client. I like that you didn't try the rough stuff to get me to talk. Ask me anything you want, but first I have to take this off."

Her hand went behind her back and undid her bra. She got out of it and threw it across the room onto a chair.

"Oooh, that feels so good. These bras look super sexy for you guys, but for us girls, they're the most uncomfortable thing in the world to wear. I couldn't take it anymore. Hope you don't mind."

"I'm not complaining."

She smiled, but hers couldn't shine a light on Samantha's patented serpentine grin. "You're welcome."

She headed for the closet and pulled out a matching emerald satin robe and sat back down next to me.

"We started in the escort business a few years ago. Addison took to it like a fish to water. Had a ton of regular clients—they booked her for hours, and that's what every girl wants. Regulars. They're reliable, you know them, and you know what they like. Addison would book up fast. She's gorgeous. Some girls have limits, they won't do certain things, but not Addison. 'Anything goes' was her motto. She even had female clients."

"Anything goes?"

She took my hand in hers, looking at it and caressing it. "She is the poster child for the girlfriend experience. For the regulars she liked, it was bareback full service all the way." She saw my confused look. "Sorry. Bareback is no condom, which is the first big no-no in this business. If a client wanted to stick it in her butt or role play, like that *Fifty Shades* stuff, it was no problem for Addison. She'd let the guys... finish... anywhere they wanted— face, tits, feet. Hell, she told me she had one particular guy she'd let finish inside her. Which is so wrong on so many levels in the escorting world. And I think she was in love with that guy. But Addison had this one ability that made her the best."

"What's that?" I asked.

"The ability to liberate men from their life savings."

"I see."

"My clients have reached the top of their earning potential. Their kids are close to graduating or they're already out and working. They don't want to leave the wife—divorce is too expensive—so they come to me, get their rocks off, and leave.

Lunchtime and right after work are my busy times. Most are just looking for affection. Once the kids show up, their wives start looking at them more like they're furniture.

"The key to being successful is listening and giving off the impression that the entire world revolves around them for that hour. They like having a young girl dote on them, it makes them feel like they've still got it. The downside is, they're older, so some are harder to get off than glitter."

She reached up and touched my face, running her fingers over my cuts and stitches.

"So, she left? Do you know the guy's name?" I asked.

"Addison never told me his name. She was a big earner, and to throw it all away over a guy…"

"Maybe she'd had enough, wanted to settle down with this guy and find a new job?"

"You just paid twelve hundred dollars for one hour. To fuck or not. I get fifty percent, and Mike gets fifty percent. I work six hours a day, which is thirty-six hundred dollars. That's Monday to Friday, so now I earn eighteen thousand a week. I work about forty weeks a year between Chicago and Vegas, making my annual income seven hundred and twenty thousand dollars. Cash. And that's without tips. And I have twelve weeks off. What other job can offer me that without a degree? I've got a few years to go, and by the time I'm thirty-eight, I'll be retired, living someplace warm, and then I'll have time to look for Mr. Right."

"Does Mike ever hurt any of the girls if they get out of line?"

"Mike's not capable of hurting anyone. He's a big geek with glasses and a pocket protector—the whole thing. He likes his freebies, but he wouldn't hurt a fly. Plus, his boss wouldn't stand for it."

"Freebies?" I asked.

"Mike does a great job of getting us scheduled and screening the clients so no one gets busted by the cops. So, every now and then, some of the girls give him an hour for free."

"You said something about his boss?"

"Mike works for someone—he doesn't own the business. And the owner loved Addison. If you're looking for a person who could make Addison disappear, well, her client list was impressive—lots of men with money and power. How would you feel if someone you'd drained your kid's college fund for just up and left?"

My first thought was the congressman. He had the money and power to make people disappear. With the truck bomb happening just after our meeting, he was definitely suspect number one. My second thought was Frank. Was he the guy that Addy had fallen in love with?

"When's the last time you talked to Addy?" I asked.

"Last week. She was in Vegas and planning on heading out here. Said we would have dinner one night and do some shopping. Look, I love Addison. I'd just figured she'd run off with someone. But now I'm worried."

"I'll find her."

Erika started running her finger around the edge of my ear. "Are you in pain? You look uncomfortable. I could make you feel so much better if you'd let me."

"Doing fine, thank you." I removed her hand from my head.

"You don't have to pay the extra. Let's have some fun." She started to unbutton my shirt. I stopped her.

"I'm sorry. You're very beautiful, but I'm on business." I rebuttoned my shirt.

"Sammy's got her hooks in you pretty hard. I've never met a man who didn't want to fuck me," Erika said.

"Not sure who you're talking about." How did she know Samantha? My breath quickened and my heart beat faster.

"Addison let only one person call her 'Addy,' and that is Samantha Rhodes. So that must be who your client is. Right?" I didn't answer, and she continued. "You're much older than the guys she's used to going out with, but I can see why she's into you. The last guy she was with was a total asshole. Treated her like property. Took her long enough to leave the bastard. You're different, and you're strong—protective, but not possessive. Rough around the edges, and it looks like you can take a punch or two. I've seen guys with fewer cuts and bruises stay in the hospital for days. You're more of a... man." She played with her hair, proud she'd made the connection.

"I'd rather talk about Addison."

"Word to the wise: Sammy's an obnoxious flirt, likes playing games, and gets bored easily. She gets the boys all flustered and the girls even more so—a real tease. You know she's bi, right? I think that all started in her cheerleading days. But come on, her in that outfit? Who wouldn't want that? She hooked up with Natalie on the squad, and that led to Colleen. Then that fizzled out. I've dabbled a bit in girls, but I like men. Plain and simple. You probably don't wanna hear this anyway."

But I did. I wanted to hear all about Samantha in her early years. But I had an obligation to keep her identity secure. I had only just met Erika—I couldn't risk Samantha's safety by exposing her as my client. This could be a test. Erika might be working for the two thugs from the alley. As engrossing as this biography was, I had to come back to matters of the present.

"Not sure who this Sammy is, but she sounds fascinating," I said as I stood up.

"You know who her dad is, right?" Erika tilted her head and played with her hair.

"Again, I really don't know who you're talking about."

"Well, tell her Rachel Cavanaugh said hello. That's my real name. She'll know who I am."

She followed me to the door.

"Just one more thing," I said. "Is there any place you know of where Addy might hide out?"

"Every chance she got, she went to… that town with the funny name…"

"Kickapoo," I guessed.

"Yes, that's it. If I had to guess, I'd say her guy probably lives out there."

CHAPTER

SIXTEEN

Outside of the hotel, the hustle and bustle of Chicago's nightlife was still going strong. Big Al's escorts weren't street girls working corners. They were well put together, mannered, and educated women. I walked along Superior toward Michigan Avenue to hail a cab. Halfway past the mouth of an alleyway, I was hammered from behind. A blow to my sore ribs crippled me. Big arms swamped me, lifted me up, and threw my already battered body against a brick wall. A kick to my face exploded my brain. I groaned as my assailant's fist punched my side, causing the air to escape from my lungs.

"Stop," I wheezed, holding up my hands in defense.

The man took me by the lapels, his breath smelling of onions and puke.

"Listen, shit for brains, I woulda thought the bomb yesterday woulda sent the message loud and clear, but no, you gotta go snooping around these whores. What are you up to?"

My puffy eyes focused. An overripe thug was leering at me with crooked teeth, bloodshot yellow eyes, and a hook nose big enough to singlehandedly keep Kleenex tissues in business if he ever got the flu.

"If you keep pushing this thing with this whore, I won't just come after you, I'll go after that slut you hang out with. Pay more attention to her ass than the whore's. Got it?"

He released me to the ground, my face dropping into a puddle slick with oil. Some of the foul water entered my mouth. I coughed most of it up, but some I inhaled. Not good for my asthma. The coughing compounded the pain.

"Hey, what's going on down there?" Someone shouted. I looked up, expecting to see a gun, but the thug had vanished.

The applause made by the sound of shoes pounding pavement drew closer, not stopping until they reached me.

"Holy shit, are you okay?" said the voice. "Do you want me to call an ambulance?" he continued.

"No. But can you hail a cab for me? Attempted robbery. I'll be fine, thanks for the assistance," I said as he helped me to my feet and into a cab.

"Lake Point Tower," I said, before spitting up blood and passing out in the back seat.

The guys from the front desk helped me up to my apartment, and I passed out in a chair for about an hour. My head and all my bones and muscles hurt. I checked my phone. Samantha had called a few times and left a message, and Jill had called as well.

A hot shower felt good. I poured some bourbon and sat in my recliner. Took a puff from my inhaler. With my achy ribs, sucking it down was painful, but it opened up my lungs. Night blanketed the city as I looked out my window. I had no idea what time it was and didn't care. Some comfort would be good right about now. I sought out my cell and listened to Samantha's voicemail.

"Hey Tiger, how are you? Feeling okay? If you're having pain, take the meds the doctor gave you. Jill's kids are a lot of fun, we've been having a good time." She ended with a sexy impersonation of some movie star that I didn't recognize.

I drank some more bourbon, licking my wounds, and waited for sleep to overtake me. I'd stay in the recliner tonight. My hope was to dream about Samantha.

The sound of a ringing phone jolted me upright.

"Ty, it's Margaret. Julius told me you were in the hospital. Why didn't you call me? How are you, dear? I'm so worried about you. Do you want Julius to send a car? You can stay here with us. I can take care of you. Poor dear." Margaret sounded concerned.

"I'm fine, Margaret, thanks. I'm all set, ready to rest here tonight."

"What's this I hear about a woman in your life? I would like to meet her—bring her by sometime. I'm happy for you, Ty."

"Thanks, Margaret. I love you."

"I love you too, dear. Julius wants to say hello."

"Ty, listen. Don't worry about work, take all the time you need to heal up. If I need anything, I'll use Ian. I want you at one hundred percent."

"I'll take it easy. Thanks."

We hung up after a few more minutes. It felt good, talking to them. I was about to doze off when the phone rang again.

"Please hold for Congressman Ainsworth."

What the fuck is he calling me for? My anger was beginning to build.

"York?"

"What the fuck do you want, old man? I got your message yesterday and today. Next time I won't be so nice."

"What are you talking about, psycho? I'm calling to tell you I've got your money. Remember the two mil in cash for the book? We'll do the exchange tomorrow morning. Eight o'clock at the Bean in Millennium Park." He waited for an answer.

I was thrown for a loop. What the fuck was going on? If the congressman hadn't blown up my truck and sent that thug to attack me, then who had?

"Are you there?"

"Yes. Yeah, tomorrow. The Bean. Eight o'clock. Got it."

Despite the soreness and bourbon haze, I fought to get up. Making my way to the safe, I retrieved the book and began browsing its pages. I must have missed a name. I made a copy on my printer, just in case.

I looked at the copy, but no names jumped out at me. Tomorrow, I would hand over the book, receive the two million, and be finished with the congressman. I wanted Samantha to see the names again—maybe she would recognize something or someone. I needed to find Frank. Maybe Erika or Rachel, her real name, would know someone on the list. I could make another appointment.

But first, the congressman. Then we'd pick up Samantha's car from Frank's garage in Kickapoo. Maybe I'd get lucky and Frank would be around. I could ask him straight up if he was Addy's boyfriend.

NEWS FLASH – WXNG-TV, CHICAGO

"... Meghan, there's been another night of active violence in the city."

"Yes, David. In the early morning hours on the CTA Red Line, a twenty-year-old male was shot at Harrison station. Police say the gunman was waiting for the victim at the stop and opened fire on the train. The shooter shot the victim in the leg and shoulder, and then taken by ambulance to Northwest Memorial Hospital where he later died.

"Just after 3:40 a.m., a twenty-one-year-old man was shot multiple times while riding his bike in a neighborhood on the Northwest Side. One witness told WXNG-TV News that three people approached the man before knocking him down. They began arguing and then opened fire while the man lay on the ground. They took the victim to Loyola University Medical Center in Maywood in critical condition, with four gunshot wounds to the shoulder, torso, hip, and back. He is still fighting for his life at this hour.

"And finally, at around 5:20 a.m. a drive-by shooting occurred in the 4800 block of West Ferdinand Street, resulting in three people being shot, but further details regarding the circumstances are not immediately known. An assailant shot a thirty-three-year-old male in the leg, the victim then transported to West Suburban Medical Center in Oak Park. The second victim, a twenty-seven-year-old female, suffered a gunshot wound to the left shoulder and she was taken to Mount Sinai Hospital. Stroger Hospital received the third victim, a twenty-one-year-old female, who was shot in the pelvis and is listed in serious condition.

"Sources tell us the women were prostitutes working for a gang, and it's possible that the shooting was retaliation for the women working a rival gang's turf. However, police have not confirmed this.

"No arrests have been made in any of the shootings.

"Reporting live from police headquarters, I'm Meghan Orr for WXNG-TV News."

CHAPTER

SEVENTEEN

I t weighs one hundred and ten short tons and is sixty-six feet long. It cost a whopping twenty-three million dollars. The stainless steel structure has no visible seams and is polished to a high degree. Besides reflecting and distorting the city's skyline, the structure is inspired by liquid mercury. They say it will last a thousand years. It sits in Millennium Park, and the official name of the mirrored sculpture is the Cloud Gate. To us locals, it's called the Bean.

Congressman Ainsworth's limousine pulled up right on time. I was surprised he got out of the car. I thought he might have someone else do it, this must be important to him.

"You look like shit," he said.

"I feel worse."

"Let's see it," he scoffed.

I tossed the book to him.

"Nice catch. Drop the bag, and you can call off the dogs, okay?" I said.

I picked up the bag and looked at its contents.

"What dogs? You're talking crazy."

"The bomb, and the guy in the alley last night. You didn't send them?"

"Think about it. If I were going to harm you, I'd use the fucking power of the US government. And I still might. I've been a congressman for over twenty years, and it comes with some privileges that the average person doesn't enjoy. But I just got off on one murder charge, why would I want to go through that again? And there'd better not be any copies." He waved the book at me. "Good day, Mr. York. Our business is done. But it appears you've pissed someone else off." He turned and left.

The park was filling up with tourists and locals wanting to take pictures of their reflections in the Bean. I hailed a cab and headed home with two million in cash.

I took three gym bags full of money down to the lobby with me, each holding five hundred thousand dollars. Jill was dropping off Samantha so we could get an early start to pick up her car.

Jill pulled up in her SUV, and I went to the driver's side window.

"How'd things go?"

"We had... fun?" Jill's face went crimson. They giggled like adolescents with a secret.

"Can I give you some gas money?" I reached into my pocket for my wallet.

"No problem, Ty. Everything worked out. I'll see you later. Sorry if we were late." Samantha got out, and Jill drove off with a little screech of the tires.

Samantha gave me a big hug and a kiss, which hurt my lips and ribs. But I didn't mind.

"I missed you so much." She kissed me again. "Jill's fun. We had a blast, but I missed you."

"Hello to you, too. What's with you guys and all the snickering?"

"Girl stuff. Her hubby's coming home, and she's a little on edge," she said with a weary look. "So, where's your car?" Samantha looked around confused, and then she looked at me.

"On edge?"

"I don't think they have a perfect marriage. She avoids talking about him or their situation. I think Donny comes home from work trips with some stress. Has she ever mentioned anything to you?"

"No."

"Have you met him?"

"A few times at work functions. He did not impress me."

"It's odd, there are no wedding pictures in the house. Just photos of the kids. And then the..." she trailed off.

"And then the what?"

"Oh, just girl stuff. Where's the car?"

"In the garage downstairs." We went to the elevator.

She'd decided to wear black boots over her tight, torn, blue jeans. It was apparent to me that no matter what this girl wore, she just oozed sex appeal. Her full and wavy hair was loose, spilling over her shoulders and dancing with every move she made. That scent of strawberry and mint filled my sore nostrils and made my blood rush.

"So, which one?" she asked.

"Right here," I pulled off the car cover.

"No way," she said, wide-eyed. "This is a 1970 Chevy Chevelle 454. It's yours?" She took a step back, checking out the car.

"You know cars?"

"I know some—this one, for sure. I love this car." She walked around looking at the detailing.

"Frank and I fixed her up. It's an LS6 V-8, to be exact. With a couple of mods we added, it can get close to 475 horsepower. It has the original Holley four-barrel carburetor and the Muncie M22 Rock Crusher four-speed on the floor," I boasted.

"Is this original Fathom Blue paint? That's my favorite color for this car," she gushed.

"Sure is, and the twin white stripes on the hood, top, and trunk. She loves cold air, and it's cold today." There was some excitement in my voice, but I always felt that excitement when I knew I was going to be driving this machine. Frank and I had worked hard on finding its parts, not to mention the blood, sweat, and tears we'd put into it.

I threw the bags of money into the trunk and we got in. With a quick turn of the key, she started up and rumbled to life.

I gunned the gas, making the back tires spin to catch their grip on the rough concrete. When they did grab hold, the force pinned Samantha to the seat. Her eyes shone and her serpentine smile twisted.

The car jetted out of the garage, and the ghost-gray tire smoke followed.

It was cold but sunny, with no precipitation in the forecast. A great day to go for a ride in a hot car with an even hotter babe. The deep blue sky that Mother Nature provided us with rivaled my vehicle's infinite blue paint. I told Samantha we'd make a few stops along the way—business. With my Beretta packed and a Baby Glock strapped to my ankle, I wasn't taking any chances. Not anymore. The Mini Uzi, fully loaded, was in the trunk for good measure.

Samantha was sitting close, but she was silent. I squeezed her hand tight and brought it to my lips. She smiled and continued to look straight ahead. We were out of the city and heading west on I-80.

"So, when are you going to tell me what happened?" Samantha finally asked.

"Erika and I met, and she shared a lot. I actually wanted to go over a few of those things with you."

"I'm talking about the new bruises on your face. When I hugged you, I made sure not to touch your sore ribs, but now the other side hurts, and I felt you wince. You got beat up again, didn't you? Did you think I wouldn't notice, Ty? If we're going to find Addy, it's going to take both of us. But I can't stand by and watch you suffer. I can help, but you need me just like I need you. We need each other. We found each other on the road that night. Fate is what it is."

We looked at each other, listening to the drone of the engine.

"Okay, yes. After I saw Erika, I got jumped. I didn't see his face, but the guy threatened to come after you if I didn't stop looking for Addy." I filled her in on what had happened with the congressman, the exchange, and what he'd said about using political power instead of brute force. She agreed that the congressman didn't fit as the guy behind the truck bomb or the messenger.

"How *was* your date last night?"

"It wasn't a date," I said as the gas pedal took a punch from my foot, the throttle lever opening the choke valve and letting the barrel suck in the cold air. The Holley carburetor responded, the polished chrome exhaust answered with a deep throaty sound and the thrust knocked Samantha back in her seat again.

"Hey," she protested.

"It would appear your friend fell in love and left the escort business. I can also say she made a boatload of money, not only for herself, but for her pimp, Mike, as well," I explained.

"So, it's Mike that wants her back and is looking for her?"

"I don't think so." I filled her in on why I thought that wouldn't work. "Erika also said things like Mike's a wimp and wouldn't hurt anyone. She also said this stuff happens all the time."

"Maybe it's this boyfriend she fell for."

"Could be. By the way, Rachel Cavanaugh says hello. Rachel is Erika, and she knew all about you. Of course, I never admitted to knowing you, but it was pretty obvious."

"Oh, wow. The three of us used to be called the Triple Threat back in the day. Rachel, Addy, and I would always hang out together. Now both of them are escorts. I must have missed that memo. I've done some crazy shit, but nothing like that." She squeezed my hand.

We pulled up to a three-story house just outside of Kickapoo. Samantha stayed in the car, and I went up to the door and knocked. A woman answered the door.

"Hi, Susan. The chief's expecting me."

"I didn't know you were coming over." She combed her hair with her fingers and straightened her blouse.

"You look great, by the way."

"You're too kind, but thanks. He's in the study with John."

A short walk down the hall put me in the company of Kickapoo's chief of police and John Evans, the district attorney for LaSalle County.

I shook hands with both men. "Bourbon?" the chief offered.

"Not this time, I gotta fly. But I wanted to drop this off." I threw three duffel bags down on the desk.

The chief opened one, looked in, and held it open for the DA. He zipped it back up and put it under his desk. "Just a little something for your favorite charities. I'm hoping some will go to the youth center and the disabled vets. Can I trust that you'll see to that Robert gets a bag?" I always thought it was a good idea to keep Robert's friends happy. I was lucky that my two best friends knew lots of people. More often than not, they were people in the right places.

"I'm not going to ask where this came from. Anytime you need a favor, just let us know." the chief said.

"Oh, I will."

"Robert is supposed to be here soon," John said. "I'll make sure he gets it. He'll use it for that food pantry project he's working on. And like always, I'll say it's from an anonymous downer. Why you don't want the credit is beyond me, but thanks."

Next up was Frank's garage. The place sat on a curve in the road. It was a bit isolated from town, lying just north of it. Upon leaving the road, the uneven ground from the street to the filling station created a bumpy exit. The car's tires made a crunching noise as they passed over the ice and snow covering the gravel lot.

The sign on the office door said CLOSED, and no lights illuminated the inside.

I maneuvered the Chevelle around the back to where Samantha's car was parked. Both cars were out of sight from the road.

"Come on. We can get the keys from in here," I said.

We made our way to the back door. I had a key. Jiggling the lock with the key inserted, I turned the handle, and the door opened. The beeping sounds from the pre-alarm rang out, but I knew the passcode and killed the alarm. Brown cardboard boxes that had seen better days filled the cluttered storeroom area. The shelving was a weak attempt to keep things off the floor and organized. Auto parts were everywhere, and only Frank knew what was in each box.

Entering the office, the stench of rubber and oil filled my nose, almost making me sneeze.

The waiting area, with its four chrome-framed, red vinyl upholstered seats, was empty, waiting for customers. Standard items that people would run in for, such as wiper blades, light bulbs, and gas treatment products, hung on dusty racks. None were in high demand these days. There was even a rack with fold-up maps and big book atlases. Hard to believe there was much need for that stuff with cell phones and GPS technology.

"Watch yourself," I warned Samantha as we stepped into the garage area. "Lots of things in here to trip over and bang your head on."

I found the spot where Frank left all the keys. It was dark, as the sunlight was unable to reach this far inside the building. A chill went through me as I fished around, looking for Samantha's.

"Are these yours?" I handed her a set.

"No." She handed them back.

"These?"

"No."

"Last ones. It's always the last one." I handed her the set.

"No, those aren't them either."

"Well, that's it, babe." I emerged from the darkness.

"No keys? Now we have to go back and get my spare set. I should have known you just wanted to lure me out here to an abandoned auto garage." She folded her arms under her breasts, boosting them a bit. Annoyed, she turned back to the office.

"You're cute when you're angry. You know that?" I said, trying to ease her tension.

"I'm cute all the time," she shouted back.

Even after another thorough search, I couldn't locate any other sets of keys. It was odd.

Avoiding the dangers of the garage, I went into the office. Samantha stood in front of the mirror, fixing her hair.

"Look, I'll try and call him, but he told me they'd be there." I got out my cell.

"Can I have the keys to your car? I want to get my bag out of the trunk and get my brush."

"Honey, you look fabulous just the way you are," I said, but she gave me an 'I'll be the judge of that' look, letting me know she was still pissed and that I had no sense of style. I handed her the keys.

She came back in with the brush and started working on her hair. She was focused on her task, so I went through Frank's desk drawers, thinking that maybe the keys would be there. After a few minutes of looking, my search came up empty. I sat in the office chair, leaning back and listening to the sound of squeaky springs and watching Samantha brush and fix her hair.

I got up and stood behind her. She looked at me in the mirror's reflection. I moved closer and spun her around.

"Am I pretty?" she asked playfully.

"Yes, you are."

"Well, I know we haven't been on a date yet, but you could have at least sent flowers, Tiger. No date, no flowers—why, what's a girl to think?" She batted her eyelashes at me a few times. I laughed out loud.

Looking around the room, I said, "Well, will wiper blades do the trick?"

"Don't think so." She pursed her lips.

"How about this then?" I gently took her in my arms and kissed her. She surrendered without a fight, not that I expected one. We made out in the garage office for a little while. "Hey, I had a thought—"

"If it's not about sex, I don't wanna hear it," she panted, then gasped as my hands roamed under her leather jacket, sliding along her tight white t-shirt.

"I'll pull the car in and—" She interrupted me with a hard kiss. Her lips moved to my neck. "Put it on the hoist and raise it up," I continued. "Ever fool around in the backseat when the car's suspended in midair?"

"Well, not in a '70 Chevy Chevelle before." She tossed her head, whipping her freshly brushed hair over her face. A flick to the right, a quick one to the left, and her beautiful face was visible once again.

"Get the car, and I'll find some rope." She flashed her serpentine smile.

Just then, the sound of a crash echoed through the garage. The Beretta was in my hand instantly.

"Stay here," I said.

EIGHTEEN

"Hey, who's there?" a familiar voice called out. "I'll call the cops. I have a gun."

"Frank?" I said. "It's me, Ty."

The light clicked on in the garage. Frank appeared—sweaty, anxious, and holding a gun.

"Mind pointing that the other way?" I kept my voice calm. "We came to pick up Samantha's car."

"Sorry," Frank said. "Just jumpy, I guess. Hi, Ty. Did anyone see you guys come in?"

"I don't think so. We didn't hear you pull up. We were uh, um, distracted, looking for the keys. You didn't see my car out back?"

"No, which one? What happened to your face?"

"Never mind about my face. What's wrong? You said you were leaving town. Where did you go?"

"I haven't left yet. Going to." Frank slipped the gun into his pocket. He was still noticeably nervous.

"Frank, where are my keys?" Samantha said sweetly and calmly.

Frank looked at Samantha, seeming to notice her for the first time. It was clear that something had happened. Something was going on.

A female voice emerged from the darkness. "I have them, Sammy." A figure stepped out from the shadows of the garage.

A woman about Samantha's age with long brown hair entered the room. She had tan skin and striking features. She was casually dressed in slacks and a sweater top, her hair and nails looked professionally done. All the minute details were in place.

"Addy?" Samantha said. "Where have you been? Your mom and dad are so worried. I've been worried." The women embraced, the lost friend was found. Tears streamed down Samantha's face.

She looked Addison in the eyes.

"I know, honey," Addison said, wiping a tear from Samantha's cheek.

Frank seemed to relax.

"What the fuck's going on, Frank?"

"Maybe we should discuss this at the cabin. I don't think we're safe here," he said.

"Sure."

"So, Sammy, who's this?" Addy nodded in my direction. "Has my Sammy been too hard on you, sweetheart? She can play rough."

"Addy, this is Ty. He's saved my life a few times. He also said he'd find you, and he has." Samantha leveled a finger at her. "Girl, you've got a lot of explaining to do. We're all in danger, and someone's after you and us as well because *we're* looking for *you*. What's going on?"

Car tires crushed the frozen gravel out front, making a popcorn sound. All eyes turned to the dust-coated windows. A car as dark as night rolled to a stop outside. I was still evaluating the situation when Frank opened the office door and stepped out.

"Frank? Frank!" I said.

I turned to Samantha. "Take Addy around back, and wait in the car. Be ready to start it." She nodded in agreement.

I stepped out of the office and stood next to Frank. The air was crisp, like the night of the shootout in Hyde Park. A familiar tall man eased out of the car, slamming the door closed and making his way around the front of it. His short friend also got out of the car, smiling.

"Fill 'er up, my good man," he said.

"We're closed, and the pumps are off," Frank said quickly.

"Well turn 'em back on. We're payin' customers." The short guy's hands became lively as he spoke.

"Hey, don't we know you?" The tall man pointed at me and rubbed his jaw.

I stood silent, my finger flipping off the safety on the Beretta in my overcoat pocket. It felt cold and heavy.

The tall man snapped his fingers as if he were triggering a memory. "Yeah, you're that guy from the alley the other night. Remember this guy from the other night, Artie? He was with that good-lookin' broad from Idaho, or some shit place like that." He pointed at me. "Right?"

"Yeah, I remember," the short guy said. "Hey, where's the babe? Boy, that was some piece of ass. Hey, what happened to your face? My buddy worked you over pretty good in that alley. Did the girl dump you 'cause you got your ass kicked? Does she know you was fuckin' around prostitutes? I'm sure that would piss her off."

I stood silent.

"You know, that ain't nice, you not answerin' his question," the tall one said.

"We're closed," Frank said.

The tall guy raised his hands. "This is what's wrong with this country today. No customer service anymore. My friend told ya, we're payin' customers. Our money's good just like everyone else's. I feel a bit discriminated against."

"Please, just go. I don't want any trouble." Frank was stern, and his military voice was making itself heard.

The stare-down began. A ticking clock from *High Noon* was the only thing missing from the scene. The wind died down a bit, and no birds sang their afternoon songs. A single cloud passed over the sun. What had been bright moments earlier had turned to gray, muscles tensed, and I exhaled.

The men stood side by side and made one more plea.

"Okay, fine. You know we're just here for the girl, Addison. Just tell us where she is, and we'll be on our—"

He never finished the sentence. In a flash, the two men went from gazing at us threateningly to wide-eyed panic. They scrambled awkwardly for the protection of their car, heading in opposite directions, slipping and sliding clownishly, struggling to gain traction in the loose gravel.

I turned around. Samantha had appeared from around the side of the building, her stance open, boots dug in, and arms braced against the hail of gunfire she was about to unleash from the Mini Uzi she'd taken from the trunk.

She squeezed the trigger, spraying bursts of lead at the dodging targets while a cascade of empty brass rained down around her. She looked amazing and perfect. What wasn't perfect, however, was her aim.

Bullets flew everywhere, splintering trees, churning up asphalt, pinging off concrete, and kicking up gravel. The effect bought Frank and me enough time to get our guns out. I leveled the

Beretta and fired on the move, angling for the dubious cover of a gas pump.

Samantha's shoulders vibrated with the juddering recoil as she fired. The Uzi clicked empty. She ejected the magazine, and crouched to reload. She ripped a new magazine from her belt and slammed it home.

The two men reached the other side of the car, but Samantha's Uzi had already shredded flesh and fiber on the shorter man. He tensed and stumbled, but he made it into the vehicle. A few rounds pocked the door and fender. Frank moved to the opposite side of the building. I dashed toward Samantha.

"Where'd you learn to shoot that thing?"

"YouTube. You can learn anything on YouTube." She ran back to the building.

By the time Frank and I had made it to cover, the two men had sped off. Samantha had caught them totally unawares, and I was sure she'd at least clipped the shorter guy. Meanwhile, Frank and I had barely gotten off a shot.

"You're the best, baby." I gave her a high five.

"You nailed one, Sam," Frank said. "Pretty sure you got him in the leg."

"Which one?" she asked, stone-faced.

"The short guy."

"Good. That bastard made my skin crawl."

I looked around for Addy. She came out from behind the garage on shaky legs.

"You okay, Addy?" Frank asked. She nodded.

I turned to Frank. "Let's lock up and go. Samantha, take your car and follow me to the cabin. We'll hang out there and figure this out once and for all."

We pulled up to the cabin after a ten-minute ride. The weather was still clear, and traffic was light. We got situated inside, and I asked Frank to keep an eye on the outside for a while, just in case our friends showed up.

Since I kept the furnace on low when I wasn't there, I started a fire while Samantha helped calm Addy down—the gun battle had affected her much more than it had the rest of us.

Within minutes, the cabin had warmed up. I opened some wine and put the bottle with the glasses on the coffee table by the fireplace. I made sure the security system was working so we'd know if someone came onto the property.

Frank reached out his hand. "I need your cell phones."

"Why?" I said.

"I believe they're tracking you through the cell service."

Once Frank had our phones, he took them to the kitchen, tore off two pieces of aluminum foil and crushed them into balls. He spread open the foil, then wrapped our phones up like a Christmas present.

"This will deflect any incoming service or tracking. Nothing can get in or out. We did the same. You guys are ghosts now." He handed back the phones and rejoined the girls.

I sat in my usual spot, and Samantha sat close by.

"How are you feeling?" I asked Addy. "I have some pretty good security around the place, so if anyone comes, we'll know."

"Okay, Addy. Let's have it." Samantha's patience had been exhausted. "Tell us why you're in hiding, why Ty's truck blew up, and why he got hurt and beat up over it. I shot someone today, and Ty shot maybe killed someone in self-defense a few days ago. What kind of trouble are you in?"

The room was silent except for the popping and hissing of the fire. My arm was around Samantha, and I squeezed her closer to show her my support.

"I'm sorry the two of you got mixed up in this," Addy said. "That wasn't my intent. I would never hurt anyone, especially not Sammy." Addy looked to Samantha for some acknowledgment, but I didn't see any.

Samantha rested her head on my shoulder. I could feel her heart beating.

"I've met lots of people through work," Addy continued. "Men and women, some celebrities, even. It's easy to get caught up in all of it. I started going to parties with some big-name people—and I'm not just talking about movie stars. Politicians and CEOs started showing up, and they were by far the worst guys around. They really think they own you and can control you." She lowered her head, and hot tears ran down her face.

Frank took Addy's hand. "It's okay, honey." He took over telling the story. "We met through the escort service. I was lonely and needed someone to talk to, you know?"

"It's all right, Frank. You don't have to explain it to me," I said.

"Well, our first session was great," Frank said. "We talked."

"I couldn't get him to shut up. He brought me flowers," Addy laughed.

"See, Ty? Flowers," Samantha said.

"We had a few more appointments, and things just took off from there," Frank said. "We had a real connection."

"Never thought I could have such deep feelings for an older guy." Addy poked Frank's ribs.

"I know what you mean." Samantha looked at me.

"I'd started seeing this client on a regular basis. He had an apartment in Chicago—a nice place in the River North neighborhood. One night, he gets a phone call. He was in another room, but I did a little eavesdropping. I thought it was his wife or something. But it turned out to be someone else, and he said a lot of 'Yes, ma'am' and 'No, ma'am.' He spoke very politely and with deference." She took a drink of wine and paused a moment before continuing.

"I went back to the bedroom, and for some reason I started looking around. I found this book with names, numbers, and dates in it. Like a codebook. It looked important, so I decided to take it. My desire was to no longer be involved in the business. I thought taking that book might be a way of getting some extra cash for us. In exchange for one of his freebies, I convinced Mike to give me the client's number. I called him with an offer to make an exchange, and he sent those two guys instead. The same guys from today. They roughed me up a bit, but I kicked the shorter guy in the balls and was able to get away. I hid the book, and Frank helped me disappear."

"I found a book on your desk that I took. Is that the one you're referring to? Have you seen the book, Frank?" I asked.

"No, she won't even tell me where it is."

"And I want to keep it that way. It's for everyone's protection. I'll tell the police exactly where it is. Maybe they can make sense of it. The one you have is my client book. It's not this one."

"We could get it and take a look." I said.

"No, you've done too much. I need to go to the police, and you need to take care of Sammy."

I asked, "Do you know what the call from the woman was about?"

"Guns, and the book I believe has something to do with it, but I don't know what," she said.

"Who was the client?" Samantha asked.

"I don't know who he was talking to on the phone, and the only name he mentioned was someone he called 'old man.' The client I was with, his name is Christopher."

NINETEEN

called Chicago PD from the cabin's landline and asked for Lieutenant Craig Capone. I'd dealt with Craig in the past. He was a decent guy—he took me under his wing when I started investigating for the law firm. I was on a case surveilling a cheating husband. What I didn't know was that the husband had his friend surveilling me. I took a bad beating, and Craig was the cop that came out when I called 911. After that, Craig taught me the finer points of surveillance. He'd been a mentor of sorts to me over the years. He gave me an earful for not notifying him sooner about what had been going on with Addison, but he agreed to meet. I left mine and Samantha's involvement out of the discussion.

My next call was to the office. I spoke with Julius and had him arrange a lawyer for Addison. She was going to tell the police her story and would let them know where to find the book. Julius said that because she was giving them evidence, she wouldn't be in serious trouble, and a good lawyer would see to that. The lawyer could also get police protection for her. I made arrangements with Julius for Samantha and me to come over for dinner that night. Before heading back to the city, we stopped and picked up a couple of burner phones.

Samantha drove her car back to the city with Addy. I followed in the Chevelle, and Frank went back to the shop to check on things and pick up the ammo casings. It gave Samantha and Addy some time to talk things out. I figured Samantha would have a hard time understanding what Addy had been doing, living a secret life she knew nothing about. Sometimes the signs are right in front of you but you still can't make the connection.

It was the middle of the day and traffic would increase as the day wore on. I thought about how Samantha had handled that Uzi. The girl could clearly take care of herself.

The burner phone buzzed, and I picked it up.

"Hello, Tiger. Thinking about me?" I could just picture her serpentine smile.

"Julius wants us over for dinner tonight so you can meet Margaret. Do you have plans?"

"What about Addy?"

"She'll be tied up with the police for a while. Frank is heading out soon. She'll be safe."

"Margaret can tell me all about your most embarrassing moments growing up." Addy laughed in the background.

I called Julius back and said we were on for dinner. He sounded happy. Margaret was an excellent cook and liked fussing over company.

Soon, Addison would be in police custody. She'd tell them what she knew and end all this. Samantha and I could start a real relationship, and maybe Frank and Addy could as well.

We rolled into the city and made our way to District 20, where Craig was waiting for us. Elizabeth Simpson, the lawyer from WAR, was also there to meet us. She was one of the firm's best, and she wasn't Randolph.

I made the introductions.

"She'll have to get processed so she can get the protection. I'll keep you posted as we go." She looked at Samantha. "You may not see her for a while."

Samantha and Addy said a warm goodbye. Craig gave me the rundown on how they'd been looking for these guys for a while.

"Ty, can I have a word?" Addy asked.

"Sure, what's up?"

"Thanks for helping Sammy. I know I should have called her, but I was scared, and Frank wanted me to disappear."

"It's fine. Frank's a great guy. No apology is necessary."

"One more thing." She gave me a slow, soft kiss on the cheek and whispered, "Take care of Sammy. She's my bestie, you know?"

"I will. We'll have a big party when this is all over."

We headed to Samantha's apartment so she could pick up a few things. I wanted her to stay safe with me at my place until this was all sorted out. Her apartment looked the same. No one seemed to have tampered with anything.

She packed a bag and then we were off to Lake Point Tower to change and head to the Ackermans'.

I showered and threw on a shirt and sports jacket while Samantha made a few calls. She wore black slacks with a gray blouse and elected to leave the Louboutins in the closet and go with flats. The conservative approach.

"Do I look acceptable?" She adjusted her outfit as she spoke.

"You look exquisite."

"You still owe me a date. Maybe dinner and a play. You could take me to see *Hamilton*."

"It's been sold out for weeks."

"Look around. I think you can afford the scalper ticket prices, Tiger."

"I'll see what I can do."

The Ackerman residence was a two-story co-op home in the 1500 block of Lake Shore Drive. Margaret insisted on incredible handcrafted finishes, some of which she had salvaged from old French dwellings on her annual spring visits to Paris. The home and its roughly 12,000 square feet looked and smelled like old money.

Margaret greeted us at the door. "Well hello, my dear. Don't you look precious?" She gave Samantha a big hug and European-style air kisses. "Welcome to our home. Please, make yourself comfortable."

"It's nice to meet you, Margaret. Ty has told me so much about you."

Margaret took Samantha by the arm and led us both inside. "Oh, my dear Samantha," Margaret said, "I've been waiting so long for Ty to bring a girl home. Finally, I have a woman to talk to. I know we'll get along so well."

"You can call me Sam, if you'd like. Everyone else does."

"Well then, my dear, sweet girl, that is why I must call you Samantha."

"I see where Ty gets his manners."

"Well, we did our best, my dear. So, tell me all about you. I want to know *everything*." Margaret ushered Samantha into the living room.

Julius yelled out to Margaret, "Ty and I will get some drinks and meet you there, my love."

"Alrighty." Margaret waved and disappeared with Samantha around the corner.

Julius and I walked into his study, and he went over to his beautiful oak bar and pulled out a bottle of Blanton's bourbon. He didn't even need to ask me. He just poured two glasses.

"Here's to mud in your eye," he said. We raised our glasses for a brief second and took a drink. "So, Ty. Will you be coming back to work? I miss seeing you. Did everything get straightened out with Sam's friend?"

"Well, I think so." I didn't want to give Julius all the gory details or a rundown of how the escort business works. "She got into a bit of trouble, but with Elizabeth's help, things should work out. And yes, I'll be back to work next week."

"Good, good. I know Randolph has some work for you—"

"What could he possibly need?" I interrupted.

"Ah, let's not talk about work right now. How are you feeling?" He poured us another.

"It gets better daily. Thanks for asking."

"Oh, boys. Bring in some wine for us. Make it the '79 Lafleur Pomerol," Margaret said using her best theatrics.

"Yes, yes. Will do, my love," Julius said.

"It's in the little wine cellar off the kitchen," Margaret replied.

Julius and I walked to the cellar, and Julius pulled out two bottles and an opener.

"Grab four glasses. Here we come, dear," Julius said.

"Come on, everyone. Let's sit down." Margaret waved her free hand while her other held tight to her wine glass. "Time for dinner."

She set out lemon chicken, green beans, and baked potatoes served family style on big platters. We started moving the plates around clockwise when Margaret exclaimed, "Oh my, I forgot." She flew off the chair and hopped away like a gazelle with a hungry lion on her tail.

"What's going on?" Samantha asked in a hushed voice.

"I don't know."

Margaret reappeared with a pot and set it down on an enameled trivet beside me.

"Here you go, my good boy. Your favorite mac and cheese. The kind you like—from the blue box."

"Oh my," Samantha laughed.

"Margaret, you didn't have to do that. I eat other things now. I have for a long time," I said, feeling more embarrassed than ever. It's true what they say, the past always comes back to haunt you.

"When Tanner was a little boy, all he wanted to eat was mac and cheese, and it had to be from the blue box. Nothing else would do." Margaret paused to take a sip of wine. "Have you tried it, Samantha? It's god-awful. I've had some of the finest chefs in the country come in and make mac and cheese. Some with meat, others with freshly grated cheeses—I even had one made with lobster, but he'd turn his nose up at all of them. He was a very fussy eater."

"Well, I like what I like." I scooped a big spoonful of the golden macaroni and put it on my plate.

"I warned him that if that was all he ate, he'd be chubby someday. And from the look of him—"

"Margaret, now, now, let him be," Julius said. "He's not nine anymore. And he brought a guest. I apologize, Sam."

"No apology needed. This sure is an education in the world of Tanner York that I haven't seen yet. And I think it's cute he likes his mac and cheese." She reached over and pinched my cheek.

"I like chicken wings, too, but you don't see those on the table," I said with a sarcastic smirk.

Margaret swirled the last gulp of wine around in her glass. "Julius, Samantha tells me she's from Winter Park, Florida. We've been to Florida so many times. It's a lovely state, especially this time of year."

I thanked the powers that be that she'd changed the subject.

"Yes, yes. Great, great golfing weather down there now," Julius said.

"Winter Park is where they have that big art festival. Remember, dear? We went through there one time and looked around. Some beautiful art pieces they had. Just some stunning work." She reached for Julius's hand, and they stared at each other while sharing a private memory to which we weren't privy.

"It's one of the oldest and largest art festivals in the country, and it's a lot of fun. We would go every spring. I'd love to go again. Maybe we could go next spring?" Samantha looked at me, her face glowing with excitement.

"Sure, just as long as I can meet your family and dig up some embarrassing memories of yours," I said.

"You won't because there aren't any, and I'll call ahead to warn them that if they do..." She let the last bit trail off.

The evening wound down. The after-dinner cocktails were kicking in, and I finally felt relaxed. Samantha and I would finally be alone tonight. A lot had happened since that night we'd first met. Some emotional walls I had built up after Karin's passing were coming down. I'd found someone who meant something to me and was thinking of a future with her in it. My beautiful daydream was shattered when the Ackermans' phone rang.

NEWS FLASH – WXNG-TV, CHICAGO

"... now we go live with our reporter, Meghan Orr, who is outside police headquarters."

"Thank you, David. Just a few days ago, Superintendent Cooper stated that the city had zero tolerance for violence, suggesting that police need to work with the community, starting with parents, judges, and neighborhood and city leaders to stop the violence, since we all have a role to play in achieving the goal of zero violence. He also said that people need to respect the lives of others, as well as their own, that stricter laws need to be in place to prevent violent crime, and that fewer guns should be on the streets.

"But just a few blocks away from here in the Bronzeville neighborhood, just last night, two people were shot, and one died in the hospital. The pair were coming out of a Starbucks in the late afternoon when shots rang out, hitting a twenty-five-year-old man in the leg and a woman in the chest. According to the man, a lone gunman approached them and fired several shots before fleeing, as he informed the police. The woman, whose name has not been released, was taken to Stroger Hospital where she died from her injuries.

"According to sources from WXNG-TV News, the man who was shot is affiliated with a gang." Police are currently reviewing CCTV footage and interviewing witnesses."

"Meghan, did the superintendent say anything about his rumored retirement?"

"I was able to ask, but it appears that he has not made decision at this time."

"Thank you, Meghan. In the political world overnight..."

TWENTY

After the phone call at the Ackermans', all hell broke loose. From what the police had told us, they were moving Addy to a safe house and were ambushed on the way there. The shooting took out Addy, Lieutenant Capone, and our lawyer, Elizabeth Simpson. The cops were quick to blame it on gang violence against the police perpetrated by two gangs—the Vice Kings and the Gangster Rebels. I tried to convince them that Addy had been the target, not Capone, but Capone had had run-ins with several of the gangs' members, and he was responsible for putting many of them behind bars.

Samantha was a wreck, and it took Jill to calm her down. I didn't know whom else to call. It was rough on the Ackermans as well. Everyone at work wanted answers, and they were looking to me to have them. Samantha and I stood outside Lake Point Tower.

"I'm leaving," Samantha said with absolute certainty. "I have a cab coming. Thanks again for the airline ticket."

"Not a problem. Are you sure I can't come with?" I asked almost pleadingly.

"I just need time. This is difficult enough, and I'll have my hands full with family and friends at all hours." Her tone was a bit demanding, considering what had happened. But I couldn't blame her.

"What did work say?"

"I have an indefinite leave of absence. They understood and said to call them when I get back, and maybe there'll be an opening somewhere." Her brown eyes blinked before continuing. "I guess they like me enough to make special arrangements."

"What's not to like?" I tried to loosen the tension. It didn't work.

"Look," she said. "I'm sorry we never got our evening alone after dinner, but I was too upset, and I just needed your support and a shoulder to cry on."

Her somber mood scared me. She was always spirited, quick with her thoughts, and full of life. But for the last two days she'd been tense, reserved, and angry.

"I'm not worried about that."

She looked at me, and I drew her in, kissing her—soft at first, then firmer.

"Ty, stop." She touched my face. "I have to go."

"I think you're a wonderful woman. You brought joy back into my life." Tears trickled from her eyes as I spoke. "I know this is crazy, and we only met a few weeks ago—we haven't even gone on a date yet."

She let out a forced laugh. "You owe me *Hamilton* tickets. I won't let you forget that. You're right. It has been crazy and sad these last few days, but you've been the bright spot."

"I know I'm not the most handsome guy around, especially now that I've earned a few more battle scars. You could have any guy you wanted."

She held her hand up to stop me. "Do you think I'm shallow?" She looked at me quizzically.

"Of course not."

"I see more than just outer beauty, the inner beauty you possess shines through and obscures any superficial flaws you might think you have. You're loyal, trusting, and care for me and others. You lived through challenging times after you lost your parents. But you came through, and I'll be back. I need to spend time with family right now, other people are devastated by this, too, and I want to be there for them. I'll be back, and I love you."

She kissed me one last time. Before entering the cab, she turned and said, "Find out who killed Addison so justice can be served, Ty."

"I will."

The cab drove off.

I spent hours beating myself up over having gone to the police. But what else could I have done? It tore me apart seeing Samantha so distraught. All I could do was support her.

I headed into work, went straight to my office, and fired up the computer. I wanted to get the ball rolling on who had killed Addison and get some leads so I could tell Samantha and get her to come home.

As soon as the computer booted up and my Skype for Business account showed I was available, there was a soft knock on the door. It was Jill.

"Did she get off okay? How are you?"

"She took a cab—didn't want me to go or take her to the airport."

"She lost her friend, along with two others who were just trying to help her friend out."

"I guess, but…"

"Give her time. Now, I need to tell you something, and I want you to promise me you'll be calm about it."

"Just tell me."

"Sam wants me down there. I leave tonight."

My heart sank. *Why Jill and not me?*

I took a deep breath. "Okay. Thanks for telling me. Tell her… tell her I'm sorry." I turned around and went back to work, hoping Jill would leave. But she didn't.

She placed her arm around my shoulder and said, "We became friends, and I think she needs friends right now. It would cause too much of a distraction if she showed up with a new guy. She'd worry about you getting along with her friends and family. Other people need her now."

I kept staring at the computer.

"I'll keep you posted from Florida." She left.

If Samantha wanted Jill there for comfort, I was okay with it. Whatever it takes, and Jill would give me updates as to what was going on.

I checked the computer systems for everything—police files, gang motives, and eyewitnesses. So far, the knowledge I had about Addy's situation led me to believe her death wasn't a gang shooting. Maybe there had even been a cover-up going on in the police department. How deep did this go?

And where did this leave me? I knew that the codebook that Addy had was locked away; had she been able to tell Capone where it was? Did Elizabeth know? But they were both dead now. If the codebook had something to do with guns, was someone buying or selling them? There was a loud knock on the door.

It was Randolph. "Ty, finally back at work? Regarding this list of names I have, I need some background checks.

"I'm a little busy now. I'll get to it later," I said, annoyed.

"Ian said you could do it now."

"Excuse me?" I turned and glared.

"Ian. Ackerman put him in charge of investigator operations."

"Investigator operations? But it's just me. When did this happen?"

"A few days ago. So, you gonna get this done today?" He held out the list. "Hey, Elizabeth's death has affected everyone in the office, but they're all pushing through it. You should too."

I tore the list out of his hands and left.

"Hey, where you going? Want to do lunch today, buddy?" Randolph said.

I walked past everyone and marched toward Ackerman's office. He didn't say anything about this at dinner the other night or when I called yesterday. I was just about to knock on his office door when I thought better of it and stopped in the men's room to cool down a bit. When I pushed open the door, Ian was standing by the sink.

"Move," I said harshly.

"He doesn't want to be disturbed," Ian said. "Take a deep breath and calm down, buddy."

"I'm not sure what you did to sway Julius, but you're done here." I planted my index finger in his chest. He threw his hands up.

"What would Julius say about your assault and battery?" he smirked.

I washed my hands and said, "I'm not sure what your story is, Ian. But I'll find out. I'll find out what gives between you and Randolph, and I'll take you both down."

"I'd like to see you try," he said, walking away.

"What a day," I said to my reflection in the mirror. I grabbed some tissues and cleaned my face. Perhaps it would be better not to confront Julius right now.

I went to my office and sat in front of a blank computer screen. I couldn't do this anymore. There was nothing to go on. Why didn't Samantha want me to go with her to Florida? Why Jill, for that matter? They seemed to have a strong connection, but why? They barely knew each other.

The computer didn't answer back. Against my better judgment, I called Samantha.

"*Bonjour*, it's Sammy. I'm off doing something awesome. Leave the deets after the beep."

I hung up. Hearing her voice had a tranquil effect on me.

Two hours after the Ian incident, I headed out of my office. Most everyone had already left as it was getting late. I looked down the hall to see if Julius's door was open. It was. I stood in the open doorway.

"May I have a word?" I interrupted.

"Ty, yes, come in. Randolph still needs those background checks."

"I'll get to them."

"That would be excellent."

"About Ian..."

"I've asked Ian to help organize your workload so you can get this murder solved. He's only going to give you work on the important current cases going on, and he'll handle the rest. I know you care about Sam and want to help, but I want to know who killed Elizabeth as well. I hope you understand. Margaret and I are counting on you."

"So, I work for him now?"

"No, no, my boy. He's just filtering the work to give you time to solve Elizabeth's— Addison's—incident. Once that's done, it'll all go back to normal. That's what we need around here. Normalcy."

My brain debated whether I should tell him about my encounter with Ian in the men's room. But it would be his word against mine, and I knew that would put Julius in a difficult position. So I decided to let it go. I'd deal with Ian after this was over.

TWENTY-ONE

"So, how are you?" Dr. Renfro asked. But just looking at me answered that question. Chicago was pushing hard into spring, and the weather was pleasant for the time of year. I had heard little to nothing from Samantha, and I was nowhere on the case.

"I'm good," I lied, "and you?"

"Fine," she said.

The scent of the vanilla candle that was burning floated through the air, assaulting my senses and making me long for the smell of Samantha's strawberry and mint fragrance. I missed her terribly, and that infuriated me.

"Why did I come here?" I groaned, looking at a blank wall.

"What? I didn't catch that," she said.

Dr. Renfro's voice broke my train of thought. "Nothing, it was nothing, just like my whole life," I muttered.

After a long pause, she broke the silence with a question. "I can't help but notice that you have some cuts and bruises. Why don't we talk about that?"

"Oh, this?" I waved my hand in front of my battered face. "I'm fine. Fell down some stairs." I could tell she noticed my gruffness.

"How did it happen?"

"You know, I'm clumsy. Didn't have my shoe tied." I threw a half-smile her way.

"Why didn't you have your shoe tied?" If the time I'd spent in her office had taught me anything, it was that she'd never give up until the truth was out.

"Okay. Look, I got in a little fight. I got jumped in an alleyway. But you should see the other guy," I laughed, pain shooting through me.

"Did you call the police—"

"No, no cops. Look, it's over, and I'll heal up." My mood soured by the second.

"Why did you feel you needed to lie to me?" Her voice was so even-toned that it was getting on my nerves.

"I don't know. I just, well, I just..."

"It seems hard for you to talk about. Did you know the person that confronted you?"

My leg started to move, hammering out a silent rhythm. The caffeine overdose I'd taken that afternoon was kicking in. Unaware of how fidgety I was, my whole body became an S.O.S. signal.

"What's upset you?" she asked.

"I met someone—a woman."

"That's great. Is it the bookstore woman you mentioned last time? How did asking her out go?" She seemed pleased, even excited, for me.

"Bridget? Naw, someone else."

"Who then?" She tilted her head.

Another pause.

She continued, "Is there a possibility that the woman you met is triggering your current behavior?"

"No, I love her." It slid out of me faster than a striking cobra.

"How do you know it's love? Do you want to tell me how you met?"

I rubbed my jaw, feeling the stubble on my face, trying to remember the last time I'd shaved. Taking a pause to collect my thoughts, I decided to tell her everything. But I left out the gun battle parts.

"I saved her life on the side of the road, out in Kickapoo…" and I went on. I told her about the hospital, the snowed-in cabin, the story of her missing friend, and Addy's death. How Samantha had left without knowing when she'd return.

"Well, that's quite a story. I can see why she means so much to you. But how do you know you're in love? What is it about her that has you feeling this way?"

I twisted in my chair. "Because my heart hurts that she's gone. Because I had that exact same feeling when Karin was gone. I just know." Relief flushed through my body. It felt good to get that out. "Why can't I be there? With her?"

"The death of a friend is never easy, and introducing someone new to her family and friends might be stressful for her." Her voice was even-toned and clinical. "From the way you describe her, she sounds lovely. I take it she's young?"

"Yes, Samantha's younger by… twenty-three years," I said, embarrassed.

"Does she feel the same way about you?"

"Yes." Again, it came out like a shot out of a cannon. Wringing my hands was another signal I'm sure Dr. Renfro had read something into. My stomach churned, and I could feel my temperature rise. Beads of sweat formed on my forehead. I leaned forward, my head in my hands.

"Are you sexually active?"

She waited for me to respond.

"We haven't... had any." I brushed it off, but she did not.

"She might have intimacy issues because of her past. It might be a good idea to go to couples therapy at some point. I can recommend someone. Do you know if she's talked to a professional in the past or is doing so currently?"

"No."

"It might be worth finding out. For homework, I'd like you to think about what intimacy means to you. We could talk about it in our next session. What about Frank and Robert? What do they think of her?"

"Why would it matter what they think?" I questioned.

"They're your friends, and sometimes getting a friend's opinion is insightful." She threw me a judgmental look, as though I should have known that.

"Jill has met Samantha," I said. "They seemed to have hit it off well. They've had lunch a few times. When Jill's husband was out of town, Samantha stayed over at the house and got to know the kids. It was a good place to hide out." That slipped out.

"Jill from your work? You said something about hiding out? Hiding from—"

I thought fast. "Her ex-boyfriend. He's called her a few times, and I thought it might be good for Samantha to be away from her apartment." I barely got out of that one. No sense telling her that we're being hunted down.

"Well, that's good that she's made a connection with Jill. I'm happy for you, but don't let the progress you've made slip because she isn't here. She said she'd be back and has not given you any reason to doubt her. Stay positive. It will work out as it should."

I nodded, we discussed a few more things, and I left to continue to hunt down Addy's killer.

TWENTY-TWO

"Gentlemen," Ian said. "Behold, the new XM2010 long-range sniper rifle. It's designed for the modern battlefield, with state-of-the-art corrosion-resistant metal. It has the Remington Arms Chassis System, or RACS, and a folding stock, allowing for perfect length for pull and cheek height, making it custom for each shooter. The Titan quick detach sound suppressor is what separates it from all the other United Optics system weapons. In case you don't know what that is, it means that the sight optics can be sent to a satellite, so what the shooter sees appears on a monitor miles away." Ian turned on a thirty-two-inch smart TV next to the weapon.

The audience of three Arab men marveled at the sophistication of the setup, nodding their heads and uttering words of satisfaction. This cast of characters and their toy were stationed in an abandoned farmhouse on the outskirts of Oregon, Illinois, surrounded by farmland. Yet another sign of the graying of rural America. Cities offer attractive jobs for the young, and they leave behind the small towns that can't compete with major corporations.

Out across the field, some 600 yards away, three wooden chairs stood on frozen, unplowed, muddy corn fields. In those chairs sat two men and one woman wearing different colored shirts: one blue, one red, and the woman in green. The man in red still fought the zip ties that held him to the chair. The others had given up the struggle some time ago.

"Can you move the sight around so we can see, please?" one of the Syrians said, moving his hand in the direction of the firearm.

Ian moved to a shooter's position, sighting the optics. The scope picked up the details of a target—a cat sitting in the open field watching the red-shirted man struggle. The TV screen showed the cat along with information that put the target at 587 yards out.

"Perhaps a demonstration?" another client asked.

Ian peered over his shoulder, not liking the question so much. But if he were the buyer and spending millions, he would demand the same.

He again got the cat in his sights, then he moved the barrel to his right, finding the woman in the green shirt. The screen read 605 yards. She was sobbing, with snot and tears running down her face. One client gasped at seeing the woman's head in the crosshairs. Ian moved the barrel again, this time stopping on the man wearing the blue shirt. He let the crosshairs linger for a few seconds. This target appeared more in control. He was mouthing words that they could not hear from the farmhouse. Ian had some talent in lip reading and concluded that the man was begging "Please, please... please." Moving yet again, he found the red-shirted man who was still trying to work himself free. Ian knew exactly what he was saying: "Fucker."

He switched between the targets, going back and forth, unsure of which target to offer his clients. Ian once again moved the weapon back to the cat. He heard impatient noises coming from the three men.

He decided on his target and sighted in. Exhaling slow and without wavering, he pulled the trigger.

The barrel's muted pop pleased the three men. On the screen, blood sprayed on the blue-shirted man sitting beside the woman. The bullet had hit her square in the chest. The force of the impact had flipped her body and the chair backwards, causing them to topple over onto the ground. One of the buyers clapped, seemingly elated.

"One down, two to go," Ian said.

The cat never flinched.

"We thank you for your hospitality; the royal family and our president will be pleased with the report. Perhaps you could help us on another matter as well?"

"Certainly." Ian sat down next to the man.

"A sheikh has a... collection of... exotic creatures and would like to add to hie collection. I know this hobby of his is rather expensive, but he assures me that if you acquire what he's looking for, he will pay you handsomely." He waited for Ian to respond.

"Go on."

He handed Ian a piece of paper, who, after reading it, looked at the man with a whimsical smile and said, "Please tell His Highness that I have just what he's looking for, and with any luck, I'll be able to deliver it with the gun shipment."

"Excellent. He will be quite pleased. He has wanted one in the worst way. I knew I could count on you."

The men left separately in black Mercedes. Ian picked up the paper and re-read the request.

"If at all possible, I would like a light-haired, mid- to late-twenties American girl with brown eyes who was or is a cheerleader. She would fit into my collection of women from around the world nicely."

"I know just who you're looking for, your Majesty," Ian said, followed by a laugh.

TWENTY-THREE

I stood there staring, not much caring if anyone was watching me. Her lines were fluid, wavy, and her headlights sleek. The metallic blue paint reminded me of the Pacific Ocean in Hawaii. Looking back, the Audi RS7 dared me to buy her. The Audi dealership was a stunning showcase of what Audi had to offer. Their customer service was impeccable—every detail was attended to. I was there on impulse; that was what depression did to me. If I could buy something I wanted, I'd be happy. It would fill the hollowness I felt inside. That was the thought process, anyway. It hadn't worked yet.

A young salesperson approached. "It's a great-looking car, isn't it?" He held out his hand. "Ronald Hudson."

"Tanner York." We shook hands. I still had some of the congressman's cash left over, so why not put that back into the economy?

"I'll take the blue one if it has the sports package," I said dryly.

"It sure does. Would you like to purchase or lease?"

"I'll buy it."

"Great. Do you have a trade-in? Can I offer you a refreshment while I write up the contract?" We walked over to his office.

"I'll take a bourbon, please. And no on the trade-in. I took an Uber here."

"Uh, this is a car dealership. We can't serve alcohol."

"Water, then."

I took a seat in his office, and he handed me a cold bottle of water.

"The car lists at a hundred and fifty-two thousand." He looked at me with raised eyebrows.

"Let's just make it an even one fifty, and we'll both have a Merry Christmas."

He chuckled, "Why not, Mr. York."

After a few hours, I tore out of the dealership and headed for the expressway. The engine growled as I hit each gear, pinning me to the seat. The response in the steering was tight and easy as I weaved in and out of traffic, effortlessly heading into the city. Richard Wagner's "Ride of the Valkyries" blasted through the supped-up stereo system. I caught myself smiling—the power of the new car made me happy, but I was still empty inside.

I walked into the law firm and headed for the kitchen to get a cup of coffee. The thrill of the ride in was still fresh in my body. I took a few sips before heading to my office.

There was a list of names on my desk waiting for me to carry out their background checks. That was something I did for the lawyers so they knew everything about any possible witnesses in upcoming cases. I went through my emails first and found nothing important, so I started on the names. I put on a Mozart CD: "Symphony No. 25 in G Minor." A few minutes later, I heard a knock at the door. As I turned, I saw Jill standing in the doorway.

"Ty, how's it going?" Her voice was husky.

"Hello. You okay? You sound different,"

"Must have picked something up from the plane," she said. "Are you upset with me?"

"We're okay. How was it?"

"It was good. Nice to get away to some warmer weather. The kids had a blast at Disney, of course. The funeral was fine, lots of people." She walked into the room and took a seat beside my desk.

She told me a little more about some travel problems she'd encountered, but nothing important—nothing that I actually wanted to hear about. I noticed there was some change in her. She seemed nervous, like she was keeping something from me.

"So, I have to ask..." Jill glanced down as if she knew what was coming. I tried not to hold my breath. "How is she?"

"She's good, considering. I met a lot of her Florida friends at dinner one night. Since we work together, they wanted to know about you. I guess she's been talking about you to them, so they knew who you were. Of course, I had to tell them the truth about what an asshole you are." She smiled and laughed.

"Thanks, friend-o," I smirked.

"Seriously, she does miss you and wanted me to let you know that she appreciates your understanding. And she wanted me to reassure you that she will be back. She promised." She touched my arm in encouragement. "How are you?" She leaned in close, invading my space.

"I'm fine. Bought a new car."

The tip of her tongue slipped out and made a circuit of her lips, drawing my attention to their deep red wetness. Her green eyes were locked onto mine. A surge of guilt flashed through me, like the time Samantha caught me glancing at her breasts.

"Wow, that's great. Which one?"

"It's an Audi, metallic blue."

"Nice. You'll have to give me a ride in it sometime." Her teeth bit into her lower lip.

I was confused. Was I crossing over into the fantasy world again? Nothing had ever happened between us. Well, there was that one kiss in the hospital, but I thought that was more of a joke—wasn't it?

"Maybe we could go out for lunch one day?" She got up, walked behind me, put her hands around my neck, and started to massage my shoulders.

"Oh, you're tight up here." Her fingers worked through my tendons, pressuring the knots to release their hold. I found the massage puzzling for the same reason the lunch offer had been.

"What's with all this?"

"Sammy asked me to look out for you, make sure you're doing okay, remember? Just doing a friend a favor." She stopped with the massage and walked around to face me.

"Any news on who killed Addy?"

"Nothing, really. I'm stumped as to where to look."

"If you need any help, let me know. Anyway, I need to get back. I'll check on you later, okay?" She walked to the door and spun around. "Bye." With a quick wave, she was gone.

"See ya," I mumbled. I tried not to think about that kiss at the hospital and refocus on the case. That kiss *was* memorable, however.

I sat at my desk, thinking about where to start. Whether the cops really didn't know who was responsible or they were covering up the shooting, I thought my best bet would be to check out the crime scene. I could canvass the area; start asking questions. But first, I needed to see Julius.

This time, I called ahead. Julius had time to meet, so I went to his office and ended up running into Randolph Rockwell on the way.

"Ty, how are you this fine, fine day? Did you get a chance to run those names?"

"Yes, all the names are done, Randolph."

"Great. Come here, fella," He slapped his arm around my shoulders, pulling me into his chest for an unreciprocated 'bro hug.' "Can you do me a huge favor? Can you bring two cups of coffee to my office? I have a special guest," he said, releasing his grasp and then punching me in the arm. "You're the best, Ty." Then he walked away, his voice still echoing down the hall as if it were the Grand Canyon. I couldn't refuse and make a scene, since that was the last thing I needed to do at work. After all, Randolph's special guest could be the US president. Instead, I went to the kitchen and set up a tray with coffee, cups, and all the trimmings.

I brought the coffee into his office, only to discover that his special guest was Ian. "Really Randolph? Ian?"

Ian started laughing, "So, you get his coffee?"

"Ty's the best. We're buds. Hey, just playin'." Randolph said.

It took just about everything I had to turn and leave without a word. Next time, I'd bring cyanide, but I vowed there wouldn't be a next time.

The door to Julius's office was open. He sat behind his big oak desk.

"How are you, Ty?" He stood and moved out front.

"I'm okay."

"Margaret's worried you've fallen back into a bit of a depression."

"I'm fine, just upset that Samantha's friend got killed and I can't do anything to help."

"Such a young girl, the officer, and our sweet Elizabeth. I hope you got a chance to sign the card that was going around."

"Are you going to fire Ian? I told you not to hire him," I said, abruptly changing the subject.

"He's working on some investigations with Randolph. He's a good man, Ty, I've been getting to know him. He's a bit rough, but if you give him a chance—"

"Why am I always the one that has to give someone a chance?"

"That's how we raised you." He put a hand on my shoulder. "Be the bigger man, remember? I taught you that. Your father did, too. Besides, with Ian helping Randolph, that means you don't have to."

"All my life, that's all I've done. It feels like losing."

"Don't feel that way, my boy. How's Sam doing? Have you heard from her?" Now Julius was the one changing the subject. Ian was doing more for Julius than he was willing to admit. I sensed it.

"She's in Florida, helping out with Addison's family and her own."

"Such a lovely girl. Why not surprise her down in Florida? Take the private jet and go see her." He picked up the phone and started dialing the airport.

"She doesn't want me down there, Julius. I tried talking to her, but she needs space and time away, and I'm going to give her that. If she doesn't come back... well, I'll just have to deal with it." I sounded like I was convincing myself more than him.

"What are you going to do?"

I raised my hands in a gesture of helplessness. "Look for the killer."

His brow furrowed. "You can't go around this city chasing ghosts. The police are handling it, and that's that. Let it go." The lines on his face danced as he spoke. Being close to eighty, those lines ran deep.

"But you wanted me to look into the murders." I'd promised Samantha that I would find the killer and get justice for Addison, so that was what I was going to do. "So why the change?"

"Rethinking it, now you may be too close to the situation. It might be best to let the police handle it. Have you anything to go on?"

"No, I don't right now."

Julius seemed relieved, maybe more than he should have been. I wondered why he was getting so upset with me for looking for the killer. Didn't he want justice for Elizabeth? And the lieutenant? I sure did. It was policework, true, and not exactly the job of a law firm investigator, but I just didn't trust the situation. There had been too many pat answers, too many coincidences, and too many details swept under the rug. I would not give up. It was better to ask forgiveness than permission. For now, I'd keep my cards close to my chest.

"You should call Sam. Maybe she's changed her mind. You can have the jet anytime."

TWENTY-FOUR

I shaded my eyes against the burnt orange color of the morning sun. Addy was shot here, at the corner of Western Avenue and Moffat Street. Although Logan Square was a decent place, the crime rate had risen over the last few years due to street gangs competing for the same turf. What I was hoping for was someone I could talk to—eyewitnesses don't communicate with cops all that well on the street. They were too scared of retaliation. But I'm not a cop. I'm just a guy looking for something that will bring me closer to the truth.

Across the street was a little bodega—that would be a good place to start. I looked around and saw a young man approaching. His walk had attitude; it was telling everyone that he owned these streets, or at least that he was connected to those who did.

"Hey," I said with a nod.

"Fuck off."

"Looking for info on a shooting that happened here a few days ago. I'll pay if you or someone you know saw anything."

"Oh, you gonna *pay*, motherfucker? The cop had it comin'."

He brushed passed me. "Hey man, one of the girls that got killed was a friend of mine. I'm no cop."

He stopped and looked back at me, "Which bitch was your friend? And I know you ain't no fuckin' cop, prick. You shouldn't be here."

"Her name was Elizabeth Simpson. She was a wife and the mother of a little girl, and she was just here helping someone out," I said.

"You tryin' to guilt me, motherfucker?" He looked at me a minute, thinking. "All right, I'll help you out. I gots somebody you can talk to. Follow me."

He started to make his way down the street. I hesitated.

"Comin', motherfucker? This is what you wanted." He headed off.

Cautiously, I followed him down Moffat Street. About two bungalows down, we headed down a gangway through a yard and into the alley. I looked around and saw no one.

"Where is he?" I said.

"Behind you."

The blow to my head scared me more than it hurt. I was on the ground, kissing the dirty concrete again. Two men stood near me. I rolled away and got to my feet. I assume a defensive posture. They were smart and fanned out to my left and right. But I was getting tired of taking a beating.

"Stop," shouted a deep, husky voice.

My foggy vision cleared, and I saw a large black man standing before me.

"To whom do I have the pleasure of addressing this fine morning in the City of Big Shoulders?" said the robust man.

"Tanner York." I tried to reach my arm out to shake his hand, but the man pulled it back.

"Mr. York, I'm Ramon. Why do you come here? This is not a good place for you to be. My wannabes are a little overprotective of our turf, and they don't take kindly to strangers. Not even white ones."

"I can assure you, I am no threat. I'm looking for some information relating to a colleague of mine, she was killed here a few weeks ago."

"Mr. York, may I ask your occupation?"

"I work for Westcott, Ackerman, and Rockwell law firm; I'm an investigator. My colleague, Elizabeth, was a lawyer."

"Oh, so you know Randolph Rockwell. He and I did some business together a while back. He helped me out on a legal matter that ended favorably for me. I owe Randolph a lot, and now so do you."

"Why me?"

"Because Randolph is a friend of ours, you shall live today." His white teeth showed once more.

"I'll take that," I said.

"I will allow you to ask two questions. Then it would be best for you to be on your way, Mr. York."

I thought a minute about what to ask. "Do you know who killed her?"

"I do not."

I thought another minute. "Can you tell me who would know?"

"Yes. Across the street there is a mini food mart. Ask for Skunk. Tell her Ramon sent you, and she will have something for you."

"Skunk? That's an odd name. Didn't her parents like her?"

"You will know why when you meet her, Mr. York. I will give you one hour, then you should leave—for your own safety."

"Great. Thanks."

Mini was the correct word for the place. It was tiny. A stale smell filled the air. I walked up to the woman behind the counter. I felt a little ridiculous asking for someone named 'Skunk,' but the clock was ticking.

"Skunk? I'm Tanner York, Ramon said..."

A phlegmy voice interrupted me. "Yeah, I'm Skunk. I know; he called and said to give you this with no fuckin' hassles." Skunk was an elderly black woman who looked like she was in agony. Everything about her was crooked, from the way she did business to her appearance. Her hands were bent every which way, with veins that popped off the skin, creating little highways on her hands and arms. She had a bump on her nose and rotten gums with missing teeth. She spit when she talked and had a wretched cough. And she smelled pungently of skunk—marijuana skunk. It was strong enough to trigger my gag reflex.

She tossed me a flash drive.

"What's this?" I asked.

"The fuckin' video from the outside camera," she sneered.

"Of...?"

"The shooting, dipshit."

"What did the cops say when they saw it?"

"Cops don't know about it."

"Why? Are you afraid of gang retaliation?"

"This was no gang thing. Why do ya think Ramon, that cocksucker, gave this to ya?" Her dislike for Ramon showed. "The Gangster Thirty-Eights are at war with the Satan Soldiers for this turf. They're making a dent in Cribland."

"What's Cribland?"

"Boy, you white people really are clueless. You know that cemetery near Maywood?

It took a second to connect, "Yes, Lady of Our God, right?"

"That's it. They donated an eighth of their land. We call it Cribland. That's where the mommies and daddies of victims of gang violence can bury their kids for free. Last I heard, it was almost full up. That was a year ago." Her voice was solemn, her gaze distant.

"So, what makes you think this shooting wasn't gang related?"

"The dude doin' the shootin' was white. This was a hit, probably ordered by the Producer." She started stocking shelves. I figured I didn't have much time left.

"Who's the Producer?"

"That's what we call the person who supplies the trophies for all this madness you hear about daily. Guns."

TWENTY-FIVE

Nobody seemed to notice I was late. Jill's office was empty, so no update on Samantha. I decided to give her a call, letting her know I might have something. Even if I got her voice mail, just hearing her upbeat tone would reassure me of what I was fighting for.

"*Bonjour*, this is Sammy. I'm doing something awesome right now. Leave your deets. Later."

"Hey, it's me. Just needed to hear your voice. I have news." That was enough to give me the energy I needed to go to work.

After grabbing a cup of coffee, I inserted the flash drive and watched the video. It was short. The white guy that Skunk had seen in the car was the tall man with the neck tattoo. These two guys keep showing up in all the wrong places. The video showed him shooting while he was driving, but it also showed one other important thing. As the car passed the camera, it captured the license plate, clear as a bell. I plugged the number into the software on my computer and found a name. The plate was registered to a woman by the name of Mary Miller, who lived in the Rogers Park neighborhood.

I didn't care who Mary Miller was or how her car was involved in the shooting, but tonight I would pay her—or whoever lived at her address—a visit. My hunch was that the car was stolen. She'd show me the police report and that would be that. But at least it was a lead.

A thundering knock startled me into sitting up straight and boosted my heart into overdrive.

"What?" I said.

In walked Randolph. "That's the best greeting you have for me?"

"What's so important that you just had to knock like Godzilla?"

"I have some work I need done," he said as he handed me a slip of paper.

"How many more names do you need background checks for?"

"It's for the civil suit for Ainsworth."

"Why are you doing this? You don't work civil suits. Don't waste my time. Have douchebag Ian do it." I tried to hand the paper back, but he wasn't biting.

"It's a favor. The congressman's going to have a dinner party in a few weeks. I'll make sure you and that hot little girlfriend of yours get invited."

"I have other stuff to do tonight, so this will..."

Jill walked in. Randolph threw a big arm around her shoulders and squeezed her into one of the gropey, vice-like hugs she hated. "Jill's going. And she's looking forward to it."

"Take it easy," she said. "I'm still a bit sore. And remember, we talked about the touching, Randolph. I don't like it." She squirmed and removed his arm.

"Sorry, Jill. Jeez."

"What am I looking forward to? I'm afraid to ask."

"The congressman's dinner party. Hey, gotta scoot. Thanks for doing this, Ty." His exit was just as loud and obnoxious as his arrival. Jill and I both shook our heads.

"Have you heard from Samantha?" I asked.

"No, she must be busy, that girl."

"I think something's going on. I haven't heard from her at all since she left, but you have." My tone was accusatory.

"We're friends, and she's going through a hard time. Sometimes women just want to talk to or be comforted by other women." She folded her arms across her chest, and her jaw tightened.

"I'm sorry for taking my frustrations out on you. I miss her. This might sound weird, but I need her right now. It just..." I left it there.

"Hang in there." She moved to the door and turned around. "How about we do lunch tomorrow?"

"Sure. Why not."

TWENTY-SIX

Mary Miller had no clue that her car had been stolen. She had just gotten back from an extended vacation to Europe. The long travel compounded with jet lag was too much for her, so she had gone straight to bed without looking in the garage when she had arrived home that day. Mary had just woken up an hour before I showed up. After a brief introduction, she welcomed me into her home.

Rogers Park was a decent neighborhood with a diverse mix of residents. Folks of Irish, German, English, and Jewish heritage had had a big presence there in the forties and fifties. Now it claims representation from eighty countries, which makes for a great variety of ethnic restaurants. Big oak trees line the streets and stand in front of brick bungalows. It borders Lake Michigan and is home to Loyola University, making it the location of some prime real estate. But even in this nice neighborhood, there is still crime.

I told her about her car being involved in a deadly shooting.

"Thank you for letting me know about my car. That's so awful, I'll call the police right away. They'll be able to use my tracking system to find it."

"Tracking system?"

"Yes, when I bought the car the salesman talked me into having one installed. He wanted twelve hundred dollars, but I got him down to nine hundred." A smile of pride creased her face. "But I never used it, until now."

My brain went off like a Fourth of July fireworks show. "If I may suggest, why don't we locate it ourselves?"

"We should call the police and let them handle it. They may need it for evidence."

"But if we could tell them exactly where it is, it would save them time. In fact, I could meet them there and tell them you are completely innocent of any wrongdoing." I smiled, trying to be polite and professional. Looking around the room, I noticed a few medication bottles.

"I have asthma." I pointed to the bottles.

Mary shifted uncomfortably, stood, and walked to the door. "Well, thanks for letting me know about the car. If you don't mind, I'm still a bit tired."

Her uneasiness mixed with the abruptness of her showing me the door got me thinking, and I started to put two-and-two together. "Mary, do you happen to deal in illegal prescription drugs, like opioids?" I picked up a few bottles. Sure enough, each bottle had a different name and none were made out to Mary Miller, if that was her real name. "All I need is one hour—that gives you time to clean up here and for me to search the car before the cops impound it."

It didn't take much else for Mary to be persuaded. I used her laptop to locate the car; it was a mere four blocks away.

I found the car parked in an alley. The property didn't have a garage, so it was right there in plain sight. I went around to the front of the house and stood at the door, ready for anything. I could see lights and movement in the place. But I wasn't sure how many people were inside. It was a standalone house with a manicured lawn, bushes, and a fresh paint job. Being a hired gun must be profitable.

I was about to ring the bell when I realized that I hadn't brought a gun. "Damn it," I cursed under my breath. "I'm the worst investigator there is."

I took a puff from my inhaler, pushed the doorbell, and remembered why I was doing this.

When the door opened, the tall man with the neck tattoo appeared before me, wearing a white tomato-stained cooking apron. The smell of dinner wafted through the air, and he looked at ease.

"Can I..." Not hesitating for a moment, I lunged forward, catching him off guard. My left arm grabbed him around his neck, and I threw several quick punches to his torso. My fist caught a few ribs, and a few punches landed in his soft belly. It took the wind out of him. We fell to the floor. I pinned his right arm down with my knee, and my left and right fists became my instruments of mass destruction, taking turns trying to rearrange his face.

His survival instincts kicked in, and in one fluid motion he flung me off him, my back taking a blow from hitting the hardwood floor. It stunned me for a few seconds. My inner voice commanded, *get up, get up!*

He was still on his back when I made it to my knees. I looked around to see if someone had heard the commotion, but no one else appeared to be home, unless they were upstairs. The sounds of our scuffle would have woken anyone up who might have been sleeping.

He started to rise. I needed a weapon. I got to my feet and gave him a kick to the ribs, like so many had done to me recently. It felt good being on the giving end, and that put him back on the floor.

I looked around the living room and saw some lamps, a TV, and some knickknacks, but nothing that could be used as a weapon. I ran to the kitchen. In desperation, I rummaged through the kitchen drawers and cabinets. A knife block sat on a shelf across the room.

I moved around the table, but just before I could reach the knives, the tall man came into the kitchen and slammed me hard against the refrigerator. The handle of the refrigerator door dug into my back, sending shockwaves of pain down my buttocks and legs.

"I knew I should've smashed that car over the edge. Then you woulda never been involved."

"She's alive and well, thank you."

"I'll kill you, then her."

With the kitchen table between us, we circled, each of us sizing the other up. He turned around and drew a large carving knife from the block and lunged. I reached out to grab his arm, but he pulled back fast.

"Who do you work for?" I said. "Is it the congressman? Is he the old man?"

"Screw you."

He lunged. I missed his arm once again.

"Tell me who you work for."

He jabbed again, faster this time. I reached out, but instead of his arm, my hand closed hard around the steel blade. His laughter echoed in my brain, and before I could let go, he was already pulling the knife back, carving out a slice of my fingers.

I screamed and opened my hand. The blood flowed quickly. But I couldn't pass out now.

"Got you good. All I have to do is wait till you lose enough blood."

I had two choices, go out like the tall man said or do it on my terms.

I chose the latter. Rushing at him, I overturned the table, causing him to brace for impact. I took his arm that was holding the knife and twisted—the knife fell, but he shoved me hard against the stove. I hit my head, and my vision began to tunnel. If I blacked out now, it was game over.

He came at me again with the knife in hand, thrusting low. I moved with more speed than I even knew I possessed, like a starving man at an all-you-can-eat buffet.

I grabbed his knife arm with both hands, staving off another attack, but I didn't have much strength left. We stumbled to the floor. He pinned me up against the stove, its heat radiated into me. He had the upper hand as he was above me. He pushed down with all his weight, and my arms, holding his knife hand, began to buckle. The blade was inching closer to my chest.

I thought of Samantha and the words she'd spoken just before she left. She was relying on me to get justice for Addy. Above my head was the handle of a skillet on the stove. I made a desperate grab for it with my bloody hand but missed. The blade ripped open my coat. I threw a punch, and it connected. That gave me enough of an opportunity to reach for the pan again. This time,

I closed my fist and heard the sizzle of burning flesh as I bought the pan downward. It was heavy; striking his head created a gong sound. Like wielding a tennis racket, I hit his head again... and again... and again. He released the knife, and his hands went to his head. A stew of some sort spilled all over the floor. I leaped to my feet, and he got to his knees, clutching his face. Blood ran everywhere, and my hand was burnt, but it had cauterized the cut. Adrenaline raced through me faster than the Indy 500 time trials, which helped to mask the pain.

"Who do you work for?" I huffed out.

"You're all gonna die, asshole." Through his bloodstained face, I saw his lips curl up and his white teeth turn dark red.

It was clear we were done talking. Like a big-league hitter, I gripped the pan with both hands and swung it with all my might, connecting right with the sweet spot on his forehead.

He hit the ceramic tile hard, his body twitching and his arms moving, but without any real meaning or purpose. Blood poured down his forehead like the river Nile. His feet started to move, but just like his arms, they no longer posed a threat to me. The blood began to pool.

I thought of Addy and what must have gone through her mind during her last moments of life. I stood over him—watching, thinking—as Samantha's instructions to seek justice for her friend echoed in my mind.

I washed my face at the kitchen sink. Using a towel, I wiped it clean and then placed it in my pocket. I found some bleach and poured some down the drain. I'd have to do some clean up to cover my tracks.

Satisfied, I went into the living room to leave, but a picture caught my eye. It was a family portrait, and the tall man was with a woman and three kids. The kids' ages ranged from one to eight. My stomach started to turn like that time in the alley. My eyes scanned past the frame, and my emotions switched from queasy to enraged as I spied who was in the picture behind the portrait of the happy family. It was the tall man with his arm around none other than Ian Smith.

TWENTY-SEVEN

Jill wanted to have lunch at La Lumière de Paris on Wells Street. She'd studied French at the University of Illinois at Chicago while getting her degree in business administration. She was thrilled when I'd agreed to go. It had been a long time since she'd experienced French culture. Her husband had never cared for French food, so doing something like that with him was out of the question. She'd warned me that it was a French-speaking restaurant, which had made me a bit nervous.

"*J'ai une réservation pour deux,*" she told the host.

"*Le nom, s'il vous plait, Madame?*" he replied.

"*C'est Sinclair, Monsieur.*"

He checked his list. "*Suivez le jeune homme, s'il vous plait.*" He snapped his fingers, and a young man jumped over to the host stand with two menus.

"*Par ici.*" He motioned for us to follow.

Our table for two was small with white linen and cane chairs. The place buzzed with excitement but had a relaxed feel. Open space was minimal as the patrons were tucked in close together. The music that played was heavy on the accordion and the French lyrics were belted out by a female singer. The walls were adorned with old French movie posters and photos of the Eiffel Tower. A server stopped by and placed a basket of sliced baguettes and a saucer of black olives on the table. The menu was all in French. I could make out a few things, but it was all foreign to me.

"I can order for us if you'd like. I mean, I don't want to over—"

"I'll leave it to you." I put down the menu.

"I just love speaking French, and I never get to do it much anymore." The music caught her attention. "Edith Piaf."

"Excuse me."

"A famous French singer from the forties, that's who's singing."

A slender man appeared and asked, "*Boissons?*"

"*Eau gazeuse.* Um, do you just want water, or..." Jill looked at me for some direction.

"I'll make this easy for you. Order whatever you want, and order something good for me. I'm here to eat and enjoy your company. That sound okay?" I didn't know she could speak French, and from the sounds of it, she spoke it well.

"Sounds fantastic." Her face brightened.

If there was one thing I always took pleasure in, it was making a woman smile.

"*On va commencer avec une bouteille de vin blanc, le Château Salmonière Muscadet Sèvre et Maine Sur Lie, année 2009.*"

"*Oui, madame.*" He spun around and left.

"Wow, Jill has skills," I said. "The only French thing I have is my chaise lounge. It sounded like you ordered some type of wine from the word blanc. Is that right?"

"Yep. It's a white wine, and this one is a little discreet—rather thirst-quenching but low in alcohol so it won't affect us going back to work, I hope. And um, that's not all the skills I have."

"I think you've been hanging around Samantha a bit too much," I said.

"I see there are some new bruises on your face. You're getting as bad as me, if not worse. And your hand is bandaged. What have you been up to... or is it something you can't talk about?" She waited for my answer.

"I'd rather not say right now. Maybe when the time is right."

"You're a mysterious man, Tanner York." The temperature in my face rose, and I knew I was turning red. "She's a mighty lucky girl, that one."

"What about you? A new bruise on your forearm?" I pointed it out.

"Preston. Who else?"

"You must bruise easy."

"He's a strong kid," she laughed.

The waiter was back with the wine. He opened it with speed and ease, poured some into a glass, and handed it to me.

"Please," I gestured to Jill for her to try it.

"*Merci*." She took the glass by the stem, twirled the liquid around a few times, and sipped. "*Excéllent*."

He poured our wine and asked, "*Prêt à commander?*"

"*Oui. Nous ont chacun le salade de saison; Je vais avoir la quiche lorraine classique. Et pour monsieur.*" She glanced at me and cracked a smile. "*Le steak au poivre et les frites, merci.*"

"*Merci.*" And off he went.

"I am simply in awe of your French."

"It was my favorite class in college. Had a little of it in high school, but it wasn't until college that it just grabbed ahold of me." The expression in her face matched the passion in her voice.

"So, you're having the steak and fries in a cognac and black peppercorn sauce, and I'm having the quiche—a classic French dish."

"Excellent," I raved, which we both laughed at.

Our salads arrived, we talked about work a bit, what was going on in the world, and a little sport, but no substantial conversation.

"So, have you been to France?" I asked. Her face lit up like the Eiffel Tower on a summer's night.

"Back when I was young, just twenty, I went over for the summer. Spent a lot of time in southern France, stayed with my dad's friends in Nice. It was beautiful, with near-perfect weather every day and the most amazing seafood. I was able to travel, so I hit Cannes and saw all those luxurious yachts at the Vieux Port. I went to Marseilles, with its rich history, culture, and architecture. And oh, Saint-Tropez is soooo sexy." She paused, gazing off as if reliving her time spent there.

"I explored the medieval vistas in Dijon, and I found this little place, Barcelonnette, with amazing views of the French Alps. It was spectacular. Every night, when I go to bed and close my eyes, I transport myself there and relive it all over again. It never gets old." She took a breath, savoring her own story.

"And then there's Paris..." she giggled with bright eyes.

"What's so funny? What happened in Paris?" I said.

"Oh, just stuff—Notre-Dame was neat."

"Don't gloss over the good stuff. Come on, let's have it."

"Well..." she giggled once more. "I guess you could say I got my brains fucked out." Her smile was as broad as the English Channel.

"This is starting to get good."

"It must be the wine. I haven't felt this free for so long. Anyway, a young girl on her own in a foreign country with a wildly different culture, meets a stranger—someone more mature—while gazing at the Eiffel Tower on a summer night in the City of Lights? Can't get any more romantic than that."

"Probably not. Well, maybe in one of those romance novels," I sighed.

"If I were writing a romance novel it might go something like, *I tried to resist at first, but my efforts to walk away were futile. The wine, the freedom, and the music in the air were just too much for me, a young woman. Before I knew it, a brief decadent weekend of love and romance was upon me. We were both oblivious to our surroundings; only the two of us existed in a world of historic architecture, marvelous cuisine, and memorable lovemaking. We walked hand in hand down the Avenue des Champs Elysées to the towering Arc de Triomphe.*" She waved a hand in the air to add flair to the drama.

I laughed out loud, "Boy, you'd make a great romance writer. He must have been some lover."

"Don't laugh," she said in a mock scolding tone. "I couldn't walk straight for a week after." Her laughter drew me in.

"I think about that weekend so often and the possibilities of what could have been." The light faded from her face. Her green eyes lost their sparkle but locked onto mine. "You and my grandmother are the only ones I've told that Paris story to. My grandmother was a really cool person—sophisticated, funny, and open-minded. She wanted me to go back and see how it would all play out. She was very encouraging. But if I brought it up with my parents, I knew they wouldn't stand for it. Me leaving the country for good and shacking up with someone they didn't know? I'd be disowned." Her tone was bleak.

"But they'd see how happy you would be, right?"

"It's better this way. Peace in the family. You know, I've lived my whole life being the peacemaker in our family. Anyway, I have two of the best kids anyone could want. That's my life now, with them. But you can bet on one thing—I'll never interfere in what my kids want to do with their lives. It's their decision to make, and I'll just go along for the ride."

"How is the family?"

"The kids have their moments, but I love 'em. Donny is good, he's been traveling a lot, as always. Tired when he's home. People think he's a jealous person, but he's just concerned that I work downtown. With all the shootings that have been going on in the city, and now there are shootings on the highways... it's just scary. I wish someone could put a stop to it."

"It would take more than one person to do that. Besides, it's not the shootings you need to worry about, it's Preston and the kitchen cupboards, right?" I said.

"What?"

"You know, you're always bumping into things, wrestling with the kids." I simulated bumping into the table with my arm.

"Oh yeah, sorry. Clumsy Jill, that's me."

When our lunch arrived, we ordered another bottle of wine. Everything was delicious, as expected. The lunch crowd was beginning to thin out. The waiter picked up our empty plates and poured the last of the second bottle of wine. Neither of us was in a hurry to get back.

"That sure is a nice car, Ty. Preston would love it for sure."

"You should come by the tower with them, and we'll go for a ride," I said.

"Yeah, we'll have to get out there. I'd also like to see that cabin of yours, if I may be so bold as to ask. Sam's so lucky. Maybe the wine's kicking in." She smiled at me.

Jill flagged our waiter down and said, *"l'addition, s'il vous plait."*

Our waiter put the check down, and without hesitation, I grabbed it.

"You did all the work, so I'll pay for lunch."

"You don't have to."

"I know. I know where you work, and they do pay pretty well. But I enjoyed it, and you did a fantastic job with the ordering—it's my treat."

"Merci, Monsieur York."

While waiting for my change, we enjoyed the last of the wine.

"I'd like to ask you a favor. Just between you and me—can you find out what you can about what Ian Smith is doing with Julius and Randolph? I think Ian is up to no good, and I fear Julius may be in danger."

"Really?"

"Really. Just keep an ear out for anything unusual, but don't engage. I'm serious. Just let me handle it."

"Okay. I'll let you know." She sounded concerned. "I'm going to freshen up. Excuse me." I watched her walk away from the table. A few moments later she returned.

"So, I'm surprised our girl hasn't come up in conversation yet," she said.

"I called, no answer, so..." I let it hang. "You know, in her voice mail message she changed *Hello* to *Bonjour*."

"It's a sexy language. Ty, look at it this way. A faint heart will not win a fair maiden, but a persistent heart will win her hand forever," she said.

"Well, aren't you the romantic one."

"I have my moments," she said. The wine had definitely kicked in. "I've known you for five years, and when you put your mind to something, you see it through. You have such passion for things. What gave you that drive?"

I sat there a few moments, collecting my thoughts. "My parents were killed in a car crash when I was nine. Julius and Margaret Ackerman were my parents' best friends, and they pretty much raised me. That's why I have no fear of getting fired. Margaret won't let that happen, no matter what."

"Nice to have job security."

"The day of the crash, my dad was trying to cheer me up because I couldn't go with them to his work party, and I'd had a tough day at school. In gym class, my team had lost a game because I'd struck out. I was so down about it. So, he told me about Winston Churchill.

"He was known as the lion, and a lion has courage, he told me. My dad quoted me something that Churchill had said, 'Do not let us speak of darker days. Never give in. Never give in. Never, never, never, never—in nothing, great or small, large or petty—never give in, except to convictions of honor and good sense. Never yield to force. Never yield to the apparently overwhelming might of the enemy.' He then told me that he loved me.

"I watched my mom and dad get into the car and drive away. And less than an hour later, they were gone from this world. Those were the last words that my father said to me, and I carry them with me wherever I go."

"Oh Ty, I'm so, so, sorry." She put her hand on mine, and I didn't pull away.

"Hey, I didn't want to sour the mood," I said. "We should get back."

The valet pulled the Audi around; I opened the door, and Jill slinked her body into the seat. We headed for the office.

"Thanks again for lunch. Next time, it's on me. And thanks for sharing your story—for trusting me enough to tell me. It means a lot."

"Likewise. Your stories about France were great," I said.

Late afternoon traffic was just gearing up for the evening rush home.

Jill followed me to my office. I was surprised that she had. I turned around as she was closing the door behind us.

"Sorry, did you need some—"

She was on me quick. Jill put her arms around me, planting her mouth on mine. My baser instincts kicked in before common sense could stop me, and I responded in kind. Our tongues swapped mouths; her thin lips were astonishingly sensual. I pulled her into me tight, throwing us off balance. She fell against the wall, my body pinning her to it. I kissed her cheek, working my way down to her neck.

"Oh, *oui, oui*," she sighed.

My hand slid over her skirt, its fabric coarse against my bandaged palm. Her thigh was firm—my fingers raked across it. My hand enjoyed its pleasurable journey north as it passed her soft leather belt and reached up to her blouse. The smooth silkiness did little to shield her body's heat; Jill's adrenaline was contagious as it raced through her body.

My hand reached its final destination—her breasts. The thin material of her blouse yielded to my touch the lacy bra she wore beneath. My fingers climbed up the mound of her breast like a spider cautiously scaling a wall.

"*Oui*," she whispered, my mouth moving down her cleavage.

Without warning, my common sense suddenly kicked in, and I pulled back.

"We can't do this," I said.

Her heavy breath slowed. "I know, but ever since that kiss I gave you in the hospital, it's been all I can think about. It... it won't happen again. I'm sorry. Maybe the wine wasn't a good idea after all. I'm sorry, Ty, please forgive me." She adjusted her clothes, trying to hide the evidence of where my hands had just been. She ran her hands through her hair and walked to the door.

"Wait," I said. She froze with her back to me. "You do not need to apologize—I'm to blame. But something is going on with you, I saw it days ago. You've been... off. Can I help? I want to help you, Jill."

She stood in silence—hand on the doorknob, head down. A moment passed, and the ticking of the wall clock boomed like a kettle drum. She took a deep breath and sighed, "You can't." She left, closing the door quietly.

Ever since Jill had returned from Florida, things between us had been odd. And now she was literally throwing herself at me? She knew better than anyone how hard I had fallen for Samantha. Was she jealous? Maybe she had always had a thing for me, and now that Samantha's around she is feeling threatened? The bruises and the pain she was always in were finally beginning to add up. She had a long history of clumsiness, sure, but it was starting to seem like more than just the occasional run-in with a cabinet door.

NEWS FLASH – WXNG-TV, CHICAGO

"On Chicago's warmest weekend of the year so far, six people were fatally shot and thirty-seven more were wounded. That includes two homicides involving high-powered rifles in the Back of the Yards neighborhood and another where nine people were shot in a single location in the Lawndale neighborhood.

"In one rifle incident, a seven-year-old boy was playing in a park when he was struck by a stray bullet. The mother called 911, and he was rushed to a local hospital where doctors worked on him for two hours before he died.

"In Lawndale, police were called to a house party when a brawl got out of hand. Police broke up the fight and sent the partygoer's home. But hours later, the party recommenced and erupted in even more fights—only this time, someone had a gun and used it to open fire on the crowd. As some people scrambled to escape, others helped get the wounded into cars bound for the hospital. As those cars left the residence, they were met with a hail of bullets. In all, nine people were shot. Their conditions range from critical to minor.

"The Chicago Police Department has released some startling numbers on gun crime in the city. To date, 275 people have been killed and 1,520 have been wounded by gunfire. These numbers exceed last year's. Police have also confirmed that high-powered rifles are becoming the norm, especially in the Back of the Yards neighborhood where this year alone, six people have been shot— including a nineteen-year-old, a twenty-four-year-old, and now a seven-year-old.

"Standing outside police headquarters, I'm Meghan Orr for WXNG-TV. David, back to you."

TWENTY-EIGHT

Mozart's "Symphony No. 40 in G Minor" filled the cabin's spacious living room with the sweeping and powerfully rugged sounds of wind and string instruments. It was in its third movement: the Menuetto, Allegretto-Trio. Grim tones led my ears on a musical voyage to the fierce and fiery finale that Einstein had called 'heroically tragic' and others had claimed Mozart wrote in his own blood.

April turned to May, and I still hadn't heard from Samantha. I started to wonder whether I'd imagined the whole thing, but Jill kept telling me to keep the faith. Bridget was looking more and more like a relationship option worth pursuing. The rest of May passed like molasses. Everything dragged—my security checks, university records for prospective new hires, court testimony, delays, and appeals. It was mid-June before I came up for air. And through it all, Samantha buzzed in the back of my brain.

It was late June before I finally heard from her.

Dashiell the owl, or Dash, as Samantha and I had named him, was in his tree keeping watch over the cabin and looking for a possible easy meal. A glass of bourbon in my hand made for a beautiful summer night.

Frank and I had had dinner earlier—he was still a bit out of it, missing Addison terribly and still deep in mourning. I tried my best to comfort him, but I couldn't be much of a friend. My own self-pity over Samantha's prolonged absence wouldn't allow for it.

I jumped when the phone rang, breaking the symphony's perfect three-quarter time. I didn't recognize the number.

"Tanner York," I said, lowering the volume on the stereo.

"Hello, lover." Her sultry voice sent a thrill down my spine, and my hand clamped firmly around the phone.

"Seems a bit presumptuous, don't you think?" My voice was as tight as my grip on the phone.

Her voice was bright and cheery. "Easy, Tiger. I've let you down, and I apologize for it. You're right, and I should have called more. But I have some good news. I'm coming home."

"When?"

"Friday—this coming Friday. How 'bout we plan that long-awaited date? I'll spend the whole weekend with you. I won't leave your side. Promise. Can you forgive me?"

I wanted to make her wait for my answer, but I caved. "Yes, I can get those *Hamilton* tickets, if you still want to go."

"Mmm. You don't even have to ask. Can I meet you at your place in Chicago Friday evening?"

"See you then. We have a lot to catch up on."

"Listen, I know I'm in no position to ask, but I need a favor—a place to stay. My apartment is gone; I couldn't keep up with the rent. More than anything, I just want to be with you. I've missed you, Tiger."

That threw me for a loop. My mind raced with the various scenarios and situations this could cause. I didn't want to seem too eager, and I didn't want to put her off. "Well, er, I guess that would be okay. We can work out the details later. I've got the room and some storage space on a lower level, so—"

"Don't sound so enthusiastic. I'm not asking for you to change the name on the deed."

"Uh, it's fine. Yes. Yes, please stay as long as you want."

"Thanks, Ty. That's a weight off my shoulders. Now, I need to tell you a few things."

A stab of anxiety went through my chest, then suspicion crept in. "What have you been up to?" I asked, almost not wanting to know the answer.

"Well, I'm in Vegas right now—"

"Vegas? What are you doing there, vacationing?" My body temperature rose. What the hell was she doing in Vegas?

"Addy had an apartment out here, remember? Her family doesn't know what she did for a living, and Addy left me a note and a key to the place. I had to clean out her stuff. Besides, I've got something else that you're gonna wanna see."

"What is it?"

"Not over the phone. I'll show you Friday, and have more surprises for you, too."

"I don't want anything, just get here, and call me daily. Do you hear me?"

"Yes, I'll call you, and stop yelling, Tiger. How's Dashiell?"

"He's in the tree, wondering where you are."

"Give him a wave for me. How's Jill? Have you seen her? Well that's a stupid question, you work with her. Anything happening with you two?" she asked. What an odd question. Did she know? Did Jill tell her? I decided to be vague for the moment.

"Huh? Anything? No. I mean, I think she's good, I guess." I began to fidget, and guilt was creeping up on me. "Haven't seen much of her." That part was true, at least. Well, I hadn't seen her much since the brief incident we'd had after lunch—maybe that was why I couldn't bring myself to be mad at Samantha.

"That's all?" She seemed surprised. "I'll have to call her."

"Uh, she might be busy with the kids, or something. You seem busy. I wouldn't bother her. You'll see her when you get back."

She laughed, "Sure. You're funny."

Our conversation lasted about an hour as we talked about random things. It was so good to hear her voice again. She told me about the funeral and her family and friends. She'd spent some quality time with her parents and sister. I was glad for her.

"I made a discovery when tracking down someone—a photograph of Ian and a person connected to Addy's...situation. Someone you've met before at Frank's garage." I tried to be vague over the phone, but hoped she got the meaning.

"I see, so you were able to do what I asked you to do before I left. Ian, you say, is in a partnership with that party?"

"Looks like it, so just keep an eye out. Be vigilant."

"I worry this thing might not be over just yet."

I thought about that too—especially about the tall man in the house in Rogers Park and wondered when, if ever, I should tell Samantha about him. There was still the Producer, the mysterious Ian Smith, and a whole nest of vipers to uncover and deal with. I'd hoped to get that all settled before she'd come back.

"You be careful, too. Are you going to call me?"

"Yes, every day. Promise. Bye, Tiger."

TWENTY-NINE

By Monday, I was back in the city. I went into the office, did some work, and planned to tell Jill about Samantha's imminent return. I ran into Julius, who told me that Jill had called in sick. That seemed a bit out of character for Jill, but even the most dedicated employees still get sick. I must have been in a good mood because I told Julius that Samantha was coming back. He laughed at my giddiness and said, "There must be love in the air." He patted me on the back and headed for his office.

I made some calls and landed *Hamilton* tickets for the coming Friday.

I left work about three and decided that some new duds were in order, so I headed over to Gustavo's Men's Shop. Family owned; the old place was just off Jackson on Dearborn. Walking through the doors was like being transported back in time. The wood floors offered no more shine or luster. Every board creaked in protest from your footsteps. A black cast iron Singer sewing machine stood in one corner, along with thousands of thread spools. A sizeable three-panel mirror stood in another corner. Gus did a great job, and all kinds of celebrities came in for his tailoring, from movie stars to sports stars. Gus made everything by hand.

"Tanner York, how good to see you. Let me see..." He came out from behind the back curtain. He was a small man and getting up there in age, but he had a big heart and an even bigger talent when it came to tailoring clothes.

"Gus, how are you?" I shook his hand.

"All good, thank you. What can I do for you?" He looked me right in the eye.

"Well, I have a date with a young lady this Friday, and I need a new suit. Can you help me? I know it's short notice—"

"For you, I work all night if I have to. Let me see you, what is this?" He grabbed my suit jacket, feeling the material and taking it off me.

"No, no. Tis no suit jacket, it's piece of garbage. Throw away!" He tossed it in the corner.

"But..."

"No buts. You want to look good for your lady friend, no? Then you let Gus take care of you. Let's see, you got fatter than last time. No?" He poked my belly.

"I don't think so," I balked.

"You did."

He measured me. He was right, I had to go a size up.

"Tanner, I just got tis in, new color gray, not too light, not too dark. No?"

"Nice, but maybe black?"

"No, this bring out your eye color, always black, you want always black."

"Okay, Gus. I trust you. A black shirt maybe?"

"No, white. Classy, clean. You want to impress this girl not scare her off." He shook his finger at me.

"Somehow, I don't think that's possible."

Gus went behind the old glass display counter and looked through his selection of ties. He pulled out a selection.

"Now, Tanner, look. I have three ties. You tell me which one you like."

I wasn't sure if Gus was testing me or if he really wanted my opinion. A red paisley would add some color, and the silk lavender tie would be a nice touch for summer. Then there was a gray tie a shade darker than the suit.

"Well, Gus, I like the simplicity of the gray one. Good choice?"

He looked at me, and slowly his wise face brightened, and his teeth became visible. "Yes, a grosgrain silk tie. You will knock her socks off." He raised his index finger in the air.

"So, will it be ready by Friday?" I winced, expecting to hear a no.

"Come back Thursday, and I will have it ready for you to pick up. Now, no more gain weight." He poked my belly again, laughing.

I left Gus's place before heading back up to Lake Point Tower. I stopped and got a haircut on the way. All set now. New clothes, fresh cut. I felt good.

Dinner tonight would be a salad.

The next day, I stood in line in the Uptown Corner Coffee shop on Wabash near Jackson; I could hear the clamor of the overhead El train. For people new to Chicago, the noise could take a bit of getting used to, but for locals, it was an expected element of the Loop's atmosphere. I was checking my phone for the latest emails, completely unaware of my surroundings. I ordered my latte and reached into my pocket for some money when the barista surprised me by saying, "It's already paid for."

I looked up, saw a striking blonde woman standing over to the side, and waved. It was Rachel. I walked over to greet her.

"Well, thank you very much, this is an unexpected surprise," I said.

"Yeah, how are you doing? Looks like you healed up." She surveyed my face for scars.

"Good as new, how about you?"

"Great, been busy. Business picks up this time of year."

"That's good, I guess."

"Are you in a rush? Do you have a minute?"

"For you, yes." I got my drink and sat down with her. We talked a little about the weather, work, and a trip she was going on.

"So, I must ask, are you and Sam still together?" Her tone was optimistic.

"Yes. Things have been interesting."

"That's Sammy." She told me a few more stories of their college days as we finished our coffee.

"Does Michael have security for you? In case something were to go wrong during an appointment?" I asked.

"Why? Looking to start trouble next time?" She chuckled. "No security. We either handle it ourselves or hire someone to be in the next room just in case. But that gets expensive, and like I said before, most guys want to be invisible—they just want to come and go. Literally."

"So, he won't send anyone out to *teach someone a lesson*?"

"No, not Michael. He just wouldn't book the guy anymore if we complained about a client."

"Good to know."

"I'd better get going. But here, take this. It's my private phone number." She handed me a piece of paper. "Call me, and maybe we can go out for coffee again, or lunch. Something. You know, just as friends. I like talking to you."

"That sounds great. I would like that, friend." Before she got up, I said, "Can I ask you one question before you go?"

"Sure."

"Who hired you? For the escort job, I mean. I know Michael is the organizer, but did he do the actual hiring, or how does it work?" At this point I was grasping at straws.

"I was recommended by Addison. She vouched for me. That helped. But I did have an interview—I had to give them some information, like STD results."

"Did you meet them in person?"

"No, it was over the phone. With Addison's recommendation, I didn't need a face-to-face interview. I did have to give Michael a few photos for the website," she said.

"Do you know his name? The guy you talked to on the phone?"

She laughed and said, "No."

"What's so funny?"

She was still laughing. "Ty, the person I spoke with was a woman. Calls herself Madame Zoe."

THIRTY

had to admit it, Randolph's office did have a magnificent view. I looked out over Wabash Avenue and remembered standing in the same spot looking out the same window as a kid. The people below looked and moved like a colony of busy ants. I glanced in the window's reflection and saw Randolph approaching. I turned to face him. I was here to find out the truth about his relationship with Ian. The picture of Hal, the tall man, with Ian, indicated that danger lay ahead.

"Ty, what can I do for you, brother-in-law?" he roared. "Get it? We both work at a law firm, so we're brothers in the workplace, so we're brothers... in... law. How funny is that?"

Not very. I did a mental eye-roll. He took a seat at his desk. Made of beautiful solid oak, it was two desks in one. "Man, I love that joke. Never gets old. Sit down." He gestured toward the chair. "What's on your mind? Hey, the weather's supposed to be great this weekend, wanna go golfing at the club?" He stood up and took a mock swing.

"No."

"Come on, what else are ya gonna do but sit up in that cabin all weekend reading? Well, at least think about it. Here to collect on the favor I owe you?" He sat back down again.

"No, not yet. Listen, I need to ask you something." This was my lead-in. I wanted to try a new tactic to find out what information I could. I wasn't sure if it would work, but it was worth a shot.

He held up his hands. "I never had sex with that woman."

"What woman? What are you talking about?"

"Oh, I just thought you were going to tell me you got another one of those calls. You know, the ones where they say I'm the daddy." His voice had lowered to a whisper.

"No, not that. Not sure how to say it, but..." I took a deep breath. "I need you to tell me why you wanted Ian to work here? Are you related? He doesn't seem the type you'd hang out with."

"He had it rough a few years ago, and I helped him with some legal issues."

"Nothing shows up in the public record."

"Well, I helped him out, and now he wants to move on with his life. Start a family, maybe."

I ran my fingers through my thinning hair. "What kind of trouble was he in?"

"Ty, just because people need a lawyer doesn't mean they're in trouble. Besides I can't tell you. Attorney–client privilege. Come on, man. Let's golf this weekend. Don't worry about anything. It's all good."

I wasn't about to let it go. "I just sense something is up, and I'm worried about the firm getting in trouble because of someone's past."

"I'm surprised to hear you say that. Everyone deserves a second chance." He looked into my eyes. "Even me."

I shifted in my seat uneasily. I'll admit that I had chosen my words poorly. Best to push forward and see if I can find out anything useful.

"By chance, you don't happen to have a tall friend with a tribal tattoo on his neck?"

"Let me see, male or female?"

"Male."

"Nobody comes to mind. I know a guy named Bob who's tall, but no neck tattoo." He looked off, still thinking.

"When's the last time you saw him? How old is he?" I said.

"I saw him yesterday, and I'd say he is about seventy-five."

"Have you seen Ian with a guy like the one I just described?"

Ian appeared before Randolph answered and I could probe any deeper. He stood at the doorway and pointed. "Randolph."

"Ian, old buddy. Just the man I wanted to see. Golf this weekend?" Randolph said.

I clenched my teeth and made an awkward departure, leaving Randolph's office with nothing. Raucous laughter followed me down the hall. I passed Jill typing at her desk. "Hi, Jill. How are you?" She almost jumped out of her skin.

"Oops. You caught me off guard. Again."

"Samantha's coming back Friday, in case she didn't tell you," I said.

"Okay, great. Good for you. You are happy, right?"

"Yes, we had a good talk on the phone. Looking forward to it. Bought a new suit, and we're going to see *Hamilton*." I stepped a bit closer, and she didn't shy away.

I looked around and lowered my voice. "We, okay?"

"Yeah, why?" She resumed typing.

"Oh, no reason, I guess." We both knew very well why, but it was probably better not to discuss it. "Looks like you're busy."

"Got to get the billing done, and Julius needs meeting notes typed up. So, no worries. We're okay, just busy."

Ever since Samantha had called, I'd been in a better mood. Even the Randolph and Ian thing hadn't bothered me all that much. Things seemed to be back to normal—nobody was shooting at me, nobody was beating me senseless, and Samantha was finally coming home.

THIRTY-ONE

Darkness edged out the day, and the flickering city lights replaced the fading sun, giving a sense of hope and promise to the city's burgeoning nightlife. Warm breezes cleared the air of the leftover decay of the dying day. Plenty of people would be taking advantage of the beautiful night ahead.

I stood in front of the window, adjusting my tie in the reflection. I returned the gaze of the face staring back at me; self-doubt crept into my mind as to who I was and why this woman affected me so much.

My new suit fit perfectly, but Gus was right—I could stand to lose a few pounds. Maybe I should give this exercise thing a shot. Brahms's "Symphony No. 1 in C Minor" filtered through the apartment. I tried to focus on the music instead of letting my mind wander. At least it would be a clear evening, based on what I'd heard on the weather report. My asthma shouldn't be much of a problem. Buzzing from my phone broke my train of thought.

My worst fear leaped into the forefront of my brain: She wasn't coming. I glanced at the phone cautiously. It was a text from her. The screen read: *I'm on my way up, are you decent?* 😈

I texted back: *Yes.*

She replied: *Too bad!* 😒, *see you soon.*

I did one more check of the place, one more look in the mirror, and headed for the door. Down the hallway to the elevator bay, I waited. A few seconds later, the bell rang and the elevator doors opened. Tony got out first with the luggage. He put the bags down beside me and went back to the elevator, holding the door open. "Ma'am."

Samantha leaned against the back wall, arms braced on the railing. She wore a cream-colored light summer jacket. Underneath, she wore a short jet-black dress, Louboutin shoes, and that slippery serpentine smile that could excite a eunuch. Her hair was lighter blonde and straight, pulled back in a ponytail. She sported large, black-framed glasses, making her appear more refined, yet sensually nerdy. She kept her eyes trained on me as she slithered out of the elevator.

"Thanks, Tony," she said.

"Anytime, Ms. Rhodes. Do you need a hand with the bags, Mr. York?"

"I can take it from here, Tony. I'll catch you later, okay?"

"No problem. Enjoy your evening," he said.

Samantha stopped in front of me. I fell deep into her eyes and her strawberry mint shampoo wafted around me.

"Hi, Tiger."

My tension was erased with just one look at her. I scooped her up in my arms, and our lips met for a slow, lingering kiss. We broke for air. From what that kiss told me—it looked like I'd have my hands full tonight.

"How are things?" she said.

"Better now that you're here."

"Well, I can promise you that things are gonna get a whole lot better," she said. We each grabbed a bag and rolled down the hallway. "Especially with what I have planned."

We spent more time getting reacquainted with each other's mouths. She took off her coat, and her sleeveless black dress revealed her skin to have a shimmery, deep bronze glow, kissed by the Florida sun.

"You've changed," I said.

"Good change or bad?"

"It's good... glasses, hair. You look... sophisticatedly gorgeous."

"I was shooting for 'you look good,' but a girl will take gorgeous any day of the week." She touched my face. "Did some thinking while I was gone. I finally know what I want to do with my life."

"Really?" I wondered about that and hoped her plans wouldn't take her away from me again.

"Let's talk about reality tomorrow and live out our fantasy tonight. For now, I just want to enjoy our date and evening together. Now let me guess." She put a finger to her cheek and glanced up. "Brahms's Symphony... Four?" She bit her lip, looking at me for an answer.

"Wow, Brahms it is, but it's the First. You've been doing some homework." I felt happy she'd taken an interest in the music I enjoyed.

"Which guest room can I use?"

"Just put it the master bedroom." I led the way with a bag.

"I don't want to crowd you, and I'm grateful you're putting me up." Her tone shifted from playful to serious.

"It's fine, and really, you can stay in my room."

"Are you sure?"

"Yes."

She unzipped a bag, took out some clothes and toiletries, and held up a rope. She looked at me and cracked her cunning smile.

I went to the nightstand, pulled the drawer open, and took out a set of police handcuffs. "How about we use these?" They dangled from my index finger.

Her jaw dropped, and her eyes went from half to full moon. She took them for a closer inspection.

"These are the real deal."

"Well, if we're gonna do it, let's do it right." I winked.

"I think someone else has been doing their homework, too."

We talked a little more about her trip while she put away her stuff. I caught her up on who'd killed Addy and told her that he wouldn't be a problem for us anymore.

"I hated those guys. Thanks. Do you think we'll be safe tonight?"

"I think so, I hired a driver. We'll be in crowded public places, so we should be good." I felt confident.

"Great, I feel safe around you. Do we have time for a glass of wine before we leave?"

"Sure."

We went to the kitchen where I uncorked a bottle, and she made a call.

"Hey babe, what are you doing? I'm at Ty's. We're getting ready to go. I think we'll get something to eat after." She looked at me for a nod.

I whispered, "Whatever you want to do."

"Hey, Ty got me real police handcuffs."

I shot her a quick look.

She giggled. "Sure babe, I'll text you when we're done with the show. Bye."

"Jill wants to know all about the play," she said.

My phone went off a few minutes later. "The car's here," I announced.

"Off we go," she said.

A large black SUV awaited us.

"Are we still going to the Private Bank Theater on Monroe, sir?" the driver asked.

"Yes, thanks."

It wouldn't take long to get there. Samantha was glued to my side, kissing my neck and making it difficult to sit still with all the blood rushing to the lower half of my body.

The theater was bustling, and the energy of the crowd was electric. The din of myriad conversations echoed off the old walls of the building. I marveled at the architecture. These old places fascinated me, and I could stand there for hours thinking about the past.

She approached me with two drinks in hand. "Great place. Here ya go."

"You know, I did some research on this place," I told her.

"Of course you did."

"They built it in 1906. It was called the Majestic Theater, and was the first building in Chicago to cost more than a million dollars."

"It's cool."

"Harry Houdini performed here in the twenties. I would've have loved to have seen that."

We moved from the lobby to the stage area. The inside was decadently decorated in reds and golds—it was one of the most elegant theaters I'd ever been in. Constructed with two prosceniums, ground-level patrons were blocked from seeing the patrons above them. It reminded me of an ancient Roman theater.

We had main floor seats on the right, half-way up. Samantha was very affectionate, even with her usual sexual innuendos toned down. It was a special night—magical and fun.

The play was lively and energetic, old American history told in a new voice. The music was inspiring, fresh, and worth the price of admission.

Arm in arm, we left the theater with Samantha getting her share of looks as we strolled by. We were in no particular hurry to get to the car.

The driver met us out front. "Where to now, sir?"

I turned to Samantha. "Are you hungry?"

"A little. But I don't want anything heavy—I still have plans for you tonight. How about a hot dog?"

"A hot dog? Really?"

"Sure, why not? Chicago has the best, right? And I haven't been in the city long enough to have already had my fill."

"Okay. My kinda girl." I turned to the driver. "Take us to the Wiener Circle on Monroe."

"Sir, are you sure you want to go there?"

"She's never been."

"Got it. On our way." Apparently, he knew the score about the place.

Wiener Circle was a Chicago landmark that was particularly popular late at night. The hot dog crowd was light for a nice summer's evening, but it was still early—the place was open until five in the morning.

It was small inside, with battleship gray walls, some stools, and a counter to eat at. A menu hung over the order and pickup windows. The real appeal of Wiener Circle was its late-night atmosphere and the rapport between the staff and its patrons. The tip jar read: BITCHES NEED TIPS TOO. You couldn't be timid in that place. The staff would cuss you every which way—up and down, left to right. And the customers gave it right back.

We dined outside on one of the four red picnic tables.

"Not too bad, eh?" I asked.

"Delicious," she replied with a full mouth while looking around.

"What are you looking for?" I asked.

"Where's the ketch—"

"Stop! Don't even go there." I barked.

We watched the crowd build and the commotion inside escalate, but the patrons came out happy.

The ride back to Lake Point Tower was short. In the elevator, Samantha decided to heat things up with a quick make-out session.

I took off my coat and tie, poured us some drinks, and headed to the living room couch. Samantha lit some candles on the coffee table; the soft lighting helped the mood and feel of the place. It reminded us of our first night by the fireplace in the cabin.

"So," I said.

"I'm getting your surprise ready, babe. It'll be here in a few minutes." She was texting on her phone.

"Late night delivery?" I asked.

"Sort of. While we wait, this is for you." She pulled out a bottle of Pappy Van Winkle's Family Reserve bourbon, aged fifteen years. Expensive, hard to find, and smooth as silk going down.

"Nice, thanks. How'd you find this?"

"My dad has connections to get stuff like that." Her phone went off. After texting a few words, she kissed me. "It's here."

She ran down the hall. Someone was at the door, and I could see them hugging. Samantha led the person down the hall and into the living room. It was Jill.

"Hi, Ty."

"Hey, what's going on?"

Samantha gestured with a flourish. "Your surprise."

I looked at Jill and then at her hands, which were empty. Samantha had a devious gleam in her eyes.

"I don't get it," I said.

Samantha came up to me and slipped her arm around my waist.

Jill took a deep breath and said, "Uh, I think what Sam's trying to say is... your surprise is... me."

THIRTY-TWO

"**Y**ou? I still don't get it."

Samantha looked at me and commanded, "I need you to do me a favor and not ask any questions and just go with it, okay? Sit, relax, and…" she looked around and saw Jill refreshing my drink. "And enjoy."

"Sure, I guess," I said.

"I came up with a playlist for tonight." Samantha hooked her iPhone up to the stereo and hit *play*.

The music started with the piano chiming twelve times, simulating the twelve strokes of midnight. The violinist's bow began scratching the strings, creating a horrible screeching. I knew the piece: Camille Saint-Saëns's "Danse Macabre."

Jill crooked her finger at Samantha and said, "*Petite chatonne.*"

Samantha sauntered over, moving in close to her on the couch opposite me. The music came alive, creating a haunting tone to set the scene in the room. Jill leaned into Samantha, their eyes locked, and faint smiles creased their faces. Jill moved closer, and their lips brushed ever so softly. Samantha wanted more, but Jill pulled back. "*Non, chatonne!*" she scolded in French.

Samantha's smile faded, and her eyes lowered. She spoke in a flat tone. "*Oui, Madame.*"

Jill flicked a finger, causing the spaghetti strap on Samantha's dress to fall off her shoulder, almost exposing one of her breasts. Jill raised Samantha's chin with her finger and spoke to her. I could not make out the dialogue, but whatever it was, put a smile back on Samantha's face.

They rubbed noses together, and Jill's tongue darted over Samantha's lips. A flush of adrenaline tingled through my body. I leaned forward, trying for a closer look. My tongue darted out of my mouth, licking my dry lips as if to imitate Jill's tongue action. I took a sip of bourbon, and its hard bite irritated my parched throat.

Samantha's dress slid down further, exposing a single breast. My pulse quickened. Jill's tongue traveled down Samantha's neck, leaving a glistening trail of saliva to her nipple. As Jill's tongue reached its goal, Samantha let out a soft moan.

Samantha eyes locked onto mine; hers were heavy with desire. The music continued its ghoulish dance as I watched the girls engage in their chilling tango.

"*Bonne chatonne*," Jill muttered. Samantha began slowly moving her hand across Jill's blouse, taking her time to finger the soft fabric. She lingered on Jill's breasts for a moment, then unbuttoned the top button. The girls looked at me, giggled, and smiled.

I blurted out, half unexpectedly, "What's going on? Aren't you marr—"

"No talking, baby," Samantha said. "You'll get to have us soon." They continued to look at me.

As the last of Jill's buttons were undone, Samantha ran her finger along Jill's cleavage, moving her finger in and around the curvature of Jill's breasts, along her bra, and so tenderly across her skin.

"*Oui, chatonne*," Jill said. Samantha unhooked her bra. To my surprise, silver bars pierced Jill's nipples. She yanked Samantha's ponytail, jerking her head back.

Samantha's mouth shot open, mirroring the surprise apparent in my own. Her eyes squinted tightly, as if she were looking directly into the sun. I went to move out of my chair to stop the performance. Jill held her hand up, halting me in my tracks. In a stern voice she said, "Kitten likes to play. *Chatonne* is kitten in French. She is our *petite chatonne*—little kitten. She is for us to play with, correct *chatonne*?"

"*Oui, Madame*," Samantha said in a strained voice.

"You're hurting her," I said.

"No," Jill said. "We use safe words when we play. *Chatonne*, what's the word to stop play?"

"*Rouge, Madame*."

"To slow down play?"

"*Jaune, Madame*."

Jill gave Samantha's ponytail a quick jerk. Samantha grimaced but did not use a safe word to halt the proceedings.

Jill looked at me. "We good?"

I nodded, took another gulp of bourbon. This time it went down smooth. Part of me was totally disturbed by what was going on. This was not how I'd pictured the evening going. Another part of me was exhilarated. The music was in full sway, and the girls' bodies were reacting to it. Their conversation with the music reminded me of a work of art—delicate, naturalistic, and intimate.

Jill was at Samantha's side, still holding Samantha's ponytail taut with one hand. Jill's other hand slid along Samantha's leg, slowly peeling back her dress and revealing what was underneath. Samantha's legs parted willingly at Jill's touch. Like a surgeon in an operating room, Jill's fingers moved with precision.

"*Non, pas de petite chatonne.* You must wait, *chérie.*"

"*Oui... Madame.*"

Jill looked at me. "She is eager, this one. She needs to be taught her place." Jill slipped the other thin strap off of Samantha's shoulder. Now both breasts were exposed, showing off their natural wonder.

"*S'il vous plaît, Madame, oui, oui,*" Samantha sighed. Jill's hand went between Samantha's legs, disappearing under the dress. Samantha arched her back, inhaling hard, and moaning sensually. Her breathing was labored, and her chest heaved up and down. My pulse quickened. Jill's hand found the timing of the music and her fingers did some conducting of their own, causing Samantha's moans to create their own music.

Samantha's legs started to tremble; her inner thighs shook, and she breathed deeply to regain control over her body. Her cries of passion drowned out the music. Once she'd climaxed, Jill let her go. Samantha slumped over, catching her breath. Her legs relaxed.

"Stand," Jill commanded. Samantha stood, removing her dress and throwing it at me. I caught it, feeling the lingering warmth of the soft fabric.

Samantha undid Jill's belt and skirt. When the skirt fell, both women were completely naked. Jill had a Pepé Le Pew tattoo on the right side of her abdomen below her navel.

My glass was empty. I reached for the bottle and poured myself a healthy serving.

They kissed—their free hands exploring each other, and their intensity reaching a fever pitch. My eyes caressed their curves with lustful, invisible fingers.

The "Danse Macabre" ended and Ravel's "Boléro" started up. It was a bit clichéd but still effective for the purposes of what was playing out before me.

I started to undo my shirt when Jill stopped me, her voice oozing sex. "*Chatonne le fera.*"

Puzzled, my brow furrowed.

"Kitten will do that."

Samantha looked at me, her wet mouth lustrous from the candle glow. She sprang up, faced me, and I kissed her hard, tasting Jill in the process. I could feel a delicious shudder that shot through Samantha. She started unbuttoning my shirt, slowly as she'd done before, but after each one was undone, she kissed my chest. When my shirt was off, we all moved to the bedroom.

"Remember, baby," she whispered. "It's only kinky the first time."

In the bedroom, she dropped to her knees, unfastening my belt and pants. They fell around my ankles. She grabbed my shorts by both hands and moved them down, freeing my erection at last. I was as hard as an Egyptian obelisk. She used her tongue to tease me, and I almost lost control right then and there. I threw my head back, changing the thoughts in my mind to distract myself so I could last as long as possible. But Jill joined in, making it more difficult. My knees buckling a bit, and I caught myself on the edge of the bed.

"Lie down, baby," Samantha said. She moved onto the bed with me.

She looked down at me. I closed my eyes, and in one fell swoop, Jill devoured me. Her hot, wet mouth taking no prisoners, she sucked hard and fast. I opened my eyes and looked right into Samantha's cognac-brown ones; her serpentine smile coiled with pride. She held up a finger. Dangling from it were the handcuffs.

"I think it's time to let your freak flag fly. Do you want to tie me up now, Tiger?"

"Yes," I said.

Samantha's hands were above her head, handcuffed, and with some creative thinking by the two conspirators, secured to the headboard. Her legs were free to move around, and she lay there squirming with delight. Jill handed me protection and sat in the chair, playing with the vibrating friend she'd brought along and watching us closely.

I reached for Samantha's leg—she kicked it away just before I could grab it. "Naughty boy." She giggled.

"Remember, kitten likes to play," Jill said.

This time, I snatched faster and caught her ankle.

"Ooh," she uttered. "Yes, fuck me. I know you want to." I slid in between her legs, and she wrapped them around me tightly. We were both good and ready, and as I eased into her, a soft gasp of surprise escaped her lips. Our eyes locked until she rolled them back and moaned, "Uhhhhhhh, yes, nice and slow, Tiger."

Her face scrunched up in painful pleasure as I pushed in deeper.

"Don't stop. Yes!" I was not surprised with her vocal... enthusiasm.

It took a bit to find our rhythm, but once we had it, the world disappeared.

My muscles began to constrict. One last thrust led to my explosion, and I heard Samantha growl, "Yes, baby." As I caught my breath, my body relaxed, and a bead of sweat rolled down my brow. Samantha's body was slick with a glossy sheen from the workout. I leaned in, kissing her, savoring the moment.

"My turn." I looked over and saw Jill standing next to the bed. I had forgotten she was there.

"You mean you want to—with me?"

Hand on her hip, she said, "Yes, of course."

"I'm gonna need some time, darling." I exhaled.

Jill looked at Samantha, who was still bound to the bed. "I'll keep myself entertained with our *petite chatonne* while you rest up. We have all weekend."

Samantha giggled, "*Oui Madame.*" Her serpentine smile grew large.

THIRTY-THREE

Our naked bodies lay interwoven like we were playing a very X-rated version of Twister on the bed. I awoke to find a derrière pressed against my face that had been my pillow for the night. I certainly wasn't going to complain, even though my neck was stiff, my back was achy, and my crotch screamed like it had been in a medieval torture rack. One of Samantha's legs was meshed in between mine, her arm lay over my chest, and her head hung off the bed. My leg was under Jill's head, and the bed covers were all askew. Another night like this would surely kill me.

I gingerly extricated myself from the pile of limbs, got out of bed, and immediately stepped on the handcuffs. "Shit," I said. I hopped on one foot to fetch my robe. Hanging behind my robe was a Miami Dolphins cheerleader outfit. I guess I knew what we'd be doing later.

I surveyed the carnage from our sexcapades the night before. Clothes were everywhere, furniture had been relocated, and the occasional sex toy lay here and there. Nothing like my usual Saturday morning at the cabin.

I shook my head. Coffee. I needed strong, strong coffee to clear the fog from my head before I could make rational decisions—if that's even possible to do with two naked females in your bed.

The kitchen island is where I had my first cup of morning joe. The strong aroma of Hawaiian Kona coffee filled the room. It was Saturday, and Irish coffee was a tradition. I strained my brain, trying to think of what would come next, but my thoughts were interrupted by noise coming from the bedroom. Jill appeared wearing nothing but one of my t-shirts—a very worn and faded, but still beloved, Pink Floyd *Dark Side of the Moon* shirt.

"Mmm, I thought I smelled coffee." She was peppy for a Saturday morning, but I guess when you're a mother of two young kids, you'd have to be.

She came right over to me and greeted me like a long-lost love. She made the embrace linger, and I didn't object. "Where do you keep the cups?" she said.

My head spun from her enthusiastic greeting. "Excuse me?"

"The coffee cups?"

"Oh shit. Right here." I showed her the cabinet.

She poured a cup, wrapping her hands around the mug to warm them. "Nice and strong. Excellent job." She winked.

"I thought maybe we'd order breakfast later from the diner down the street, unless you have to go?"

"Mom's got the kids, and I have all weekend to spend with you guys. Unless you want me to leave?" Over the rim of her coffee cup, her eyebrows arched as she waited for an answer.

"No, feel free to stay as long as you'd like." I had so many questions to ask her. The silent pause was lengthy. I poured my second cup of coffee and a shot, and I searched for the words I was looking for, hoping the caffeine would kick in soon.

Jill finally spoke. "So, how awkward do you think this will be for us at work?"

"It's going to be as awkward as we make it, I guess. I've never... cheated with someone before. Maybe I should have stopped. But you guys were so damn hot, and I just couldn't. I'm sorry."

"No, don't be sorry, I *wanted* to do it. I knew full well what was going on, and for the record, that was the first time I've ever cheated on my husband with a man." She paused and glanced down. "And it took a long time for me to get the courage up to do it. But I'm glad I did."

"Come here." I took her hand, and we headed to the window in the living room. I set up two chairs, and we watched the flow of life down below.

"So, I'm guessing that that great sexual experience you had in Paris was with a woman, not a man?"

"Yes."

"I just assumed it was an older man. Did your grandmother know it was a woman?"

"Oh yes, and she was all for it. But I knew my parents would've freaked out and disowned me if I'd told them. So, I never did. Sometimes I wonder what might have been if I had?" She took a sip of coffee. "But then I wouldn't have had two great kids that I love so much, or a fantastic job with friends like you and Sam."

"When did you and Samantha... um..."

She grinned. "When you first brought her into the office, there was an immediate spark. Then, when she stayed with me for those few days, I could feel something brewing between us. One night, we put the kids to bed, talked, drank some wine, and... well, things happened."

"If you don't mind me asking..."

She looked into her coffee cup, anticipating my question. "My marriage is okay, but it's not great. We don't make love anymore—I'm not desirable enough, he says. He travels, or I'm tired, the kids have school activities... it goes on and on. I think he cheats on me, but..." She shrugged. "I'm sure most marriages go through the same problems after so long. Let's just drop it."

She stared out the window and seemed a million miles away as she took in what the morning light was revealing. At thirty-five, she still had a lot to offer. I felt angry that her husband didn't find her desirable and had the nerve to tell her so.

"Stop staring at me, Ty," she said, looking out the window.

My voice rose. "Jill, you're gorgeous. Any guy who can't see that isn't worth being with. The bruises..."

"Shh!" She held up her index finger. "I'm in enough trouble with my emotions right now, and I don't need you adding to them with your sweet talk. I'm not looking to leave him or replace him with you. You and Sam are an item, and she loves you. She talked about you to her family and friends in Florida non-stop. Last night was an escape for me—that's all it was. I'll be back to reality soon." She paused. "And the bruises are my fault. Donny has nothing to do with them."

"I didn't mean to make you feel uncomfortable, but..."

"Look, Sam's been doing some work on Addy's case, and she has an idea for you."

Jill was making a hard effort to change the subject, so I let it slide for now. "What is it?"

"She's worked hard, and I support her, but Sam needs to tell you herself. And if you listen, and really think about it—instead of just reacting—you'll realize that it sounds like a great idea."

"So, you're ganging up on me?"

"In more ways than one." We laughed.

I made another pot of coffee, and we talked some more. Samantha eventually walked in, naked as the day she was born. Her hair was tangled, and sleepiness lingered in her eyes.

"Coffee?" I asked.

Samantha walked up to me, hugging herself to shield her body from the air conditioning. I wrapped my arms around her. My hand skated down her back, stopping at her firm round behind.

"I'm cold," she said.

"Why don't you have any clothes on?"

"'Cause... what were you guys laughing at?" she muttered.

Jill and I replied in unison, "You."

By mid-afternoon, we were all somewhat clothed. Jill was helping Samantha finish her unpacking, and I was reading in the living room. Jill and Samantha walked in, with Samantha looking very serious in her black-framed glasses.

"Can we discuss business?" Samantha said.

"Sure." I put my book down.

"We need to find out who was behind Addy's death. We know who the killer was, but I think there may be more to the story."

"I agree. But maybe I should just be the one doing the finding. It's too dangerous for you—"

"Stop. I'm, excuse me, *we*," she wagged her finger back and forth between Jill and herself, "are fully aware of the dangers. And we can handle it. Just like you can. Haven't we so far?"

"Sure, but Jill?"

"She's going to work the inside. Can you get some communication worked out without being traced, so we can all talk to each other?"

I was skeptical, and I knew my face showed it. "All right," I said. "As long as I can bring Frank in on this." I rubbed my jaw, searching for an answer.

"Bringing in Frank is a great idea. We can use him," Samantha said.

"Who's Frank?" Jill asked.

"One of Ty's friends and Addy's boyfriend," Samantha said.

"But we still need a starting point."

"I did some digging on my own. This is why I really went to Vegas." She handed me a book.

"The codebook, *Monsieur*." She handed it to me. When I took it, a chill shot through my arm to my chest, causing a heavy heartbeat.

I skimmed through it, but it didn't improve my mood. "You know, now that we have this—"

"I know," Samantha said. "We have a target on our backs. It has numbers. Lots of them, a codebook. I think I know what it's for, but not the details. We'll need to crack the code. Now, let's talk about Ian Smith."

She passed me a file with several papers in it. "When you told me about the picture you saw, the one with Ian and the tall guy, Hal, I did some checking. Ian Smith's real name is Christopher Walsh. Born in Columbia, Kentucky, he attended local public schools and graduated from Green County High School." She got up and walked around slowly as she laid everything out for me.

"He enlisted in the Marines in 2010 and completed basic training at Parris Island. Tours in Iraq, Afghanistan. Tons of medals and awards."

I paged through the file. Two Bronze Stars, a Purple Heart, assorted Navy and Marine commendations, sniper training, and various marksmanship badges. I set the file down. "I get it. He's a fucking war hero. Just our luck."

She held up a hand. "But wait, there's more." She took a swig of water. "He entered a treatment facility for PTSD at Hines Hospital in Maywood. There, he met a guy who got him hooked up with a street gang in Chicago—the Gaylords, who are allied with the People Nation. The Gaylords are the biggest white gang in Chicago. Their heyday was back in the late seventies, but they're still active in the northwest suburbs. They keep a low profile these days. They're rivals of the Folks Nation." She peered over her glasses. "Are you with me so far?"

"Yes, I'm following."

"After connecting with the Gaylords, he was introduced to high-ranking members of the Latin Kings gang. He was never a member, but he could offer something that the Latin Kings were after: guns. It all began when he started supplying them, and it grew from there. He supplied the People's Alliance for years, mostly handguns. But these were not squeaky clean, fresh out of the box guns. These were knockoff guns made in China."

I was a little stunned in not only the detail but also her delivery.

"Now, here's the good stuff. Eventually, he got busted. Gun running charges are serious, but he never saw the inside of a jail cell. Any guesses as to who his lawyer was?" Again, she peered over her glasses at me, her brown eyes waiting for an answer.

"Randolph Rockwell," I said.

"I'm impressed," I said. "But I don't think I want to know how you got this information."

"All I did was ask," Samantha said.

"Who?"

"The Winter Park Police Department. I showed them a photo of Ian that I got off the firm's website. Told them he was stalking me, said who he was but didn't believe that was his real name. They ran the photo through facial recognition, and Christopher Walsh showed up. Two hours later and I was back on the beach."

"You just walked in, and the police did this for you?" I was skeptical.

"Ty," Jill said. "Look at her. Who's not going to help her?" Jill waved her hands around Samantha like a game show model showing off a new car.

I shook my head. Despite Randolph's efforts to sanitize Ian's record, with overlapping jurisdictions of law enforcement agencies, a lot of things tended to get lost, fall through the cracks, or mis-communicated. We'd lucked out.

"All right, point taken," I said. "You found the connection between Ian and Randolph, but I still don't think Randolph has anything to do with this." He might have been a buffoon, and he might have been sleazy, but he tended to toe the line when it came to following the law. He valued his pompous ass too much to risk doing anything that would sully his reputation or put him behind bars.

"Agreed."

"So, what happens next?" Jill said. "What do we do?"

"We? You're a wife and mother of two small kids. This is dangerous. I can't be worrying about your safety while going after Ian and his crew."

"Now wait," Samantha broke in. "Jill has a purpose here. She can get information for us from the inside. She's close to Julius and Ian in the office. Can't you tap his phone or something?"

"I can watch what he does," Jill said. "Who he's with and when he leaves. You guys can tail him when he's outside, see where he goes. I'm not going to do anything that'll put my kids in jeopardy, but I can still help."

"If we can get Frank to assist, we could cover it," I thought out loud. "All we would need is a location. Once we know where the weapons are, we could call in the cops. He might not serve time, but at least the rifles would be off the streets."

They put their arms around me in a sort of group hug.

"We can do this, baby," Samantha said. "We'll watch each other's backs, stay in contact, nail this guy, and put it all behind us."

"Let me think on it awhile," I said.

I moped around the apartment and spent a good deal of time looking out the windows. I imagined the cabin's fireplace. It was funny but staring into a blazing fire had always helped me think. It focused my concentration—the flickering flames helped me formulate new ideas and new approaches to difficult problems—I wished I were at the cabin. I poured a shot of bourbon and paced around the kitchen, barely aware of the girls quietly tidying up last night's mess. The sun had moved across a good chunk of the sky before I called them into the living room.

"Okay, but we have to do what Frank tells us to do. Got it?"

"We got it," Samantha said. "Right Jill?"

"Right."

"And no more secrets." I looked at Samantha. "Is there anybody else coming over this weekend?"

"No, not this weekend," Samantha said with her serpentine smile.

The weekend wound to a close. Jill was collecting her stuff; soon, she would be picking up the kids and heading home. We would start surveilling Ian Smith on Monday.

The front desk called, saying Frank was downstairs. I told them to send him up. I met him at the door, got him a drink, and laid out the plan.

"So, is this doable?" I asked.

"Yeah, it just might work," Frank said.

Samantha entered the room. "Jill's just about ready." She gave Frank a friendly hug. "How are you doing, Frank?"

"I miss her, but I'm getting along, I guess. How about you?"

"About the same, but I have Ty, so that makes it a little easier."

Jill came in. "Okay. I'm heading out."

"Jill, this is Frank. He'll be giving us a hand," I said.

"Then I guess we'll be seeing a lot of each other over the next few days," Jill said as she shook his hand.

"I reckon so. I'll get you a comms setup—it will be a more secure way for us all to communicate," Frank said.

"Super," Jill said. "Well, it was nice meeting you. Uh, Ty, thanks... for everything." She hesitated, but I moved toward her and kissed her goodbye. The inevitable awkwardness between us seemed to have started.

While Jill and Samantha had a long goodbye, Frank and I talked.

"Do you want me to follow her to make sure she gets home okay?" he said.

"That would be awesome. Text me when she gets there. And here, look at the book. It's the codebook Addy had." I handed him the book that Addy had stolen from Ian.

"Do we need to get Robert involved?"

"Not yet."

Samantha's warm naked body lay next to mine. Holding her put me at ease, feeling her breath while she napped. The gentle in and out hush and whisper of her breath was the sweetest sound I'd heard in a long time.

I was falling hard, and I knew it. I'd been in trouble ever since I saw her lying in that hospital bed so long ago.

She stirred and whispered, "What are you thinking about, baby?"

"You, and why you'd want me."

She rolled to her side and looked at me. "Because when you touch me, my heart flutters. When you hold me, I feel locked in your fortress. And when you make love to me, you love me like it's our last day on earth."

I brushed a few strands of hair from her face.

"You want to know something else? I'll tell you a secret."

"No secrets, remember," I said.

"I love you." She ran a finger down the side of my face.

"I love you, too."

We lay in silence, listening to Beethoven's piano sonatas in the background. The piece was Opus 27 with Sonatas 13 and 14, the fourteenth being the famous "Moonlight Sonata."

"Were you weirded out by this weekend?" she said.

"A little. But for some reason, I'm glad it happened."

"I think Jill's more of a lesbian than straight."

I thought about what she said. "Perhaps?"

"Do you find Jill attractive? Would you date her?"

"She's a very attractive woman. But because she's married, dating her has never crossed my mind."

"But what if she weren't married?"

"We could play 'what if' all night. What difference would it make? Besides, I have you, right?"

"How would you feel about me and Jill getting together from time to time? Just us girls. I mean like..." she took a deep breath, and I sensed she was nervous. "Like, you know, in an intimate way."

"Do you still want to be with me?" I asked.

"Yes, of course." She replied without hesitation.

"I guess that would be fine. Just tell me when you do see her... it's kind of a turn-on thinking about you two together." I paused with a mental image of them naked in bed. I came back to reality quick. "Seriously, though, I worry about her husband. What if he finds out? Does he approve of Jill being with you?"

"I've never met him. Jill doesn't think it's a problem. That's what she told me, anyway."

"But if she wanted out of her marriage..."

"Her kids... they're still young, and divorce is hard—so I think she just settles."

"I have something to tell you. When you were gone, Jill and I..."

A bright smile illuminated her face and deepened her dimples. "I know! Who do you think told her to do that, silly? I wanted to know if you guys liked each other in that way. Because if there wasn't chemistry, this wouldn't have worked out so well."

I shook my head. "Wow, you are devious."

She laughed like a mad scientist. "So, you're up for more weekends like this in the future, then?"

"All day and all night, *ma chatonne*."

Her lips creased in that serpentine smile. She leaned in and kissed me, biting my lower lip. Her hand jetted down my lounge pants, grabbing a firm hold of me.

"Ooooh, I just love a man with stamina."

NEWS FLASH – WXNG-TV, CHICAGO

"... The Fourth of July holiday can be fun, hot, and thrilling, with the big fireworks show held at Navy Pier, but it can also be a violent long weekend for police and emergency services around the city. Let's go live to Meghan Orr for the story."

"Thanks David. Yes, the streets of Chicago can light up with not only illegal fireworks but illegal gunfire as well, especially if you're on the West and South Sides of the city.

"Last year, the long Fourth of July weekend saw fifty-two shootings with four fatalities. This year, the number of shootings has almost doubled, and the number of fatalities tripled. There were one hundred and two shootings and seventeen related deaths. The youngest victim was a fourteen-year-old girl from the Lawndale neighborhood; the oldest was a sixty-six-year-old male from the Austin neighborhood—both were just outside their homes with family celebrating the holiday when they were shot.

"Another startling fact is that most of the shootings happened in a single twelve-hour period—sixty shootings took place between 1:45 p.m. on July 3rd and 1:45 a.m. on July 4th. In a brief press conference, Superintendent Cooper had this to say."

"We stepped up our police presence this weekend with 1300 more police officers on the street, and although results were marginal, we still need to establish a culture in which people think twice before pulling out a gun. There were three major factors that contributed to this weekend's shootings. We have found that these factors are commonly related to high numbers of gun violence. The first was the warm weather. The second was people drinking or doing drugs. And the third was the availability of guns on the streets, including rifles, which we are now seeing in growing numbers."

"According to WXNG sources, the shooting of the sixty-six-year-old male, Reggie Clifton, was in retaliation for a fight that had broken out earlier in the day between two rival gang members. The gunman pulled up in a black sedan and started shooting wildly into a crowd when Clifton was hit in the back of the head. He fell to the ground dead, right in front of his wife of thirty years. She made the following statement."

"We were just outside our home, wrapping things up, when it happened. It... it happened so fast, I really didn't hear anything. One second, he's beside me holding my hand and the next he's gone, lying there bleeding. I thought he fell at first. He wanted to hold my hand because it was dark, and he didn't want me to fall... I... I don't know what to do."

"No arrests have been made in relation to that shooting. The violence from the long weekend overshadowed a massive police effort that resulted in the raids of several known gang hideouts, leading to the arrests of seventy people who police say are responsible for driving the violence in the city. They also seized over one hundred illegal firearms and some of the rifles that the superintendent mentioned earlier. So, it seems that some fine police work has gone nearly unnoticed due to the high number of shootings that took place over the weekend.

"Reporting live from outside police headquarters, I'm Meghan Orr. David, back to you."

"Thanks, Meghan. In world news..."

THIRTY-FOUR

My red Honda with Oklahoma license plates paled in comparison to my new Audi. Samantha had insisted that I rent a less flashy car that would not draw attention. Since I was down to my '70 Chevelle and the Audi, I could see her point.

Samantha was hanging out at nearby Uptown Corner Coffee, working the laptop in case we needed quick information. Frank was in a Ford Focus opposite my position on South LaSalle Street in front of the WAR Building. Jill kept us up to speed on what was happening inside.

Frank had hooked us up with some sweet communications equipment—small earpieces let the four of us listen to one another and talk hands-free.

"Seven Mary Three, come in," I said over the comms.

Frank: "Seven Mary Four, you're loud and clear."

Samantha: "Uh, what are you guys talking about?"

"Those are the call signs for *CHiPs*," I said.

Samantha: "So, you guys are hungry? Do you need me to get some potato chips?"

"No," I said. "*CHiPs* was a TV show back in..."

Frank: "Ty, forget it. Don't embarrass yourself. It was before her time."

"I suppose you're right," I said. "Jill, any news?"

Jill: "He's been in a meeting with Randolph for the past hour."

I said, "Samantha, how's it going? What are you doing, babe?"

Samantha: "Having a second latte. I got hit on twice, and now I'm shopping on Amazon. I found a great deal on shoes. They're so cute."

Jill: "You go, girl. I'm a size seven, if you think they're my style."

I said, "I thought we were going to be professional about this, ladies?"

Samantha: "We are, I take shopping seriously, honey."

Jill: "Randolph's door just opened, Ian is coming out. He's headed this way."

Frank: "Be cool, Jill. Try to get him talking."

Ian's voice came in faintly over Jill's comms. *"Hey, Jill. How are you? How are the kids?"*

"Shit," I said.

Jill: "Shit... Uh... sorry, I meant great... uh fine. You know, the usual. How's yours?"

"What?" Ian said. *"I don't have a family, like a wife or kids, I mean."*

Jill: "Oh well... uh, that's too bad. You'd make a great wife... uh, husband. Sorry, I'm a little distracted. Lots of work to do."

"Do I make you nervous, Jill? Sorry, you know, I hadn't realized how attractive you were until now. Your husband's a lucky man."

Jill: "Uh... thanks, but he likes to think I should be happy to have him."

Samantha: "That's fucking crazy."

"That's crazy," Ian said.

Jill: "Well, I guess I could stand to lose a few pounds. Gotta keep him wanting me."

Samantha: "Oh, please. Fuck him."

"Hmm," Ian said. *"I'm not sure how it works in married life, but I wouldn't change a thing."*

Samantha: "You're gorgeous the way you are, baby."

Jill: "Thank you."

Ian said, *"Hey, is Ty around? I'd like to talk to him."*

"Jill," I said. "Tell him I'll be there in about half an hour."

Jill: "He's coming in soon, Ian. Maybe a half an hour or so."

"Great," Ian said. *"Let him know I need to see him, okay?"*

Footsteps faded as he walked away.

Jill: "Guys, he's gone. Sorry, I panicked. He caught me off guard."

"That's okay, Jill," I said. "You did great. I'll come in and see what he wants."

Frank: "Hey, Ty? We may be able to use Jill to talk to him, get his day-to-day schedule."

Samantha: "No, Frank. I don't want Jill near this guy."

Jill: "Frank, he seems interested in me. Do you think if I got friendly, he might slip up?"

Frank: "It's worth a shot, you're already off to a good start, Jill."

Samantha: "Ty, Frank. We'll discuss this later—"

Jill: "Sam, I can handle this."

Samantha: "Don't forget, this guy does bad things to people."

Jill: "I won't."

I headed into the office. It was business as usual; no one seemed to have missed me.

My first stop was Jill's desk. "You, okay?"

"Yeah, I'll do better next time."

"You did great."

I walked off, looking for Ian. He was in his office, and I cautiously entered. "You looking for me?"

"Ty, yes. Sit." He indicated toward an empty chair.

I sat down, half expecting to get jumped.

"I want to mend fences. We got off on the wrong foot and, well, we need to work together for the greater good of the firm."

It took me a few seconds but then I burst out laughing. "You want to be pals with me?"

"I'm extending an olive branch here..."

Frank: "Ty, don't fuck this up. The more relaxed and calmer he is around the office, the more likely he'll be to slip up. Keep the enemy closer."

"... so, you see why it's better that we work as a team?" Ian finished his speech and stared at me.

I swallowed my pride and said, "Sure, I get it. Let's start over. Why not?"

"Great, put her there, friend." He extended his hand. Reluctantly, I took it.

A few hours had passed. I was in my office, Jill was in hers, Samantha was at Uptown Corner Coffee, and Frank was in the car. Ian was still in the building when I received word that Julius wanted to see me. I passed by Jill, gave her a wink, and went into Julius's office.

Julius got up and went to the front of his desk to greet me. "Hello, hello, Ty. Come in. How are you?" He wore a light gray suit with a tie that almost matched.

"I'm good, how are you and Margaret, sir?" I asked.

"Good, good, excellent. Thank you for asking." He beamed.

"So, what's up?" I was a little anxious.

Samantha: "Mmm, why don't you let me tell you what's up, baby?"

"Excuse me!" Startled, I stirred in my chair, trying to find a comfortable position.

"Ty? Are you okay? You seem edgy. Do you need some water? Uh, just a second." He stuck his head out the door.

"No, no. I'm fine, Julius," I protested.

"Jill? Jill, can you get Ty some cold water? Please, thank you." He returned to his desk. Jill shot me a quick smile and a raised eyebrow.

"I wanted to talk to you about the new security software being installed. Now, do we need everyone to have access or just some select people? Now, the way I see it..."

Samantha: "Ty, guess what I'm doing?" She giggled.

I said nothing. Despite how boring it was, I maintained my focus on Julius and his words. I wasn't going to let her win this game.

Julius was in full speaking mode, with his arms and hands flailing away, adding dramatic emphasis like he was arguing in court.

Samantha: "I'm touching myself inappropriately in this public place, and no one seems to notice. I'm just thinking about you and last weekend, I just couldn't help myself, baby."

"Um," I cleared my throat, thinking she might get the hint.

Samantha: "My wrists are still sore from the handcuffs. They left marks."

"Here's your ice-cold water, Ty. Hope it cools you off." Jill handed me the glass. She seemed to be enjoying the conversation.

"Please continue, Julius." I took a few gulps of water.

"So, like I was saying, if only we had some way to monitor the workflow better, we might have a better..."

Samantha: "Wasn't Jill so sexy this weekend with her little purple lace teddy? Mm-mm, she's a sexy bitch."

I started to fidget; I just wanted to get out. Julius was rambling on about low-priority work that didn't need my approval anyway.

Jill: "Did my little kitten likey? *Tu es une mauvaise petite chatonne.*"

"Great," I shouted.

"You like that idea, Ty? I didn't think much of it, but if you think that's best, I'll have to reconsider." Julius scratched his head and sat back down at his desk. "Now, let's go over one more thing..."

Samantha: "Oh, you know little kitten loves it when you talk French to her. I just shiver when you kiss my neck and say sweet things to me in—"

Jill: "Uh-oh, guys. Ian is on the move. I think he's leaving."

I rose from my chair, "Ty, what's the matter now?" Julius said.

"Nothing. I just have a lot of work to do. Can we finish this later?"

Jill: "Yes, he's leaving. He's at the elevators. I'll see if it stops at another floor or goes down to the lobby."

"Oh, come on now. We never get to talk. I give you full permission to sit and talk with me." Julius continued to talk, but my mind and heart weren't in it. I needed to know what was going on with Ian.

"Sorry. I really have to go, Julius." I started to get up again.

Jill: "He's past the tenth floor, no stops."

"Sit," Julius insisted. "What about..."

"Julius, I really, really have to go." I started making my way to the door.

"Are you ill, boy?" Julius asked.

Jill: "He's past the fifth floor. Still no stops."

"Yes, ill. My stomach, you know. I should eat better. Margaret always says that, right?" I let out a fake laugh, easing my way out the door.

Jill: "He's past the first floor now, looks like he's going to the garage."

"Sorry, Julius. I gotta hit the washroom."

"Sure, sure. I'll tell Margaret to make some chicken soup for you."

Jill was returning from the elevators as I passed by her desk. I flashed her an angry look and said, "Frank's on comms listening, too, remember?" I continued walking but couldn't help noticing her face grow bright red.

Jill: "Oh, fuck."

"Jillian Sinclair. Language, please!" Julius replied as he walked out of his office.

I hit the elevators, then raced out the door. "Frank, what you got?"

Frank: "I got em. He's just turning on Monroe, heading east. And ladies, that was awesome, thanks. You can fill me in on the rest of the weekend later."

Pedestrian traffic was thick. I bumped into a few people and apologized, but it seemed not to matter judging by the expletives they shouted back. As soon as I entered my car, I found a break in traffic, and off I went. I was several blocks behind Frank when he offered an update.

Frank: "Ty, he took a left on State Street. I made the light, so you're good."

"Got it. I'm just turning on Monroe." Traffic bogged down, and I got stuck by the light on Dearborn. The light turned green, and I was moving again.

Frank: "He's turning left on Madison. I'm two cars behind."

"Okay."

Frank: "Whoa. He made a sharp left down the alley. Wait, it's the entrance to the parking garage. Ty, he's going to the Hines-One Building, I'm following right behind, but you might lose me when I enter. I need you to stay back..."

That was all I got. He was in the garage, and we lost the comms signal. I hung back, parked illegally, and waited. I watched the entrance with an eagle eye. The people around me were oblivious. I started biting my nails, trying to anticipate what might come next. Five minutes passed.

Samantha: "Ty, what's going on? What should Jill and I do?"

"Samantha, head back home, but stay in touch. Jill, stay in the office. Do your normal routine and keep an eye out for anything unusual. When Frank comes back with an update, we'll go from there."

Jill: "Roger that."

Samantha: "On my way out. Take care, baby."

I kept looking around for any signs of being followed. I could have used the soothing tones of Bach's "Keyboard Concerto in

D Minor." It was playing in my head when the sound of a cop's nightstick rapping on my window made me quickly jerk around.

"Gotta move, buddy," he yelled curtly.

I rolled down the window and said, "Just waiting for a friend."

"There's public parking just down the street, man."

I nodded and pulled away. I didn't need to cause a scene, not when we were so close to wrapping this up.

Frank: "Ty, it's Frank. You hear me?"

"Yeah, yeah, I got you. What the hell's going on?"

Frank: "He's having lunch at the Rosebud Prime restaurant with two people. I'm at the bar; I've got eyes on 'em."

"Great. I had to move the car. Who are the two people?"

Frank: "One appears to be a woman, but I can't get a good look. Her back is to me, and she has a hat on. Let me move a bit. Oh shit, you're not going to believe it, but think we know who the old man is now."

"Ainsworth, the congressman?" I guessed.

Frank: "No. Old man Superintendent Cooper."

"Uh... what? He's the old man? That's not good news," I said.

I found another spot to park a few blocks away and waited. The waiting was the hard part. I'd always hated waiting for anything. Bach was back in my head, along with thoughts of Samantha. Forty-five minutes later, Frank had an update.

Frank: "He's on the move. Shit, he's going out the front."

"Frank, where's he going?"

Frank: "Damn it, he hailed a cab. By the time I get back to the car he'll be gone. Ty, where are you? He's headed north on Dearborn."

"I'm near Clark and Monroe, on the move. Any make on the cab?" I turned down Dearborn, heading north. But it seemed everyone was leaving lunch and heading back to work. Moving the car was slow.

"Frank...?"

Frank: "I can't. I can't give you a taxi description, we've lost him."

The silence was hard to hear.

"Damn." I turned the car around and headed back to the office. I'd wait there for Ian's return. But I doubted he'd show up the rest of the day.

I headed up my building's elevator with Chinese takeout. It was late, and Frank had convinced me to go home—there was no sense in waiting any longer. I had Jill text Samantha when she got home to make sure she was safe. Frank was going to check out Ian's private residence, just in case something was brewing. He'd call me if needed. I had Samantha waiting for me. I was beat. Dead tired.

I entered the apartment, and she met me with just one of my dress shirts on. It appeared that these girls liked wearing my clothes.

"Oh, baby, you look tired. Come here, let me take your jacket. Why don't you take a shower, and I'll take care of dinner? And Jill got home okay."

I didn't protest, but I needed something first. I held her in my arms in a long embrace. She let me cradle her. I smelled the freshness of her clean skin and the familiar scent of strawberry and mint. The tension in my body immediately eased. She was the calm in the center of the storm—my rock, and my purpose.

I let go and headed to the shower. The hot water soothed my muscles, making my legs wobbly. Our first recon mission was deemed a success. No one had been hurt, and our cover hadn't been blown.

We spent the rest of the evening on the couch, with my feet on the coffee table and Samantha tucked underneath my arm, never far away. We sipped wine with minimal conversation; we were comfortable—relaxed and content with the silence between us. Day two of our mission would start early. Frank and I were thinking about having Samantha in a car as well.

"What are you thinking about?" she asked.

I thought briefly, then I said, "If this was how the rest of my life was going to be, I'd take it, gladly."

She got up and held out her hand. "Come on, Magnum, P.I., let's put you to bed."

We headed to the master bedroom. I crawled under the cool sheets. My eyelids were heavy as I fell into the dark abyss. Samantha turned out the lights, curled up next to me, and as the day wound down, I heard her whisper an Irish poem:

"Feel my heart as you shut your eyes.

Sleep more tight as we reunite.

All the stars that are so bright,

Forget all the worries and the fright.

Stay calm with me as I recite,

May you have the sweetest of good nights.

Sleep tight, my Tiger."

THIRTY-FIVE

The alarm rang, waking me from my slumber. I rose from the bed, and my muscles screamed in disapproval. Samantha, to my surprise, was up already. I took a puff from my inhaler to jolt my lungs awake.

She was in the kitchen, still in my dress shirt, fixing coffee and toast. "Morning," she said, wrapping her arms around my neck and bringing her lips to meet mine.

"You're up early," I said. "Thanks for doing this." I raised my cup in salute. It had been a long time since someone had made coffee for me in the morning.

"Margaret called." Julius had told her I was sick, and she was concerned. "I told her you were fine, not to worry, and that you'd call her."

"Thanks." I dialed the number, and Margaret picked up.

"What does Julius have you working on? Maybe it's too strenuous a task. I only ask because I'm concerned about your asthma, dear," Margaret said.

"Oh, just some surveillance things. Boring stuff, really, if you ask me."

"Oh, I hope Ian is helping you. Is he?"

"I have Frank helping me. You know Ian?" I hadn't thought of it previously, but Margaret could be a good source of information on Ian. She might be a bit naïve, but working through her could be a way of avoiding arousing Julius's and Randolph's suspicions.

"I know everyone at the office, dear. How long will you be doing this surveillance?"

"As long as it takes, I guess."

"Well, you be careful. And that lovely girl of yours? Is she well? Where is she staying?"

"She's great," Samantha buzzed in and out of the kitchen. I decided to just rip the band-aid off. "She's living with me now."

"Oh, I see." I sensed a frosty disapproval on Margaret's end. Her views were not very enlightened. My living arrangements would have been frowned upon back in her day.

"Well, I guess it's all right. You do have extra bedrooms she can stay in, right?"

"I have plenty of space."

"Good. You two must come by sometime soon." We said our goodbyes, and I got ready for the day ahead.

At the office, work was slow. We decided to switch things up a bit. Samantha was now in a backup car, just in case Frank or I got stranded somewhere. Jill was still overseeing office operations, like the day before, but there wasn't much going on because Ian was in meetings with Julius and Randolph for most of the morning. I had a call to make.

"Stevens' Jewelers, may I help you?" A man's voice said.

"Yes, do you make custom jewelry?"

"Depends on what you have in mind."

"Something like a bracelet."

I spent the next twenty minutes ordering Samantha's birthday gift. The man seemed sure they could do it. I just hoped she would like it.

Ian took a quick lunch break, but after that, he stayed in his office.

At four, Jill went to get her kids and Samantha went to my place. We were wrapping things up around five when Frank said he needed to see me, fast. Ian was still in the office when I left.

I met Frank and jumped into his car. We headed out, bogged down in traffic on the way to my place.

"Ty, there's something you need to see." He handed me his phone. "I couldn't say anything until I had confirmation, and I just got a text from an ex-SEAL buddy of mine. That codebook. Looking at it, you see numbers, but it goes deeper. It's a code used by terrorists. From what my friend can gather, Ian Smith is trading in guns, rockets, and acts of domestic terrorism in exchange for money. Lots of money."

"Rockets?"

"Yes. He also told me that various Syrian factions are very much in play here. Which means ISIS. This is big time shit."

"No kidding."

"It looks like tomorrow's going to be a big day," he said. "Something's going down, so we need to get on it. Are you sure you want to do this?"

"Yes, I'm sure. How the fuck did we end up here, Frank?"

"Good question. It's a long way from drinks on the weekends at the Bison Head Tavern. Based on that lunch meeting Ian had yesterday with the police superintendent and the mystery lady, it looks like we won't have the cops for backup. We're on our own, buddy."

"What about Robert?"

"No time. This is going down in a few hours from what my buddy got off the codebook. We need to get those guns before they get shipped out."

"Let's keep the girls out of the action," I said. I knew they wanted to be a part of things, and I was sure I'd hear about it later, but I couldn't put them at risk. If anything happened to them, I would never be able to forgive myself. "I'll put Samantha in a car a few blocks away."

"And Jill can stay in the office," Frank said. "I need to see her before work. Can you arrange it? I can meet her in the parking garage."

"Sure."

We called it a day. Frank dropped me off, and I headed up the elevator, looking forward to seeing Samantha. She was making life more bearable.

A quick bite to eat, a shower, and off to slumber land we went, but I couldn't sleep. I was deep in thought about the news Frank had shared. Samantha stirred and cuddled up to me, extracting some of my body heat.

"Tell me something," she said.

"What do you want to know?"

"Your one piece of great advice."

"I don't have any advice, let alone great advice."

"Come on, no life lessons for a young woman just starting out in life? There's got to be something." She sighed.

"Don't fuck around with an older man, how's that?"

She pouted. "No, I'm being serious."

"Okay. Let me think." I thought about the life lessons I had learned over the years. Money, health, and love all had their lessons worth sharing. But the one truly hard lesson that I had learned and lived through was the right one to tell her about.

"There is one lesson I had to learn the hard way..."

"What's that?"

"Don't take anything for granted. I know you've probably have heard it before, but it rings true on so many levels. Don't wait to appreciate all you have until it's gone. Health, family, friends, jobs, money—all of it and life itself. When you're young, your parents are always there, or you feel you have plenty of time to do things or make amends. But nothing, and I mean nothing, in life is guaranteed to be there tomorrow. I guess that would be my one life lesson."

Her big cognac eyes peered into mine as if she were searching for a lost soul. It took her only a few moments to find it. "Who was she?" Her voice was soft. I had no response for her. We had a big day ahead, and I didn't really want to get into Karin. But she had a right to know—no secrets. She sat up, the sheet falling down, exposing her perfect breasts. Her eyes were serious. "Ty, who hurt you? Do you want me to kick her ass? I will."

Her posture radiated stubbornness, waiting for an answer. I told her about Karin, my parents, and just about everything else—including my best friends, Frank and Robert. I was free; there was nothing hidden between us. I could meet tomorrow head on. I had a clear focus, and this would all be over soon.

"Say, don't you have a birthday coming up soon?" I said.

"Why, yes, I do. What do you have in mind?"

"Well, you've made mention of missing your co-workers, so why don't we have a dinner party here? You could invite whomever your little heart desires. I've been known to dabble in the culinary arts from time to time. I'll cook for you."

"Really?" Her eyebrows almost hit the ceiling. "That would be special, but I'd want Jill to come and that could get a little awkward." Her mood was getting heavy.

"How so?"

"Well, if all four of them come, it might get weird having her husband there. But we could do it when her husband's out of town." I could see the wheels spinning in her brain. Her mood began to lighten. "Nothing says it has to be on the actual day, right?"

"Works for me."

She slid under the covers next to me. Her talented hands worked their way down my lower body.

"Oh my," she said. Her voice was wickedly playful. "Someone's rising to attention."

"We need to get some sleep, it's late." I didn't protest too hard.

Her body slithered down mine, and her head went under the sheet. Her serpentine smile was the last thing I saw before her mouth had my full attention and began constricting.

THIRTY-SIX

Superintendent Cooper was at his weekly appointment at the Golden Palms Massage and Spa in Chinatown. The clock was ready to strike midnight. He was with his favorite masseuse, Lu Li. She had a velvet touch and knew all his secret places. The conclusions to her massages were second to none and just what he needed after a long, exhausting week. Secretly, Lu Li couldn't stand him—she found him repulsive but managed to hide it well.

He was lying face down on what was known as a 'milking table,' which was a massage table with an extra hole in the middle, making it easy for Lu Li to finish her work by 'milking' Superintendent Cooper until he'd climax.

Lu Li did her massages topless, which also appealed to the superintendent. She was twenty minutes into the massage when the door opened. A pale man stood there; he was a good-looking man and someone she'd seen around the Golden Palms before. He raised his index finger to his lips. She understood what he meant and remained silent. He handed her a robe and motioned for her to leave. She did so with pleasure.

The superintendent heard the door close, "Lu Li, are you still there? I'm waiting for you to finish." There was no answer. "Lu Li, are you—"

"She left, old man. You'll have to settle for me."

Cooper turned his head to see the man standing beside the table. "Oh, it's you. Send the slut back in, and I'll be out in a minute. Unless you want to watch, you kinky bastard."

"I don't think she's coming back, and I need to terminate our business arrangement."

"Hey, what are you doing?"

Ian wrapped his gloved hand around what was sticking out of the hole and squeezed tight. "Here, let me give you a hand."

"Hey, that's too tight! What the fuck are you doing? Let go! Aaaaaaagh."

The superintendent couldn't get up off the table. The more he tried to push against it with his arms, the harder Ian pulled on his genitals. "Stop. Nooo!" Ian yanked harder. Superintendent Cooper felt like his whole body was being pulled through the hole.

"It's been fun working with you, chief, but we've decided to move in a different direction."

"No, no. Stop, god damn it." Tears poured down his face.

Ian pulled down, the wet ripping sound proving to be too much for Cooper. On the brink of passing out, he was suddenly free. He rolled off the table and flopped onto the floor. His crotch was on fire; his hands were frantically searching in vain to find his male member—his pride and joy—and make certain he was whole. But he found nothing but thick, sticky fluid.

Ian stood over him. Hanging from his hand and dripping with blood was the precious organ Cooper had been searching for. Cooper's brain registered what Ian held in his hand. He looked into Ian's liquid blue eyes and directly down the barrel of a gun.

"Enjoy your retirement," Ian said before he pulled the trigger.

THIRTY-SEVEN

"Nooooo." The shrill cry came from the living room. Half-dressed, I hustled out of the bedroom to see a distraught Samantha awash in the morning light and holding her phone, her thumbs a blur as they hammered out a text.

"No, no, no," she yelled.

I kept my voice level, fearing the worst, whatever on earth that might be. "What's up, honey?"

She froze, reading the answer to her text. "No, this can't be happening." Her phone took more abuse from her thumbs. Again, she waited for a response, biting her fingernails.

She looked up, wide-eyed in terror. I thought she would soon be ejecting that morning's breakfast.

Slowly, the words came out of her mouth. "It's my mom."

"Is she okay?"

"She's coming up and not only wants to have my birthday dinner this weekend but she also wants to stay here... with us." Head bowed in dejection; her chin dropped to her chest.

I guessed that was a bad thing.

The day was bright, clear, and cloud-free. It was a splendid summer day in Chicago, one of those flawless days where the sun's radiance makes for the perfect temperature for any number of activities, thus creating a nightmare on the city's streets. The Loop was full of pedestrians, and navigating the traffic was a challenging and demanding task. Not the best conditions for tracking someone.

Samantha was in a car at Jackson and Wabash, four blocks east of the WAR Building. Her mother's impending arrival was a distraction for her, so I tried to keep her out of harm's way. Jill was in the office. We were back on comms, all set and ready for action. Or so we'd thought.

Frank: "Okay, check-in time. How's everyone doing today?"

"I'm good," I said.

Jill: "Super, Preston won his game last night, so an ice cream celebration was had by all. And what about darling Sammy Bear?"

Samantha: "Oh, I'm fine. Did I tell you my mother's coming up for a visit?"

All: "Yes."

Samantha: "Ty and I are having a birthday dinner. You're all invited, and you have to come. It is mandatory."

No one could confirm their attendance due to the short notice.

Frank: "Hey Jill, were you able to do that favor for me?"

Jill: "It's done. No trouble."

Frank: "Thanks. I owe you one."

Samantha: "I need more caffeine... I'm gonna hit Uptown Corner Coffee. It's right where I'm parked."

"Keep an eye out, just in case."

Jill: "It's showtime. Looks like Ian's heading out; he's in the elevator. He's all yours."

I started the car and waited for Frank to get eyes on Ian.

"Frank, you there?"

Frank: "I read ya. Nothing yet."

Jill: "The elevator went to the parking garage. You'll see him soon."

"I'm ready. Come on, come on. Show yourself," I muttered.

Frank: "Got him. He's out of the garage. Turning off LaSalle onto Jackson, heading east."

"Headed that way." Might have just been the coffee jitters, but I sounded more excited than I should have been under the circumstances.

Frank: "He's stopped at a light on Jackson and State."

"Got it. I'm turning down Jackson."

Big busses loomed and blocked my view ahead. Public transportation was booming, the nice weather was bringing out all the tourists, shoppers, and the workforce. It was hard to cover much distance quickly on the streets.

Frank: "We're back moving. I'm four cars behind."

"I'm at Clark, two blocks away."

Frank: "They just passed Wabash—whoa, a quick pull off and park. I'll have to pass him and pull over. Ty, where are you?"

"I'm on State Street, a block out. Lots of people. I won't make this light. Maybe the next."

Frank: "It looks like they stopped for... Uptown Corner Coffee?"

The noise from the street made it a bit hard to hear Frank, so I rolled up the windows and flipped the air to low. It hit me like a gunshot. Uptown Corner Coffee? Why would he stop there? But wasn't that where...

"Hey, Frank. Say again."

Frank: "Three guys just met Ian outside the van. Wait a second, that looks like Sam. Two guys are approaching her. They got her by the arms."

Samantha: "Get off me."

"What?"

Jill: "Frank, what's going on?"

Frank: "They're forcing her into the van."

Samantha: "Get the fuck off me, asshole."

Frank: "Looks like Sam's trying to fight them off. She kicked one of them in the nuts; he's doubled over, but Ian hit her from behind, and she went limp in the other guy's arms."

"Frank, can you get out and help?"

Jill: "Ty, Frank, what's going on? If this is some joke…"

"Samantha, we got you, we're coming to get you, baby."

Jill: "Oh god."

Frank: "Okay, they got her in the van, and it's moving past me. I'm on them."

Jill: "Ty, answer me. What's going on?"

Frank: "Jill, it looks like they picked up Sammy and roughed her up a bit. But our girl fought back hard. We're blowing past Michigan, eastbound."

"I'm stuck at the fucking light, and I can't blow it, there's people all around. Fuck."

Jill: "Ty, this is scaring me. Get her back."

Frank: "Sam, if you can still hear us, scream, yell—anything to let us know."

Samantha: "What the fuck are you looking at, asshole?" There were some grunts and inaudible sounds. "Don't you touch me. My boyfriend's going to kick your ass. Ian, you fuck."

"Hey, shut up; you had plenty of time to stop this little spy game. And your boyfriend can't kick anybody's ass. Maybe it's time you were with a real man." We heard Ian say through Samantha's comms.

Samantha: "Get your hands off me, hey." We heard some inaudible sounds. Then a haunting voice came through.

Ian: "Hello, everyone out in spy land. Just letting you know that we have your girlfriend. Or is her code name Double-O-69? I took her earpiece out so we could chat a bit."

"Ian, you better not hurt her, I swear—" I said.

Ian: "What are you gonna do, Ty. Huh? Listen, we can end this peacefully. I want the codebook in exchange for your slut." We heard a hard slap followed by scream of pain from Samantha.

"Fine, done. When and where?" My voice was dry with cotton.

Ian: "I'll call you, but for now, it's silence for you guys. Don't worry, Ty. We'll keep the lovely Sam here entertained in the meantime, and I'll find out if she's a wiggler. She's pretty feisty, so I'm guessing yes." We heard laughter from inside the van, and then the line went dead.

Frank: "They just turned on Columbus Drive, heading south—do you want me to keep following? Ty, what do you want to do?"

"Kill the motherfucker. Keep eyes on the van."

Frank: "You got it."

Jill: "Ty, Frank. Go get our girl back."

Frank: "Will do, Jill. They're past Congress Parkway."

I was able to work my way onto Columbus Drive, southbound, my heart beating out of my chest. We'd been so stupid. Ian was ahead of us every step of the way. My brain filled with thoughts of what they were doing to her.

Frank: "Okay, we just reached the Field Museum. They might be going to Lake Shore Drive."

"I'm past Balbo Drive."

Frank: "Yeah, Ty. Lake Shore Drive, coming up on Soldier Field."

Once I hit Lake Shore Drive, traffic moved at forty. The turn onto I-55 surprised me.

"I think I see you up ahead, Frank. Keep on 'em."

Frank: "They're getting off LSD and onto the I-55 South ramp."

"Great, we're doing good. Frank. Keep your eyes peeled for that van."

Frank: "Ty, they're taking the I-90/94 South ramp."

I almost missed it and had to cut off a few people to make it, but that was the norm in Chicago.

Frank: "Ty, you there? Where are you?"

"Just at Sox Park. I can't see you anymore."

Frank: "We're getting off on 43rd Street, Wentworth Avenue exit."

My heart pounded. Just last night, my life had been perfect, and now it was being ripped apart. "Hey, aren't there a bunch of warehouses down on 43rd? And the train yard?"

Frank: "Yeah, they could be going to the Back of the Yards neighborhood. Lots of old buildings and warehouses down there. They just passed 43rd—looks like they're going west on 47th."

They drove down 47th, and headed up Ashland Avenue north to 43rd, heading west again.

"Hey, Frank, what's the update?" No reply.

Jill: "Ty, what happened to Frank?"

"I don't know, Jill. I'm pulling over." At least we were out of the Loop, and traffic was scarce.

Frank: "Ty, they're on... and looks like... so I'm moving..." Frank's comms were breaking up.

"Frank, repeat, repeat." I got out of the car, hoping for better reception.

Frank: "I'm stuck... can't see where... went... too... I... Sorry..."

"Frank, I can't make out what you're saying. Where are you?" No answer. He had to be somewhere nearby. My pulse raced, and my breathing was fast and shallow. I knew this could lead to an asthma attack, so I had to get it under control.

"Jill, are you there? Anyone, please." My voice shook.

Frank: "Ty, are you there?"

"Yes, I'm here."

Frank: "Hey, they're around 43rd and South Damen, but a truck pulled out and I didn't see where they went."

"What?" I couldn't believe it. I thumped my fist on the roof of the car. Shallow breaths came fast and hard. My lungs tightening, despair twisted and turned in my stomach. I shook uncontrollably. In a last-ditch effort I clutched my chest—for what, I had no idea. Barber's "Adagio for Strings" played in my head; it was the saddest piece of music I knew. With the violins weeping, the street rose up to greet me. My breathing stopped, and my eyes peered down a tunnel, looking at the face of blackness closing in. The abyss opened wide. I plunged in, and everything stopped. A voice spoke to me and faded away.

Frank: "I'm sorry, Ty, she's gone. Samantha's gone."

THIRTY-EIGHT

an sat Samantha down on a wooden chair in the middle of a warehouse filled with crates. The crates were in perfect rows, like streets leading to a traffic roundabout. She came to with the metallic taste of blood in her mouth and felt a thick fluid oozing down her chin. With her eyes still closed and her head foggy, her senses began assessing the situation. Ian zip-tied her wrists, causing runny plasma to flow from the tight restraints. Her eyes focused, and she tried to speak, but bloody drool was the only thing that came out.

The large room had only a single overhead light, fighting to beat back the shadows in the warehouse. The scene reminded her of something out of an old film noir. All that was missing was some fog, men wearing fedoras, and a girl in a tight black dress with a gun.

Someone said, "She's awake," confirming that she was still alive.

Shuffling footsteps approached, and her head was raised by someone. A splash of cold water hit her face. She shook her head, flinging beads of liquid into the air. The reality of her situation had sunk in, and she began to struggle against the restraints.

"Easy darlin', you ain't going anywhere," a voice called out.

Her body hurt too much to fight, anyway, and she needed to conserve her energy.

Someone set a wooden chair in front of her with its back toward her. She strained to lift her head. Ian came into view. He straddled the empty chair, his arms resting on the back.

"Sam, can you see me?" he asked.

She blinked hard several times, and he came into focus. She smirked.

"There you are. Hello, Sammy Bear. Sorry about the situation here, but you put up a pretty good fight. We had no choice." He raised his hands, palms out, like a priest at Sunday Mass.

"Where am I? You asshole—" Red liquid spewed onto her pants.

"Easy, Sammy Bear. We have some business to discuss, and I would like to handle it in a professional manner. Do you think you can do that?"

"Why would I, ass wipe?"

"Because your life depends on it."

That got her attention. Adrenaline masked her pain. She struggled in her seat, the zip ties cutting into her wrists. She remembered what her father had told her when she was a kid: *Don't show 'em you're afraid. Stay strong.*

"You know, I've got to hand it to you guys. I underestimated you right from the start. First, Ty guns down one of my guys in a moving car, making an impossible shot. Then you take out Artie with a fuckin' Uzi—a fuckin' Uzi—can you believe it?" He turned to the others in the room for approval. "Then Ty takes out Hal, which, by the way, was just downright wrong. Come on, man. Hal was a great guy. And how the fuck did Ty take him down? Hal was twice his size." He shook his head.

"And the way Ty killed him—with a damn frying pan? Who does that? Hal deserved to go out better than that. He was a loyal man... You shoulda seen 'em at the funeral saying how a burglar had broken in and beat him with a frying pan. It was almost hilarious."

"Give me one chance and I'll do it to you, too," she said.

"Look, it's quite simple. Your friend, Addison—who, by the way, could fuck like a goddess." He glanced skyward. "She had something of ours that we would like back. It's a codebook with some information that we would rather keep private." He forced a grin.

"Well, all you had to do was ask." She tried to laugh, but it quickly turned into a coughing fit.

"Easy, I know we got off on the wrong foot, so why don't we start over? We need the book, so just give it to us."

"What makes you think I have it? Me and Addison lost touch a few years ago. Why did you kill her? Why not just kidnap her and get it that way?"

"We tried, but she went to the cops. You guys got her to go to the cops, so really *you* killed her by doing that. The cop and the lawyer, too.

"We tried to send a message when we blew up Ty's truck, but no, you still had to pursue it. You made a mistake thinking it was the congressman, just like we made a mistake thinking that Addison was in the car that night when it was actually you. The boys pushed you off the road, and when they checked, they discovered you weren't Addison. I think Artie copped a good feel while you were passed out, if I remember what he told me correctly."

His eyes peered up again, checking his memory. "By the way, what do you see in Ty? Come on, you could have any guy in town, and you go for him? A classic case of beauty instead of brains." Bemused chuckles echoed through the room.

"I get that a lot." She fought the restraints again, while her mind sought out other options.

She looked around the room, surveying the layout and calculating an escape, when suddenly she saw a figure, a dim silhouette, sitting in the back.

"Who... who is that?" She nodded her head in the person's direction.

"What are you, a fucking owl?" Laughter filled the room again. "That's my boss. Taking an interest in you."

"Maybe I should be talking to him instead of you. Cut out the middleman."

"No, you'll have to deal with me. My boss is shy."

"You fuck face." She arched her back against the restraints, tilting the chair. It began to fall. A hand caught the chair and pushed her upright.

"Give us our property back, and we'll give you a hefty sum."

"Just like that?"

"Don't worry, I'm not going to kill you. You're way too valuable for that. In fact, we have to be careful how we handle you. At least your face. You have a few cuts, but nothing that won't heal quick."

"What do you mean?"

"I have plans for you, little cheerleader. The people that are going to buy these guns are also in the market for a youthful blonde cheerleader." He pointed at her chest. "That's you."

"You've got one messed up head. A hero to zero. But you were always a loser, weren't you?"

He jumped to his feet and screamed, "Shut up."

"What's the matter? Mommy didn't love you enough. Daddy beat you?" An evil smile creased her face.

"Lies, all lies."

"Who lies?" she asked.

"You, your friends, the government."

"The government?" She chuckled.

"The lying bullshit that the politicians spill out of their mouths is constructed to sound like the truth. They throw the word freedom around to defend their actions. It's used as a defense mechanism when they're confronted, questioned about their actions. They use freedom to terrorize people into thinking we need to go in offensively to prevent a pretext for war.

"Good men died. There were no weapons of mass destruction. They led everyone to believe there were. People died, my friends died, because they said there were WMDs. Fucking 9/11. Take your head out of your ass and see what's going on. They lie. The government lies to you." His teeth clenched, and beads of sweat formed along his hairline and upper lip.

"Take it easy, we're just talking here. If I'm not mistaken, 9/11 happened years ago. You must have some issues about letting go," Samantha said.

"I was in the Marines because of 9/11. All that patriotic bullshit got to me. Then what? Here come the lies. Do you know how many people I blew away? Kids and women—do you know what that does to you? It makes you a hard man; it makes you soulless. They tell you it's us or them. The truth is, they had no chance."

"You were defending our freedom—"

Ian's next diatribe came out in almost a single breath. "Do you really think nineteen men with box cutters could overpower flights full of passengers and trained ex-military pilots on four commercial aircraft? Fly, off-course, mind you, for over an hour without being intercepted by even one U.S. fighter jet? These hijackers, who like to drink alcohol, snort cocaine, and visit the local strip club, we are told, are devout religious fundamentalists. These are the guys who could knock down three buildings with two planes in New York City. And here's my favorite part, the plane in Washington D.C., the guy that flew that plane couldn't handle a little single-engine Cessna. Yet he flew a 757 in an 8000-foot descending 270-degree corkscrew turn to come exactly level with the ground and plow into the Pentagon? Wow, that's some magical stuff. And the ringleader, what about him? Well, turns out he's directing all this halfway around the world while on dialysis using a satellite phone and a laptop? That's right, the most sophisticated penetration of the most heavily defended airspace in all the world was brought to you by a guy in a cave."

"You're a conspiracy theorist?"

"Look at the evidence they gave you, Sammy Bear. It basically fell into the FBI's lap a day later when one of the hijackers' passports was found just a few blocks away."

She battled hard against the zip ties.

"Easy, little cheerleader." He walked over to the figure in back, and they spent a few minutes talking. Then he came back, leaned in close, put his hand under her jaw, and tilted her head back.

"Change of plans. After the buy tonight, we won't need the book. So, I just wanted you to know that your boyfriend will die tonight, and you'll be leaving the country. You'll be bought and sold many times in what is left of your life. You know those Middle Eastern kings and sheiks—trading women is like a hobby for them. You'll be passed around like a big, fat joint. Everyone will get a turn. It's over. You lost." His laugh sliced through her like a knife.

THIRTY-NINE

"Tanner... Tanner... Tanner York, you wake up right now." I'd heard that voice before, but it was from a long time ago. "Ty, she needs you... now, son."

"D... D... Da... Dad? Is that you?"

"Yes son, I'm with you. I've always been with you. Get up, Ty. Stand. Remember, have courage, my boy. Be a lion—the lion, son."

"O... o... okay, Dad." My eyelids flickered open, and my eyes began to focus.

"Ty, hey Ty. It's me, I got you." The voice had changed.

"F... Frank?"

"Yeah, it's me, Frank." My eyes were now sharp. Two bodies were on the ground next to me, lying in a pool of blood. We seemed to be in some sort of warehouse.

"Let me help you up. We gotta go," Frank said.

"What happened? How did you find me?"

"You were unconscious on the street. I pulled you into this empty warehouse and had to take out these two guys and give you your inhaler. Take a few more puffs." Frank looked around frantically. "We gotta move."

I grabbed his arm. "Frank, I can't ask you to do this. This has gone too far, the killing..."

"Hey, remember when we were kids? Me, you, and Robert—all three of us made a pact to have each other's backs forever, even if it killed us..."

"But we were just kids."

"No buts. You've been there for me plenty of times, and so has Robert. We have a bond no one can break. Do you want to get your girl back or not?"

I looked at him and saw the determination in his face. Arguing with him was useless, and I didn't have the breath to spare. I nodded. "How?"

He held up a small electronic device. "With this. It's a tracking receiver." He handed it to me, and on the screen was a small flashing red dot.

"I don't get it," I said.

"Remember this morning, when I wanted to see Jill? Well, I got her to plant a tracker on Ian. The flashing dot means she was successful. That's how we're going to find Sam."

"Frank, that was risky." I didn't like Jill taking such risks.

"Yes, but well worth it now, don't you think?"

We headed out of the warehouse and into the sunlight. It hurt my eyes, and my knees buckled, but Frank caught me. It looked like Ian was two warehouses down from where we were. Frank handed me my Beretta—he had mounted a suppressor on it.

"Thanks," I said.

"Look, let's go in quiet." He looked around and pointed. "There, we'll go in that door. Let's see what we're dealing with, and with any luck, you and Sam will be home tonight."

"Fine by me." I took the safety off and racked the slide of the Beretta. I was ready to go; ready to get my girl back.

Frank picked the lock and cracked the door. We heard voices, but we saw nothing. We worked our way in, sneaking behind some crates. It would be hand signals only from then on.

When I moved forward, my foot clipped something, and I stumbled. I got my legs under control right before crashing into a pile of loose scrap wood.

"Watch it," Frank whispered. "There's wood scraps all over the place. Watch where you step." Two-by-fours, one-by-twos, and pieces of plywood were strewn about.

I nodded and motioned to Frank to move to the far wall. As I watched, he disappeared into the darkness. I hoped it wasn't the last time I'd see him alive.

I walked down the aisle between the mountain of crates on either side. The smell of wood filled the air, and I missed the scent of strawberry mint shampoo. At the end of the aisle, I peered around the corner and saw nothing. I went further into the warehouse, my hand tight around the Beretta, my mouth dry.

I moved from one aisle to the next, working my way toward the center where the crates weren't stacked as high. The overhead light revealed someone tied to a wooden chair and surrounded by five men. One of the men lifted the slumped head roughly, revealing a familiar mop of blonde hair. It took all that I had to control my trigger finger. A stray shot now would be disastrous.

I moved to another aisle, working my way closer to the group in the center. I saw Frank in the shadows on the other side—we now had them in view. But attacking them from this vantage point wasn't the best idea. The man in the middle was Ian. He was flanked by four armed guards; they were more focused on Samantha than their surroundings, so that gave us a bit of an edge.

I gave a quick wave to Frank. He acknowledged it and motioned for me to move back and around. I slipped back into the shadows and went around as quietly as I could to meet up with him.

"Hey, did you see her, did she look okay?" I whispered softly.

"Couldn't tell from the back. Let's move around so they have their backs to us—that way we'll get two of them by surprise, and we can get the other two as they spin around."

"What about Ian?"

"The guards first."

We parted ways. Frank would send me a signal once we were in position, then it was open season. Frank would start on his two guys. He had more training than me.

When I headed down one of the aisles, my chest began to tighten, and my hands started to shake. I reached for my inhaler, but it wasn't there. I must have dropped it on the street. I closed my eyes and took some deep, even breaths, trying to stave off another asthma attack. After a few deeper breaths, I opened my eyes and began to move. In a couple more feet I'd be in position. I was starting to hear their conversation.

Ian let out an evil laugh.

"You'll be sorry." Samantha choked back a sob. "Just wait, assholes."

"The boss left. It's just me and you and the boys here."

"Who's your boss?"

"Well, if I told ya, I'd have to kill ya. And I need you so I can't kill ya, which means I can't tell ya." Ian laughed at his childish wit. The others laughed as well.

"Fuck you," she spat.

"Easy, hellcat. Come on, you have two options. One, get sold to the sheik, where you'll live in luxury and want for nothing. It'll be like a vacation for the rest of your life, or at least until your looks fade. Or two... I could give you to these guys." He gestured to the four guards, all of whom smiled, laughed, and high-fived each other.

"Settle down," Ian said. "She's worth more than you guys can afford." He turned to Samantha and moved in close enough to kiss her. "You see, it's just business."

Samantha reared her head back and lunged forward, head-butting Ian so hard that he fell over. He held a hand to his face, blood trickling between his fingers.

"You bitch," he said, his voice a little more nasal than it had been.

"I'm not going anywhere," she said. "And I'm sure as hell not getting sold. Who are you? You sell guns to kids to kill other kids. You used to be an American hero. What the fuck happened to you?" Samantha yelled, maybe hoping the outside world would hear.

Ian got to his feet, holding a finger under his bleeding nose. Profanity blazed out of him like a dragon breathes fire. He shouted, "All these guns here? They're not going out on the streets of Chicago, they're going to the President of Syria."

She looked at him with revulsion.

I was now behind them and in a great position to shoot—the guards would never see it coming. I raised, leveled, and sighted my Beretta. Shots from a weapon might confuse them momentarily, so I could take them out before they knew what hit them. I now had the one guard lined up. My sight was hot, but even with both hands supporting the gun, my right hand couldn't stop shaking. I had to make these two shots.

I took a deep breath, exhaled slowly, cleared my mind of all doubt, and squeezed the trigger. The Beretta coughed and spit flame. Red mist shot out five feet past my target.

From the corner of my eye, I saw Frank's man fall. My other guard reacted in slow motion. A slight turn and my sight was hot again—no time for a breath—so I squeezed the trigger once more. Again, the red mist signaled a strike on a target.

I took a quick glance that told me Frank's second guard had fallen right on cue. Head shots are always the best way to go when disposing of an enemy. Ian was covered in blood. It was all over Samantha, too. Frank and I came out of the shadows with guns raised and locked on our next kill.

Ian didn't even flinch when the blood had started to spray. Instead, he whipped around Samantha, cowering behind her. He pulled out a big knife, and its blade sliced through the zip-ties without much effort. He put the deadly blade up to her pretty neck. In one swift motion, he lifted her off the chair using her body as a shield. The knife began to draw blood, which ran down Samantha's slim neck. Ian pulled her backwards, slinking into the shadows of an aisle between the crates.

I fixed my sights on Ian. "Stop, stay in the light."

"Easy there," Frank murmured.

Samantha said, "Ty, Frank. Good timing, guys. I had it handled, but nonetheless, glad to see ya." Her sigh of relief said a lot.

"Shut up, bitch." Ian jerked her back, hard. He readjusted his left arm around Samantha's chest so his hand got a good grasp of her right breast. Bile climbed up my throat. Ian's actions enraged me, and he knew it.

"Easy, Ty," he said. "If I'm gonna die, I might as well get in a cheap thrill first." He stuck out his tongue and slowly licked up her cheek, leaving a trail of saliva and blood. Her face soured as she wrestled uselessly against his strong grip and the sharp blade. He laughed. The blood from Samantha's neck now reached her chest; the stream flowed down her cleavage.

"Ian, Chris... whatever your name is... just let her go. Let her go, and you walk free. We're not cops, we couldn't care less if you disappeared." I put the gun down and held up my hands. Frank remained still with his gun trained on Ian.

"It's not that easy," Ian said. "I have a delivery to make. People are depending on me. You're in my way."

"Shoot him, Frank," Samantha hissed.

"Ty?" Frank asked for permission.

My throat was dry and tight. "Don't do this, Ian."

Samantha struggled, and the blade at her throat cut a little deeper.

"Samantha, easy, honey," I said.

He jerked Samantha around a bit more.

"Shoot him, Frank," she said.

"Ty? Just give me the word," Frank insisted.

Ian crouched behind Samantha. "No, easy Frank, please. Everyone, just hold on," I begged.

Ian began to rock back and forth. This had gone on for too long. Our plan was going all to hell.

In a split second, Ian's demeanor had totally changed. His eyes rolled back like a shark's—they were blank, soulless eyes. "We can't go around forcing our will on people in their own country, taking them from their homes and saying it's justified by our government's lies, the government's hidden agenda." Ian spoke slow in a monotone voice. "It's not honorable or dignified. Right, Frank? You look like a military man. Marines? It's not what we, as American soldiers, should do. They need to stop drawing lines. Us or them. Frank, you've seen the torture—the mass graves we dug. How many kids did you bury and then were told to never question or speak of it again? They could have prevented it. We knew they were out there. All we had to do was put air marshals on every plane before 9/11, and it would never have happened. It was that simple."

I glanced over at Frank, whose arms were going slack, his gun no longer fixed on Ian. "Frank," I shouted. "Stay focused. Stay with me, Frank."

Ian took another step back and started laughing. What appeared to be a wooden two-by-four began to rise vertically behind Ian's right shoulder. It rose slowly, floating behind and above him. The board looked odd in the light. I saw Frank staring at it with a furrowed brow. The board reached a certain height and then fell back into the shadows, only to reappear and come crashing down on Ian's head. The board cracked in half as wood chips and slivers mixed with blood and brain matter. It made me wince. His eyes locked on mine, frozen. The knife held against Samantha's throat fell as Ian's grip on her loosened. She stepped toward me; I scooped her up and set her down behind me. We were all transfixed by Ian. With his eyes wide open in shock and his mouth twitching, he crumpled to the floor.

Jill emerged from the shadows holding a splintered and blood-stained two-by-four. "Nobody touches my bitch, asshole." She clubbed Ian in the head again as he lay there.

"Jill," I said.

Jill took the two-by-four and raised it over her head once more, slamming it down on Ian's already bashed-in skull.

Samantha screamed. Jill tossed the board away in disgust and wiped Ian's blood off her face.

"Good going, Jill," Frank said, nodding to me.

"Are you okay? Is anything broken?" I checked Samantha over, arms and legs, relieved she seemed okay. I found a towel and wrapped it around her neck.

Jill started shaking and looking at me rather confused. "I saw you... on the street. You died? No?"

"Well, I'm here, aren't I? So, I guess I didn't."

"Did I kill him? I just wanted to distract him, I didn't mean to kill anybody." A horrified look crossed her face. "Have I murdered someone? I have kids—I can't go to jail."

Frank checked Ian for a pulse. He looked at me and shook his head.

Frank walked over to Jill, grinning broadly, and put his hand on her shoulder. "Glad to see you, you saved us. I could kiss ya."

"I agree. And I will." Samantha nudged Frank out of the way and kissed Jill softly on the lips. "You did great, baby. You killed the bad guy; nobody's going to jail. We'll protect you." She put her arms around her. Jill seemed to be calming down.

"How did you find us?" I asked.

"With this. Frank gave it to me." In her hand, she held a tracking receiver. "When I lost you guys on the comms, I got scared and followed the red dot."

"I knew that was a great idea," Frank boasted. "Why don't you take Sam and go to Ty's place? We'll meet you there."

I helped get Samantha into Jill's car and said, "Go straight to the tower, Jill. Text me when you get there."

"Ty," Samantha said. "There was someone else in the warehouse. Ian said it was his boss. Did you see anyone come out?"

"No. Frank and I will check it out."

"This might not be over yet. I was so scared, but I knew you would rescue me."

I looked deep into her eyes, gave her a crooked smile, and said, "I had to. What would I tell your mother?"

FORTY

We had a problem. Crates filled with guns were everywhere—not handguns, but rifles. We found a few other surprises too: handheld rocket launchers, grenades, and a few boxes of C-4 plastic explosive.

"How do they get this stuff in and out?" I asked without expecting an answer.

"Payoffs would be my guess, and having the police superintendent on your side surely helps. I wonder what the price for selling out your country is these days," Frank said. "Wow, would you look at this." He held up a rifle. "Do you know what this is?"

"No, assault weapons aren't my thing."

"It's an HK—Heckler & Koch 416 assault carbine. It's based on the AR-15. Do you know what it's famous for though?"

"Again, no."

"This is the type of weapon that was used by SEAL Team Six to kill Osama bin Laden." He gave the weapon a long look over, checking out all the moving parts and looking through the sight as he engaged in a mock shootout.

"Beautiful," Frank said.

"Your definition of beauty differs drastically from mine, my friend."

"Yeah, I know what your definition is—long legs and blonde hair with a nice rack."

"Hey, watch it. You're talking about my girl, man. Can you believe I can actually say I have a girl?"

"About time, old friend."

We hit a few more crates, and it seemed the HK was the rifle of choice in that row. We opened one crate from a different aisle.

"Hey, buddy. Wanna come here and tell me what this is?"

Frank came in a flash. "Oh man! This is a Remington M2010 enhanced sniper rifle—it even has a Leupold Mark telescopic sight. Who's buying this stuff?"

"What's its range?"

"I would say up to 1,500 yards, and I believe these fire a magnum hollow-point boat-tail bullet."

"What does that do?"

"Decreases wind deflection on the bullet, reduces muzzle flash, and has a low drag coefficient. It's got performance and lethality on its side. If this rifle were a car, it would be a Ferrari."

We found other crates with more rifles, more HKs, and some SIG 516s designated for civilian and law enforcement use.

Frank nearly climaxed in his jeans once again when he found the AAC Honey Badger assault rifle with built-in suppression and subsonic ammo.

"Tough to find this one," he said. "There's enough here to equip a small army, like a rebel group looking to overthrow a government."

"Or for a government to defeat an uprising," I added.

"True. Ian was in it for the money. Your scenario is more likely. A big oil country could afford all this, no problem. Let the people starve while the government buys guns to support the cause, isn't that how it works?"

"But Ian would need money for such a large haul to begin with. I doubt the supplier takes credit cards. So, who's the backer? Samantha mentioned another person being in the warehouse. Ian's boss, according to what she was told."

"With this shipment most likely not going where it was supposed to, I doubt they'll be looking for us. They'll be headed for the hills—somebody's going to want what they paid for."

"So, what do we do now?"

"Call the cops, I guess."

"If we do that, these guns will be on our streets instead. We know the superintendent is in on this. You know how it works around here," I said. "If there's money to be made, someone's going to exploit the opportunity."

"So, what do you want to do? We have five dead bodies here and two more in the other warehouse, along with all these guns, grenades, and bombs being shipped to Syria today. I don't have room at the garage to store all this—"

"Funny," I said.

"But I have an idea. We have C-4, and I know how it works."

FORTY-ONE

can only imagine what the eruption of Krakatoa was like, but in less than an hour, Frank and I had set up Chicago's version. We plastered C-4 around the building and the crates. Frank wired the blocks in a series to set off one blast at a time, like demolishing a skyscraper. This would limit the collateral damage.

"Let's do one more sweep of the inside before we go and pack up the car," he said.

We counted nearly two thousand crates filled with guns, rifles, explosives, and ammo. Frank figured the blast wouldn't destroy all the guns, but it would certain draw Homeland Security to the location, and once they saw the amount of firepower in the warehouse, they'd take care of the rest.

I looked around, eyeing the corners, the ceiling joists, and the overhead pipes. Something caught my eye—a sheet of plywood that had been laid on the ceiling support beams.

"Hey Frank, did you check up there?" I pointed. "Help me with the ladder." We moved the ladder over, and I climbed up to the plywood platform to discover a heap of canvas bags.

Frank called up to me. "Anything?"

"A few duffel bags."

"Toss 'em down."

One by one, I shoved them over the platform. There were six in all.

"Well, let's have a look." Frank hefted one onto a crate.

"All right, here goes nothing." I unzipped the bag to find it stuffed with cash. "Holy... shit."

"We could've blown that up. Are they all—"

"Let's find out." We opened all the bags, and each one was filled with cold, hard, tax-free money.

"So... halfsies?" We high-fived with grins on our tired faces.

"No—a four-way split. I insist. We all earned a slice of this."

"You'll get no argument from me," he said.

It was finally dark enough to load up the car. Frank took a few souvenirs to add to his collection. We were isolated from the nearest residential neighborhood, but if we heard a car or a noise, we were at the ready. It had been a long day, and our nerves were shot.

The cool night air hit me and put a spark in my beaten body. I called Samantha.

Jill answered. "Are you guys, okay? I was getting worried."

"We're fine, Jill. Is Samantha all right?"

"She's fine. I finally got her to lie down. She's sleeping now. She has some cuts, bruised ribs, a bump on the head, and some restraint marks on her wrists and ankles, which I'm sure won't bother her—she's used to that."

"You're probably right. How are you?"

"A little shaken. Glad I figured out that tracking device Frank gave me. Glad I was there for the team." She sounded better than she had the last time we'd talked.

"Frank and I are wrapping things up here, so I'll be home soon." I hung up.

"Let's go, lover boy," Frank said.

"Here." I tossed the keys to him. "Put the cash in the cabin. You know the hiding spot?"

"Consider it done."

"And uh, hey, if you ever want to talk about what happened when you were in the service—"

"I'm okay. We're not all nuts like Ian. But thanks, maybe I will take you up on that one day."

We checked one last time to see if anyone was around and found that all was clear. We drove down a block down the road and got out of our cars.

"Fire in the hole," Frank muttered and pressed the remote button.

It took a second before the bright detonations flashed, turning night back into day. Another second later, and the blast had ripped the warehouse roof apart. The sound was deafening, and my ear canal tickled. The supersonic high-temperature shock wave sent Frank and I airborne. Flames and columns of smoke rose high overhead. We landed hard, with our asses bearing the brunt of the impact.

It took a moment for me to regain my composure and scramble back to my feet. Car and building alarms were blaring, and aerial debris was making its way back down to the ground.

"For fuck's sake, Frank." My ears were cottony, numbed by the explosion.

"I guess I overestimated the amount of C-4," he yelled back.

"Ya think? We could've just started the second Great Chicago Fire."

The flames started to lick at the building. The heat that engulfed us was strangely comforting. We stood watching this image of hell on earth that we'd created. It was an arsonist's wet dream.

My ears were still ringing when I shut off the engine of the rental car. The underground garage at Lake Point Tower was cool in contrast to the warm summer night and the blast furnace we'd created. I sent Jill a text, letting her know I was on my way up. Frank said he'd wait down in the lobby for Jill and make sure she got home.

Jill met me at the door. "What happened? What'd you guys do?"

"Let's just say that Syria won't be getting any guns anytime soon. How is she?"

"Sleeping. You want me to get her?"

"No, let her sleep. I'm gonna hit the shower. You better go. Frank's down in the lobby; he'll make sure you get home safe. You can't say anything about this, Jill. What we did could get us locked up for a long time."

"We did a good thing, didn't we? We saved a lot of lives."

"I think we did."

She left, and I looked in on Samantha. All seemed good. Then I hit the shower. The warm water washed away the day's grime, but could it wash away the guilt I felt for having put the lives of those I loved in danger?

Samantha was in a deep sleep. I kissed her forehead and went into the kitchen, put three scoops of French vanilla ice cream in a bowl, and poured some bourbon over it. I headed for my recliner. With the TV on, it took no time at all for me to fall asleep with my vanilla ice cream melting in my lap.

A subtle noise roused me from sleep. My eyes opened to see Samantha's angelic face. She wore her usual attire—one of my dress shirts and nothing else. This one was light green. I remembered what Rachel had told me about blondes wearing the color green; it certainly worked on Samantha.

"I made coffee." She took my bowl of melted ice cream away. "Don't get up Tiger, I'll bring it in."

"Thanks."

She reappeared, handed me the steamy brew, and cuddled up beside me.

"Your face is puffy. You should have woken me up; we could have put some ice on it last night."

"You look great. Really. Damn, you heal fast. The young have it all," I grumbled.

"Here, feel." She took my hand and put it just above her forehead where I could feel a knot.

"Sorry. Does it hurt?"

"Only when I laugh." She grinned. "You guys are all over the news. Jill's called several times."

She took the remote and turned on the TV.

"... And you can still see the flames coming out of the warehouse. Evacuations have been ordered for a four-block radius, giving emergency crews room to attack the blaze. So far, five are confirmed dead, but fire officials won't know if there are any more fatalities until the fire is out and they have deemed it safe to inspect.

"In another warehouse east, two bodies were found shot to death. Police don't know if these incidents are related."

"Meghan, have the police given any indication as to what the warehouse contained or whether this was an act of terrorism?"

"No, David. There is a press conference scheduled for ten this morning, so we'll get more information then. Reporting live from 43rd and Ashland in the Back of the Yards neighborhood, I'm Meghan Orr. David, back to you."

She switched it off.

To lighten the mood, I asked, "Hey, would you like your birthday present?"

Samantha screeched, kicking her legs. "Yes, yes, yes."

I pulled out the end table's drawer, reached in, and produced a medium-sized, deep red velvet box. "Happy birthday, sweetheart."

She took great care in opening it. Her eyelids shot to the ceiling when she saw what it contained. "Aw, it's a charm bracelet. Ty, thank you." She looked into my eyes, bit her lower lip and kissed me.

We came up for air. "Here, it has four charms on it. I had it custom made from white gold."

Samantha took it out of the box, rolled it in her fingers. "I see a heart, oh, I love it. And my school logo from FIU, it's Roary the Panther." She threw a fist in the air and shouted, "Go Panthers." Samantha saw the next charm and laughed. "An owl, it's Dash. I love this." Her face was so bright with joy. A tear slipped from the corner of her eye. Her biggest reaction came from the last charm. A little set of handcuffs.

"Oh my, you're a bad man *Monsieur* York. And that's what I love about you." She kissed me with soft tender kisses. "Thank you, I love it."

"You're welcome." I helped her put the bracelet on. She looked at it, admiring how it laid on her delicate wrist.

"So, is my hero hungry?" she said. "Do you want to go out or fix something here?"

Although my body screamed, I fought its protest and jumped up, taking Samantha in my arms.

"Yeah, I'm hungry," I growled as I carried her to the bedroom.

"Our reporter, Meghan Orr, has been on the scene of the warehouse explosion all day. Meghan are you there?"

"I'm here, David. As you can see from the live footage provided by Sky Chopper WXNG, smoke is still billowing from the carnage that befell the warehouse. We've been told to stay back as police and fire are still unsure as to the cause and whether more explosions are yet to come. Police have not said if this is a terrorist attack. But I can tell you this for sure—debris is everywhere. We are about five blocks away, and we are surrounded by all kinds of rubble that presumably came from the building. Next to my foot—if Diego can get a shot of this—is what looks like a pipe about two feet in length. But upon closer inspection, it is apparent that this is a gun barrel from a rifle. We've notified police of this discovery.

"Could this warehouse be the source of all the firepower we've been seeing on the streets for some time now? Could this explosion be linked to gang violence? We are waiting on word from the superintendent's office... oh, wait. Ma'am? Excuse me. Did you witness the explosion?"

"No, I didn't see it. I heard it though. It was big and loud. Scared me, I came runnin' out, you know that's all warehouses back in there, don't know what shady business goes on over there."

"Did you see anybody coming from that area?"

"I saw two cars come from that direction, and they be haulin' some ass."

"Did you get a look at the drivers?"

"Naw, nothing that I could be sure about. One was white and the other black."

"Okay, thanks for talking to us. Well, that adds a little more to the story. I'm sure police will be checking for witnesses and any video from street cameras. Reporting live from 43rd and Ashland in the Back of the Yards neighborhood, I'm Meghan Orr. David, back to you."

"Thank you, Meghan. We will keep you updated as this story develops."

FORTY-TWO

Frank made it to the cabin in short order. Not long after I'd finished my morning coffee, he sent me a text:

The bags are locked away.

Perfect. I knew I could count on Frank.

Great. Thanks! On a serious matter, are you coming to Samantha's birthday dinner next weekend at the tower? Her mom will be there.

I'll pass, keeping low for a while.

Hmm. It wasn't like him to turn me down. Yesterday must have taken more out of him than he'd let on. I couldn't say I blamed him. We'd had enough excitement for a lifetime. But I wanted him there. And I didn't want him being alone.

No sir, can't let you do that. I'll need you more than ever. Please come. I invited Robert.

Maybe.

The ice was cracking. I took a gamble and sweetened the deal.

Jill's coming. Maybe the 4 of us can discuss the future.

?? He replied.

What to do next, new business endeavors.

His reply was delayed by about a minute.

Okay. See you next weekend.

Sweet.

Later, I found myself back at work in the office, puffy face and all. Several people stared, and a few asked what had happened. A simple car accident with airbag deployment was an answer that satisfied all. I knew that Julius would go nuts and so would Margaret, so I stayed out of sight.

My thoughts were broken by the ringing of my phone.

"WAR Investigations Department. York speaking."

"Ty, this Dr. Renfro. I'm just calling because you missed your appointment yesterday. Is everything all right? It's not like you to miss an appointment without calling to reschedule."

"Uh, sorry, I was in a bit of a car accident."

"Are you all right?"

"Oh, I'm fine. I just completely forgot about our appointment. It's been crazy here at work."

"Do you have time next week?"

"Uh, sure. That should be okay," I said

"Great, I look forward to talking to you."

Jill had called in sick; she'd said that one of the kids had come down with something and that she wouldn't be in for the rest of the week. I was glad she was taking some time off. I was at the coffee machine getting a cup of joe when Randolph walked in. For some reason, for the first time ever, the sight of him didn't bother me.

"Have you seen Ian?" Randolph said.

"No, I haven't."

"Hey, what happened to your face?" His eyes were wide open, giving my injuries the once-over like a doctor would.

"Uh, car accident."

"Not the Audi—"

"What?" Now I was starting to get bothered.

"Your sweet new car, man."

"Oh, no, not the Audi, just a rental," I remarked.

"Good. I need one of those. I think I would look good in it." His eyes went glassy as he stared into the distance. He put his arm out and moved it back and forth like he was driving his imaginary car.

"What can I do for you, Randolph?" I interrupted his fantasy.

"Well." His demeanor changed, and a more somber Randolph appeared. That was something I'd never seen from him.

"I... well... it's like this..." And that's where he left it.

"Just say it."

His eyes began to well up with tears, and my back stiffened in preparation to hear bad news. "Julius? Margaret?" I asked.

"No," he shook his head. "Abella left me."

"What?"

"Abella. My girlfriend. She left me."

They all came to their senses sooner or later. Apparently Abella had been quicker than most. "Randolph, you have a new girlfriend every other month."

"But I bought a ring, and I loved her."

"I didn't know. I'm sorry, Randolph." He grabbed me, wrapping his long heavy arms around my chest. I had to use every muscle I had to hold him upright.

"You treated her good, right?"

"Like a princess." He let go of more tears, and I could feel them soaking through my shirt. I thought of Karin and briefly shared his pain.

"You didn't hit her, did you?"

"No, I'm not a monster."

"Then why did she leave?"

"She took off with a younger guy—one of her model friends. They were always pretty chummy." He lowered his voice to a whisper and said, "But I just thought he was gay."

"Oh, I see."

"She said I disgust her, and I'm too old and too overweight. Now, come on." Randolph started flexing his biceps and sucked in his stomach. "Do I look overweight? I'm as fit as any twentysomething."

"You're kidding, right?"

"Okay, thirtysomething. I'm not as out of shape as you are, though."

I didn't feel the need to answer that.

He used half a box of tissues just to get his face liquids in order, and I saw my opportunity to make an escape. But then he hit me with something I hadn't seen coming.

"Ty, you're a great friend and a wonderful person. I treasure our working together."

"Excuse me?"

"Are you still going out with Sam? You guys make a great couple. I wish I had that."

"Thanks." That was all I could say.

I was frozen, and I couldn't move. Hearing kind words from someone I'd despised for years was completely unexpected. What with the trial of Karin's killer and hiring Ian, the list of his offences was long. I should have turned and walked away. But I just stood there.

"Well, she's gone, my Abella. What's gone is gone, and you know what that means."

"No." Now I was scared.

"Strip club, baby." Again, he slapped a huge paw against my back. "Let's go next weekend. VIP all the way—my treat. Bring some friends."

"I can't make it. Me and Sam—"

"Just tell her you'll be working with me. Bring a change of clothes, otherwise you'll reek of perfume and be covered in glitter." The old Randolph had returned in full force.

"I'm not going to lie to Samantha, and besides, her mother is in town, and it's Samantha's birthday, we're having a dinner party..." I realized my mistake immediately. That was the worst possible thing that I could have said. I stopped speaking and hung my head.

"Awesome. A dinner party. I'm in. That's just what I need. Hey, is Sam's mom hot? You would think she has to be, right? Thanks for the invite. Sam's birthday, I'll bring the champagne. Hey, does Sam have a sister?"

"Yes, she has a sister, but she lives in Florida."

"Oh well. Can you imagine if we married them? We really would be brothers-in-law."

"Randolph, it's just a small dinner party with some of Samantha's friends from where she used to work. You'll be bored out of your mind—I'm not even looking forward to it," I lied.

"Man, that's perfect. I'm the life of the party, you know that. That's why you need me there, buddy. You're welcome in advance. Glad to help you out." He laughed and started to walk out of the kitchen. "See you at the party." As he left, Peter from payroll walked in. "Hey, Peter," Randolph said. "I'm going to Ty's dinner party. Yahoo!"

"You're having a dinner party? Can I bring a date?" Peter asked.

I shook my head and muttered, "She's gonna kill me."

FORTY-THREE

Samantha used the Audi to pick her mother up at the airport and bring her back to the apartment. Cynthia Rhodes was slightly taller than her daughter, but they shared the same build and good looks. She dressed casually but stylishly.

"Nice to meet you, Mr. York." Samantha's mother said. She extended her hand.

"Call me Ty, and it's a pleasure to meet you, Mrs. Rhodes. We'll get you upstairs, and you can make yourself at home. You must be tired from your trip."

"Nothing a good glass of wine won't cure," she laughed.

"I'm sure we have something you'll like. I hope you had a pleasant flight," I said.

"It was fine. The first part of the flight was a little bumpy, but it smoothed out after that. I was sorry to hear about your accident. I hope you have a speedy recovery."

I set up Cynthia in the guest bedroom. "Is there anything else I can get you, Mrs. Rhodes?"

"Nothing right now, thank you, Ty. Um, is that Handel I hear?"

"Yes, ma'am. Do you fancy classical music?"

"Well, Sam's father does, so it's on all the time. He tells me who's who and what's what. I guess some things stick occasionally."

"Very well. I'll leave you to get settled."

"You two will get along," she sighed.

"Ma'am?"

"Sam's father and you. You both like the same music. You'll have plenty to talk about."

"Yes, ma'am." I closed the door.

From what I'd been told, Cynthia Rhodes was fifty-four. She'd lived in Florida all her life. She'd married young and had Samantha's sister, Tiffany, at twenty-two. Samantha came along three years later. While raising two kids, she'd gone to community college, taking general studies. When she graduated, her husband had put up the money for her to open a shop for women's fashions. It was so successful, she opened up two more shops.

"How is she?" Samantha said.

"She's great, and I might dump you for her."

"Oh, shut up."

"I'm gonna get started on dinner."

"I'll help."

We'd invited eight, and all but Robert had accepted. Frank, Jill with her kids, and some of Samantha's co-workers from the TV station. The others had invited themselves—Peter, his plus one, and Randolph. Our theme was Italian, so we told our guests to bring wine or an appetizer or dessert if they were so inclined, but nothing was required.

Cynthia finished unpacking and came into the kitchen. "This sure is some place you have here, Ty. Beautiful views all around."

"Thanks. Would you like that glass of wine now?"

"Oh, I'll wait for everyone else to get here."

"Oh, Mom. Have a glass and loosen up already." Samantha handed her a glass filled to the brim.

"Well, all right." Cynthia sat on a kitchen stool and watched us work.

Samantha and I were great as a team. She worked on the bruschetta appetizer, and I worked on the toasted ravioli.

The first of our guests to show up was Jill with her kids. Cynthia was a bit surprised that Jill was able to let herself in. It was a small detail we'd all forgotten about.

The front desk called up to announce that Samantha's work friends had arrived. They were shown to our door, where Samantha greeted them with hellos and hugs.

It was my turn to be surprised when she introduced me to Meghan Orr and her crew, editor Jason Williams and cameraman Diego Ramirez, whom she called *el perro grande*, explaining that he was 'the big dog.' He was big in every sense of the word. His shoulders were so wide they barely fit through the doorframe.

We sat in the living room, getting acquainted. Preston and Caprice were still a bit shy, but they were slowly warming up. Caprice was tentative about getting too close to the windows at first, but her little brother had no fear whatsoever.

"So, how's little Sammy doing?" Meghan looked around. "Not too shabby, girlfriend."

"When are you coming back to work, *gatita*?" Diego said.

"I'm not sure, Diego. I miss you guys."

"What does *geheta* mean?" Cynthia said.

Diego explained. "Oh, I'm sorry. *Gatita* is kitten in Spanish. That's the nickname I gave her because she's always curious and getting into trouble. But not bad trouble." He waved his finger at Samantha and laughed.

"No tall tales, Diego." She laughed back.

Next to arrive was Peter Pozniak and his plus one—yet another surprise.

"Ty, this is my date, Erika."

"Hi, it's nice to meet you. Thank you for inviting me." She shook my hand, gave me a genteel smile, and showed no flash of recognition toward me. She was a pro at what she did. And I had my answer as to how Peter got all those attractive women to 'date' him.

"Um, let me give you a quick tour of the place so you know the layout," I said. It was a stall tactic so I could separate them from Cynthia. I needed to have Samantha prepare for her mother's reaction to her friend Rachel being mysteriously referred to as 'Erika' tonight.

I steered them away from the crowd and waved Samantha to come over. Her eyes nearly popped out of her head when she saw who was standing next to me. She came right over.

"Why hello, Peter. Do you remember me from the office?" Samantha said.

"Yes, I do, and happy birthday. This is my date."

"Erika. Nice to meet you," Rachel said with the same professionalism she had shown me.

"Hi Erika, I'm Sam. Peter, I'm going to steal her away briefly and show her where we..." Samantha looked at me for a finish to her sentence.

"Um," my mind raced, "the girls' powder room?"

"Perfect, the ladies powder room." Samantha repeated and whisked Rachel away.

"Nice place, Ty," Peter said.

Before I could answer, I heard Samantha call out, "Mother, can I see you in the bathroom, please?"

"Oh, coming dear," Cynthia said. I didn't know how Samantha and Rachel were going to handle the situation, but I did know not to get involved.

A couple of minutes passed, and the three ladies seemed to have it worked out. Crisis averted, I thought.

Just before dinner, the one and only Randolph showed up. Of course, Randolph had to make a grand entrance, but he'd also brought a couple of bottles of Dom Pérignon from House Moët and Chandon.

"*Buona sera*, everyone," he bellowed. "Ty, put these on ice, they need a chill before we can open them." I envisioned myself smashing one of the bottles over his head.

Frank was the last to arrive, we shook hands and the tension in my body released. He was an important person in my life, and it meant a lot that he was here.

"Robert?" He asked.

"Sadly, no."

Our family-style dinner featured our toasted ravioli and bruschetta to start followed by chicken parmesan with penne pasta marinara, along with roasted peppers and potatoes. Everything was a big hit. We had two special requests—Caprice wanted plain pasta, while Preston didn't want cheese on his chicken. We managed to accommodate both.

Once the cannoli and lemon cookies had been brought out, the conversation picked up. Different groups had discussions going on simultaneously. The odd couple thus far was comprised of Randolph and Cynthia—they seemed to have hit it off well. I sat back watching all the people smiling, laughing, and enjoying themselves.

Samantha reached across the table and squeezed my hand. "Having a good time?"

"Yes, thanks."

"Thanks for what?"

"Being here."

I cleared the plates and got them in the dishwasher. Frank helped. "How's it going?" he asked.

"I look worse than I feel."

"Good, 'cause you look terrible."

"Gee, thanks, buddy."

"My source tells me the police have no leads on the explosion," he said. "That's good for us."

I was still mentally holding my breath about the whole ordeal.

Frank continued. "I still think there's one major player we haven't seen yet—the money backer."

"The woman in the restaurant?"

"Yes."

"Do you think we're in danger? Do you think the woman Ian met for lunch is the same person Samantha saw in the warehouse?"

"I do, and I think we should be okay. Whoever is behind this needs to worry more about the Syrians than exacting revenge on us. But keep an eye out."

I poured each of us a glass of bourbon, and we headed back to the party.

Samantha was sitting in the living room with her work friends and her mother. The rest were in the dining room finishing up the desserts. The seat next to Samantha's was open, so I gladly took it. She slipped her hand into mine.

"So, Sammy," Meghan said. "I must ask, when are you coming back? We miss you."

"I'm not sure. I've been rethinking what I want to do."

"What could be better than telling the news with us?" Diego chuckled.

"We could use an assistant director, if staying in the studio is something you'd be interested in," Jason said.

"That sounds like a fantastic opportunity, dear." Cynthia looked at Jason and said, "I won't have to worry about her being out on the street. There's so much violence out there. Now they're blowing up buildings. Why is this city so infested with gangs and violence?"

No one wanted to field that particular question.

"Well, there's a lot of debate about that," Jason finally said. "Meghan did a piece on it about a year ago. Didn't you do some legwork on that, Sam?"

"I think I did."

"I remember," Diego said. "We found that child abuse, alcohol abuse, and drug use—except for marijuana—are the main drivers of violent crime."

"And it's not just boys," Meghan said. "Most females committing crimes have a history of being abused. Of course, poor parenting plays its part as well."

"But it's not all on the criminals' side of things. What the police do and don't do are reasons for the high crime rates, too," Samantha said.

"True. Use of force issues and not putting oneself at risk through aggressive tactics have been found to have connections," Jason said.

"What about racism?" Frank asked. "Black-on-black crime gets little or no attention in the media as opposed to black-on-white crime. The media plays a role in this, too."

Jason cleared his throat, a bit uneasy at Frank's last comment.

"I would think politics is also a factor. Political power is often misused to take advantage of weaker groups and people. And the rise in disharmony that comes out of such situations often forces the victims to resort to crime. Politics is more related to crime on a larger and a much more heinous level than anything else," I said.

"True," Meghan said.

"That makes sense," Cynthia said. "But why does New York, a much larger city, have a lower crime rate?"

Jason was the first to answer. "New York has smaller areas or neighborhoods of poverty, public housing. Chicago has larger areas."

"The unofficial Chicago Police Department motto is 'Be reactive, not proactive.' I was told that by a cop, believe it or not," Meghan added.

"It's always been a high-crime city with corruption in politics, police, and business. Once the government bans something, like the prohibition of alcohol, drugs, you open up a new avenue for organized crime. If people want it badly enough, they'll find it through gangs," I said.

"So, crime is a byproduct of poverty, poor parenting, unemployment, racism, drugs, and alcohol abuse. Does that about cover it?" Cynthia said.

"Well, let's not forget that ours is a society of selfishness and greed," I said.

"Also, the other side is what happens after the shootings. The victims. If you put a price tag on it, it costs a hospital on average fifty thousand dollars per injured person. That's with no follow-up or long-term care. Last year, it cost the city two and a half billion, which then gets passed down to taxpayers. We figured this amounted to about twenty-five hundred per Cook County household.

"I interviewed the chief of trauma surgery at one of the busiest hospitals in the city that sees a lot of gunshot wounds. He said that even if you survive, you could be paralyzed, need one-on-one care for the rest of your life, lose arms or legs, or be permanently disabled. Most don't get shot and then walk out of the hospital," Meghan said.

"Remember when he told us about fearing the bag? Man, I don't know if I could deal with that myself," Diego said.

"What bag? Like a body bag?" Cynthia asked.

Meghan looked at her. "No. They fear the colostomy bag. When one gets shot in the abdomen, they must operate and check the insides out. That's procedure. So, when they do that, the intestines stop working temporarily. They'll install a colostomy bag on the outside of the body. Gang members all know about it, and sometimes they shoot for the abdomen on purpose, just for that."

"That's horrible," Cynthia said.

"When they come in gut-shot, they beg the doctor not to give them the bag. But he has no choice—it's that or die."

We changed the subject to something lighter: movies. Samantha's co-workers stayed another hour and then left. Randolph said a long goodbye to Cynthia at the door. Peter and 'Erika' followed shortly after. All evening, Rachel had been good at her job. She was attentive to Peter's needs, laughed at his jokes, and acted like everything he said was profound. She and Samantha found some time away from everyone to catch up, and she only winked at me once the whole night.

We were down to Frank, Jill, and the kids. Preston and Caprice had their iPads to keep them occupied while the adults talked.

"Your kids are so wonderful, Jill. You and your husband must be proud. I can't wait to have grandchildren," Cynthia said.

"Thanks. They're a handful, but all in all, I can't complain. Isn't that right?" Jill took her hand and mussed up Preston's hair. Preston shrugged it off, engrossed in his video game.

"So, what are you and Sam doing tomorrow?" Jill asked.

"Shopping. All up and down Michigan Avenue, then a nice lunch. Would you like to come with, dear?"

"Oh, I would love it, but we have a soccer game and a cookout birthday party at Preston's friend's house. Are you going back to Florida on Sunday?"

"Yes, Sunday afternoon."

"Well, I hope you enjoy your stay, and don't worry about all the crime stuff we talked about. Sam's in good hands." Jill winked at me.

Jill and I were sitting at the dining room table when Caprice came running up.

"Mom. Preston says we're up so high that we're in the clouds. Is that true?"

"Well, yes, I guess that's true." She looked at me and smiled. "Sometimes we could be in the clouds."

"Then if we're in the clouds, then I guess we're where the angels are, right?"

"Uh, I guess that's right." Jill took the girl's hands in hers.

"Well, we should live here then, with the angels."

"Why do you say that?" Jill glanced from her daughter to me. "I don't think Mr. York has room for all of us. We have our own home, a nice big one, and you love our house. You have your own room and lots of stuff to play with. And Grandma comes over all the time to see you. What's bothering you, sweetie?"

"I don't need my own room, and I don't need all that much. And Grandma can visit here." Caprice had started to look worried.

"Why, my baby?" Jill brushed Caprice's hair with her hand.

"I want to live with the angels." She crossed her little arms over her chest.

Jill laughed a bit. "But why? Why do you want to live with the angels so much?"

"Because then the devil can't come here. Right?" Jill's warm expression turned stone cold. Jill scooped up Caprice and wrapped her arms around her. Caprice hugged her back, and mother and daughter shared a tight embrace.

"Oh, baby. I'm sorry. It's not your fault." Jill closed her eyes, and a single tear took a crooked path down her cheek.

Caprice hugged her mother a little tighter and said in a soft angelic voice, "Don't cry, Mom. This is where the devil don't go."

FORTY-FOUR

Samantha decided to call it a night shortly after our last guest had left. She hugged her mom, kissed me, and headed off to the master bedroom. I wanted to catch the late news for an update on the explosion.

Cynthia drifted into the living room. "So, Ty. Can I talk to you?"

"Sure, what's up? Did you have a nice evening?"

"Yes, I did, thank you. Dinner was great, and everyone was so nice." She sat up straight and put her hands on her knees. From her posture, I knew what was coming wasn't going to be good. "But I must be honest and tell you that I disapprove of you dating my daughter."

"We've only known each other for a few hours. Perhaps by the end of the weekend, you'll have gotten to know me better, and then you might change your opinion of me," I said.

"I doubt it."

"May I ask why you disapprove of me?" I'd thought we were past this hurdle. I was taken aback by her blunt approach.

"Oh, it's not you per se; it's just the age difference that is a bit disconcerting. The older rich guy with the younger girlfriend. It must be fun to show her off to your friends." Her eyebrows rose as she spoke the last few words.

"So, you're more concerned about how this looks than if we're happy together? Or whether your daughter is living the life she wants with whom she wants to live it?" I rubbed my jaw for effect.

"Sam has always been hard to tame. She'll act out to spite us. Her father and I thought she was a lesbian; she was always hanging around this one girl—a bad influence. She finally brought home a boy. We were glad, and he was a nice boy, too."

Samantha came into the room like a heat-seeking missile. "Mom, please. My relationship is my business. Who I date is my business. I love you and Dad but stop trying to control me." She came up to me and wrapped her arms around me.

"Well, I didn't mean to upset you, dear. But we are your parents, and we'll never stop looking out for you and Tiffany. But you know how our family image looks to the general public. This could be trouble down the line."

"I'm happy, Mom. That should be all you need to focus on."

"I'm happy, too," I said. "I understand that you married at an early age—maybe you're feeling like you missed out on some things? You raised two daughters, and I know being a parent never stops. I would like to say that I've been looking out for your daughter, but in reality, she's been looking out for me."

"Each other," Samantha said. "We look out for each other."

I crawled into bed and stared at the ceiling, collecting my thoughts. Samantha turned to me and wrapped her arms around me, her warm naked body pressed against mine. My pulse began to race.

"My mother can be a handful," she whispered.

"Oh, she's just being a mom."

"I love you," she said.

With that, her hand only needed a few quick strokes for me to be ready. She climbed on top and moved her hips.

"Aren't you tired?"

"Yeah, but I want you now. And forever."

FORTY-FIVE

"No, Mother. Forget it. You're not going." Samantha's voice had enough intensity for the seventh game of the World Series. It was just a slight disagreement between mother and daughter before heading out for their day of shopping.

"Don't tell me what to do, young lady."

Cynthia had offered to clean up a bit the morning after the party, which she had said was a wonderful time. I was hoping I scored some points for that.

"Need I remind you that you're still married to Dad? I'm texting Tiffany right now."

As Cynthia moved about the apartment, Samantha followed. As soon as Cynthia rearranged things, Samantha would reset them to suit her taste.

"We're separated, dear, there's a difference. And your sister will side with me. She always does."

They floated from room to room, made their way back into the kitchen, and then retraced their steps. I heard bits of the conversation, but my experience with Karin and her mom had taught me that it was better to stay out of the way.

"Separated is not divorced, which means you're still married. Your circle of friends must have put the separated word in your brain. Is that the *in* thing this month? Separation? Have you made *that* public? I don't see Dad gallivanting around with other women. And Randolph's twenty-some years your senior, so why is it okay for you, but not for Ty and me..."

I was scrolling through the news on my phone to see if there had been any updates on the explosion. The *Chicago Tribune* had something.

"Well, maybe your father should start dating. It might make him more human. And our age difference is different than yours, sweetie, believe me."

I skimmed the article, picking out the highlights.

A Chicago police spokesperson made a brief statement, delivering an update on the explosion of the warehouse in the Back of the Yards neighborhood three days ago.

"The Chicago police would like to again thank all of the first responders for their efforts in containing what could have been a much worse incident. We can confirm that five fatalities were found inside the warehouse. The bomb and arson squads are investigating the cause of the explosion, and that investigation is still ongoing."

"I just don't think it's a clever idea to be dating right now when Dad's still trying to save your marriage. And why does Randolph get to call you Cindy when Ty has to call you Mrs. Rhodes?" I watched Samantha walk by, still wearing my dress shirt. My eyes wandered back to the article.

Currently, there is no one in custody. Search and Rescue are still sifting through the warehouse for evidence. There doesn't seem to be anything indicating thus far that this was a terrorist attack. The city has not raised its terrorist alert level. Officials are still gathering facts to determine the warehouse's contents. Reports from credible news sources say that military-grade weapons were stored there. Because it is an ongoing investigation, the authorities have no comments to make on those reports.

They will be releasing the names as soon as all the victims have been ID'd and next of kin have been notified. Police are still looking to see if there was a connection to the bodies of the two men found dead in a nearby warehouse.

The article had nothing major to report so far. I put the phone down and went into the kitchen for a cup of coffee.

"Your father's not working that hard at the marriage, dear. And Cindy is Randolph's pet name for me."

I stood at the window sipping my coffee. The early morning boaters were out in the calm waters. Traffic was light on Lake Shore Drive, but that would change as people headed to the beaches.

"Sammy, get dressed. We can hit Starbucks on the way there," Cynthia shouted. Somehow, she'd lost Samantha.

Cynthia stood next to me. "It sure is a wonderful view, Ty. Don't mind us girls, this is nothing compared to when Sammy and her sister are together." Samantha squeezed in between us.

"I just don't think it's a good idea for you and Randolph to go out tonight for dinner and drinks. And you told him to call you Cindy. Remember?" Samantha grinned at me and gave me a wink and a kiss before heading into her mother's bedroom. "I'm wearing a white top, so I want to borrow your sapphire necklace."

My phone went off, and I answered quickly. "Hello, Frank. Save me."

"Oh no. You made your bed, pal. You're on your own."

"Great."

"Hey, so, we got a problem. My connections fizzled out. We still don't know who's really behind all this."

"We just have to keep looking."

"True. Anyway, I had a good time last night. Thanks for pushing me to join you."

"No problem. We'll have to do it again soon," I said.

"Boy, did Cynthia and Randolph hit it off or what? How's Sam doing with it?"

"It's been an interesting morning."

Frank laughed.

I dressed and met Samantha and her mother in the living room. "Don't you guys look stunning? The stores on Michigan Avenue won't know what hit 'em."

"Well, thank you, Ty," Cynthia said.

"Aw, you're sweet." Samantha slipped her arm through mine. "Escort us down, baby." She flashed her serpentine smile.

"With pleasure."

We rode the elevator down together. The chatter between the women was deafening. They planned to take an Uber to Water Tower Place and then work their way south. I needed to stop by the office. I hoped Julius would be there, and I wanted to bounce something off him.

The car pulled up, and Cynthia got in first. Samantha turned to me and asked, "Did you remember your inhaler?"

"Yes," I said, patting my breast pocket.

She gave me a hot and heavy goodbye, whispering, "Think of me often. I'll fuck your brains out later."

"I'll get the whip and handcuffs ready," I whispered back.

"Don't tease me."

"Come on, Sammy, you're wasting time," her mother barked. "For God's sake, it's not like you won't see him for days."

"Love you." She bit her lower lip, and her eyes said a sinful goodbye. She left me there, flustered and disheveled, while I watched them pull away.

After I had collected myself, the guys from the front desk brought my Chevelle up from the garage. I buckled up and thundered off.

I'd had no luck connecting with Julius at the office. It was midafternoon when I opened the door to the apartment and put on a pot of coffee. I grabbed my book off the nightstand, poured a hot cup of joe, and headed for the recliner. I tried to read but Julius not being in the office had me worried. He said he'd be there to edit an opening argument from one of the upcoming cases. I hadn't heard from either Julius or Margaret since the explosion, so I called them at home. No answer. I'd go into the office tomorrow, Sunday, on the off-chance that he'd be there then. If I didn't see him at work, I'd go to the house.

Hours later, the girls showed up with a dozen or so shopping bags.

"Hi, babe. Miss me?" Samantha's faced beamed.

"Of course. Did you guys buy one of everything?"

"Just about. You're looking at professional shoppers," Cynthia said.

The rest of the afternoon was low key. They told me all about their shopping adventures. They suddenly seemed more like sisters than mother and daughter. It was a totally different scene from what had gone on that morning.

Cynthia stood up. "Well, I hate to break this up—"

"Then don't," Samantha shot back.

"We talked about this, dear," Cynthia said softly.

"And you know how I feel about it."

"I know it's not my business," I said. "But I hope you have a good time tonight, Cynthia. Have fun."

"Why, thank you," she said.

Samantha pouted. "You're right. It is none of your business."

Cynthia left to meet Randolph. Samantha was on pins and needles. She spent an hour on the phone with Jill, then we watched a movie, or rather I watched, and she asked questions every half hour about what was going on. She was clearly preoccupied.

I fell asleep on the couch and woke up alone. I saw her staring out the living room window.

"It's one a.m.," she said.

"They must be having a good time." She gave me the evil eye. "You're cute. Stop worrying. Randolph won't let anything happen to her. He's a lot of things, but he's also responsible."

"When did you guys become such good friends?"

"We didn't. But your mom, just like you, can make her own decisions," I said.

"I'm worried about my dad. He doesn't deserve to be cheated on. He's a great guy. You'd like him."

"I'd like to meet him, but do you really think Randolph and your mom are doing it?"

Just then, the door opened. Samantha grabbed me, pulled me down the hallway to our bedroom, and hid in the shadows.

We watched her mother take her jacket off and head to her room to go to bed.

"There. You, see? Safe and sound."

Samantha and her mother were at the kitchen island the next morning. Samantha was holding her mother's hands in hers. It looked like Cynthia had been crying. I approached with caution.

"Morning," I said.

All I got in return were half-smiles. I took a few sips of coffee, and once the caffeine hit, I started the dialogue. "Where'd you go for dinner?"

"Chicago Cut, I'm not sure where it is."

"Excellent." I nodded.

"It was very good, and then we hung out at the bar till closing."

"It's okay, Mom."

"Uh oh, what happened?" I was almost afraid to ask.

Cynthia sniffled a bit. "Everything was fine. He was a perfect gentleman. But after dinner, he..." Her tears fell on the cool marble tabletop.

"We were sitting at the bar and all he talked about was his model ex-girlfriend or whatever—how great she was and how broken up he felt. Then he called her while I was sitting there, and they made a date for next week."

"Oh, Mom." Samantha rubbed Cynthia's shoulder.

"I'm so embarrassed. I made a fool out of myself."

"No, you didn't. He's just an ass," Samantha said.

I nodded in agreement.

FORTY-SIX

Passing by the large plate glass windows of Uptown Corner Coffee shop, I heard a tinny tapping noise. My attention diverted to the source of the annoying sound, I looked in the window and saw Rachel waving frantically, urging me to go inside. She was wearing just a hint of makeup—she didn't need much—and workout clothes. I nodded and went in.

"Hi!" Rachel cheered, hugged me tight, and followed up with a kiss. She smelled great, like a fresh spring rain.

"I want you to meet someone." She took me over to a corner booth.

"Ty, this is Jennifer, a new girl in the... the office."

"Hi. Pleasure to meet you," I said.

"Likewise," she said.

I sat down next to Rachel. Jennifer was eye-catching with her light brown hair, very tanned skin, and blue eyes. She had workout clothes on as well.

"That was a great dinner party. I didn't know Peter and you worked together. But thanks for not blowing the whistle on me."

"Hey, I would never do that, but let me know if Peter gives you any trouble, or if anyone else does for that matter."

"Aw, see Jen? There are some real men left out there. Would you believe that Ty passed on a freebie because he's in love with someone?" Rachel beamed with pride.

"Nice. Good for you, and good for her. She must be something else."

"She is," I said.

"Can you stay? I'm getting another round," Rachel said.

"I can for a bit." She left to order and her absence created a silence between Jennifer and me. After a few moments, I initiated the conversation. "So, Jen, are you part of the Florida group? Did you know Addison?"

"No, I'm originally from Texas. My dad was in the Army, so we moved around a lot. I was an Army brat, you might say."

"How do you like Chicago?"

"It's nice. Tough though, but the lakefront is really cool. When I save up enough, that's where I want to live. One of those condos on Lake Shore Drive. Have you lived here all your life?"

"Yes, but now I split my time. Weekdays I live and work in the city; weekends I have a cabin along the Illinois River."

Rachel came back with our coffee.

"So, what are you guys talking about?" She sat down on my side of the booth and slid right up beside me. I felt trapped.

"Oh, just where we come from," Jennifer said.

"Are you working on any big cases right now?" Rachel asked, her eyes wide with curiosity. "Ty here is an investigator for a big law firm. What are you working on?"

"I just finished with one. I can't say much, but it made a big impression on a number of people."

"Sounds exciting," Jennifer said. "Do you solve murders and stuff?"

"Based on our clientele, it's mostly white-collar crimes. But on occasion, a murder case may come my way. But my job's not nearly as action-packed as it is on TV." I hid my grin behind a sip of coffee.

"Well, I need some gossip time," Rachel said. "How did you get along with Sam's mom? What was that like?"

"Uh, fine. She's a nice lady."

"Oh, bull." Rachel leveled a finger at me. "I know her, and she didn't look crazy about you two being together. So deal, mister." They laughed.

"Actually, it was rough in the beginning, but after her date with Randolph—"

"Wait, shut up! She went out on a date. Sam's mom? But she's married."

"Separated, I think," I said. "You didn't know?"

"No, this is news to me," Rachel said. She dribbled some cream into her cup. "That's gotta hurt Tim. Did Sam say how her dad was doing? What's he going to do now? Is the campaign still on? I was thinking about working on it, maybe it's time to change careers."

"Now I'm confused. What are you talking about?"

Rachel seemed surprised. "You do know what Sam's dad does, don't you?"

"No, not really. He works for the state, somehow. Samantha was pretty vague about it."

Rachel's mouth fell open. "You mean to tell me you didn't background check Sam?"

"Yeah, I did, but not her family." After I said it, I hated myself for it.

Had I been lazy or stupid? I wasn't sure which. I wondered if he was a media guy or something. Maybe that was where Samantha got the bug for working in television.

"He's just a state senator, is all. Senator Timothy Rhodes."

"I could see her wanting to keep a lid on that, I guess." Then I thought about Randolph. "At least he's not a lawyer."

"He travels around a lot, so maybe their marriage isn't what it appears to be. The plot thickens." Rachel wagged her eyebrows. "His primary office is in Orlando, but the capitol building is in Tallahassee. Maybe he's got a girlfriend on the side."

"One of those interns fresh out of college?" Jen chimed in.

"Oh yeah, that'd be perfect—fucking someone close to his daughter's age. He does have a history of liking younger women. After all, he married one," Rachel said.

"Well, I've never met him, and it's not a great idea to put things out there without having any proof. So, let's change the subject, or I'll have to head out." Having raised my voice, I looked around to see a few people staring in our direction.

"Jeez. I was just having fun." Rachel got defensive but lightened up fast. "See, Jen? The guy's in love, defending his girl's family's honor. Why can't I meet a guy like you?"

"Yeah, me too," Jen said.

The conversation faded. The girls talked about some of the shopping they could do in the city. I decided to skip the office for now and just head straight over to the Ackerman residence. My mind wandered to Samantha and the cabin. I hadn't been there in a few weeks and was itching to go. Maybe I'd tell Julius I was taking two weeks off and head out there with Samantha, relax, and enjoy the isolation. We could plan our future.

"I wanted to ask, what did you and Samantha tell Cynthia about your name not being Rachel?"

"Oh…" Rachel started to laugh. "Well…"

Two cops entered the coffee shop. My pulse quickened, my body stiffened, and I eagle-eyed them all the way to the counter. Rachel was telling her story, but I didn't hear a word. My focus was on the two cops and why they were asking questions.

They showed the attractive barista a sheet of paper. She took a look at it and nodded her head. They talked for a minute, then the cops split up—one was heading away from us, and the other was heading in our direction. I could feel my lungs constricting as he drew closer. I wondered how well asthmatic people fare in prison.

"Excuse me folks, I just wanted to let you know that the Chicago Police Department is offering full immunity through a gun return drive we are having. It's no questions asked if you bring in a firearm for disposal. Can I leave you with a flyer?"

"Sure, officer. You're kinda cute—will you be there?" Rachel asked. The officer flushed, smiled, and handed her a brochure. She took the flyer, looking at it with interest.

Considering what I'd done in the past year and the fact that I was just then sitting with two escorts, that guy had missed the perfect opportunity to meet his arrest quota for the month in one fell swoop.

The cops picked up their coffee order and headed out the door.

"What's with you?" Jen stared at me.

"Nothing, why?"

"You look like you've seen a ghost."

"I'd better fly," I rose from my chair.

"Hey, you got a picture of Sam I can show Jen?"

"Uh, yeah," I flipped through my phone's photo gallery. "Here's some from the dinner party." I handed the phone to Rachel.

"Cute," she said, showing it to Jen.

"Lucky guy. I can see why he passes on freebies. Girls aren't really my thing, but I would definitely go for her."

I didn't really know how to respond to that. "Thanks, I guess."

Rachel swiped through some of the pictures. "Here's Peter, my client. That's Randolph. I still can't believe Sam's mom went out with him."

"Stranger things, right?" Jen said. "Whoa. Why do you have a picture of Madame Zoe? You work for the agency?" Jen gasped.

"What? Who looks like Madame Zoe?" I took the phone and laughed when I saw the picture. "That's Margaret Ackerman." I stood up. "I gotta go." As I put the phone in my pocket, I said my goodbyes and made my way towards the door. Two steps later, I turned and headed back.

"Why did you say that?" I asked Jen.

"Because to me that looks exactly like Madame Zoe. The woman who runs our business."

Strange that she would say that. "Are you sure?"

"Yes, I'm sure."

They say everybody has a doppelganger. Odd that Margaret's would be an escort service madam. "So, you've met her? This Madame Zoe?"

"Yes. She interviewed me," Jen said.

I turned to Rachel and asked. "Why didn't you meet Madame Zoe when you got hired?"

"Like I told you before, Addison vouched for me, so I was good to go as is."

I wondered if when Margaret set me up on blind dates whether she used the women from the escort service. Was Julius involved? My mind was flooded with questions.

"Ty, hey, come back to earth." Rachel snapped her fingers. "You look more confused than a polar bear in the Bahamas. So, you know her as *Margaret*? What else do you know about her? Do you know her well?"

"Apparently not," I said in utter disbelief.

FORTY-SEVEN

The quaint two-tone chime of the Ackermans' doorbell could be heard through the thick oak door. No one answered, so I tried again. Had I missed them notifying me about a vacation or a business trip? I used my key. The entryway was dark, and my eyes needed time to adjust from the change of light from the bright sun outdoors. I took two steps, and my toe hit something hard. The surprise jolted me and got my blood pumping.

"Damn it," I yelled. I hobbled to the wall, feeling for the light switch. The lights revealed that I'd tripped over one of the several bags of luggage that were on the floor.

"Julius? Margaret?" I waited for a reply. Nothing. "It's me. Ty." Nothing.

I slowly moved into the living room. I paused this time to let my eyes adjust to the dark room. Why was everything so dark? I couldn't recall it ever being this dark at their place. I fumbled my way over to a lamp. The room was large, so one lamp did a poor job of lighting the whole room. Shadows concealed the corners, but nothing looked out of the ordinary. I headed for the kitchen.

It was also dark, but everything was neatly in its place. There were no dirty dishes in the sink; no containers had been left out. Somebody was planning on going away for a long time.

The upstairs was similarly vacant and impeccably clean. I headed back down toward the living room and stopped as quickly as I'd entered—a shadow in the corner had moved. It would have been the perfect time to have had a gun on me, but did I have one? No. I'd had all those guns at my disposal only a few days earlier, and today I had nothing.

"All right, take what you want and get out, fast," I said. "Come on, I'll give you a free pass, but if you hurt the owners of this place, I'll hunt ya down." The shadowy figure moved into the light.

"You're sweet for letting me take what's already mine, dear."

"Oh, Margaret. You had me worried. I was about to call the police. Where's Julius taking you this time?"

"He's not going, just me. I made some mistakes, and I need to leave town for a bit."

"Oh, come on." I moved closer.

"Stay right there, Ty." In her delicate hand was a small caliber revolver, the barrel pointed at me like an accusatory finger.

"Margaret, what's going on?" Was it true what the girls had told me? Was it really Margaret who had hired them? I liked to think I was pretty savvy when it came to figuring people out—seeing through any barriers they'd erected, any illusions they'd used to hide their true natures. It was part of my job as an investigator. But *Margaret*? I decided to take the direct approach. "Might you be running an escort business? Tell me, I can help you get out of whatever trouble you're in, please."

"Just stay there." She gestured with the gun. "I don't have much time. I've been the one keeping you alive, and I'll be damned if I'm gonna let them harm you now because of me."

"You're scaring me. Put down the gun and talk to me." I stepped closer.

"Stop. Now. I can't harm you, I always wanted a son." Tears rolled down her cheeks. "I loved you so."

"And I love you. We have plenty of years left together me and you. And now Samantha."

"Oh, I did something bad; something that needs to be paid for. Otherwise, they'll hurt you." More tears welled up in her eyes.

"It's, it's not so bad. Please." I reached out my hand. "Please give me the gun."

"You have to listen to me. She didn't have to take that codebook. All she needed to do was lie there with her legs spread and do what she was told."

"Are you talking about Addison? Samantha's friend? You knew her?"

"She worked for me; I run the escort business—they put me in charge. Mike runs the day-to-day stuff. We were making money hand over fist. Then she took that codebook. I had to stop her."

I felt cold—sick to my stomach. "You killed Addison, Capone the cop, and Elizabeth? *Our* Elizabeth?"

"Ian sent his guy to kill Addison. The others just got in the way. I had to, otherwise they would have killed you."

"What? *Me?*"

"You'd met Sam. Those two buffoons hit the wrong car that night out in the woods, then you came along. You couldn't have just dropped her off at the hospital, could you? No, that's not how we raised you, is it? No, you had to go and fall in love with her and dig into her friend's disappearance."

I took a deep breath and put a hand to my forehead. This was beyond belief, but it explained a lot. I was still reeling from the news of Samantha's dad being a state senator, and now this. Like being struck by lightning, a thought flashed through my head. If she knew the two men that had hit Samantha's car, then did she also know the connection between Ian and the—

"You have ties to the Syrian weapons, don't you?" I said.

"Yes."

"Does Julius?"

"No. He knows nothing."

"Ian?"

"He's part of it, and Superintendent Cooper, too. But Cooper's dead. Ian killed him."

"Why? How did you get involved?"

"A long time ago," her gaze wandered, lost in remembrance, "Julius made some investments, and they paid off big. He thought I needed a hobby, so I started gambling. Local card games at first. Then Vegas—horses, you name it. Before I knew it, I was deep in debt. I couldn't tell Julius, so I took a loan out from the wrong people."

"No, Margaret."

"You're a smart boy. I guess you can see where the story goes from there. They set up the escort business and forced me to oversee the operations. I was able to pay all the money back and make some, too. The business pays very well."

"Why didn't you leave?"

"You know you can't ever leave, son. They threatened to kill Julius and you. I couldn't have that. Now the Syrians—" A car's brakes squeaked outside, and we both turned toward the window.

"Give me the gun," I yelled.

One car door slammed, and then another.

"Come on, damn it. *Now!*"

"They're here. They've found me. And now they'll want their money and guns. Oh god, they'll kill you. They'll kill us both." Her eyes grew wide. The jitters in my stomach spread down my legs and arms. I could not run, I could not just give up. The lock on the front door clicked.

"I have to protect you, son. It's me they want most..."

"What are you going to do?"

"I love you, sweetheart. Run out the back, now."

I saw it happening, but I couldn't stop it. She was so fast, whereas I seemed to move in slow motion. She let out a deep breath and, in one fluid motion, raised the gun to her temple and fired.

The one side of her head blew open, sending a messy spray over the otherwise immaculate room. I caught her before she hit the ground, and I tried to cover the hole, but the blood poured out so fast. Haunting images of Jackie Kennedy in Dallas scrambling to put her husband's pieces back together flashed through my mind.

"No, no, no." I cried, tears blurring my vision. I could not make out who the two figures were that were moving toward me. "Back off," I screamed. "I'll kill you. I have to call 911. No, Margaret, no."

"Ty... Ty, let me see," said a vaguely familiar voice.

"No, you're not going to kill her." I started rummaging around for the gun. He grabbed my shoulder. I pulled away hard. "Fuck off."

"Ty..." With considerable force, I was pulled off Margaret and held down. Too distraught to fight, my body gave up. I felt a towel or tissue rub my eyes. My vision cleared, and I looked up to see Randolph.

"You? You're in with the Syrians, too?"

"What? No. What happened here?"

Randolph propped me up. I saw Julius stooped over Margaret's lifeless body.

"I'm sorry," I whispered.

"... we go live to Meghan Orr, who is standing outside police headquarters."

"David, some good news for a change. In one of the city's most violent years, this past weekend has proved an exception. Police have confirmed that no shootings were reported over the weekend.

"We contacted the area hospitals that see most of the shooting victims, and they've confirmed that no gunshot wounds came in.

"The acting police superintendent had this to say about the weekend's numbers."

"In a tremendous effort made by the police, we saturated the streets this weekend with a strong police presence. And because of those efforts, we have achieved our goal of no gun violence on our streets. This proves that all of us can live together and build a community with peace and love with our neighbors. The police are only one factor—it takes everyone's help for this to succeed. Let's take this and move forward and show the world we are a better people now."

"While the police have their explanation for the sudden drop in gun crime on Chicago's streets, our sources tell us something a bit different, claiming that the warehouse explosion was in fact a key factor in the absence of gun violence over the weekend. Allegedly, a plan was in place to move guns for money which was foiled by an unknown group that has everyone scared and on their best behavior for the time being. We have learned that when the warehouse exploded, it was hiding a cache of guns destined for an overseas buyer—not for neighborhood gangs as first suspected. It appears that the military-grade assault weapons, as well as sniper rifles and grenade launchers, were earmarked for the Syrian government.

"It remains unclear as to who blew up the warehouse. WXNG sources speculate that CIA, MI6, or maybe even factions within Homeland Security are responsible. Police tell us that no security camera footage exists from the hour before until an hour after the warehouse exploded. Clearly, there is much more to this story than police are officially telling us.

"But for now, the city and its residents can feel a little safer. How long will it last? We'll just have to wait and see. Reporting from police headquarters, I'm Meghan Orr for WXNG-TV."

FORTY-EIGHT

It took a while, but with encouragement from Samantha and Jill, I finally got back on schedule with Dr. Renfro. Julius and I were still trying to come to terms with Margaret's death five months after the fact.

"So, how are you?" Dr. Renfro asked.

I opened my mouth to speak but nothing came out. I swallowed some water and took three deep breaths. "Margaret killed herself back in July." I exhaled.

"Oh, Ty. I'm so sorry. It's devastating when one chooses that option. You said this happened a few months ago? How have you been coping with this? You should have come in sooner."

"Samantha's been an immense help, with a few bourbons along the way." I grinned at the halfhearted joke, knowing she wouldn't approve.

"Drinking is never the correct response to grief. I'm glad Samantha is there to help you through it.

Dr. Renfro settled back in her chair. The initial surprise had worn off, and her body language indicated that we were back to business. "A sudden death like that can be a trigger for your depression and anger. You need to be careful. I don't want you slipping back, although you seem to be handling it quite well. How's Julius?"

"Not good. We told everyone at the office it was a burglary gone wrong."

"Julius is strong. Be there for him like Samantha is for you."

"Yes, Samantha's a gift—she doesn't let me get to that dark place. We've been through a lot recently, and we've become closer."

"Well, it seems she has a tranquilizing effect on you and has gotten you back on track. How does she feel about you?"

I nodded. I started thinking about that first time in the cabin, when we were snowed in. About how that one night set a lot of things in motion. We later became killers and thieves, but we did save a lot of lives. Not the lives of anyone we knew, but lives nonetheless. I thought about Addy, Margaret, Elizabeth, and Craig Capone, and I wondered if it had been worth it. In the abstract, yes, but on a personal level, I wanted my friends back. I wanted the burning emptiness I felt inside to stop.

"Ty."

"Huh? Oh, sorry. She loves me too." I nodded. "She's said it."

I took a drink of water.

"You mentioned before that you and Samantha have gone through a lot. Do you want to elaborate?"

"Samantha's friend passed away, her mother visited, and then Margaret..." I tried not to roll my eyes. "That type of stuff." I left out her getting kidnapped and the destruction of the biggest gun running business this side of the Mississippi. Dr. Renfro didn't need to know those details.

"I see." She gave a faint smile of acknowledgement.

I took another sip of water. "For the first time in a long while, I have a clear path forward."

Her look lingered briefly. I wasn't off the hook yet.

"The death of someone close can most certainly trigger change. What makes you say that you have a clear path forward?"

"I believe there's now opportunity for me where I'd thought there was none; maybe I've found my confidence. I've found real friends. Maybe I just want to make the world a better place."

"Having a good support system helps."

"I've decided to leave the firm and start my own investigation business."

"That's a big change. Good for you. Have you told Julius?"

"Yes. We'll still work together—I'll work freelance for the firm, but we'll be able to take on more clients. Start out small, just one or two." My gaze broke, and I smiled.

"We? You said we. Who else is joining you?"

"York Investigations is a team." My smile grew. "Me, Samantha, my friend Frank, and Jill."

"Jill from the firm?"

"Yeah, she'll handle the office. Me and Samantha will do the field work."

"What about—"

"Frank? He'll do what he does best—watch our backs and clean up our messes. We already have a contract in place to do WAR's investigating."

"Great."

"Yeah, I feel pride in ownership. I think we all do, since we all put money into it." We all agreed that the money Frank and I found in the warehouse should be put into our new business, along with some of the money going to charities that each of us chose.

"Well, it sounds like you do have a path forward, a sharp vision."

"Clarity," I said.

"Yes, clarity. We only have a few minutes left. Any questions? I think we're set up for our next few appointments." She stood abruptly and offered her hand. For once I felt good. I had a clear head and a sense of direction for the future. I carried that thought all the way to the parking lot.

FORTY-NINE

had Samantha's upper body pinned against the large living room window in my Lake Point Tower apartment—naked, except for her Louboutin's. The city shimmered below in full view, exposed to our desires. A stream of headlights snaked along Lake Shore Drive. The reflected luster off the glass of Chicago's skyscrapers penetrated the dark sky.

Samantha's arms were handcuffed above her head, my right hand holding them there by the chain that linked the cuffs together. The cuffs were strong and tight. They would leave marks on her wrist... she wanted the marks. She loved being submissive, whether it was me or Jill being the dominant one, she got off on it.

"Are you going to be a good girl tonight?" I whispered.

"Yes, I'm here to please you, sir." She huffed through her serpentine smile. "Ooh, I'm ready for you," she beckoned.

I kicked her legs open wider, surprising her. She accepted it with pleasure, her lower body moving to a leisurely rhythm.

"Take me," she yelled.

My thrusting increased... not much longer now. Her hair was up for the party tonight. I kissed and bit her neck, making her moan. My grunting amplified; I released her arms, cupping her breast in my hand instead, squeezing softly. She kept her arms in place, the cuffs clanking on the cold glass with each thrust.

The sweat on my brow ran down my cheeks, my muscles tightening. My legs went weak as I emptied into her.

"I can feel you," she whispered. She turned around, throwing her handcuffed arms around my neck and kissing me. She bit my lower lip and tugged gently, then let it go.

"I love you, Tiger." Her serpentine smile was back once more.

My open hand caressed her bare ass as she walked away. She glanced over her shoulder, biting her lower lip in a show of teasing petulance.

We were going to the office Christmas party, which was nowadays called the Holiday Celebration party. A formal affair, Samantha had made me get a new black suit, shirt, and tie. She did the same and bought a new dress and shoes—Louboutin, of course.

I waited in the living room, taking in the sights of the city. I heard the familiar clicking of her heels as she approached. In the window's reflection, I saw her coming from down the hall.

"Well, what do you think? Good enough to go out with you?" she asked.

"More than you'll ever know. Stunning, my love, absolutely stunning."

Her eyes smoldered behind a smoky, copper-glitter eyeshadow. Her long lashes waved every time she blinked. Glossy cherry lipstick made her mouth inviting. A pair of chocolate diamond earrings adorned her earlobes. The little red dress was a knockout. The modest scooped neckline was framed by cute cap sleeves. A scalloped hem finished off the twirl-worthy skirt, and the back plunged lower than the front—all was held together by a little gold zipper that ran the length of the back.

She completed the outfit with a gold open heart pendant necklace that sparkled with full-cut diamonds.

She stopped and spun—the dress flared, but not high enough to reveal what was underneath.

"I have something for you." I held out a gift bag.

"Aw, for me? You're so good to me."

She took the bag, her bracelets jingling on her wrists.

She opened it and held up a pair of black panties.

"Do you want me to wear these now?"

"Yes, along with this." I showed her a smooth, contoured plastic oval about the size and shape of a small bar of soap.

"Looks like a paperweight. What's it supposed to do?"

"Here, like this." I showed her the little pocket in the panties where it fit. "It's a panty pleasurizer. When you walk around or dance tonight, it will rub those sensitive spots. Keep you warmed up all night so when we get home—"

"I'll be ready to go. Is that what's on your devilish mind, Mr. York?" She put her arms around me. "You like owning me." Her serpentine smile spread wide. "I'm yours for the taking."

We headed out of Lake Point Tower; the firm had reserved the ninety-ninth-floor event deck in the Willis Tower for the party. The view would be spectacular on such a clear night, not to mention the food, drinks, and dancing. It was a family affair, so spouses and children were welcome.

We were both quiet in the car, still recovering from the sexcapades we'd just enjoyed. The ride to the party was short. We got into the Willis Tower elevator with some people I recognized from work and we made the appropriate introductions. My back was to the wall with Samantha's arm hooked through mine—the proper way for a gentleman to escort a lady in public. The attendant pushed the button and we took off. I reached into my pocket for the remote to Samantha's pleasurizer and pressed the button.

"Woo hoo," Samantha screamed. She jumped a bit, clinging to my arm. The other occupants in the elevator turned to look.

"Sweetheart, are you okay?" I played dumb.

Laughing a bit, and looking perplexed, she said, "Yeah. Felt something a bit weird. I don't know what it was. Vertigo, maybe."

We were passing the fiftieth floor.

I had the remote in my hand and was looking at it.

"What's that?" she said, straightening her dress.

"I'm not sure."

"Looks like a garage door opener. What are you doing with it?" She took out her compact and checked her makeup in the mirror.

"I don't know, what do you think this button does?"

"Push it," she said absently.

"Naw, I'd better not."

"Oh, just *push it*." She snapped her compact closed.

I pushed and held it, hearing a faint hum. Samantha shot to attention. Her eyes and face lit up like the lobby's Christmas tree. Her fingers dug deep into my arm; her legs quaked. In fact, her whole body shivered. She groaned a bit, trying not to scream. I released the button.

She doubled over just as we hit the ninety-ninth floor, and the doors opened. A few people glanced our way but seemed none the wiser.

"Me thinks I know what that button does, Mr. York," she whispered.

I smiled broadly, proud of myself. It was going to be a fun night.

I helped her out of the elevator, and we were greeted by a hostess. We received a table number and checked out coats.

"Oh, I'm so wet now I feel it running down my legs. Dirty pool, Mr. York. You're a very bad boy." She grinned.

"I like to torture you."

"I like it when you do." She took my hand and led me to the bar. I gave her a little juice and she cried out, "Ow, stop it," and laughed.

"So, what will it be tonight? Red or white?"

"Let's do... white."

"A pinot grigio for the lady and I'll have a bourbon," I said to the bartender. "I believe Mr. Ackerman is holding a bottle of Blanton's for me. Neat, please."

We surveyed the room, looking for Jill, but had no luck. We saw Randolph being his usual self, loud and obnoxious. The lawyers and partners were required to wear tuxedos and most of the women wore black dresses. The rest of the employees wore dress attire.

We were on our second drink, and Samantha was beginning to loosen up as we stood and talked, her body swaying to the beat of the music. It was your usual dance house music mixed in with a Christmas song every now and then. Hips swaying, she flared her skirt out a bit—the wine in her glass swirling in time with her hips.

She devoured me with her eyes. We were fixated on each other. She danced over to me slowly, inching closer and closer.

Heads turned to watch, but she didn't care—I was her focus, nothing and no one else.

"Dance with me," she said, her voice sultry.

"If he won't, I sure will, you sexy bitch," said Jill, suddenly appearing.

Samantha shrieked and threw her arms around her. "Finally, it's been forever."

"Look at you two." Jill wore a black dress with a low neckline that revealed a perfect amount of cleavage. Her black hair and outfit made her look dark and mysterious.

Jill reached out and took my hand, more in a handshake than anything else. In public, it was strictly business with us.

"You two are funny." Samantha let out a full laugh.

"She's on her third wine," I told Jill.

"Oh my, she's ready to go. Aren't ya, babe?" Jill looked at Samantha.

"Hey, where are the critters?" Samantha and Jill were arm in arm.

"Let's see, they're dancing, so..." Jill looked around the dance floor. "There." She pointed out the kids in the crowd.

"Aw, too cute," Samantha said.

We watched the kids for a bit, all of us smiling.

"Girl, you do look amazing—and you reek of sex," Jill said.

"Guilty as charged," Samantha said, glowing.

Jill took Samantha's hands and slid her bracelets up, revealing the handcuff marks from earlier.

"You're such a slut," Jill giggled.

Caprice and Preston ran up and greeted us.

"You guys both looked so great out there," Samantha said.

"Thank you," Caprice said.

"Sam, do you want to dance with me?" Preston stood wringing his hands.

"Why yes, I would. Thank you, kind sir."

"But *I* want to dance with Sam," Caprice pouted.

"Let's all dance together, would that be okay?" Jill offered.

"That'll be fun," Preston said.

"We'll let Ty hold up the bar. I'll get ya later." Samantha loved taunting me.

I ordered another drink and watched the dance party. The place was decorated to the nines and very festive. It had been one hell of a year, and the spirit of the season made me appreciate all I had.

I took a walk around and shook hands, wishing everyone good tidings. I found myself looking out the window. The view was breathtaking. The liquid lights shimmered in the skyscrapers' windows, creating a cascading multi-colored waterfall. Adding to the party's décor were the red and green lights shining from the ships on the lake.

Making my way back, I saw that the kids had moved on to better things in the children's play area. And Samantha and Jill were dancing. Damn, they were sexy together, their bodies moving to the beat of the music. I reached for the little remote and pressed the button. Samantha broke from her rhythmic fluid motion to do a herky-jerky dance. I chuckled while she gave me a 'wait-til-later' look. She then proceeded to whisper something in Jill's ear. Jill's shocked expression transformed to amused as she looked at me. She gave me a thumbs up and laughed.

The appetizer table held a bountiful array of nibbles: crab and spinach dip, a chicken crescent wreath, hot wings, meatballs, salsa, and a few more items.

Samantha had returned to the bar, and she looked a bit uneasy as a guy I didn't immediately recognize spoke to her. I couldn't make him out at first, but he was holding her by the arm and pulling her closer. He was big, and suddenly it hit me who he was. I caught some of the conversation as I approached.

"You're hurting me. Let go," she said, trying to twist out of his grasp.

"So, who... who are you with? You really look good. I watched you dancin' out th... there, maybe we could take a s... s... spin around the dance floor. Who are you with again?"

I walked up.

"I'm with Tanner York," Samantha said, visibly peeved.

"What... he's like your brother? Cousin or somethin'?" He reached out to touch her.

Samantha moved away and then saw me. Relief flashed across her face. "Oh man, am I glad to see you." She wrapped her arm around me, almost painfully tight.

"Hey, Ty. Just talking to your sister or some... somethin'. She won't tell me."

Rule number one for office parties: never be the drunk guy. He'd broken the cardinal rule.

"She's my date and I think you've had a few too many."

"I'm fine. H... how did you... get some chick... like this?" He laughed while he swayed, just about ready to fall over. "Did you p-p-pay for this like that other loser?" He pointed to Peter and grabbed for Samantha again. "Come 'ere, baby girl."

"Back off," I said, swatting his arm away like a fly at a picnic.

"Is there a problem?" the bartender said.

"H-hey, I'll kick yer ass, loser. In fact... I'll kill ya."

"Just a bit over-served," I told the bartender.

"There's always one," he said.

"Who is this guy?" Samantha asked.

"Samantha Rhodes, meet Donny Sanders. Otherwise known as Jill's husband."

Samantha couldn't hide her shock.

"Are you the Sam that hangs out with my wife? She talks about you all the time." He looked her up and down. "Ya know, you should come over when I'm home, we could have some fun."

"Daddy, Mommy wants your help," Caprice said in a soft voice.

"Aw shit, I can't relax at all," he said. "Okay, pumpkin, le's go. Le's find out wha' yer mom can't do now." They vanished into the crowd.

"Poor Jill," Samantha sighed.

"Yeah, he's a real catch, if you ask me," I huffed. *Didn't know he was that bad with the booze.*

"That explains a lot. We have to help her before the situation gets completely out of hand."

"What are you talking about?"

"He beats her," she said, deadpan.

"What? Did she tell you that?"

"Not in so many words, but now that I've met this jerk, all the signs are there. I knew it." She let out a deep breath. "First, the most obvious sign: the bruises. It's not like she'll come in with a black eye or a broken nose. That's too recognizable as abuse. It's the subtle ones on the arms, her sides, and the inner thighs, where he forces or punches her legs open. The shoulders—he's constantly pulling on her arms. Those don't come from kitchen cabinets or little kids climbing all over you."

"I don't know what to say. We've known each other for five years, and I never saw it. I feel—"

"There are the emotional signs as well. She avoids certain topics on her home life. She told me she can never do anything right at home, but she's the smartest woman I know. She's totally confident at work and runs the place as if it were her own—you know that from working with her."

I nodded.

"But she can't do anything right according to her husband? Doesn't add up. Have you never caught her staring into space? And she won't tell you what she's thinking about?"

"She's told me she has some secrets, like we all do." My blood was starting to boil. *Why hadn't I noticed these things? Was I too preoccupied with Ian and my own issues? Some investigator I am.*

"Look at it this way," Samantha continued. "He's here, drunk, hitting on me, and now he's shifted his attentions to that other girl." She pointed it out to me. "While his smart, gorgeous, and loving wife, who is the mother of his children, is in the same room.

"Her house has no pictures of them together—not even a wedding photo. She says they're not photogenic people. And how come we only see her when he's out of town on business? I know the kids, but my thought is that when he's home, he probably threatens to kidnap them if she leaves—no going out with her friends and no girls' nights, or else he'd probably accuse her of cheating on him. My hunch is that he doesn't even go out of town on work trips—he's cheating on her, for sure." Samantha turned and looked at me with frosty eyes. "Jill would have never started our affair unless she'd finally had enough. This is not going to end well. We were so busy with Ian and wrapped up in us that we didn't see this happening right under our noses. Ty, I want you to promise me that you'll get her out of this situation."

That was the first time I'd ever seen Samantha look so deadly serious. "At the dinner party, Caprice said she wanted to stay and live in the clouds with the angels, so the devil couldn't get them."

"Maybe that devil is her father," Samantha said.

Jill approached. "Hey, you two. What's going on? What did you do, Ty? Sam looks like someone just kicked a puppy. You okay, sweets?" She wrapped her arm around Samantha's waist.

"We're fine, Jill. Just talking sports," Samantha joked.

"Jill..." I didn't know how to start; I didn't know which words to say.

"Yes?"

"Um..." This was not the time or place. "You really look fantastic tonight. I wish you could come home with us."

"Oh, I've been thinking about that all night. I'm trying to work it out. I'll let you guys know." She took Samantha and met up with her kids on the dance floor.

I watched them in silence for a while. My body was numb. This would not end well for him, I thought, and maybe not for Jill if she got caught in the crossfire. On the outside, I was business as usual, but a storm was brewing on the inside.

FIFTY

My body was eerily cold as we drove home, but not from the outside temperature. How could I have missed it? All the signs that Samantha talked about—she was right. But how was she able to piece it together when I couldn't? My muscle memory took over driving as I thought of Jill having to defend herself against his closed fists. I saw each of the bruises she had dismissed with an excuse and imagined how they'd got there. I thought not only about Jill but also about the kids. Had they witnessed any of this abuse? Did he beat them, too?

My hands tightened around the steering wheel as my fury grew. My insides burned as I saw the pain and distress in her eyes. I envisioned her getting into bed with him, unwilling but feeling too trapped to refuse, surrendering her body for his twisted, sadistic pleasure.

My fist hit the leather-padded wheel. "Damn it! Why wouldn't she tell us?"

"She has her reasons," Samantha said, staring through the windshield. "We all do."

"Why?" I muttered.

I felt ashamed to be a man. Jill was a decent, hard-working woman and a great mother and friend. She'd saved our lives.

"The three of us have exchanged bodily fluids. You don't think she could trust us with this? We have to get her and the kids the hell out of there," I said.

"I know, and we will, but it's not going to be tonight, or tomorrow even. She needs to come to that decision on her own. I'll talk with her—we can talk with her—give her options and let her know that we support her." When I pulled into a gas station, Samantha asked, "I'm getting a bottled water, do you want anything?"

"I'm fine." This news had triggered my PTSD, and I was boiling over. I needed an outlet.

She ran into the Quick Mart. I filled the tank, completely oblivious to the cold outside. When the pump shut off, I returned the nozzle and hit the button for the receipt. The digital readout said CLERK HAS RECEIPT.

"Damn it!" I slammed my hand into the message screen and cracked it.

With clenched teeth I stormed into the Quick Mart. "Hey, asshole," I said. The kid behind the counter sat up. Looking through thick glasses, his skinny arms dropped the paperback novel he was reading.

"What, are you too fuckin' lazy to get off your ass and add paper to pump seven? Is it too fucking cold out? What you gonna bitch about? The lack of pay you're getting or that you're too good for this job and you don't have to deal with this shit? Dickwad."

"Uh... s-sorry... I didn't know, here." He printed out the receipt and held it out to me, nervously.

I took one massive stride toward his shaking hand.

"STOP!" I froze, immediately recognizing Samantha's voice. I turned my head to see her marching toward me from the back of the store. Her long coat was off one shoulder, and her hair bounced with every step.

She licked her lower lip, "Stop it, now." Her voice was commanding, but not loud.

My jaw was still tight, but the pounding in my chest had slowed. Her confidence was appealing—I felt more attracted to her than ever. As she approached, it was like I was seeing her for the first time.

She reached the counter and said, "Hello. I'm Sam, and this is my guy, Ty. May I ask your name?"

The kid looked down at his name tag, breaking the trance in which he had found himself. "My name is Walter... Walter's my name, miss."

"It's Sam, remember? I want to apologize for my man, for him storming in and yelling at you like that. He shouldn't have done that, but he can be a bit of a... Tiger, at times." She shot me a glance.

"It's okay, I-I'm used to it. I get angry customers in all the time." His voice sounded rickety.

"Ty, would you like to say something to Walter?"

"What? Fuck no."

She turned to Walter and said, "We just received some bad news about a dear friend of ours, and we're having a difficult time dealing with it. So, we're not quite ourselves tonight. My Tiger, here, is taking it a bit hard."

I was stunned by the way she kept her voice so even and calm—it was extraordinary. She was extraordinary.

"Ty, please apologize to Walter for your rudeness."

My eyes narrowed and my brows came together. She had successfully talked me off the ledge. "I'm sorry for how I acted… Walter." I cracked a quick grin.

"Now, in the spirit of the holidays, let's shake hands, shall we?" She slipped her arm through mine and walked me to the counter.

We shook hands.

"Here's something for the water and for your trouble, Walter." She put down a hundred-dollar bill.

Walter's eyes grew big. "Jeez. Thanks, Sam." He snatched it up and put it in his pocket.

"Goodnight," she said.

I peeled out of the gas station. She reached down to my crotch.

"Man, you are rock hard." Her serpentine smile was ready to strike.

I pulled into Lake Point Tower's garage and killed the engine. She knew I wanted her bad. I made a move toward her.

"Wait." She held my arm. "Look, I'm just as pissed off as you are. I should have said something about my suspicions to you earlier, but we need to handle this slow, carefully, and think this through with clear heads."

Her eyes were earnest. I looked into them as if I were reading her mind. It took a second or two, but what she wanted to do eventually registered—we had become so close that our thoughts were practically one. I tilted my head slightly, acknowledging that I understood. But just to confirm, she said it out loud. "Let's kill the motherfucker."

FIFTY-ONE

A cold Friday found us on either end of the couch. Samantha was wearing her usual lounge attire—one of my dress shirts and nothing else. Our bare feet touching, we were deep into our mystery novels. It was mid-January, and a brief snow shower had made for a wonderful winter weekend at the cabin. I had chopped the firewood for the day earlier on and opened the first bottle of wine for the night. The smell of cookie dough filled the room as Samantha had a fresh batch cooling on the kitchen counter.

The last few weeks had made us the most boring couple on the face of the planet. Since the Christmas party, I'd worked sparingly. We'd hammered out the details of our new business venture, but mainly we'd spent our days together talking, reading, listening to music, and just loving one another. We let it all just come to us—we had no plans, nowhere to go, and no thoughts of changing the world.

I'd gotten Samantha hooked on crime and mystery novels, along with classical music. Her favorite was Mozart—although she'd never admit it. Instead, she felt she needed to profess to like some more obscure composer's works. Someone lesser known or not quite so mainstream as the Mozarts, Beethovens, and Bachs of the world. But playing at that moment was a piece she'd selected: Mozart's "Symphony No. 40." One of his best, if not the best.

She'd been on pins and needles since we'd got the call from Jill to say she was heading out to the cabin to talk to us. Jill was vague over the phone and wanted to talk in person. We hadn't seen her since the Christmas party. According to Samantha, their phone calls had been brief, friendly, and more about the new business than anything else. They had not been as intimate as they had been before the party. Perhaps Jill suspected that we'd figured out her secret and was keeping her distance to avoid a lecture. I thought that with the holidays, family coming over, and the kids being out of school it was just a busy time for everyone. But Samantha wasn't buying it. "Not even a little time for her kitten," she complained.

"I can't read anymore, I'm going to text her," Samantha said.

"She's probably driving and won't be able to reply," I answered.

"Then I'll call, no? What if she's going to tell us bad news? Maybe she wants to have no part of us anymore."

"Let's let her do the talking first. She has something she wants to tell us, so maybe it's good news. Like she's leaving him. Besides, she said she was staying all weekend—if she wanted out, would she stay for the whole weekend?"

"I guess, but if it's something stupid like she wanted to tell us she bought a new car... boy I'll really take it out on her tonight—I'll play the madame and she can be my kitten." She opened her book with force, as if the book itself was fighting back.

It was closing in on late afternoon when Samantha's phone rang.

"It's not Jill—it's a number I don't recognize," she said.

"So, answer it," I said, and she did.

"Hello, this is Sam. Oh, hi. What's wrong? What? When? How bad? Oh no. What did the doctor say? Oh God. Oh my God."

"What? What is it? Who is it?" I whispered. She waved at me to be quiet.

"I see. I'm so sorry. I'm here with Ty, yes. We're coming. It will take about an hour and a half. We're leaving now. How are the kids? Okay, good. We'll talk when we see you. Yes, just take it easy. Get some rest. We'll see you soon, and thanks for letting us know."

"What?" I asked.

I could see tears well up in Samantha's eyes and slowly glide down her cheeks. She took a deep breath to gather herself before speaking. "We're too late. That was Jill's mom. Jill was beaten up pretty bad. She's at Hinsdale Hospital in serious condition—one cracked rib, a fractured cheek bone, and a busted nose. They'll have to operate on her face." She ran to me and hugged me, sobbing. "They're going to operate on her face."

"How did it happen?"

"The police said Donny found her, and he said that she'd told him it was an attempted robbery. She was right outside her house when he found her." Her sobbing increased.

"That's bullshit," I said.

"He did it, he did it. He found out she was coming here, and he did it. You know that, don't you?"

"Yes. Yes, I do." I wrapped her in my arms and never wanted to let go.

"She's unconscious, Ty. Our girl was beaten up and is lying unconscious in a hospital. We have to go, now." She ran and got her stuff.

Traffic was light, and we made good time. We arrived at the hospital and found out that Jill had been moved from the emergency room to a private one. We found the nurses' station on her floor where we met Jill's mother, who introduced herself as Beverly. She clued us in on the latest developments. They were waiting for a surgeon to fix her nose and cheekbone. Beverly said that Jill had been floating and out of consciousness, and she warned us to brace ourselves for what we were about to see.

"Where's Donny?" I said.

"We don't know," she answered, with a stern look that only a pissed-off mother can give.

Samantha and I walked up to the half-open, dull brown door to Jill's room. Samantha entwined her fingers in mine. Taking a deep breath, I pushed open the door. We took one step in; the room was devoid of all beauty. A flaccid curtain hung open. The walls were beige in color and bare, only rubber glove dispensers and hand sanitizers adorned them. It was a stark reminder that cleanliness was the staff's priority. My nose caught a whiff of cleaning antiseptics, further drawing my attention to the myriad germs we could be bringing in. Jill was the room's only occupant. She lay on a plastic-framed bed with her upper torso propped up by about 30 degrees. She lay as still as a corpse.

Her face was swollen, welted, and all shades of purple with a lot of red thrown in. The eye sockets were puffy and saturated with a gooey substance. Her nose was an entirely new shape. Cheekbones looked raw and puffy. Her lips were fat and curled over, with deep cuts from her teeth. A patch of hair was missing from her head. I winced just thinking about someone pulling hard enough to yank the hair out, roots and all.

Samantha went to hold her hand but suddenly pulled back. "I don't want to hurt her," she said, crying.

Jill's arms were covered in bruises, the appearance of which made her look diseased.

Samantha bent down as tears fell and soaked Jill's flimsy hospital gown. "We're here, baby. You're safe now."

I set up a chair by the bed so Samantha could sit next to her. I paced. The pain in my chest went to my stomach, making me queasy. It took seven strides to reach one side of the room from the other.

"She's awake," Samantha said.

"Hi there," I said.

"Hey back," Jill said in a low voice.

"Take it easy, do you know where you are?" I said.

"Waaateeer." Jill struggled to sound it out.

Samantha got a cup of cold water and a straw. She held the cup while Jill sipped.

"If you didn't want to come out to the cabin, all you had to do was tell us you were busy this weekend. You didn't have to go to such extreme lengths," Samantha said.

Jill laughed, but it was quickly followed by a grimace from the pain. "Don't make me laugh."

"Do you know what happened?" I asked.

"Unfortunately, I do," Jill said. "And yes, what you're thinking, about who did it. It's true." She strained to look at Samantha through her swollen eyes. "For me, do nothing. For my kids' sake. We'll handle this when I can. Please, I don't want him to take my babies. He said he would."

"He needs to pay—"

"Honey, please. Not now," I said, begging Samantha to stop pushing it. Fear gripped me. Now that Jill was awake, it had all become real. And it had become my problem. And the outcome wasn't looking good.

"I know I should have left long ago. But... I just couldn't." Jill looked at me and said, "Do you want to know the worst part? You think that this is the best you can do. That you don't deserve any better."

"Jill, you are better, and you deserve so much more. You deserve to be happy." It got to me then. I started to cry. Samantha put her arms around me and cried along.

"Ty, I want you to promise me something."

"Anything."

She swallowed hard as the pain etched across her face. "When I'm better, you'll take the three of us to Paris. I want to see France again. With both of you."

"We can do that." I smiled.

While waiting for Frank in the hospital cafeteria, Beverly approached my table. I felt consumed by guilt, shifted uneasily in my chair. I took a puff of my inhaler.

"May I sit?"

"Please." I motioned with my hand to the chair opposite me and stood.

"Thank you."

"Mrs. Sinclair, I'm so sorry…"

"You're not the one at fault, Ty. There's only one asshole to blame for all this."

"Jill needs to tell the police—they can arrest him."

"He'll just get out, take the kids, and beat her again. Maybe if I'd stood up to her father, she'd be happily living in Paris now." Beverly shook her head.

"You don't know that. Besides, you have two super grand-children."

Her mood swung from soft and vulnerable to hard and certain. "Frankly, I don't know what your relationship is with my daughter, and I don't want to know. But you and Sam seem special to her. She talks about Sam all the time, and she looks up to you. Based on what she tells me, you can do no wrong. So, I'm asking. If you care about Jill, will you… can you?"

"Do what, exactly, Beverly?"

"If Donny were to have an accident, he wouldn't be missed. No one would question it, he drinks, drives—"

Out of the corner of my eye I saw Frank, so I held up my hand. He stopped.

I got up and took Frank by the arm. I told him Jill's room number and said that I would meet him up there. Frank left.

I returned to Beverly and said, "If you want me to help solve this problem, I'm going to need that man's help, and the less you know about it, the better."

"I see."

"Good. I believe I can help you with your problem. Give us an hour with Jill before you come up. We'll be gone by then. It's better that you have minimal contact with us. Don't use your phone to call us. We'll get you a phone to use. And we never had this conversation." I raised my eyebrows, waiting for an answer.

"Okay," she said.

I headed up to meet Frank.

FIFTY-TWO

I hadn't thought about dying for quite some time. Until tonight. I emptied my inhaler—I'd gone way over my limit of puffs for the day. The source of my anxiety had brought on a slew of breathing problems for me. I had to get it under control. An asthma attack now would weaken me and rob my assassin of the pleasure of facing a worthy opponent.

Slow, deep breaths. *Calm down, buddy.*

The cabin's creaking porch floorboards announced the arrival of my guest. A smile creased my face as the door was broken open by a hurricane force. A giant of a man—no less than six-six, broad shouldered, and with a beefy chest and arms—stumbled in. Confusion and disorientation were written across Donny's face due to the ease with which he'd knocked a solid oak door off its hinges. But when he saw me, like a werewolf, his face contorted with rage.

I took a step back and held up my hands. "Get back, Donny! Don't come any closer, or I'll call the police."

"I'm gonna kill you. Right here, right now." He moved closer.

I pointed my index finger like an arrow. "Don't do anything you'll regret. Leave, now!"

He lunged and grabbed my shirt with both hands, pulling and tugging. My shirt ripped as he twisted me around. My left cheek served as a landing area for his fist. Pain shot across my head, almost knocking me out, but I'd had a lot of practice getting beaten over the past year. I held onto consciousness.

The second punch landed straight in my gut. I doubled over and hit the floor hard.

He was on me again. He flipped me on my back, and before I could realize what was coming, he buried his foot deep in my balls. The pain was like a nail bomb going off inside my body. I screamed, curling into the fetal position. I wheezed for air.

He pulled me up, his large arms powerful, with my feet dangling above the floor. He threw me across the room, and my shoulder bore the brunt of the landing. I slid to a stop by the fireplace. My eyes teared up, and the thump of his footsteps vibrated through me. One thump after another, getting closer.

Air was escaping my lungs and death was filling the void.

"Don't you die on me, you piece of shit." His voice was bilious and full of hate. "I say when you die."

"I... I... I can... can... can't bbbbre... breathe," I begged. "In... inha... inhaler." I crawled slowly at first, while he stood over me. I got to the coffee table and fumbled for the drawer.

"Inhaler." My shaky hand reached into the drawer.

We'd set Donny up. Samantha had arranged to meet him at a local restaurant, plied him with a few drinks, and told him I was having an affair with Jill. Samantha said she was crushed that I would cheat on her and asked if Donny would do something about it. She told him where I'd be tonight, and that I'd be alone. Frank had rigged the cabin with cameras inside and out to capture the break-in and show that I was acting in self-defense.

My previous charitable donations would ensure that the outcome of any potential court case would be firmly in my favor. We left Jill out of our little scheme; she had just been released from the hospital a few days earlier and was still much too weak. We would fill her in afterwards; better to beg for forgiveness than ask for permission.

He'd busted my face good. I guessed that he'd broken a few of my ribs and maybe my collarbone, but he'd made two fatal mistakes.

First, he hadn't disabled my legs. Second, he'd trusted me to reach into the drawer and pull out my inhaler, not my Glock 26. With a quick roll, I was on my back and pulling my knees to my chest. I thrust my legs forward as hard as I could. My feet caught him square in the chest; his shocked face disappeared as he fell backward. I had the time I needed to pull out the Glock and slam the clip in.

Donny was back on his feet fast. Still on my back, I held the gun out in front of me.

"What the hell?" he bellowed.

White teeth flashed under his curled lips. Fists at the ready, he looked me square in the eye. "Time to die for what you did. I'm gonna kill you."

"Not today," I said.

He lunged as if the gun weren't even there. I squeezed the trigger. The gun flashed white-hot, popped, and recoiled, the bullet hitting his forehead just left of center. All sounds but the hard ringing of the blast vacated my ears. The bullet's impact snapped his head back, and then it flopped forward. An explosion of flesh and brains blew out from the back of his head. The eruption caused a liquid halo, like an electric blender making a smoothie with the top off. A geyser of red blood sprayed over the fireplace mantel and wall. He collapsed on top of me, compressing my chest. More air evacuated from my lungs. The small ragged-edged hole in his forehead oozed blood, soaking my shirt and radiating outward. As he bled, the stench of copper pennies filled the room.

It took a few minutes for me to catch my breath. I reached into the drawer, pulled out a new inhaler, and took two puffs. Instant relief. I was getting my life back.

I lay on the floor with him on top of me as his warm sticky blood flowed like a river over my body and onto the hardwood floor. My hearing came back slowly. The sweet sound of Vivaldi's "Four Seasons" from the stereo replaced the ringing in my ears. I looked around and had crazy thoughts enter my mind about how great the cabin looked from this vantage point. The ceiling fan needed dusting. My eyes wandered to the books on the coffee table. My gaze drifted to the red goo that looked like tomatoes, cantaloupe, and cauliflower sliding down the wall slapped the hardwood floor as it landed. That struck me as funny, and I began to laugh. And laugh. And laugh.

The cabin's kitchen was an open space separated by an L-shaped breakfast island. I walked over to a kitchen cabinet and grabbed my bottle of Blanton's bourbon, poured a full glass, and downed it in two gulps. It flowed down my throat like lava. The heat hit my chest and wrapped around my insides, giving me that comfort of a Kentucky Hug. Despite my desire to feel more remorse, I had none to spare for Donny, a wife-beating slug. I poured another drink.

I hobbled my way to the front porch where I knew of a blind spot from the outdoor cameras. The frosty midnight air hit me hard. From a burner phone, I texted *Done* to the team. I then smashed it and threw it into the woods, despite my sore shoulder's protest.

Picking up my cell, I called Randolph Rockwell—the best attorney in Chicago. He owed me a favor, and it was finally time to collect. "Hello? It's me, Ty."

"What's up, buddy?" Randolph's bellowing voice made me pull the device away from my ear.

"You know that favor you owe me? I'm collecting tonight. I need you at my cabin. Now."

"Wow. Okay, I'm on my way. I happen to be in your neighborhood tonight. Good thing, huh?" I already knew Randolph would be out this way based on his schedule from work. It wasn't a coincidence. "Can you give me a hint as to what this is all about?"

"I shot and killed someone in the cabin. He broke in."

"Shit. You okay? Are there others in the house? Are you still in danger?"

"I'm fine, I'm alone. What should I do?" I mustered up as much distress as I could.

"Call 911. You know what to say." This wasn't a question; it was a statement. Everyone in our line of work knew what to say to the police. "Give the cops just your info—no details until I get there."

"Got it." I hung up, took a deep breath, and dialed 911.

Swirling out of the cabin's chimney stack, smoke escaped upward into the clear dark sky. Naked trees did little to conceal the source of the haze. The giant glowing moon shined on the small central Illinois town of Kickapoo. I stood on the front porch of my cabin as the sirens approached with fervor.

From high above in the massive oak tree, Dash perched on a limb. The moonlight showed me its yellow eyes, piercing the night with a critical glare.

"Don't judge me, Dash."

He replied with a curt *hoot*.

Winter's heartbeat was strong this February, but it hadn't snowed much this season, so the roads were clear. Emergency vehicles would have no trouble arriving quickly.

I felt my eye swell, tighten, and begin to shut, but the frigid air on the rest of my battered body kept the swelling at bay.

The wailing got louder.

"Hey, you'd better scram, or they'll pin it on you," I said to the owl.

The owl's ear tufts perked up, its feet shuffled, and its feathers ruffled. Its head swiveled toward the source of the commotion. Even the trees seemed tense now. The owl knew there would be no hunting at the cabin tonight. He opened his wings and launched himself with one silent thrust from his roost, soaring into the darkness. He cleared the tree and with a quick turn, vanished without a trace.

"I don't blame ya."

I raised my head skyward, closed my eyes took a breath and exhaled.

Snowflakes began to hit my face, and I smiled as they melted. The cold water was cleansing and reminded me of this time last year. It seemed so long ago that I had found Samantha on the side of the road—or had she found me?

I took another breath.

Exhaled.

Happy.

I just killed the devil.

ACKNOWLEDGMENTS

To you, the reader, I owe a tremendous debt of gratitude. Thank you for choosing to read my book. I hope you enjoyed it and found a bit of an escape from this crazy world we live in.

My heartfelt thanks go to Scribendi for their meticulous editing, which elevated this book to a new level. Your expertise and attention to detail are deeply appreciated. Any inaccuracies, mistakes in grammar, timeline, or anything else are on me, the author. I take full responsibility for any errors.

To, Miblart for their outstanding work on formatting and cover design. Your creativity and skill brought my vision to life in a way that exceeded my expectations.

A special thanks to my beta readers, Dora, Nancy, Anthony, Jon, Ron, Greg, Heather, and Sarah Lucente. Your insights were invaluable in developing the story and characters. Your feedback helped shape this book into what it is today.

Two very special people, Claudia H and Laura Murphy, took a thorough analysis into my writing and characters, often engaging in lengthy discussions about the story. Your honest critiques, though sometimes hard to hear, made me a better person and storyteller. I am forever grateful for your dedication and support.

To my family and friends, your unwavering support in my writing journey and in life has been a constant source of strength. Thank you for believing in me and for always being there.

To Dr. LL, thank you for your invaluable insight and guidance on the psychological aspects of the book and its author. Your expertise added a profound depth to the narrative.

To my wife Debi, who is the light at the very center of my life and the reason for everything in it. I truly cherish your love and support. This book is as much yours as it is mine.

Lastly, to my granddaughter Cece, who is a smart and beautiful person inside and out, I'm afraid you can't read this book until you're twenty-one. I mean it.

ABOUT THE AUTHOR

Andrew is a passionate storyteller and dedicated writer, weaving tales that captivate and inspire readers. With a keen eye for detail and a love for exploring the human experience, Andrew brings characters to life and creates worlds that readers can escape into.

Born and raised in and around Chicago, Andrew developed a love for literature at an early age, often found with a comic book in hand or telling stories. This passion for storytelling eventually led to a hobby in writing. His poems found publication in magazines and newspapers. His short stories in anthology books.

Andrew has recently retired from his research and development job that he held for 30 years, and moved from Chicago to North Carolina.

Besides writing, Andrew enjoys wildlife photography, and has had his images and videos published in books, magazines, webpages and commercials. He often draws inspiration from these activities. He is a dog person.

This novel, Devil Don't Go, is a testament to Andrew's dedication to the craft and a celebration of his love for storytelling. He hopes it brings as much joy to readers as it did to create.

You can find more about Andrew at **DYKPub.com**

Tanner York and the crew will return.